Honey Roasted

Honey Roasted

Cleo Coyle

BERKLEY PRIME CRIME
New York

BERKLEY PRIME CRIME
Published by Berkley
An imprint of Penguin Random House LLC
penguinrandomhouse.com

Copyright © 2022 by Alice Alfonsi and Marc Cerasini
Penguin Random House supports copyright. Copyright fuels creativity, encourages diverse voices, promotes free speech, and creates a vibrant culture. Thank you for buying an authorized edition of this book and for complying with copyright laws by not reproducing, scanning, or distributing any part of it in any form without permission. You are supporting writers and allowing Penguin Random House to continue to publish books for every reader.

BERKLEY and the BERKLEY & B colophon are registered trademarks and
BERKLEY PRIME CRIME is a trademark of Penguin Random House LLC.
A COFFEEHOUSE MYSTERY is a registered trademark of Penguin Random House LLC.

Library of Congress Cataloging-in-Publication Data

Names: Coyle, Cleo, author.
Title: Honey roasted / Cleo Coyle.
Description: First Edition. | New York: Berkley Prime Crime, 2022. |
Series: A coffeehouse mystery; 19
Identifiers: LCCN 2021042532 (print) | LCCN 2021042533 (ebook) |
ISBN 9780593197561 (hardcover) | ISBN 9780593197578 (ebook)
Classification: LCC PS3603.O94 H66 2022 (print) | LCC PS3603.O94 (ebook)|
DDC 813/.6—dc23
LC record available at https://lccn.loc.gov/2021042532
LC ebook record available at https://lccn.loc.gov/2021042533

Printed in the United States of America
1   3   5   7   9   10   8   6   4   2

Book design by Kristin del Rosario

This is a work of fiction. Names, characters, places, and incidents either are the product of the author's imagination or are used fictitiously, and any resemblance to actual persons, living or dead, business establishments, events, or locales is entirely coincidental.

PUBLISHER'S NOTE: The recipes contained in this book are to be followed exactly as written. The publisher is not responsible for your specific health or allergy needs that may require medical supervision. The publisher is not responsible for any adverse reactions to the recipes contained in this book.

To the humble bee, without whom we would not be

AUTHOR'S NOTE

Honey Roasted marks the nineteenth entry in our Coffeehouse Mysteries. As our longtime readers know, our stories are often inspired by real events that happen in and around our New York home.

The inspiration for *Honey Roasted* came one hot August afternoon when a swarm of 25,000 bees descended on an outdoor hot dog stand in the heart of Times Square. On that day, we first became aware of the NYPD's beekeeping unit (Twitter handle @NYPDBees).

The unit was launched right after New York City legalized urban beekeeping—a move that quickly led to swarms invading city streets, parks, apartment buildings, and (as much of the world witnessed that hot August day) the occasional hot dog stand. The actual beekeeping unit is based out of the 104th Precinct in Queens. For this work of fiction, we kept their headquarters at its current location, but expanded the unit's size. As far as other deviations from doctrine in this story, we plead the author's defense—in the service of fiction, rules occasionally get bent.

Several print and online resources helped us in the research for *Honey Roasted*, including and especially *Keeping Bees* by John Vivian, illustrated by Liz Buell (1985, Williamson Publishing, Charlottesville, Vermont), along with Bee Culture (beeculture.com), an excellent online source of information and lore. Likewise, Savannah Bee (savannahbee.com) provided inspiration on all things honey (including their fabulous version of Roasted Honey Coffee). For specialty coffee inspiration, including a sublime Peru Cajamarca, we lift our mugs to coffee roaster Rusty Dog Coffee (rustydogcoffee.com).

A sweet shout-out goes to our publisher and the honey of a crew who helped put this book into your hands. We're especially grateful to executive editor Michelle Vega for her valuable input, which helped sharpen and strengthen our story. Thanks also to assistant editor Jennifer Snyder and production editor Stacy Edwards for keeping us on track; as well as our copyeditor Marianne

Aguiar, our designers Rita Frangie and Kristin del Rosario, and our marketing and publicity team, Elisha Katz and Stephanie Felty, for their essential contributions.

To Cathy Gendron, the queen bee of artists, who created yet another brilliant cover for our Coffeehouse Mysteries, we send our sincerest appreciation.

To John Talbot, our literary agent, we continue to treasure your patient support and consummate professionalism.

Last but far from least, we send our love and gratitude to everyone whom we could not mention by name, including friends, family, and so many of you who read our books and send us notes via e-mail, our website's message board, and on social media. Your encouragement keeps us going. For that, we cannot thank you enough.

Whether you are new to our world or a devoted reader, we invite you to join our Coffeehouse community at coffeehousemystery.com where you will find bonus recipes, our latest book news, and a link to keep in touch by signing up for our newsletter. May you eat, drink, and read with joy!

—Alice Alfonsi and Marc Cerasini
aka Cleo Coyle, New York City

When you are pretty sure that an Adventure is going to happen, brush the honey off your nose and spruce yourself up as best you can, so as to look Ready for Anything.

—*Pooh's Little Instruction Book*, inspired by A. A. Milne

If you want to gather honey, don't kick over the beehive.

—Dale Carnegie

Honey Roasted

One

"**WELL**, what do we have here?"

Matt Allegro spied the colorful brochures I'd been frowning over. Before I could stop my ex-husband, he snatched the bundle off the café table.

"Honeymoon destinations?" He flipped through the glossy pile. "So, you and the flatfoot have finally agreed on a getaway? It looks like more than the birds and bees will be busy next spring."

"Very funny, Allegro. Now give them back."

Instead, Matt shook his shaggy dark head and grinned, white teeth gleaming behind his bush of a beard, crow's-feet crinkling in his deeply tanned skin—a rugged shade acquired not in a Manhattan tanning booth but under the tropical sun of a Costa Rican *finca*, where he'd also obtained an outstanding microlot of honey-processed arabica beans. For that alone, I should have forgiven him, but I wasn't in the mood.

With a quick swipe, I tried to reclaim my happy-honeymoon dream, but Matt pulled the pamphlets out of reach and skidded away, ducking behind one of the overstuffed easy chairs in our second-floor lounge.

Straightening my Village Blend apron, I strode across the room, and stuck my hand out.

Matt viewed my open palm with amusement. "What will you trade for them?"

"How about three insults and an elbow to the ribs?"

He tapped his foot. "I'm waiting."

"Hmm . . ." Pretending to think it over, I studied the embossed design in our antique tin ceiling. Then I made my move. With a sudden lunge, I attempted to reach around his hard body, but his annoyingly muscular arm easily blocked me, and he was off again.

Okay, it's on!

As I chased my ex-husband and lunatic business partner around café tables, standing lamps, and intentionally mismatched bohemian living room furniture, my baristas scattered. So much for our after-hours staff meeting.

For a moment, a rush of nostalgia swept me back two decades: Matt and me in our twenties, happily racing our toddler daughter around this same Village Blend lounge.

But Joy was all grown-up now and (allegedly) so was Matt.

I attempted a second grab, my chestnut ponytail bobbing, but once again my slippery ex slipped out of reach. He made a show of flipping through the brochures.

"Aruba, Bermuda, Bahamas. What is this, a Beach Boys song?"

"It's none of your business, that's what it is." Abandoning pursuit, I placed my hands on my hips and produced my sternest stare. I should have known better. Not even Joy fell for that anymore—but apparently my youngest barista did.

"You shouldn't tease her!" Nancy scolded.

A wide-eyed transplant from upstate, Nancy Kelly liked to embrace her inner farm girl with a fondness for wheat-colored braids and blue gingham miniskirts. She also made a habit of crushing too easily on cute guys. Her Matt-crush was inevitable (we all fall for Matt), but I shut that down fast since he was her boss, not to mention twice her age. The crush on her coworker Dante, however, nearly killed him. (But that's another story.)

Hearing the disapproval in Nancy's voice, Matt turned to face her. "Go on, I'm listening," he said with the tone of a patient father. "You have something more to say?"

"Yes, I do! I don't know why you're giving our Boss Lady such a hard time. She's just looking for the perfect getaway after she and Lieutenant Quinn become husband and wife. What's wrong with that?"

"Nothing," Matt replied, sending me a glance. "I just didn't understand why she looked so unhappy. Now I see. She's searching for the *perfect* getaway. A nice getaway or a fun getaway just won't cut it. For the Boy Scout in blue, it has to be *perfect*."

"If you ask me, they deserve perfect," Tucker Burton said with a theatrical sigh. Dedicated thespian and darling of the Downtown cabaret scene, my lanky, floppy-haired Tuck was our oldest and most loyal staff member. "If I were planning their honeymoon, I'd send the newlyweds to Paris for a stay at the Hôtel Ritz!"

Esther rolled her eyes. "It's a honeymoon, not a money-moon."

A former NYU grad student, Esther Best had the kind of prickly attitude that was challenging to manage but extremely handy in Manhattan retail, where aggressive demands of New York customers (especially those forced to wait more than five seconds for re-caffeination) would typically scare a more timid part-timer off her Crocs.

Our zaftig, raven-haired resident poet was also a proud urban rapper, which was how she met her boyfriend—a Russian-born baker who dreamed of becoming the next Eminem. But Esther's true passion, other than Boris (and coffee), was her dedicated work with poetry slam outreach, a nonprofit program for at-risk kids.

Adjusting her black-framed glasses, she stared Tucker down with her trademark scowl. "The Paris Ritz is for bougies with bank accounts. Two weeks in those perfumed digs cost more than an Elon Musk space launch."

"Esther's right," Matt said, scratching his unruly beard. "On a New York cop's salary, the Motel 6 in New Orleans is about as close to France as these newlyweds will ever get."

Dante Silva folded his tattooed arms. "Why go to Europe, anyway?"

His comment surprised me. Most young artists dreamed of European studies. Then again, Dante had moved to New York from a little town in Rhode Island to paint quirky scenes of urban life—and he'd encountered plenty working behind my counter.

"New England is a great place for a honeymoon," he said. "There's an amazing bed-and-breakfast where I grew up in Quindicott. It's a restored Queen Anne called the Finch Inn—"

"Paaa-leeeeze," Esther scoffed. "Any honeymooners serious about their self-titled mission would want more privacy than the paper-thin walls of an old Victorian B and B. If Boris and I ever go on a honeymoon, we'll either rent a cabin in the woods or make sure our hotel room is soundproof."

"Too much information!" Dante cried, squeezing his eyes shut.

Tucker opened his wide. "Why, Esther, I didn't realize you were such an incurable romantic."

"It's not romance," she said, pushing up her glasses. "It's sex."

Matt snapped his fingers. "Speaking of great se—" (He cleared his throat.) "—romance, why not go to Hawaii, Clare? That's where we had our honeymoon. Remember those starry nights on the beach?"

I could not believe my ex-husband said that with a straight face.

"Matt, some of my wedding plans may still be up in the air, but I can tell you one thing. Whatever they are, they will not be repeating the same pattern."

"Pattern?" Bafflement crossed his bushy face. "What pattern?"

"I'll make it simple—" I raised an index finger. "Number one. This is my second wedding. This time around, I'm a mature, independent woman marrying a man I deeply love, not an infatuated, pregnant teenager with no means of support.

"Number two—" I made a peace sign. "I'm marrying Detective Lieutenant Michael Ryan Francis Quinn in a chapel surrounded by friends and family, not at City Hall in front of a bored clerk.

"Number three—" I waved my old Girl Scout salute. "Mike and I are going to have a lovely reception at a beautiful venue on the river with those same friends and family as our guests.

"And finally, on our honeymoon, Mike and I are going somewhere— anywhere—that does not remind me of my first failed marriage." I stepped up to my ex-husband until we were standing toe-to-toe, if not face-to-face (at my height it was more like my face and his sternum).

Matt looked down and grinned again. "Can't handle the memories of me, huh?"

I suppressed a groan (barely). "I simply want this wedding to be the opposite of my first one in every respect. Get it now?"

"Oh, I get it." Matt handed back the brochures. "You're honeymooning in the Arctic Circle."

"Well, if we do, I'm sure Mike Quinn will find plenty of creative ways to keep us warm."

With a snort, Matt scanned the room. "Speaking of cold fish, where is our friendly neighborhood apple-swiping flatfoot? Shouldn't your precious groom-in-waiting be here to help pick your perfect honeymoon package?"

The lounge suddenly got very quiet. Then everyone turned to stare— at me!

Two

I knew why they were staring. They were waiting for an answer. And from the looks on their faces, they appeared concerned that something was very wrong.

I couldn't blame them. My staff had grown used to seeing Lieutenant Quinn at our after-hours meetings. Mike always enjoyed the banter between my baristas, along with samples of my new roasts and the leftover treats in our pastry case. And my baristas appreciated quizzing him about police activity in our neighborhood, especially patterns of crimes—from more serious events like muggings and assaults to misdemeanor infractions like bike thefts and graffiti.

The last two weeks, however, my fiancé had been notably absent.

"Mike is working, okay?" I snapped out. "Which is what we are supposed to be doing, remember?"

I kicked myself for my tone. I had wanted to respond without emotion, but the words came out way more defensive than I meant them to be. I might as well have been wearing a neon sign that flashed *Trouble in Paradise*.

With a frown, Matt studied my unhappy expression. That's when I realized what all his teasing and chasing was really about.

My ex had noticed my anxiety over those honeymoon brochures. His impromptu "playtime" had been his way of trying to lighten my mood. Now he saw the truth. My worries could not be chased away by a few jokey remarks and an adult version of *Romper Room*.

Matt stepped close, his brow knitting with unspoken questions. But this was not the time to answer intimate queries about my relationship with Mike Quinn.

DING! The smartphone timer went off in the pocket of my Village Blend apron. The French presses were ready.

"Let me finish the coffee," I said.

As I pushed past Matt to press down the plungers, his low whisper told me he was not letting this subject die.

"You're not saved by the bell, Clare. I want to know what's going on—"

To my relief, his words stopped there. Remembering we had an audience, he faced the staff and clapped his hands.

"The Boss Lady's right! Fun time's over. Everyone, grab a cup and let's get down to business."

A minute later, I was listening to Matt and my staff loudly and dutifully slurp. (It may have sounded uncouth, but sucking air in with the coffee was essential for a proper tasting. Not only did it help spray the entire palate, it allowed the nose to get in on the tasting action.)

When Matt finally cleared his throat to speak, I held my breath. These beans were special, and this finished coffee had to be.

"Clare, this is one of the finest roasts you've ever created. It's masterfully balanced, and you've perfectly preserved the fruit and floral notes." He met my gaze with a mix of gratitude and admiration. "It's intoxicating."

I exhaled with relief. My ex was not a man who offered praise easily, especially when it came to the beverage that defined his life's work.

"What do the rest of you think?" I asked.

Esther, Dante, and Nancy all gave enthusiastic thumbs-up. That left Tucker, who sat in silence, eyes closed.

"What's the matter, Tuck?" Nancy frowned. "Don't you like it?"

Without a word, Tucker fanned his hands to catch more of the fragrance rising from his cup. Then my oldest and most experienced staff member slurped again and opened his eyes.

"I got the fruit and floral notes," he began. "Peach and candied apricot with a hint of rose petals. But as the coffee cools, there is so much more—a luscious honey sweetness. And it's a clean, bright sweetness, not heavy or syrupy. This coffee is so lively and complex, it's throwing a dance party on my tongue!"

"Don't hold back, Shakespeare," Esther cracked. "Tell us what you really think."

"I just did, dearie. This brew beats anything I've been served at a TSCA annual banquet."

Esther smirked. "The last time I checked, you were a server for the Tri-State Specialty Coffee Association, not one of the served."

"Caterers are on the front lines, sugar. We sample everything first."

"Oh, really? Does that include the Dom Pérignon?"

"Only when I'm rehearsing my Academy Awards acceptance speech for Best Actor." Tuck flipped his floppy brown mop. "You have to admit, when draped in formal wear, I bear an uncanny resemblance to a young Hugh Grant."

As Esther snapped a comeback (something about "*Notting Hill* you're not"), Matt bypassed the bickering baristas and extended his empty cup.

"More, please," he said, his furry face beaming. Clearly, he was pleased, even a bit euphoric, and he had every right to be.

At my request, Matt had traveled to Central America, where the "honey processing" of coffee had originated and was still all the rage. He'd already forged an alliance with one of the most highly regarded *fincas* in Costa Rica, and on this trip, he bought the farm—not literally, of course. But Matt did buy an entire shade-grown, certified organic, honey-processed microlot.

While my ex-husband's agricultural chess move was perfectly executed, it cost the Village Blend a hefty chunk of change, which meant Matt and I had a lot riding on the quality of this brew. Fortunately, the *oohs* and *aahs* emanating from my baristas told me our financial gamble had paid off.

My expertise in roasting hadn't hurt, either.

I had micro-roasted multiple test batches to achieve that perfect crack. This final batch was finished a short time ago, right after my regular roasting session for the shop.

Now my baristas were eagerly pouring second and third cups.

"This coffee is awesome," Dante declared. "It's sure to wow that Tri-State coffee group, including the stuffed shirts and know-it-all snobs among them."

I appreciated Dante's support, but impressing members of the TSCA was not my main concern. My primary worry was producing a coffee that served as a dazzling representation of a single person: Blanche Dreyfus Allegro Dubois, the Paris-born owner of the Village Blend, known affectionately (and respectfully) as "Madame."

Like our landmark coffeehouse, Madame had become a beloved asset to the Greenwich Village neighborhood she served. Despite coming to America as a penniless, motherless refugee and being tragically widowed twice, our grande dame had risen to become a pillar of the community.

For decades, she'd caffeinated, cajoled, and even bankrolled struggling artists, writers, actors, and musicians, some of whom rose to the ranks of worldwide acclaim.

Along the way, she birthed and raised a widely respected globe-trotting coffee hunter (our own Matteo Allegro); and she didn't hesitate to take a pregnant art school dropout (me) under her wing to teach her the coffee business from top to bottom, including the master art of blending and roasting the best beans on the planet.

In two weeks, at the Tri-State Specialty Coffee Association's annual meeting, my former mother-in-law would be presented with the Golden Demitasse to honor her countless contributions to the New York community.

Before that trophy was presented, she would undergo a surprise "honey roast," staged by some of her closest friends. The opposite of a traditional comedy roast, where the honoree is skewered with insults, a honey roast drenches the guest of honor with praise. Everyone who knew Madame agreed she deserved every sweet drop.

After I'd accepted an invitation to provide a special coffee for the event, I knew my roast had to be exceptional. Hearing the happy sighs from my staff, I couldn't help feeling relieved, though my work was far from over. I still needed feedback on my Honey-Cinnamon Latte, which I also planned to serve at the banquet—*and* my spring wedding.

On top of that, my staff needed to rehearse their honey roast speeches. Tucker and Esther certainly knew how to entertain a crowd, but Dante and Nancy had zero experience addressing large audiences.

Even now, in this small meeting, Nancy was raising her hand like a bashful schoolgirl.

"What is it?" I asked.

"If you don't mind, I have a question about this new honey coffee?"

"Go on," I said. "Speak up."

She tugged a braid. "How exactly did you get the honey into this honey coffee without making a sticky mess inside the roaster?"

Esther groaned. Tuck and Dante snickered, and my ex bit his cheek.

"What's so funny?" Nancy asked defensively.

"They are," I said. "Because they forgot there was a time when they didn't know it all." The group immediately looked contrite. When I was satisfied all smugness in the room had been snuffed, I continued to answer Nancy's (quite logical) question.

"Despite the name, there is no actual honey in this coffee. The 'honey process' term comes from the way the beans are prepared for shipping and roasting. The tough skin of the fruit around the coffee bean is removed, but the soft mucilage is left on. This infuses more complex flavor and sweetness into the beans as they dry. It also makes the beans sticky—like honey—and produces a sweet, honey-like fragrance. That's where the name came from."

"Okay, but . . ." Nancy frowned. "If there is no actual honey in honey-processed coffee, then why is the coffeehouse filling with bees?"

Bees?!

I followed Nancy's pointing finger, and there they were—a dozen yellow-and-brown-striped honeybees buzzing their furry little heads off around the ceiling.

As my staff and I watched in shock, a second, larger swarm joined the small cluster. Then a third wave buzzed up from the first floor. Instead of joining their pals, they made a beeline straight for us!

ThREE

~~~~~~

"Oh, no! Not bees!" Esther shrieked. "Bees are dangerous. If you're allergic, bees can kill you!"

"You're allergic?" Tucker asked.

"No, but that's not the point!" Esther said waving her arms. "I can't stand bees!"

"For goodness' sake, they're just little bugs."

"Little bugs with big, poisonous stingers! I absolutely hate them!"

"You never mentioned that before."

"We've never had a swarm of bees invade the coffeehouse before!"

Just then a big, fat bee dropped in front of Esther's face. As it hovered it seemed to stare her right in the eye. With a bloodcurdling screech Esther dived under the table, curled into a ball, and covered her head. The bee followed her into her foxhole and Esther yelped again.

"You ducked and covered like there's a nuclear war!" Tucker laughed at her. "Bees aren't hazardous. If you leave them alone, they'll leave you—Yeowwww!"

Tuck clutched his forearm. "One of those little buggers stung me!"

"Nice knowing you, Shakespeare," Esther called from her hiding place.

"What's that supposed to mean?"

"If you're allergic and don't know it, you're doomed. But don't fret. I'm sure they'll dim the lights on Broadway, even for an off-off-way-off-Broadway actor like you."

"You bet they would, sweetie, and now this actor is off to find a first aid kit!"

"Where are they coming from?" Nancy cried, running in a circle. "It's October! Bees should be hibernating in their hives, not harassing baristas!"

"You're right," called Matt as he hurried toward our spiral staircase. "And it looks like they're coming up from somewhere downstairs."

Before I could reply, Matt hit the wrought iron steps. The metal clanged under my ankle boots as I followed him to the main floor.

"They're coming from the basement roasting room. You didn't notice an infestation down there, did you, Clare? A hive forming?"

"I'm not cultivating honey, if that's what you're suggesting. And there are no pests, either. Not even a mouse. When I'm roasting, I bring my cats with me to see to that and—oh, no, NO!"

"What is it?"

"Java and Frothy fell asleep down there, and I didn't see them come back up. We've got to save them from all those bees!"

Matt hopped over the coffee bar, and I circled around it. Together we approached the basement door. I'd sweated up a storm for hours and left the door wide open to help dissipate the heat. Now bees were buzzing up from below and circling above us.

"I opened the rooftop vent, too," I told Matt. "That might be how they're getting in."

He nodded. "The heat exhaust is probably what's attracting them."

As we peered into the basement, I spied my coffee-bean-colored Java. She'd woken up and was now playfully pawing at a small swarm above her. While she appeared to be fine, there was no sign of Frothy, and I felt a rising panic. Where was my sweet, latte-foam-colored, soft-as-a-bunny baby?

Matt reached for the doorknob. "Sorry, Clare, we have to close the door."

"No! We have to save my cats!"

"If you think I'm going down there, you're—"

I dashed past him, descended the wooden steps, and came to a dead stop when I reached the concrete floor.

The roasting room was still uncomfortably warm—and filled with bees! The entire space seemed to vibrate with the sound of their wings. Many had settled on the big red Probat roaster. But most still circled the air in some state of bee confusion.

Just then, Java rushed a particularly large bee that seemed ready for a face-off with the frisky feline.

"Java!" I clapped my hands and pointed. "Upstairs. Right now!"

Amazingly, the cat obeyed.

I scanned the room for Frothy. When I called her name, she let rip with a heartbreakingly fearful howl. I called again, but wherever my scared little cat was hiding, she refused to budge.

Finally, through the cloud of bees I spotted a puffed white tail sticking out from between two barrels of raw beans.

"Here, kitty, kitty! Come out, Frothy! Come to Mommy!"

"Keep it down," Matt hissed. "Yelling might agitate the bees."

"Thanks for the help," I muttered—but quietly, under my breath.

Slowly and carefully, I crossed the basement, resisting the urge to swat at the plump, bobbing insects that buzzed my ears, clung to my apron, and bumped against my face. With a bee dangling off the side of my nose, I reached behind the barrels and picked up my cowering cat.

With Frothy cradled in one arm, I cautiously crossed to the control panel and tugged the handle that closed the outer vent. Then I put my head down, moved slowly through the buzzing cloud, and climbed the steps.

With a slam Matt closed the door behind me.

"What now?" I said, gasping for air.

Matt flicked a bee from my ponytail. "I'm going to check the roof."

"I'm going with you."

Dante took the frightened cat from me, and Frothy promptly buried her fluffy white head in his armpit.

Meanwhile, Matt grabbed a Maglite from the utility drawer in our pantry, and we headed up to the building's attic. There, amid the clutter of surplus chairs, tables, and catering carts, Matt extended the ladder that led up to the roof hatch. With the flashlight beam dancing madly about the loft, he climbed to the top.

After a string of Portuguese curses he'd picked up in Rio, Matt managed to pop the sticky hatch. Cool night air rushed into the stuffy loft. Matt moved through the hatch and turned to help me up.

As soon as I stepped onto the roof, I regretted not grabbing a jacket. A biting breeze was flowing off the Hudson River a few blocks away, cold enough to make me shiver in my thin T-shirt. The chilly air was a sharp shock after working up a sweat in the steaming-hot roasting room.

"Hold this," Matt said, shoving the flashlight at me. He shrugged off his loose flannel shirt, revealing a formfitting Brazilian soccer jersey.

"What are you doing?"

He placed the thick flannel over my shivering shoulders. "You know me. I'm not just hot—" He winked. "I'm hot-blooded. And you need this more than I do."

"Thanks." I handed back the Maglite and wrapped the fabric close. It was still warm from his body, and I was grateful.

As we walked the length of the roof, I realized I hadn't been up here since the Fourth of July, when Mike and I spread out a blanket for a picnic on the Village Blend's "tar beach." We ate my homemade Buttermilk Fried Chicken and Creamy Pasta Salad, sipped sauvignon blanc, and watched the fireworks exploding over the moonlit city. The beautifully clear night was summery warm, and our own mutual passion added to the heat.

Tonight was far less temperate than that lovely memory. Though a full harvest moon glowed brighter than a disco ball, it made the jagged gleam of distant skyscrapers seem even more harsh. The city's new pencil towers loomed like glass beanpoles, far less charming than the stately, old historic structures of Greenwich Village, four floors below.

A wailing siren cut through the muted roar of the city. Otherwise, the shadowy roof felt eerily silent, until Matt and I heard another sound. An ominous, almost alien-like hum. He lifted the flashlight beam and together we gasped.

Thousands of bees had clustered around the roaster's metal chimney, wrapping themselves into a big, squirming, furiously buzzing ball. The swarm was intimidating, even from fifteen feet away, and there was no way we were getting any closer.

Matt scratched his head. "Who the heck do we call about this? The Central Park Zoo? Winnie the Pooh? Terminix?"

I reached for my smartphone. "This is New York City. I'm calling 911."

Four

∂⊚∂⊚∂⊚∂⊚∂⊚∂⊚∂⊚∂⊚∂⊚∂⊚∂⊚∂⊚∂⊚∂⊚∂⊚

"They're on the way," I told Matt after I hung up.

"Who's on the way? Animal control? PETA?"

"The New York Police Department's beekeeping unit."

"Beekeeping unit? Clare, are you sure you called 911 and not Gags 'R' Us?"

"That's what the emergency operator told me. She said to keep our distance from the bees until they arrive. She also warned me that it might take up to an hour for the unit to get here because they're coming from Queens."

"From Queens or with queens?" Matt quipped. "Queen bees, I mean."

A blast of cold autumn air swept across the flat rooftop. This time it was my tropically acclimated coffee hunter who suppressed a shiver. I took hold of Matt's strong arm, spun him around, and gently shoved him toward the roof hatch.

"There's nothing we can do up here. Let's go back inside and wait for the police."

When we returned to the coffeehouse, we found order had been somewhat restored.

After Esther had fled the building, dragging her roommate Nancy along for "moral support," Dante single-handedly cleaned up the coffee service and stashed the cups and cart. He kept one wary eye on the swarm the whole time, but still managed to get himself stung.

While Dante complained about swelling, Tucker soothed his own sting with ice packs from our pantry freezer. After that, Tuck returned Java and Frothy to my duplex apartment above the coffeehouse, which he assured me was bee-free. He left my kitties fed and watered and relaxing on my living room rug.

Meanwhile most of the swarm was still locked inside the roasting room. The bees who'd escaped the cellar now congregated in one corner of the shop's second-floor lounge ceiling, where I hoped they would remain.

It was getting late, so I sent Tuck and Dante home. I tried to let Matt off the hook, too, and shoo him out the door. "I'll be fine here alone," I told him, but he insisted on staying, complaining of "body clock insomnia" due to "time zone changes."

It sounded like a lame excuse to me. "Costa Rica is only two hours behind New York."

"Okay, you got me. I actually want to see this so-called beekeeping unit in action."

I barely believed that, but I stopped arguing. Instead, I brewed us a fresh pot of the honey roast. Without a fire in the hearth, the coffeehouse felt drafty, and I was tempted to start a blaze until I saw my ex was already lighting the kindling.

Crossing our wood plank floor, I skirted empty café tables with two steaming cups in hand and took a seat close to the fireplace.

"It's a shame what happened," I said, pulling Matt's thick flannel closer around me as I watched him coax the tiny flames higher. "We didn't even get a chance to whip up my new Honey-Cinnamon Latte for everyone to sample—and I took such care in sourcing the perfect gourmet honey for the drink. It came from Madame's old friend, Bea Hastings—"

"Only to have your plans disrupted by a bee invasion." Matt laughed. "You should relish the irony."

I didn't reply, just stared into the rising fire and sipped my hot coffee.

"Look, I know you're disappointed," Matt said, taking a seat across from me. "If you like, I'll taste test one of those lattes now."

"My heart wouldn't be in it."

"Yeah, that's clear. Something's knocked the heart out of you."

"It's been a stressful day."

"Come on. I know you too well. This funk is more than disappointment over a drink test and some bee infestation. And despite those glossy brochures, you aren't acting like a woman who's planning her perfect wedding, never mind the perfect honeymoon getaway—"

"And how would you know?" I snapped, and immediately regretted my tone. "Sorry."

Unfazed, Matt stared me down. This time without a trace of taunting or condescension. Instead of snapping back, his voice softened.

"Will you please talk to me?"

I looked away. "You wouldn't understand."

"I understand that you're brooding about something. Maybe I can help. Just tell me what's bugging you?"

"*Bugging* me? Very funny. And really, nothing's wrong beyond the stress to impress the hypercritical crowd at the TSCA banquet."

Matt raised his cup. "You've clearly got that problem solved." He took a long sip and sighed. "Your roast is perfect, and you know it. On top of that, you are a lousy liar."

I shrugged, turning my attention back to the crackling hearth.

"I know the problem," Matt pressed. "You're upset because your own honey isn't here to sample the honey roast and share your triumph with the staff." He checked the time. "It's after ten. I'll bet Mike Quinn isn't coming over at all tonight. Or is he?"

"Oh, please, don't make this an excuse to throw another pass my way. I think that boat has sailed, then capsized, and finally sunk."

"Believe me, I got the memo. But I do remember something you don't."

"What?"

"Near the end of our marriage, you wore the same anxious expression you're wearing now. Back then, it was because you stopped trusting me. You knew I was keeping secrets from you, and you hated me for it."

I fell silent, considering Matt's words. Honestly, what I hated right then was my ex-husband being right about something. And I really disliked it when he was right about me. I wanted to tell him to mind his own business and take a hike, except . . . I didn't.

Maybe it was because Madame was off taking a much-deserved vacation with her old friend Babka. I hadn't spoken to my beloved mentor since she left for the Caribbean, two weeks ago, and I needed to talk my situation out with someone who really knew me.

Well, here was Matt, sitting across the table, encouraging me to open up. He certainly did know me. So, despite my misgivings, I found myself confessing . . .

"The problem isn't *us*. It's Mike."

"Mike Quinn the man? Or his job? Not that I can tell the difference. To me, your fiancé is more cop than human."

"And that's the problem."

"Really?" Matt sat back. "I thought you already knew that about him."

"I do, and I've always supported his work. But lately—the man, the one I dearly love—just won't rest. The pressures of his job are getting to him, and he doesn't see it."

"Doesn't see it how? Give me an example."

"Well, I'm planning this big, traditional wedding celebration because he wants it as much as I do. More than I do, if I'm being honest. But now he's balking at the idea of a traditional honeymoon getaway. I believe we need it as a couple—and deserve it. He doesn't see it that way and seems concerned about the time off. But he needs to step back from his work and take a breather."

"Have you talked to him about it? I mean *really* talked?"

"It's been a challenge. He creeps in at two or three in the morning, and . . ."

"And?"

I felt heat on my cheeks. Once again, I looked away.

"Come on, Clare. Don't clam up now. What happens when he creeps in?"

After an excruciating pause, I admitted the awkward truth. "Nothing happens, okay? *Nothing.*"

Matt studied my embarrassed expression and flushed face. "You mean—"

"These late-night hours have happened before with Mike: stakeouts and stings and PD actions galore. But in the past, whenever he'd come to our bed, no matter the hour, he'd . . . you know."

"Make love to you?"

I nodded. "And it used to be so good. I mean *really* amazing, some of the best—" I cut myself off, remembering who I was talking to. "What I mean to say is . . . Mike's wanting me was never in question; the passion was always there. It was a kind of therapy for him, too, a stress reliever. And now I just wake up in the early hours and find him sacked out, dead to the world. By then, I have my own work, opening the shop, and I'm off to start my day."

"What happens between you and Quinn when you're out of bed?"

"He zones in and out, doesn't matter whether we're sharing a meal or having a coffee break together. I talk, but he barely seems to comprehend what I'm saying. He's distant—until the phone rings, and he's alert again, because the phone is always the job, and at all hours, too."

Matt scratched his beard. "Maybe you and the flatfoot are drinking too much coffee."

I blinked, momentarily stunned. "I *never*—not in a million years— expected to hear those three words come out of your mouth."

"Too much coffee?" He laughed. "You never heard me say those words because it's never been true for me, and never will. I'm a relaxed guy by nature."

"You're an adrenaline junkie."

"I like excitement, that's true. But afterward, I'm completely content to sleep on a beach in Rio."

"You mean sleep on a beach bunny, don't you?"

"Don't deflect. Be a big girl and face the facts about your fiancé. Quinn's an alpha. One who continually reins himself in. The man's got repression embedded in his DNA. And the cop job only makes it worse. It's a recipe for heart-attack-level stress. Have you tried opening a bottle of wine?"

"No."

"Well, try it. Create a relaxed environment for him. You know, a cop-free, human zone."

"That's not funny."

"I'm completely serious. Quinn is a workaholic." He met my gaze. "Just like you. Just like me."

"Maybe."

"*Maybe*'s not a word that helps people face reality, Clare. Take it from a recovered cocaine addict. Being committed to your work is accept-able, as long as you can still manage your life, find a way to step away and unplug from obsessing, laugh at yourself, enjoy a walk in the park, recon-nect with people in your life. Sounds to me like Quinn's losing that battle—"

"Or *maybe* I'm feeling overly sensitive with the wedding coming up.

After all, he is still Mike Quinn, the man I love. I don't know why I'm feeling so anxious."

"The answer is easy. You're getting a preview of what it's like to be the wife of a work-obsessed cop, and you don't like it."

"That's not true!"

"It is true. You're beginning to realize—*really* realize—that you are about to hook your life to a man who's responsible for the very lives of the people under his command; a man whose own life is sometimes at risk; a man who could kiss you goodbye one morning and never come back."

Matt's words knocked the air out of me.

Part of me wanted to rage at him, but the other part feared a dreaded and dreadful truth had been spoken. Instead of responding to his assertions, I swept up the empty cups and headed for the coffee bar. As I crossed the plank floor, the night bell rang.

"I'll get it," Matt said.

He pulled the door blind back and peeked outside.

"Who is it?" I called.

Matt scratched his beard. "It's either the bee whisperers or a pair of alien astronauts."

FIVE

೦⌇೦⌇೦⌇೦⌇೦⌇೦⌇೦⌇೦⌇೦⌇೦⌇೦⌇೦⌇

"Ms. Cosi? I understand you have a bee problem?"

The stocky one spoke with a lighthearted lilt. The other one, taller and leaner, remained silent. Both were swathed from neck to toe in thick canvas overalls, their heads crowned by broad-brimmed hats draped with heavy mesh veils. If I hadn't called the beekeeping unit, I would have assumed the pair, showing up at this hour at my front door, were beings from another planet—or overgrown trick-or-treaters.

A closer inspection revealed NYPD badges clipped to their chests and duty belts festooned with tactical gear circling their waists. Noting my bemusement, the stockier man pulled his headgear off, to reveal a middle-aged Black man with a round, bald head and broad, sunny grin.

"I'm Officer Darius Greene and this is my partner Peter Banner."

Under the hat and veil, Officer Banner dipped his head but remained silent.

I invited the stocky officer and his taller, skinnier partner into the coffeehouse. I had to step aside as they lumbered by, both carrying an odd assortment of gear.

"I'm sorry for staring, but I never even knew there *were* bee police until an hour ago."

"Well, we *are* the smallest unit in the NYPD," Officer Greene informed me with a shrug. "Just last year we tripled our ranks from two officers to six. Officer Banner and I are two of the newbies."

"New bees?" I smiled. "Officer Greene, are you trying to be punny?"

The pair stood in silence. Apparently, he wasn't.

"So, you think you have a swarm here?" Greene asked. I noted the skepticism in his tone.

"We actually have three swarms," I assured him. "The biggest one by far is on the roof. There's a smaller group in the basement. And a third group upstairs in our second-floor lounge."

Greene raised his eyes, blinking in amazement. He climbed the stairs to verify my report and quickly came back down.

"This is freaky," he declared, sending a loaded glance his partner's way before addressing me again. "Bees naturally hole up in their nice, warm hives through mid-autumn and winter. They primarily swarm between May and July. Something dire must have happened to this colony's hive for them to abandon it. I'm talking fire, flood, earthquake."

The big man faced his silent partner. "Okay, Buzz. Let's get ready."

"Buzz?" I said. "I thought your name was Peter."

It was Darius Greene who replied. "We call him Buzz because of that military haircut—and attitude. Some vets leave their past behind, but not Buzz Banner. He's forever a marine."

"Oorah," Buzz said flatly. (Clearly, this was a running joke between them.) Removing his hat and veil, he revealed his pale skin and close-cropped blond hair. At least a decade younger than his partner, he was likely a recent graduate from the police academy.

Just then, Officer Greene noticed a single bee drifting down the spiral staircase. He looked at the tiny creature with pity and shook his head.

"Let's start with those little lost souls upstairs."

"Lost souls?" I said.

Greene nodded. "What we're likely dealing with at this time of year, Ms. Cosi, is a single swarm of worker bees surrounding and protecting one queen bee. The bees upstairs have been separated from the rest of their colony. That's why I call them lost souls."

When he looked up again, his dark brown eyes narrowed. "Buzz, skip the ladder. We'll use the Giraffe instead."

"Giraffe? Don't we have enough wildlife in here?" Matt cracked.

A deep belly laugh erupted from Officer Greene.

"You gotta love a man with a sense of humor. You too, Ms. Cosi. Most folks who call us are in a pants-wetting frenzy, if you'll excuse my expression."

"Actually, you've pretty accurately described the reaction of one of my baristas. She warned us all about the dire consequences of being allergic while diving under a café table."

"Violent reactions to bee stings are rare," Greene noted, "but allergic or not, nobody likes to get stung."

"It doesn't look like you get stung much," I said. "With all that gear, I mean."

"Four hundred and six times and counting." He grinned proudly. "You get used to it."

While we were talking, Banner started assembling the equipment. It was strange, DIY-looking stuff, seemingly slapped together with duct tape and string. Their function was a mystery, yet all these Rube Goldberg–esque devices appeared to be fashioned from common and recognizable household items.

I was dying to ask Banner about it, but I could see he was seriously focused as he screwed together a long pole and connected it to the longest vacuum cleaner hose I'd ever seen. Finally, he slipped a large cone over one end of the hose and attached the opposite end to a bagless Hoover vacuum cleaner with its plastic housing removed to expose the interior mechanism.

"Let's go," he said.

As the two officers carried the equipment upstairs, Matt and I followed, stopping at the far end of the lounge. From there we watched Greene and Banner slowly approach the swarm, which was humming loudly in one corner of the tin ceiling.

Hat and veil still off, Banner slowly raised the pole toward the bees until the cone was almost touching the buzzing insects. With a flick of a switch, Greene activated the Hoover. The machine hum was startling— someone had obviously tinkered with the device because it sounded way more powerful than the puny motor on my upright vac.

Within seconds the live bees began to fill the large, clear plastic holding bin. Up top, a few scattered in panic and one bee alighted on Officer Greene's exposed neck.

"Damn," he groaned, wincing. "That's four hundred and seven."

Banner coolly snapped the stinging bee off his partner's throat with one gloved hand while clutching the pole with the other. Squinting, he studied the bee.

"Greene, check it out," he yelled over the machine whine.

Banner displayed the still-squirming insect, and Officer Greene whistled again. Then he quickly put his hat and veil back on and took the pole from Banner.

"Put your own veil back on," he sharply cautioned.

Matt caught the not-so-subtle exchange and directed a wary stare at the stragglers still buzzing around the ceiling.

"What's going on?" My ex yelled loudly over the hum of the vacuum. I could hear the concern in his voice. "Are these killer bees or something?!"

"No, nothing like that!" Officer Greene yelled back. "These aren't a common species, that's all."

When Banner switched off the vacuum, I pressed the question. "Are these honeybees not native to America?"

"No honeybees are native to America, Ms. Cosi," Officer Greene replied. "Honeybees were brought here in the 1600s. Within a century, they'd spread across the entire continent from sea to shining sea."

"You mean there were no bees in this hemisphere before the seventeenth century? That can't be right. How did the trees and plants pollinate?"

"I didn't say there were no bees," Greene clarified. "There are more than twenty thousand types of bees in the world, and four thousand are native to North America. But only seven types of bees produce honey, and none come from North or South America."

"Italian bees are the most common," Banner chimed in, his deep voice muffled by the headgear as he broke down the long vacuum pole. "I'd guess that ninety percent of domestic honey is produced by Italian bees."

"And the rest?"

Greene tapped the clear plastic container. Inside, the rescued bees buzzed irritably.

"These are Carniolan bees. At least, I think they are. Some folks call them Alpine bees because Carniolans originally came from the Austrian Alps. They require more care and maintenance, but they are hearty and produce a bit more honey than Italian bees because they also gather nectar on cool and overcast days."

He glanced at the bees in the plastic bin with a look of admiration.

"This bunch, bless them, were able to survive tonight's ordeal."

I pointed to his veiled headgear. "How dangerous are they?"

"Carniolan are gentle once they get to know their beekeeper, but they can be aggressive with strangers, and when protecting their hive and queen. With their hive gone, it's the queen they're trying to protect."

"Where is this queen?" Matt asked.

"Either in your basement or on the roof."

The two officers talked for a moment.

"Is your basement heated?" Greene asked.

"Very. I roast coffee down there, so it's quite warm."

The two men looked at each other.

"We better hit the roof," Greene told his partner. "Now."

Six

WHILE Buzz Banner quickly took the canister of bees (from the lounge swarm) to their heated police van, I escorted the heavyset officer to the attic, up the ladder, and through the roof hatch.

The wind had died down, but a deeper cold had descended on our tar beach. The full moon was so bright the swarm was visible without a flashlight. By now, their buzzing was subdued, and they didn't seem nearly as active as they were just an hour ago.

Once again, Greene let out a whistle. "We've got to get this swarm to a warmer place."

Banner appeared just then, and this time he brought along a more sophisticated vacuum than the homemade machine he'd been using.

"It's a state-of-the-art Colorado Bee Vac," Greene explained. "A kinder, gentler way to suck up the bees. This machine is not likely to harm the queen."

It was a lot quieter, too, and after carefully approaching the swarm, Greene began to methodically collect them.

For the third swarm, in the basement, we led the officers back to the coffeehouse. Moving around the coffee bar area, we headed for the pantry and the basement door. When Greene opened it, a few more bees buzzed by, and Banner produced a gallon-sized steel pot with a spout that blew smoke.

"This bee smoker will help calm them down," Greene explained as Officer Banner directed the smoke into the stairwell that led to the roasting room.

After a minute, both men made the careful descent together, into the eerie gray fog, hazard suits and headgear in place, weird DIY bee-sucking Hoover in tow.

I glanced at Matt as the drifting smoke curled around us. "Is it me? Or does this look like something out of a 1950s Atomic Age drive-in thriller?"

"*Invasion of the Bee Snatchers*?" he quipped. "Or *Attack of the Killer Bees*?"

I shook my head. "Officer Greene assured us these are harmless honeybees."

"Okay." Matt folded his arms and leaned against the wall. "Then it's more like *Panic in the Roasting Room*."

"Or *From Hell It Came*."

"Don't you mean *From Hive It Came*?"

"Ha ha," I said. "How about *Angry Bee Planet*?"

"*Plan Bee from Outer Space*."

"Or *The Terror from Bee-yond* with a visit from the cast of *Bee Police Academy*?"

"That last one isn't an Atomic Age thriller," Matt pointed out. "The police thing is a comedy." He threw me a look. "Maybe not in your bedroom."

I punched his shoulder—and hurt my hand on his rock-hard deltoid. *Ouch!*

Matt just laughed. "How about *The Giant Bee-hemoth*?"

"Not as good as *The Queen Bee from Outer Space*."

"Or *It Came from Bee-neath the Coffeehouse*!"

After fifteen minutes, we ran out of B movie titles (pun intended), and the officers finished sucking up all the living bees in our basement. Their otherworldly hazard suits and veiled heads rose from the smoke-filled stairwell and rejoined us on the first floor.

WITH our swarm problem solved, Matt and I invited the bee cops to take off their protective gear and join us for a break at our coffee bar.

As I served them my Honey-Cinnamon Lattes (finally, a trial run!) and a plate of my new Honey Cookies with Honey-Roasted Almonds (which I thought they would appreciate), the two men eyed the plastic cannisters buzzing with the newly collected bees from the basement.

"What are you going to do with all those little lost souls?" I asked.

"We have rescue hives on the roof of the 104th Precinct," Greene said, as he contentedly sipped my new latte and munched a honey cookie. "We'll give them a temporary hive, feed them sugar water, and keep them warm until we can get them home again—a little like what you're doing for us, Ms. Cosi."

Banner wiped the latte foam off his upper lip. "I'll contact the Department of Health and Mental Hygiene in the morning," he told his superior.

"Why?" I asked, worried. "Did we violate a health code?"

"No, nothing like that," Greene quickly replied. "Good coffee drink, by the way. Actually, I think this may be *the* best coffee drink I've ever—"

"Thanks," I said. "Sorry to cut you off, but what is the *reason* for contacting the health department?"

"It's nothing to worry about," Greene reassured me with a warm smile. "The DOH has records for all the city's registered hive owners."

"*Legal* ones," Banner sharply noted. "Not everyone does things by the book in this town."

"Or any town," Matt pointed out, folding his arms. "Skirting the law is a global sport. I've seen enough examples."

"What's that supposed to mean?" Buzz Banner locked eyes with Matt. "Do you *know* of anyone who's illegally raising bees in this part of town?"

Matt bristled at the cop's accusatory tone, and Darius Greene placed a heavy hand on his young partner's narrow shoulder. "Forgive my partner's enthusiasm." He chuckled to break the tension. "Buzz is still operating on Marine Corps time. He's used to getting things done."

"I know someone who keeps bees in Chelsea," I offered. "And I'm sure her hives are registered. She sells her gourmet honey to high-end restaurants. Your lattes were made with it, and those cookies were baked with it."

Greene nodded appreciatively. "These honey cookies are as good as your coffee."

"Thanks again, but I still want an answer about finding the hive owner. Is the owner in trouble because the bees escaped?"

"No, no," Greene assured me. "We have no interest in punishing the owner, just finding them is all. Returning the bees to their original home is the best thing for them. And that's what we'd like to do, if it's possible."

"And it may not be," Banner pointed out. "From the sound of it, Ms. Cosi, your friend likely takes very good care of her hives. I doubt her bees would have left them. In the meantime, there could be dozens of registered *and* unregistered hives in the surrounding rooftops, so it could take some time to find the hive owner of these bees, if we ever do."

A few minutes later, Matt and I said good night to the bee whisperers, who assured us they'd rescued as many of the living bees as they could. They also warned us to be prepared for plenty of dead bodies on the floor of our basement.

While I tidied up the coffeehouse counter and kitchen, Matt (thankfully!) volunteered to check out the roasting room and deal with the aftermath. A few moments later, he returned holding a balled-up paper towel in one hand, a broom in the other.

"I was sweeping up the dead bugs downstairs and noticed something weird." He unwrapped the bundle. "I want you to check these out."

"Eww!" I cried with a shudder, suddenly channeling Esther. "I don't want to see a bunch of dead bees!"

"No, Clare, you have to come closer," Matt insisted.

I remained rooted to my spot, but I extended my neck enough to get a second peek. "They're probably just worker bees," I said. "You heard the bee guys; there's only one queen."

"It's not what they *are*," Matt replied. "It's how they *smell*."

Matt stepped close and shoved the grim bundle under my nose. Before I could pull away, I caught the whiff of a familiar scent.

"Huh? That's—"

"Lavender," Matt said. "How in the world did these bees find lavender in October?"

"Oh my God!" I cried. "I know where the bees came from!"

"Where?"

"Despite what Officer Banner said, I know I'm right. In fact, I'm certain. These honeybees belong to your mother's old friend—and my gourmet honey supplier—Bea Hastings."

Seven

෧෧෧෧෧෧෧෧෧෧෧෧෧෧෧෧෧෧෧෧෧෧෧

"Come on, Clare. How can you be *certain* these insects belong to Beatrice Hastings?"

"I'm *certain* because of something she told me the last time I visited. After we discussed flower choices for my upcoming wedding, Bea complained about a shipment delay that slowed production of a *lavender* honey she's been cultivating. Bea confided she had to grease a few palms in Bulgaria to get a quarter of a million lavender plants stateside before they perished."

"Bulgaria?" Matt shook his head. "I never equated the word *lavender* with *Bulgaria*."

"Bea said the short growing season in Eastern Europe caused their lavender varietal to produce more pollen. And more pollen means more honey and a hive of happy bees. 'Nothing but the best for my honeybees,' she told me. She said, and I quote: 'They're one of a kind.'"

Matt snorted. "No wonder they call her Queen Bea, though I'm fairly sure she coronated herself."

"She loves her bees, Matt. What's wrong with that?"

"Nothing, I guess, though she might try loving her fellow man a little more—"

"Don't get off topic." I pointed to the pile of fragrant bee bodies cradled in their paper towel shroud. "These little bugs absolutely reek of lavender. Where else could they have come from than Bea's rooftop hives?"

"You're probably right," Matt said, relenting. "Mother told me that Bea has a massive greenhouse, covering the entire roof of her building. And it's a big building. She certainly is loaded, I remember that. And I guess it's possible she's filled it with exotic plants for her bees to cavort in. If anyone could pull that off, she could. After all, before she was Queen Bea, Mrs. Hastings *was* the famous Lady with the Green Thumb."

"Bea sold that florist business over a decade ago, according to your mother. And she hasn't made a paid commercial for the new owners as that 'Lady' in years." I reached for my phone. "I better give Bea a call."

"Clare, it's almost midnight."

"That won't matter. Bea's up half the night dealing with her Asia-Pacific clients."

Matt blinked. "Asia-Pacific clients? What is she shilling, honey or heroin?"

"Bea Hastings produces some of the most sought-after floral honey varieties in the world. Gourmet restaurants pay premium prices for the nectar her bees produce. Which means those bees are a gold mine, so if something has happened to them, Bea is going to want to know about it."

I kept Bea Hastings's private number in my phone directory, along with most of the other members of Madame's exclusive Gotham Ladies club. (A reporter from the *Daily News* once told me in all seriousness that I could sell my contact list to any journalist in the city for a tidy sum.)

Ominously, Bea's phone rang six times before it went to voice mail. I ended the call without leaving a message.

"I'm worried something's wrong, Matt. In fact, I'm going to walk over there right now to see what's going on."

"Walk? At midnight? By yourself?" Matt looked about ready to have a stroke. "Clare, it's been a while since New York has been that safe. I'm calling an Uber—"

He reached for the phone in his pocket. I stopped him.

"I can walk to Bea's place in ten minutes, while I'd have to wait at least that long for a car. Forget the Uber. My feet will get me there faster."

"I came over in the Village Blend van," Matt said, blocking my way. "It's parked right out front. Let me drive you."

"Leave it," I insisted, sidestepping the block. "Tuck has to load it for a catering job tomorrow. That's a prime parking spot. We don't want to lose it."

I grabbed my coat and shoulder bag from behind the coffee bar. "I'm off!"

"Clare, this is silly! You are just trying to distract yourself from the anxiety you're feeling about Quinn—"

"Stop!" I turned to face him. "You have two choices, Allegro. Either come with me or stay here and sweep up the dead bees. Frankly, you would be doing Esther a huge favor if you did the latter. She's working the morning shift tomorrow and might freak at the sight of bees, living or dead."

"Oh, well, in *that* case—I'm going with you."

"Don't you want to grab a jacket?"

"For a ten-minute walk?" He waved his hand. "I'll be fine."

With that, I set the burglar alarm, locked up the coffeehouse, and together we hit the sidewalk.

Eight

~~~~~~

As we headed north, the Village streetlights illuminated our way up the quiet avenue. Car traffic was light with no honking horns or screeching sirens battering our ears. The golden glow from the windows of the Federal-style row houses, cozy little restaurants, and gastropubs made the neighborhood feel warm and charming, one of the many reasons I appreciated living and working here.

Several blocks later, we left the historically preserved district behind, and the buildings began to grow wider and taller. The night air grew colder, too, but with the layers of clothes I had on me, I didn't feel anything close to the shivery chill I felt on our rooftop. In fact, the brisk air was refreshing. I could even smell the ocean-saltiness from the river, just a few blocks away, ushering in tidewaters from the nearby Atlantic.

Unfortunately, when I made the mistake of praising the freshness of the cool air, Matt's reply was an annoyed gripe, something about it being a lot less hospitable than the warm, humid hills of Costa Rica, where he'd been happily romping only forty-eight hours before. (So much for my "hot-blooded" ex!)

Hands shoved deep in the pockets of his worn denims, he suggested our sluggish progress was due to the chilly headwind, which didn't bother me. But it obviously bothered Matt. And it didn't help that I'd underestimated the time it took to reach Bea's building on foot.

"You *do* know where you're going, don't you?" he asked. "It feels like we've been walking for an hour!"

"We're almost there. Cool your jets—"

"My jets *are* cool. This wind off the river is freezing!"

"Let me help you out, okay? Here—" I slipped off my coat and pushed it into his hands.

"You're kidding, right? You expect me to fit into this little thing?"

"I don't want you to *wear* it, I want you to *hold* it. I'm giving you back your flannel shirt. Now *you* need it more than I do."

Matt didn't argue. He pulled the thick flannel (now warmed with my body heat) over his bright yellow Brazilian soccer jersey. The relief was immediate.

"That's better," he said, nodding his thanks.

"Look—" I pointed, slipping my coat back on. "Our destination is right on the next block. See that big apartment building, the one with the Hastings Florist Shop on the corner? That was Bea's *original* store."

"Wow—" Matt's tone turned mocking. "A *shrine*. Just like the very first McDonald's."

"Don't be snarky—"

"Don't be naive. Hastings Florists is a crappy franchise. They sell cheap flowers to a mass market. Customers complain their bouquets are half-dead when they arrive, and their gift baskets are high priced and low quality. What they do spend money on is slick advertising—and lots of it."

"None of that is Bea's fault. The new corporate owners are the ones who bought her local chain of florist shops and turned it into a national franchise."

"A second-tier franchise. Yet Bea still collects a pretty penny for the use of her good name." Matt looked up and pointed. "And speaking of names, didn't Bea tag that pricey piece of real estate after herself, too?"

Matt wasn't wrong about Bea's real estate. Even from a block away, the Hastings was impressive. A solid granite structure with a footprint that took up an entire city block, the building was constructed as office space during the Art Deco craze of the 1930s. Today the property had retail space on the first floor and ten stories of luxury apartments above, all crowned by Queen Bea Hastings's duplex penthouse on the eleventh and twelfth floors.

"You're right, Matt. She did name it after herself, and why not? Bea started out as a renter in that humble little shop on the corner. Now she owns the entire multimillion-dollar property. Don't you find that inspiring?"

"Did Mother ever tell you how Bea Hastings acquired that building?"

"I didn't know your mother and Bea went back *that* far."

"They met when I was just a kid," Matt replied. "Bea's humble little shop provided flowers for my father's funeral."

"Oh, I'm sorry."

We walked in silence for a minute.

"So," I said. "How *did* Bea get that building?"

"Funny story," Matt replied.

"I'm listening," I said—and got the distinct impression I wouldn't be laughing at the end.

Nine

~~~~~~

"Years ago," Matt began, "Bea's little shop was continually getting hit with huge rent increases. It happened like clockwork, every five years. The excuse was always that the building had a new owner, but the person handling the lease was always the same sketchy guy."

"That does sounds shady," I agreed.

"And it was. Turns out the 'new owner' was the same grifter buying the same property, over and over again."

"Wait. That doesn't make any sense."

"It was a real estate scam, Clare, a pretty sophisticated one; and in this town, there's always somebody out there ready to run a scam. In Bea's case, her old landlord would buy a property, jack up the rents and pocket all the fees, pay no property taxes, and let the building fall into disrepair for as long as he could get away with it, usually four years or so.

"When the city finally seized the building for back taxes, they were forced to make extensive repairs to get the property up to code before they could put it on the auction block. Meanwhile that same crooked owner would create a shell company and buy the newly renovated property again, and the cycle would start over."

"So how did Bea end up acquiring the building?"

"She figured out the grifter's scam; and when the property was up for grabs again, Bea was there with enough money to buy the building in cash, right out from under the jerk. She'd mortgaged her business, sold her home in Long Island, and cashed out her savings account to beat her former landlord to the punch."

"A happy ending, then."

"For Bea Hastings. She single-handedly out-scammed the scammer and outsmarted the city, too. She bought that building for half its worth, and after she repurposed the property from commercial to residential, it tripled in value. From then on, Bea used the Hastings as collateral."

"For what?"

"To buy up little properties all over the five boroughs. Coincidentally, all those properties rented to a long-running mom-and-pop florist shop. When she bought the building, Bea evicted the original shopkeepers and turned their indie shop into another Hastings Florist. That's how Bea expanded her business enough to sell it to an investment firm for a cool billion."

"What's your point?"

"Bea Hastings might love her bees, but when it comes to people, she's not so empathetic. From what I've seen she's way more ruthless than the other Gotham Ladies, a shark in a tank of lady barracudas."

"That's a little harsh. Don't you think? Your own mother had to employ tough tactics over the years to keep the Village Blend afloat."

"But Bea will never get a humanitarian award. Mother was tough when it came to corrupt and incompetent bureaucrats, but she would never pull the rug out from under some small mom-and-pop business, and you know it, Clare."

I flashed back on my last visit with Bea. She had boasted with apparent glee about a competing local honey producer she'd tried to put out of business.

"Not only was his honey infused artificially instead of naturally flavored," Bea told me. *"The crook actually adulterated his honey with sugar syrup, then sold it as pure premium, organically produced honey. I was happy to publicly expose him at the honey fair and top off his humiliation by grabbing a few of his customers and squashing an international deal he had percolating."*

Bea never mentioned the man's name, and I didn't ask. But I realized then what Matt was emphasizing now. Bea Hastings had a ruthless streak when it came to competition—and money.

"Well," I argued weakly, "I suppose there's nothing wrong with having a good head for business."

"Which she does. Bea's public persona is the Lady with the Green

Thumb. But if you ask me, she's more like the Lady with the Midas Touch." Matt paused. "And I have to admit, she did keep my mother financially solvent."

"What do you mean?"

"Do you remember when Mother's second husband died?"

I nodded, recalling it was a particularly sad time in Madame's life. She had dearly loved Pierre Dubois. A wealthy importer, he was the one who'd purchased the lavish Fifth Avenue penthouse apartment Matt's mother still occupied today.

"The Fifth Avenue home was all Mother wanted Pierre to leave her. But when Pierre was near the end, he arranged for her to receive a large sum of money in addition to the penthouse."

"I thought all his assets except the Fifth Avenue digs were left to his children."

Matt shook his head. "Those Dubois brats took control of Pierre's company and the lion's share of his fortune. But that wasn't enough for them. Oh, no. They legally challenged their father's gift to my mother and eventually won. *But* . . . before the Dubois bunch took back the money, Bea Hastings helped Mother hide some of it through an investment scheme. And I've got to give Mrs. Hastings credit where it's due. She turned that little bit of cash into quite a fortune."

I listened with wide eyes. "I didn't know any of this. No wonder they've remained friends for so many years."

Matt shrugged. "Mother still consults with her for investment advice. With a shark like Bea in your tank, why not?"

"Enough gossip. We've arrived."

Ten

≈≈≈≈≈≈≈≈≈≈≈≈≈≈≈≈≈≈≈≈≈≈≈≈≈

WELL, we'd *almost* arrived.

The Art Deco bronze-and-glass doors provided easy access to the outer lobby, but the interior entrance was locked tight. I was hoping to sweet talk the doorman, or maybe convince him to check on Bea himself.

But apparently the doorman was out on an errand or break—a sign with little clock hands indicated he would return in thirty minutes, though I had no idea how long the doorman had been gone already.

"Look, there's her bell and intercom." Matt pointed. "Give Bea a buzz, and I'm sure the queen of bees will buzz you in."

I pushed the button once, twice, three times without a response. In frustration, I pulled out my phone and tried calling her a second time. Once again, my call went to voice mail. This time I left a message—

"Bea, it's Clare. I've come to see you. I'm right downstairs. Please call me back. It's urgent. Or at least I *think* it is."

I ended the call and Matt rubbed his beard. "Now what?"

"I guess we wait for Bea to return my call—unless there's something wrong, and she can't, which is why I'm worried. Or we wait for the door-man to get back."

"Why wait?" Matt said. "This is Manhattan. We're inside the lobby of an awfully expensive apartment building. Surely one of these night owls is waiting for a delivery of some sort. Pizza, all-night cookies, a pastrami on rye. Something—"

"You can't start ringing random buttons and bothering residents," I protested.

"Just watch me!"

Matt's grin was devilish behind his pirate beard. He rang one buzzer on each floor, starting at the top. Someone on the seventh floor finally responded.

"Delivery," Matt said into the speaker.

"Oh, you're a hoot, beefcake," a man breathlessly replied. "Now get on up here you sexy brute. I bought a new leopard-print thong, and I can't wait for you to model it. Remember, seventh floor!"

I stifled a laugh. The door buzzed, and a red-faced Matt pushed us through.

"Bea's private elevator should take us straight up from this lobby to a reception room inside her penthouse."

"Surprise, surprise," Matt said as we approached it. "Looks like the elevator is locked for the night."

"There's another way," I said, dragging him to the main elevator bank. "Your mother took me this way once when Bea's private elevator was under maintenance. We take one of these public elevator cars up to the tenth floor. From there we can easily switch to a service elevator and ride it up two floors. It opens right outside the service entrance to Bea's penthouse."

I boarded a waiting elevator, but Matt hung back.

"Come on, hurry up," I commanded my suddenly reluctant ex.

"Okay," he replied. "But under *no* circumstances are we stopping on floor number seven."

"You got it, beefcake. Now get in!"

To Matt's obvious relief (and my amusement), the elevator breezed right past seven. But when the doors opened on ten, we were both in for a surprise.

"Matteo Allegro? Is that you?"

A tall blonde wearing black leggings, a black leather coat, and matching thigh-high boots greeted Matt as he stepped out of the elevator.

"*È bello vederti*," she cooed, showing off a perfect Italian accent to convey nothing more than the equivalent of *It's nice to see you.*

"Nellie!" Matt projected a grin, but I could see his usually relaxed posture tensing up a little about the unexpected encounter. "*Stai benissimo*," he said, getting into the whole *Let's be Italian* moment. In Matt's case, he told her she looked great, and did she ever.

Statuesque and shapely, Matt's friend didn't just project sophistication, she reeked of it. Her eye-catching attire was top-shelf designer stuff. The scent she wore was subtle, almost fleeting, like a fine perfume should be. Her golden locks appeared to be expensively balayaged (i.e., hand-painted by a stylist to give her light brown hair a look of natural sun-kissed color), her diction was cultured, even her Italian accent was refined.

She gave Matt a Hamptons' hug and air-kisses to go with it. When she took a step back to appraise him, Matt turned to me.

"Clare, I want you to meet *Forbes* magazine's Queen of Start-ups, Mrs. Nellie Sagar—"

"It's Nellie *Atwood* again."

She shook my hand, then touched Matt's lips with her index finger. "Don't mention that man's name to me and we'll get along fine."

Matt raised an eyebrow. "Your whirlwind romance didn't go so well?"

"Let's just say that after a sweet honeymoon—" She paused to make a lemon-sucking face. "Things went very sour, very quickly. Fortunately, it's my second divorce so I knew the ropes—and just the right attorney to hire. Hey, I heard you visited the *un*hitching post yourself."

Given her social status, I knew Ms. Atwood wasn't referring to the ancient history of Matt's divorce from me. She was talking about my ex-husband's second mistake, his recently failed marriage to fashion maven, media entrepreneur, and fixture on the international social scene, Breanne Summour.

Matt and Breanne had a whirlwind romance, too, but as the wealthy and influential Ms. Summour saw her once highly popular *Trend* magazine collapse into online obscurity, and her influence go the way of the dodo, she felt the need for more economic security than my intrepid coffee hunter ex-husband could supply. She moved on to greener pastures—green, as in the color of money in a new (much older) companion's (much richer) bank account.

"Nellie, meet Clare. She is—"

"I know all about Clare Cosi." Nellie studied me with interest. "She's your partner in the coffee business and a master roaster, among *other* things, from what I hear."

Matt blinked in surprise. "You remembered?"

"How could I forget? You could never stop talking about that coffeehouse, or Clare." She fixed her gaze on me. "You're obviously a man who loves his . . . work."

Matt quickly jumped topics. "Is this where you live now, Nellie?"

She ran a manicured, French-tipped, and ringless left hand through her long, salon-burnished locks.

"Oh, no. I was just visiting a friend. My ex retained the Hamptons property, and I bought a place in Hudson Yards a couple of months ago. You should drop by some time—and bring a magnum of Cristal as a house-warming gift. We'll share it."

Nellie was chatty—okay, flirty—and Matt seemed reluctant to break off the conversation. But I was here to see Bea Hastings, not visit with yet another woman with an obvious Matt-crush.

"We need to go," I said, elbowing my ex.

"You go on ahead, Clare. I'll catch up in a few minutes."

With a polite goodbye to the Queen of Start-ups, I hurried down the carpeted hallway. Just around the corner, I found the service elevator. As I pressed the button and waited, I overheard Matt and his gal pal continuing to chat away.

"Look at that *wild* beard," Nellie gushed, her tone becoming far more personal now that I was gone. "May I touch?"

"Sure, I guess. I didn't have time to trim after my trip to Central America. You like it this bushy?"

"Oh, yes. It's so . . . *primal.*"

Good grief. Despite what Matt said about "catching up to me," I suspected that was the last I'd see of my "primal" ex-husband tonight.

Eleven

〰〰〰〰〰〰〰〰〰〰〰〰〰〰〰〰〰〰〰

At last, my elevator arrived. It was a service car, no frills and big as a Buick. Counting the seconds, I rode its lumbering motor two floors north to the penthouse.

The doors clanged open onto a deserted private lobby illuminated by muted torchieres. The dimly lit space was windowless, and decorated in a faux-Egyptian, Deco style that also dominated the building's design.

The service door to Bea's penthouse apartment was closed and locked. *Ring for Deliveries*, read a tasteful sign next to a doorbell, and I did, several times. Then I knocked—pounded, actually—even shouted for someone to answer.

I knew Bea had a live-in housekeeper named Ella. Her private bedroom and sitting room were located near this service door. Even if Ella had been sleeping, she should have heard me ringing, knocking, and yelling my head off.

Bea's twentysomething niece, Susan Hastings, sometimes lived here with Bea, as well, though the girl traveled so much, who knew if she was there now.

With no luck getting any response, I was about to head back downstairs and search for the missing doorman when I realized a strong draft of cool air was streaming through this service lobby—and it wasn't air from an internal source because (after a long sniff) I detected a tinge of Atlantic salt. This air was obviously coming from outside.

Turning from the apartment door, I glanced around the windowless walls and spied a second door in the deep shadows at the far end of the lobby. This second door stood wide open, and night air was pouring through it like water through a funnel.

I followed the strong breeze to the open door and found an unlit corridor with a polished marble floor. The corridor was as dark and cold as a mausoleum, and I couldn't find a light switch. With a shiver, I considered what to do next.

Turn back?

No way. Not now.

Channeling Nancy Drew and my old Girl Scout ingenuity, I reached for my smartphone (the twenty-first-century in-a-pinch flashlight) and used its bright LED glow to guide me through.

At the end of the gloomy corridor, I discovered a steep flight of stairs. I peered up the dark steps to find a thick steel door at the top. It was standing open, too, wide enough for me to see the night sky—and I realized this back passage gave Bea direct access to her roof.

I knew it was possible that Bea was up there on her roof right now, puttering around in her greenhouse. Ella could be with her, helping out. Yet the whole scene felt off to me—

The doors standing wide open.

Bea not answering her phone.

And those poor little honeybees (which I was *still* sure were hers) fleeing their hives for the warmth of my roasting room chimney.

I had no evidence that anything was actually wrong here, just a gut feeling. So, I kept going, climbing the steps to investigate further.

At the top of the stairs, I peeked around the edge of the metal door and considered calling out Bea's name, but decided against it, at least until I got a better sense of the situation. Instead, I stepped out onto the flat, dark roof.

No lights were on up here, not even decorative landscape lighting—and that seemed wrong, too. The massive two-story glass-and-steel structure was silhouetted only by the glowing city skyline.

I'd never seen Bea's greenhouse before, only heard about it. Now I stood in awe of its sheer size. It was far larger than I'd imagined. With twenty-foot-high walls and a sloped roof, its footprint took up most of the city-block-sized roof. Several small outbuildings hugged the steel and glass structure, some overhanging the roof's edge.

I didn't know if I was alone up here, which was why I found the darkness and silence even more disturbing. I mean, shouldn't a greenhouse have lights? And shouldn't there be a heating system humming away on such a cool night?

I waited for my eyes to adjust to the gloom and soon noticed that the door to the greenhouse was also wide open.

I crossed a raised wooden walkway layered over the tar roof and cautiously approached the looming structure. The greenhouse was pitch black. Even before I reached the doorway, my senses were overwhelmed by the cloying aroma of lavender. That strong floral smell was all I had to guide me, except for some ambient light from the buildings around me, and the pathetic glow of my phone.

With a deep breath I stepped over the threshold, fumbling for a light switch. Finally, my fingers closed on the control, and I flipped it.

Lights came on like a blazing sun. My night-honed eyes teared as I blinked against the glare. I took a blind step forward—and immediately felt something soft squishing under my boot.

I paused and waited.

When my vision returned, I stared in horror at the greenhouse floor. It was littered with corpses!

Twelve

~~~~~~

Little bee bodies, their tiny legs curled, covered the greenhouse floor like a tan-striped carpet. More dead and dying honeybees were scattered on supply shelves, in a deep stainless steel sink, on a folding chair, and on a long worktable table propped against the wall.

Remembering how Officer Greene described the honeybees in my coffeehouse as "little lost souls," I wanted to cry.

The cause of death was obvious—the bees' happy homes had been attacked. I counted six blocky box hives. Five were knocked off their stands, and one had been heartlessly destroyed. Frames had been ripped out and dashed to the ground. Among the splintered wood and dying bees, cracked wax combs oozed puddles of Bea's coveted honeybee nectar.

Beyond this grisly graveyard, I found row upon row of lavender plants, purple waves that stretched all the way to the other end of the greenhouse with levels rising up. And above those neat levels and rows, coffin-like planters dangled from steel cables, their contents shrouded in shadows.

But something was wrong with the lavender, too. The sea of flowers drooped; many purple blossoms withered from the cold autumn air filling the greenhouse.

I closed the door behind me, but still I felt a steady stream of air coming from somewhere. Another door? If so, I had to secure that one, too, or Bea's priceless plants were as doomed as her beloved hives.

Heat vents lined the base of the glass and steel walls, but they emanated no warmth. I soon located the thermostat, along with a lot of other controls having to do with humidity and air pressure. But none of my fiddling with switches or dials made the system kick on. Undoubtedly, the vandal had damaged the climate controls, as well.

If I couldn't get the heater going, I could at least close the other door. All I had to do was find it.

The low heels of my ankle boots echoed hollowly as I walked along the many rows of flowers. Though three levels of grow lights burned overhead, their heat would not be enough to sustain the plants for long.

At the opposite end of the greenhouse, I found a telescope mounted on a tall tripod. There was a table next to it with several pairs of binoculars and a video camera. The telescope lens was pointed west, toward the river. And it was locked in place.

Out of curiosity I peered through the lens. The view was of the Hudson River and a narrow blacktop pier with a barge lashed to it. The view was partial—just a section of the pier and the bow of a cargo barge, both framed by tall warehouses on either side. The pier was so well lit, and the telescope so powerful, that I saw with crystal clarity a stack of boxes marked with a full white moon and the name *La Luna Farms*—a fresh produce brand I saw every time I went to the supermarket.

Not a soul was on that pier, but it was late, so I wasn't really surprised, though the view made me wonder.

Was Bea bird-watching or boat watching?

A dark blue curtain rippled nearby, then a loud bang startled me. The noise and movement were immediately followed by a rush of cold air that raised the tiny hairs on my arms.

I'd found the draft.

Cautiously, I stepped around the curtain and discovered a door, wide open, and banging in the wind. There was broken glass, too. Silvery shards spilled outward, onto the roof's narrow ledge.

I wanted to close that door. To reach the handle, I carefully stepped through the doorframe. The concrete ledge was barely large enough to accommodate my feet. With a twelve-story plunge just inches away, I felt a jolt of panic when a wind gust buffeted me. But I couldn't quit now. Hugging the glass greenhouse wall, I reached out for the door handle. As I did, I realized that part of Bea's apartment balcony was directly below where I stood—maybe thirty feet down.

I glimpsed the plush furniture and lush, exotic plants from my last visit. Bea and I had sat on that very balcony, sipping refreshing Bee's Knees cocktails as we chatted about the creation of my Honey-Cinnamon Latte, her cultivation of lavender nectar, and even her advice on my choice of wedding flowers.

But one thing was different now. Bea's broken body was sprawled face-down on that balcony, among puddles of dark red blood.

Sick with horror, I backed up, almost tripping as I moved through the doorway. I turned to seek help—only to smack right into a hard wall of masculine muscle.

When two strong hands seized my arms, I couldn't help myself.

I started screaming.

Thirteen

〰〰〰〰〰〰〰〰〰〰〰〰〰〰〰〰〰〰

"Clare! Get a grip!" Matt cried, releasing me. "What's wrong?"

"Oh, God, it's you."

"Who did you think it was, Bea Hastings?"

"No." I shivered. "Because Bea . . . is over there . . . *down* there . . ."

I gave up trying to explain and just pointed. Matt squeezed his broad shoulders through the narrow doorway. Without holding on to a thing, he looked down.

"I think she's still alive."

"I'm calling 911."

"If that doorman is still MIA, they'll have to crash through her apartment door," Matt cautioned. "Unless . . ."

"Don't worry, I'll warn the operator."

But Matt wasn't listening. Instead, he scanned an array of tools and gardening equipment hanging on racks, stacked on shelves, or leaning against the wall.

My call was answered, and for the second time tonight, I rattled off the pertinent information to an emergency operator. This time she told me to wait for the police in front of Bea's penthouse door.

Matt was busy, too. While I talked, he had peeled off his loose flannel shirt and looped a long and absurdly thin rope around a steel support beam; the other ends of the rope he was wrapping strategically around his bright yellow Brazilian soccer jersey.

"What are you doing?" I cried.

"Bea's cut up pretty bad. If the fall didn't kill her, she'll bleed out if she's not treated ASAP."

"The police are already coming," I argued. "An ambulance is coming, too."

"They might have to break in through her apartment door, and that would take time. But if I get down there, I can help Bea *and* let them in."

Before I could stop him, Matt was pulling the rope ends through his legs to create a makeshift harness and backing up to the roof's edge. Powerful gusts of wind ruffled his shaggy hair.

"Tell me you're not going to use that thin little rope to climb down there!" I pleaded.

"The rope is fiberglass, so there's no chance of it breaking." He adjusted his grip. "And I'm *rappelling* down the side of the building. There's no climbing involved."

"That's crazy. You could get killed!"

"Take it easy, Clare. I'm an expert in this technique. It's called South African abseil, remember? I've told you how I use it—I even gave you a lesson once. Sometimes the best way to check out a great shade-grown coffee crop is down the side of a mountain."

"Please be careful!"

What happened to Bea was awful, and I didn't think things could get worse. But now I had a front-row seat to see the father of my daughter splattered on a Chelsea sidewalk.

As I tensely watched, Matt threw me a reassuring wink, then he backed off the roof's edge, manipulating the rope as he moved. In seconds he'd lowered himself out of sight.

I waited in frozen silence, fully expecting a scream or a bone-crunching splat. When I heard neither I risked a peek. Gripping the doorjamb like a lifeline, I peered over the edge again.

Matt was already on the balcony, sweeping broken glass aside. He knelt beside Bea to examine her injuries. He checked her pulse and breathing, then he ran inside Bea's apartment. He came out again with a bundle of towels. Quickly creating a tourniquet, he wrapped it around Bea's battered right leg.

He looked up, saw me, and shouted something. But his words were swallowed by sirens blaring on the street below.

Fourteen

⌒⌒⌒⌒⌒⌒⌒⌒⌒⌒⌒⌒⌒⌒⌒⌒⌒⌒⌒⌒⌒

TWELVE floors down, emergency vehicles were converging on the Hastings. I ran through the greenhouse, across the roof, and down the stairs.

The faux-Egyptian lobby was still empty, but Matt had unlocked and opened Bea's apartment door. I was about to enter when the service elevator dinged.

The doors opened and two burly policemen emerged, one wielding a steel battering ram. The officers spied the open door and registered obvious disappointment.

A pair of paramedics raced past the uniformed officers and into Bea's apartment. When I tried to follow, a heavy hand dropped on my shoulder.

"Hold on, ma'am," one of the policemen said. "Who are you and where do you think you're going?"

I shook off the hand and turned to face a blue serge wall, a badge, and a name tag that read *Healey*. A pair of inquisitive eyes stared at me from under the brim of an NYPD cap.

"I'm Clare Cosi, a friend of the victim. I was the one who found Bea and called 911."

"Tell me what you know, Ms. Cosi."

I did, and that took several minutes. In that time, Officer Healey did a lot of scribbling.

I finished my account just as the paramedics wheeled Bea out. Matt was with them, holding an IV bottle steady while the EMS crew maneuvered the gurney into the elevator. Madame's old friend looked gaunt and pale, her flesh stretched tightly over her skull, her closed eyes sunken.

"Who could have done this?" I said in anguish as the elevator doors closed.

"Why do you think anyone's done anything, Ms. Cosi?"

I reminded Officer Healey about the vandalism on the roof.

Nodding, he touched my elbow. "Let's go up together, and you show me what you found, okay?"

Fifteen minutes later Officer Healey and I had finished our inspection of the greenhouse. We returned to find Bea Hastings's apartment door standing open. The paramedics were gone, and I wondered if my ex-husband had come back upstairs. I didn't get a chance to ask before Officer Healey took me inside Bea's apartment and began grilling me.

"Have you been inside this apartment before?" he asked.

"Yes," I said.

"Were you in here tonight?"

"No. I told you already. No one answered when I rang."

"The doorman claims he didn't let you in."

"That's true. He was off duty."

"He takes a meal break every evening at this time. It's possible you knew that, being a friend of the victim and all."

I shook my head. "I didn't."

"How did you get through the security doors downstairs?"

"Funny thing," I muttered, ready to tell him the beefcake story.

He cut me off. "Look, I need to bring you in, Ms. Cosi. I think a detective should take your statement."

"I'm happy to help with any investigation, but right now I want to go to the hospital to check on my friend. Look, I was the one who found her in the state she's in. My business partner can corroborate my story. He came here with me. He even climbed down the side of a building to save her life—"

"Where is this business partner?"

At that moment, Matt Allegro walked into Bea's apartment, alongside two policemen. One of them was a sergeant—easily recognizable by his white uniform shirt (well, "easily recognizable" if you're engaged to an NYPD detective).

"Sarge," Officer Healey said. "I was about to detain Ms. Cosi—"

"No need, Gil. I've spoken with the paramedics, and I just checked the scene with Mr. Allegro. It looks like it might have been a terrible accident. It appears she knocked over several hives and stirred up the bees, who went after her. To escape, Mrs. Hastings went through the door to get to the roof ledge and lost her footing. The Crime Scene Unit is on the way to better evaluate the situation. And detectives will be assigned to follow up."

I thought that "attack-bee accident" theory was absurd and was about to contradict the sergeant. Matt knew it, too, but he shot me a very sharp warning look that said, *Please keep your mouth shut!*

For once, I did.

"It seems these two just happened onto the scene," the sergeant continued. "And a good thing they did. The paramedics tell me this man risked his own life to save the victim."

Matt shrugged. "I just applied what I know, Officer. Basic first aid comes in handy when you do what I do. There's no 911 on a mountainside in the Andes or the highlands of Ethiopia."

Healey's eyebrows rose at that. "Then I guess I should . . . ?"

"You've got Ms. Cosi's statement. And I understand from Mr. Allegro that she's Detective Lieutenant Quinn's fiancée, so we'll know how to find her."

"Mike Quinn of the OD Squad?"

"The same. Now cut her loose."

Five minutes later, Matt and I were on the sidewalk again.

"You don't believe what happened to Bea was an 'accident,' do you, Matt?"

"Honestly? I don't know what to believe. But I *never* argue with a cop who's about to set me free."

"Well, what's done is done. And you heard the sergeant, the Crime Scene Unit is on the way and detectives are going to follow up soon. They'll want to talk to me *and* you, so don't disappear into the highlands of Ethiopia, okay?" I checked the time. "Now I've got to go—"

"—to the hospital," Matt finished for me. "I know you do, Clare. So do I. They took Bea to Beth Israel. Let's grab a cab together."

Fifteen

꩜꩜꩜꩜꩜꩜꩜꩜꩜꩜꩜꩜꩜꩜꩜꩜꩜꩜꩜꩜꩜꩜꩜

I've visited far too many intensive care units over the years, and they all seemed the same: the antiseptic smell; the beeping machines; the whispering nurses and the heavy sense of sadness, worry, and even fear.

In the waiting room, the RN told Matt and me that Bea Hastings had been stabilized and was semiconscious. I felt we had to see her, but when Matt asked, he was informed that only a family member, clergy, or a legal representative was permitted to visit a patient in the ICU.

Matt spoke up. "But I'm the one who saved her—"

"I'm her niece," I loudly interrupted. "My name is Susan Hastings and I live with my aunt."

I hated lying, but I told this whopper for two reasons—the first because I wanted to know what happened to Bea! The second because the police would need time to evaluate the scene, and though the sergeant informed us that detectives would "follow up," nobody from the NYPD was here *now*.

Getting Bea's statement would not only help me help Bea, it might help the police investigation, and that's what I intended to do.

I also knew that Susan Hastings only lived with her aunt sporadically. A freelance Internet marketer by trade and flighty by nature, Suzie had a generous trust fund—courtesy of Aunt Bea—and she traveled extensively, all the while working remotely for several companies, large and small. There was little chance Ms. Hastings would barge into the ICU and dispute my borrowing of her identity.

Lucky for me no one checked my ID. Instead, I was immediately ushered to a bed surrounded by medical devices and IV tubes. Bea looked small and fragile, but her eyes were open, if unfocused.

Before I could get close enough to address her, a doctor pulled me aside.

"We're putting Mrs. Hastings into a medically induced coma to reduce the swelling on her brain," she warned. "You can talk to her, but remember, Mrs. Hastings is groggy, and she appears to have short-term memory loss. Don't tax her too much. And please keep your visit as brief as possible."

After that, the medical staff hung back, and I was allowed to speak with Bea in private.

"Bea?" I whispered. "Can you hear me?"

With surprising abruptness, Bea's eyes focused on me.

"Clare?" she rasped, the tubes in her nose and throat making speech difficult.

"What happened to you, Bea?"

Her eyes moved from side to side. She tried to lift her arm, but it became entangled in IV tubes, and she lowered it again.

"Take care of my bees, Clare . . . My bees . . ."

Obviously, Beatrice either didn't know about or didn't remember the vandalized hives, and now certainly wasn't the time to mention it.

"What about your housekeeper, Ella?"

"My Ella? Ella is gone. Back to Austria. I told her to go . . ."

I heard rustling. Someone came through the wall of curtains behind me, but they kept their distance. I assumed it was a doctor or a nurse who came to chase me out, so I didn't acknowledge them. Instead, I pressed Bea for more answers.

"What about Susan? Where is your niece?"

Bea seemed disoriented for a moment, then she became agitated. "I don't know . . . Suzie . . . Suzie . . . I . . . can't . . . reach . . ."

Her choking voice failed for a moment. Her lips moved but no sound emerged. Then Bea's eyes focused on me once again.

"You *must* take care of my bees, Clare. You're the only one I trust."

I took Bea's hand, alarmed by how cold it seemed.

"I don't trust anyone . . . Only you and Blanche," Bea continued, weakly squeezing my hand. "Promise me you'll do it."

"I'll do it, Bea. I promise. I'll do my best to protect your honeybees."

Bea relaxed when she heard that. She settled back on the pillow and within seconds she seemed to fall asleep.

Suddenly, a machine at Bea's bedside began to ding repeatedly. The curtains were immediately swept aside, and two nurses circled Bea's bed.

"You'll have to leave now," one of them insisted. "We'll take care of her."

I turned to go and bumped into a stocky, ginger-bearded youth with a mop of red hair crowning an elfin face. He wore an untucked Hawaiian shirt and baggy denims. Around his pudgy neck he wore a metal chain with a rectangular bauble of some kind dangling from it.

"I guess you're in charge," he declared.

"Excuse me?"

"I heard Mrs. Hastings put you in charge and I have to tell you that's a relief. I know nothing about bees except they have stingers."

"Who are you?"

"I'm Todd Duncan, Mrs. Hastings's IT chief. Actually, I'm chief of me, as I don't have a staff."

"You run Bea's business computers?"

"And her security system, along with the greenhouse, which practically runs itself thanks to my software."

"How did you get in here?"

He grinned. "I'm also a lawyer. I just passed the bar . . . barely. My degree's only from a night school, but you wouldn't believe how far that shingle gets me."

"What are you doing here? How did you find out about Bea's . . . accident?"

"Bea's doorman Freddie rang me up, told me what happened. I was on my way to the greenhouse to make things right again. I stopped here first to find out if Bea had any instructions for me. And I just heard them— Mrs. Hastings put *you* in charge, Ms. . . . ?"

"Cosi, Clare Cosi. I'm one of Bea's culinary clients, and my employer is one of her oldest friends."

"Okay, then." He shuffled his Nike-sandaled feet. "No offense, but I better get going before the cold damages Bea's hothouse flowers. I'm going to get things up and running, even if it takes me all night."

"Wait! Do you know Susan? Bea's niece?"

"Yes, of course."

"We need to reach her. Do you have her phone number?"

"I do not." He shrugged. "I tried to ask her out once. Thus end-eth the conversation."

"Well, we need to find her. As far as I know, she's next of kin."

Todd agreed. He and I exchanged phone numbers, and I promised to call him in the morning. Then Todd Duncan was gone. Meanwhile, I remained somewhat dazed and confused by Bea's request.

I had no clue how I was supposed to transform myself from a coffee roaster to a beekeeper overnight. But I had to make a plan, manage a way to fulfill my promise to Bea.

Returning to the waiting room, eyes downcast, my head was hanging as low as I felt. What I needed more than anything at that moment was an emotional rescue—and sometimes you do get what you need.

"Hi, Clare."

Hearing that deep, familiar greeting, I looked up, right into Detective Lieutenant Mike Quinn's cobalt blue eyes—as sharp and cool as arctic ice when he was working, now warmed by his worry and compassion for me.

Quinn's short-cropped sandy brown hair glowed like a halo under the harsh florescent lights. He greeted me with strong arms wide, and I was relieved to step into his embrace. As he held me close, I hugged the man's sturdy frame like a tired swimmer hugs a rock in a storm.

"Are you okay?" he whispered.

"I'm okay. But Bea isn't. And neither are her little lost honeybees." I stepped back and swiped at a tear. "How did you know I was here?"

"Allegro called me."

Quinn dipped his head in the direction of the nurses' station, where my ex-husband was focused on talking with a smiling RN. He was ignoring us—or pretending to.

Quinn shrugged his broad shoulders. "I think he's still trying to do right after all the wrongs he's done."

"I'm so glad he called you."

We hugged again, then Quinn asked about Bea.

"Take me home and I'll tell you all about it."

Sixteen

"Hey, Allegro," Quinn called, "do you need a ride to Brooklyn? We can drive you."

"Three's a crowd." Matt displayed his phone. "And my Uber is on the way. Thanks anyway."

I was relieved that Matt declined the invitation to join us, and I suspected Quinn was, too. Though things were going smoothly now, the tension between the man I was about to marry and the father of my only daughter would likely always be there.

Quinn was parked right near the hospital entrance—in a no-standing zone—which was risky business in a town where parking tickets appeared as if by magic. But the official NYPD plaque on the man's dashboard had a magic power all its own.

"So, what happened to Mrs. Hastings?" Quinn asked after he slipped behind the steering wheel and I poured myself into the passenger seat.

My words tripped over themselves as I told him everything—starting with the swarm at the Village Blend, the visit by the NYPD beekeeping unit, Matt smelling lavender and me sniffing out enough clues to find the vandalized greenhouse and Bea Hastings.

"Allegro doesn't believe what happened to Bea was an accident?"

"No, but he pretended to accept a preposterous theory about attack-bees the police sergeant spun out of thin air. I wanted to object, but Matt insisted it wasn't smart to contradict a police officer who's about to let you go."

Quinn actually laughed, melting away hours of toil. "Allegro isn't as stupid as he acts."

"The challenging part is that Bea begged me to protect her bees. And she did it in front of her IT guy, Todd Duncan, who also happens to be a lawyer. Mike, I certainly want to help. But I don't know a thing about the care and feeding of honeybees."

"There's no one Bea worked with?"

"A woman named Ella is her housekeeper. She assisted Bea in the greenhouse, but Bea said she went back to Europe. I don't know why."

"Bea has no family?"

"Only her niece, Susan, but the woman's a nomad. Bea couldn't tell me where she is, and neither could Todd."

"Well, if I were you," Quinn said, "I'd try to find her—and fast. If Susan lives with her aunt, even part-time, she likely knows something about the woman's business, and she might be able to provide some leads for the police investigation—you know what I mean, whether Bea had any enemies or was in a dispute with anyone."

I considered Quinn's words. "What if Bea was in dispute with someone, and that person was Susan?"

Quinn sat back. "That would be sad. But don't worry, the detectives will look into that, too. And they'll review the security camera footage. The footage will likely provide their strongest leads."

"Okay. In the meantime, I made a promise to Bea. I'll have to figure something out—"

A loud, static *buzz* from Quinn's police radio drowned out my bee talk (which I found ironic). He offered an apologetic frown before responding. He talked for several minutes, but I didn't even try to eavesdrop. My mind had temporarily exceeded its capacity to deal with pretty much anything.

When the call ended, Quinn tucked the phone away and apologized. "Duty calls. A body was dumped; looks like another OD. Two of my people are heading there, but I'm going to meet them. I need to look at the scene itself, not just a report and photos. I'll drop you off at home—"

"No. I don't want to be alone right now. Take me with you."

Quinn shook his head. "It's so late, Clare. This could take an hour or more."

"I don't care."

"Well, you should. You have to open your shop in the morning, don't you?"

Sitting back, I folded my arms. "I'm not leaving this car."

Quinn let out a breath. "I *could* arrest you for defying a police officer's directive."

I held out both wrists. "Make my day."

Quinn's cop mask finally cracked. "Don't tempt me, Cosi."

"Come on, start the engine."

Miraculously, he did. *First round to the Coffee Lady.* As we drove up First Avenue, I felt victorious—at least for a moment.

"So where are we headed? Brooklyn? Queens?"

"Both," Quinn said with a cryptic glance. "And neither."

"What's that supposed to mean? Are we entering the Twilight Zone?"

"In a way. We're going to a slice of old New York called the Hole."

"The Hole? I never heard of it."

"It's real, unfortunately. A miserable little neighborhood between Brooklyn and Queens that's not part of either—a place so problematic neither borough will claim jurisdiction."

"You make it sound like a border town in the Wild West."

"Most city agencies won't let their people go down there, either."

"Down? You mean it really *is* a hole?"

"Thirty feet below sea level. So deep the Department of Environmental Protection can't connect the neighborhood to the sewer system. Every time there's a heavy rain, the streets flood, which causes sporadic power failures and undermines streetlamps, which either fall over or go dark."

"You make it sound almost romantic."

"Hey, you're the one who insisted on coming," Quinn warned, completely missing my attempt at humor.

I took a breath. "Why don't you tell me more. I need the distraction."

"There's not much more to tell. Thirty years ago, the Mafia used the Hole as a dumping ground for their victims. There used to be horse trailers there, too, and cowboys."

"Okay, now you're pulling my leg, just because I made that Wild West border town joke—"

"I swear, Cosi, I'm not pulling your leg. This is actual New York history. You've heard of urban cowboys, right?"

"Not to be confused with midnight cowboys?"

"Definitely not."

"Kidding aside, I know there's a horsey culture in the wider tristate area. But the city?" I scratched my head. "There used to be horseback riding on a bridle path in Central Park. And didn't Madison Square Garden once host an annual rodeo?"

"Yes, to both, and the Hole is part of our urban cowboy history. At one time, it was used by the New York City Federation of Black Cowboys. The group was organized to keep the memory of the African American cowboy tradition alive. They managed Cedar Lane Stables in Howard Beach, gave riding lessons, and ran programs for inner-city kids. Good stuff. They don't run the stables anymore; it's under new management. But some of the old cowhands still live and ride in the neighborhood."

The police radio buzzed again. As Quinn began a new round of talks with the dispatcher, we crossed the 59th Street Bridge, made famous by the old Simon and Garfunkel song. The span connected Manhattan and Queens and offered a spectacular view of both boroughs and the East River flowing between them.

On each side of the sparkling dark waters, high-rise buildings stretched out before us with millions of windows looking out on the world. Some were in shadows, but others glowed brightly, even at this late hour because New York was—and always would be—the city that never sleeps.

Traffic on the bridge was still coming and going. Slow-moving barges kept floating down river, and planes continued to cross the clear night sky. This was our hive, packed with countless little souls whose buzzy energy seemingly never flagged.

Ironically, my own was beginning to. Between the drone of the wheels on the pavement and the gentle motion of the car, I started to feel drowsy. Heavy eyelids closed and I dozed off—only to be jolted back awake after what *felt* like a few brief seconds.

Clearly, I'd slept much longer.

While I had dozed, Quinn had crossed the borough of Queens and was now plunging the car into a steep drop that threw me forward, against the shoulder harness.

We'd left the highway behind and were now surrounded by flat-roofed row houses—a landscape that quickly vanished from view as we rolled down bumpy pavement into a dark valley.

"Where are we?" I asked, rubbing my eyes.

"The Twilight Zone," Quinn said, throwing me an arctic glance. "Welcome to the Hole."

Seventeen

After going down that steep incline for a hundred yards or more, we finally reached bottom where a puddle that could pass for Lake eerie (pun intended) had collected in the middle of the road. A single streetlight burned above the murky pool, its glare reflecting off the water.

"This area was a bog once." Quinn shook his head. "Developers tried to make it livable but failed. Now the swamp is reclaiming everything. It's hard to believe this seedy neighborhood is only a few miles from some of the most valuable real estate in the world."

Quinn cautiously plowed through the shallowest part of the pool without flooding the engine. Next we passed the unfinished remains of a failed development. The walls of a row house leaned drunkenly on a sagging foundation that was completely submerged in murky water. Dangling branches from weeping willows and wild outgrowths of low scrub choked the pavement around it.

On the opposite side of the road, half-concealed behind a wall of thick brush, I spied a for-sale sign, the house in question a ramshackle silhouette nearly obscured by overgrown weeds.

After that we drove by a formerly empty lot surrounded by a rusty and broken chain-link fence. The muddy strip of land was piled high with empty produce boxes, all bearing a full white moon and the words *La Luna Farms*.

It looked like a grocery or warehouse was shamefully using this area for their personal dumping ground—which only encouraged more lawbreakers. Among the heaps of cardboard boxes, a faded white van—tires missing, windshield smashed, plates removed—had been abandoned to rust away.

Quinn braked to allow a trio of roaming dogs to scurry furtively through the beams of our headlights. Before he inched forward again, I swear I saw the silhouette of a cowboy on a horse in the rearview mirror.

I blinked, opened my eyes again, and the reflection was gone.

I must be more tired than I thought, I decided. *Mike's urban cowboy talk has got me hallucinating the Lone Ranger.*

One thing I did not hallucinate was the flicker of red emergency lights up ahead. I counted a pair of police cars, a van from the coroner's office, and a truck from the Crime Scene Unit. All four vehicles were jammed into a cul-de-sac with a dilapidated garage at its center. A faded sign that read *Dan's All-Nite Car Repair* was still visible on the ruined façade.

Off to the side of the dead-end road, a pair of uniformed officers stood over a plastic tarp spread on the muddy shoulder. The impromptu shroud was surrounded by crushed beer cans and broken liquor bottles.

Quinn cut the engine and faced me. "Wait here. This shouldn't take long."

When he opened the door, the car was flooded with cold, damp air and the smell of rotting vegetation. As Lieutenant Quinn approached the crime scene, I removed my seat belt and settled in for more of my interrupted snooze.

Before I closed my eyes, however, I glanced at the rearview mirror, where the reflection of a cowboy on horseback had reappeared. The rider looked much closer than before, and he was getting closer all the time.

Okay, Clare. Maybe you're not crazy after all.

I stepped out of the car. The air was cool and misty. It felt damp against my skin. I pulled my coat closed and took several paces away from the car, where I came face-to-face with a middle-aged Black man, slim and tall in the saddle. As his horse loped toward me, the man astride the mount tipped his Stetson.

Despite the chilly fog, the cowboy wore only a flannel shirt under a light hoodie, his neck wrapped in a red bandana. When he reined his horse, the sleek ebony animal snorted, blowing steaming breath from both nostrils.

"Either you're very lost, or you're with those gentlemen up the road," the cowboy said in a melodious voice.

"My fiancé is over there. He's a police lieutenant."

The cowboy nodded and pushed the Stetson back on his head. "Excuse me if I don't get off my high horse."

He smiled. It was a kind smile.

"That's okay," I said. "It's a pretty horse. I wouldn't want to get down off it, either."

"Missy's a beauty," he said. The horse's ears perked up when she heard her name. "But you misunderstand, ma'am. I'm not trying to be rude. It's just that my legs aren't all that cooperative, courtesy of a roadside bomb overseas."

"I'm sorry to hear it. And I thank you for your service. My name is Clare. Clare Cosi."

He leaned over the saddle and extended his hand. "I'm William Moxley."

I shook his calloused hand, and he nodded toward the emergency lights. "I suspect there's trouble up ahead, if a police lieutenant is involved?"

I nodded. "Someone dumped a body near that old garage."

He sat back in his saddle. "I'm sorry I didn't see anything that would help. And that's too bad because I was out tonight looking for assholes—excuse my French. But that's what I call people who dump garbage illegally."

"I wouldn't argue with that. Are you part of some kind of citizens watch group?"

He laughed. "What I am is one of the last cowboys in the Hole. Most days, I go it alone—except for Missy here."

Again, the horse reacted to her name with ears twitching and a stamp of her hoof.

"You wouldn't be a member of the New York Federation of Black Cowboys, would you?"

"I would. I started riding horses as therapy to strengthen my crippled leg. Then I decided I liked it." He smiled again. "But it really started when I was a boy. A teacher gave me a book on the Black history of the American West and the contribution Black cowboys made to it. That blew my mind."

"I don't doubt it." I nodded. "And all that brought you to horse patrol tonight?"

He leaned on the saddle horn. "That lot you passed back there was empty until a few months ago. Then it started filling up with those crates. A couple of days ago an abandoned van was added to the mess."

Moxley shook his head. "There's another lot just like it a block from here. Well, I don't like my neighborhood used like a garbage dump, so Missy and I mean to stop it."

The horse nickered, and the cowboy patted its neck.

"Missy sure likes her name. Don't you, Missy?" Unconsciously, I used my high pitched "cat voice" and Missy responded instantly. The horse nudged me with her snout, then shook her mane.

"She does love her name, it's true. But she wouldn't mind an apple or a carrot."

"I'm sorry, Missy," I said, still speaking in cat-ese. "I didn't bring anything."

Missy dipped her head and nudged me again.

"I think she likes you."

"Well, I like Missy."

The horse nickered.

"I think this girl is impatient to get home, and with the police around I doubt anyone will dump trash tonight. So, I'm going to say good night, Miss Cosi."

"Good night, Mr. Moxley. It was very nice to meet you."

"It's been a pleasure."

And with the touch of his hand to his Stetson's brim, one of the last cowboys in the Hole rode off on his Missy into the misty night.

Eighteen

꩜꩜꩜꩜꩜꩜꩜꩜꩜꩜꩜꩜꩜꩜꩜꩜꩜

Ten minutes after I returned to the car, Quinn arrived with a new layer of concern etched on his already grim expression. He was tired, too; I could see the weariness in the slump of his broad shoulders.

"I've just clocked out," he announced, trying to sound upbeat.

"Are you hungry?"

"Now that you mention it, we could grab a bite on our way home."

"Let's just *go* home," I suggested. "I have those leftover stuffed shells in the fridge with my Homemade Ricotta, remember? You loved it. We can eat in privacy and relax."

He nodded distractedly, then got quiet. But I knew his mind was still racing.

"What's wrong?" I asked. "Do you want to tell me about it?"

"You've got your own problems, Cosi."

"And I told you I needed a distraction. I talked through my dilemma; now it's your turn."

He snorted. "Dilemma? More like a paradox."

"Give me the facts, Detective."

"Okay, here they are. In the past thirty-two days, four bodies have been dumped in the Hole. All males between the ages of twenty-five and forty, all presumed homeless, though we have no record of them in any shelter for the past year. No attempt was made to hide the bodies; they were simply tossed onto the side of the road, just like the one tonight."

"Were they murdered?"

"Three out of four of these men died from an overdose of XS12, a type of synthetic opioid. I'm betting the toxicology report on tonight's victim will be the same. But that only leads to another mystery."

We'd hit a red light and Quinn faced me. "The OD Squad took that very same batch of poison off the streets and out of clubs ten months ago, or we thought we did. With these OD DOAs, it looks like someone hoarded a stash and now they're dealing it, which puts my team in a high-pressure spot."

"Are you sure it's the same drug?"

"I have three corpses and three toxicology reports to prove it. It may be four as of tonight once we get the lab results."

He shook his head. "When that crap first hit the street, it was easy. Every beat cop got the memo. If they spotted that distinctive blue smoke, they knew it was XS12. Now it's all underground. We can't even find a single dealer selling it, yet XS is still killing people."

I sat back in thought. *No wonder Mike has been so tied up in his work . . .*

For several years now, the small unit of detectives Quinn oversaw was tasked with investigating any drug overdose within New York's five boroughs, lethal or not, and following up when criminality was involved. It was a complicated tour of duty that involved liaising with medical professionals, DEA agents, and local precincts. Nicknamed the OD Squad, Quinn's team had been instrumental in battling wave after wave of pharmaceuticals flooding the streets of New York. The unit was so respected by the police brass they'd been immune to recent cuts imposed in the department. But an unfinished job like Quinn just described could hurt that reputation—not that he was a glory hog. He simply knew that every defeat his team suffered was a win for the wrong side.

"Someone in or around the Hole must be dealing that XS12," I said.

"No. And that's another paradox. None of those victims died *here*. Forensics analysis of their clothes and shoes suggests they died at the same— as yet undetermined—location, and their remains were brought here and dumped."

"But that doesn't make any sense."

"No, it doesn't," Quinn agreed. "A junkie corpse is usually found wherever he or she overdosed, but not in these cases."

"What did they find?"

"Who?"

"Your forensics people. You said they found something on the victims' clothing—"

"And on their shoes, an oil solution used to finish roadways, as if these men spent time walking on fresh tar or asphalt. On their clothes they found recent food and beverage stains that are exactly the same, which suggests the men shared meals or ate at the same place. We're figuring that happened at a food pantry or homeless shelter and we're looking for a match, but no luck so far."

"Are the victims' backgrounds similar?"

"Only that they were addicts. The first victim was a longshoreman from Newark. He started using and couldn't stop. Lost his wife, his family, his home. His own mother hadn't heard from him for over a year before we found his remains."

"And the others?"

"We have yet to identify the second victim. Number three was a short-order cook up in the Bronx who'd fallen on hard times.

"There was no wallet or ID on the guy we found tonight, but we took his fingerprints, so we should know more in a few days."

Quinn stifled a yawn.

I was glad I'd kept him talking and alert all the way across the bridge. With Manhattan traffic so light, we reached the Village Blend in only twenty minutes.

Even after he parked the car, I could tell Quinn's mind was still on duty, even if he wasn't supposed to be.

"The finest police commissioner I ever worked for used to say that the first time something occurs it's likely happenstance, the second time could be coincidence, but the third time definitely indicates a pattern." He released a breath. "After victim number four, I don't even know what to call this."

"With everything you described, Mike, it sounds deliberate."

"If it is, Clare, then we both know what to call it."

"Murder."

Nineteen

By the time Mike Quinn and I walked through the front door of my duplex apartment, I suggested he skip the food and go straight up to bed.

"You look wrecked, Lieutenant. Get some sleep."

He surprised me with a low, firm "No."

Shaking his head, he peeled off his trench coat and sport jacket, revealing a white dress shirt with some serious wrinkles, primarily from the leather straps of the shoulder holster that held his service weapon in place all day.

"I'd like us to have a *little* time together," he said, hanging his clothes on the coat rack. "You know, other than outside an ICU or beside a crime scene perimeter."

"That's nice. But you've had a long day and a tough night."

With calloused fingers, he touched my cheek. "You've had a long day and a tough night, too."

That cheered me up. So did the lingering kiss he gave me. It had been so long since he touched me like this, I wanted to cry. But the kiss didn't last long enough; and as our lips separated, I felt a vibration of need go through me, sharp and sweet.

Curling my arms around his neck, I pulled his lips back onto mine. I wanted more, and Mike did, too. With a quiet moan, he pressed closer.

The stubble on his cheeks felt rough against my skin as he deepened the kiss into a moment drenched in honey, and I flashed on some spectacular couplings we'd shared in this apartment, when our passion was so raw, we couldn't wait. He'd back me against the stairwell wall, or lift me onto the kitchen table, or pull me down onto the living room rug. Clothes came off, we came together, and the weary world fell away.

But that didn't happen tonight. Instead, Mike pulled away.

"I should clean up," he murmured, voice hoarse. "I'm pretty rank right now."

"You don't need to pull rank on me." I forced a smile, trying to hide my disappointment. "I just want us to be together. It's been a while."

He looked away. "Tell you what. Let me shower off, get cleaned up, shaved." He rubbed the cactus growth on his cheeks and chin.

"You don't need to make yourself pretty for me."

"You deserve a little romance, Clare. Not a brute who gives you brush burn."

It was my turn to touch his cheek. "You're not appearing in court tonight, Detective, and I have no objection."

With a little smile, he covered my hand, took it in his, and kissed my palm. "I'll be back down in ten minutes. Then we'll inhale those stuffed shells, and after that—" He arched a sandy eyebrow. "Start a little fire in the bedroom."

Or a big one, I thought. The night had been cold, and I was looking forward to us (finally!) warming each other up. But first I'd need to warm up our way-past-midnight snack. As I pulled my leftover stuffed shells (with my extra creamy homemade ricotta) out of the fridge and prepped two plates for the microwave, I began to worry that Mike's shower wouldn't wash away his worries.

You need to create a relaxed environment, Clare.

Matt Allegro's annoyingly confident advice echoed back to me, and I didn't disagree.

Relaxed environment, okay . . .

As I waited for the microwave bell to ding, I put a cloth over the table and set it nicely, including two silver candleholders with cream-colored tapers. I turned the track lighting low and lit the wicks.

The flicker of flames combined with the fragrant smell of tomato sauce turned my apartment's kitchen into a little Italian restaurant.

Very romantic, I thought. What else?

Maybe you and the flatfoot are drinking too much coffee. Have you tried opening a bottle of wine?

Okay, I'm on it.

I reached into the back of my fridge and chose a red sangria that my daughter, Joy, had suggested. It was a nice little California concoction with a conveniently *low* percentage of alcohol, so it was perfect for tonight, since I was aiming for a relaxed detective, not a passed-out drunken cop. (That was *Joy's* assessment, and she would know, given her boyfriend.)

I was so proud of my daughter, especially after the ordeals she'd been through. She'd worked hard in her culinary studies and after a horrible incident was thrown out of school. But that didn't stop Joy. She took a lowly apprenticeship at a Paris bistro and worked so diligently and brilliantly that she'd proved herself worthy of a job offer from a Michelin-starred restaurant. Now she was running our Village Blend DC (and its casual "Jazz Space" gastro-lounge) while continuing her romantic relationship with a young detective on Mike's OD Squad.

Sergeant Manny Franco was such a good guy, and I hoped he and Joy would find a way to make things permanent. Not that my ex-husband would agree. Matt could not stand Franco—not his shaved head or his cocky attitude or (especially) his occupation. Or maybe it was simply that Joy was madly in love with the young sergeant, and Matt couldn't do a thing about it.

Was there *ever* a daddy who approved of his little girl's boyfriend?

Seriously doubting it, I poured a glass of sangria for myself and savored the sweet, chilly fruit-forward fun of it. Yes, this would do nicely!

Up the carpeted staircase I went, toward the master bedroom. The bathroom door was open, the hot shower running. I saw Quinn's used razor was on the sink, a can of shaving cream next to it.

"Mike!" I called. "I have something for you!"

Quinn drew back the curtain. He was still soapy, but I saw he'd shaved. His strong jaw was smooth and square and very kissable. But he wasn't smiling. His expression looked as grim and distracted as ever.

I held out the glass of red sangria. "I just opened it. Drink up. I think you'll love it."

"Wine tasting in the shower? This is decadent."

"That's the idea, big fella."

He returned my smile, but it was a weak one.

"Joy suggested this California vineyard. She says Franco loves it. It's delicious, don't you think?"

At the mention of my daughter and her boyfriend, Mike's smile suddenly fell away.

"What is it?" I asked. "What's wrong?"

He shook his head. His mind was still racing; he couldn't let go. I hoped the sangria would help and maybe this wee-small-hours-of-the-morning supper would, too.

"I've got the food warming."

"That's great. I'll be right down."

I sat at the table, everything ready, including the Sinatra playlist on my phone, which I set into my kitchen speaker dock.

Five minutes went by.

Ten minutes.

At fifteen, I left Frank at the Vegas Sands and climbed the carpeted steps again, second glass of wine in hand.

I found Mike in the master bedroom, passed out on the four-poster, his empty wineglass on the side table. My royal blue bath sheet was still wrapped around his hips, dewdrops of water clinging to his broad, naked chest.

I sighed the sigh of a hungry dieter salivating at a Thanksgiving dinner with all the fixin's. Then I drained my wineglass of red sangria. Every. Last. Drop.

I knew very well I could have kissed Mike awake, pulled that towel away, and given him something to dream about.

But I just couldn't do it—for a lot of reasons, one of which I wasn't too keen on facing at this wee small hour.

And so . . .

After lovingly spreading a blanket over his big, powerful body, I went back downstairs, put away the food, and blew out my candles.

Twenty

‽‽‽‽‽‽‽‽‽‽‽‽‽‽‽‽‽‽‽‽‽‽‽‽‽

B*zzz* . . .

Bzz-Bzz-Bzzzzzz . . .

Oh, please, not again!

Roused from a dreamless sleep, I sat bolt upright. The room was still dark. Not even dawn's early light was peeking through the cracks between my drawn curtains.

Bzz-Bzz-Bzzzzz!

Arms raised, I frantically searched the air for winged invaders, ready to swat them away, *until* I realized the buzzing wasn't coming from a confused swarm of little lost souls.

My mobile phone was vibrating on my nightstand.

Great.

Grabbing the device, I peered at the screen. *Unknown number?* I picked it up anyway. "Hello?"

"Clare?"

Though the voice was weak and distant, it sounded like Mrs. Hastings. "Bea? Is that you?"

"It's me."

I couldn't believe it. I was so glad to hear from her! "How are you? Are you calling from the hospital?"

"I need you to go to my greenhouse, Clare. I need you to take care of my bees."

"Of course! I didn't forget. I'll do it first thing in the morning—"

"No! Go now! You *must* go now, Clare. That's all I have to say."

"Wait! Don't hang up!"

I knew Mrs. Hastings's short-term memory was a casualty of the trauma she'd suffered, but I had to try again: "Listen to me, Bea, this is important. Do you have any idea who attacked you? Think. Do you remember *any-thing* about last night?"

I waited for her response, but there was none. Had she gone already?

"Go *now*, Clare. To my greenhouse. Don't waste another minute!"

And that was the end of the call.

Throwing off my bedcovers, I rose and dressed quickly, trying not to disturb Mike on the other side of the four-poster. Not that I could. The man was still sawing wood pretty good.

In no time, I was on the street. The chill was still in the air and in my bones. The mist had turned into full-blown fog. As I hurried along the Village sidewalks, I felt as though I were flying through a cloud bank, miles high. I saw no people, heard no traffic, just a ship's horn in the distance. That lonely sound, crying out in the dark, sent a new shiver through me.

There was no problem getting into Bea's building, but that wasn't necessarily a good thing. The front doors stood wide open. The lobby was empty, no doorman, not a soul in sight.

My skin felt prickly, but I didn't stop. I *had* to do what Bea asked. I couldn't explain why, but I suddenly felt as though her life depended on it.

Skipping the private elevator, I hurried instead to the building's public lift. On the tenth floor, I stepped out onto the carpeted hallway and began walking toward the service elevator around the corner, but I stopped when I heard laughter—*female* laughter.

"Look at that wild beard. May I touch?"

The voice of the woman sounded familiar—along with her beard fetish, or was it just *Matt's* beard that fascinated her?

Nellie, the "Start-up Queen," that's what my ex called her, and I assumed he was with her now, around that corner. But *why* was he back here?

"Matt!" I cried out. "Did Mrs. Hastings call you, too? Are you going up to her greenhouse?"

I hurried to get an answer, but as I rounded the corner, I saw no Matt and no Start-up Queen. The hall was empty—and very different. The carpeting was gone. The service elevator doors weren't there, either.

What in the world was going on?!

A darkened doorway stood at the end of the hall. I stepped through and found the staircase that led up to the roof.

One person was already on those stairs, a petite young woman with sunny blond hair flowing past her shoulders. She looked like Bea's niece, Susan Hastings.

"Suzie!" I called, assuming she must have heard what happened to her aunt and came back to check out the damage to the greenhouse. Was that the reason why Bea wanted me to come here right away? Was she worried about Suzie's safety? I called to her again—

"Suzie, wait!"

But the young woman didn't stop. She didn't even turn her head.

I began to follow her up the stairs when I heard a voice call my name—

"Ms. Cosi! Don't go up there! You won't like what you find!"

"Todd? Todd Duncan?"

I turned at the sound of the young man's voice. But saw no one. Then I heard something else, something disturbing. Bea Hastings was shouting at someone up on her roof. I had to see what was happening—and try to help.

I rushed to the top of the staircase, raced onto the rooftop, and stopped dead.

I expected to enter Bea's massive two-story glass greenhouse, its steel structure silhouetted by the glowing city skyline. But I saw no greenhouse. Not even the wooden decks and walkways were left. There was *nothing* here, only flat black tar, stretching out in a square nearly as large as the city block below.

Bea's greenhouse was gone.

Twenty-one

Cautiously, I stepped across the darkness, searching for Suzie or *anyone*. And that's when I saw it. The only thing of Bea's that was left behind—

Her telescope.

I walked up to the standing tripod and touched the optical tube. Bea's telescope was locked into place, as it had been before.

Once again, I peered through the eyepiece, expecting to see the same view—a lighted Hudson River barge and dock with crates of La Luna Farms produce stacked high.

But that's not what I saw.

Rubbing my eyes, I looked again. The produce boxes were still there. I could clearly read the La Luna Farms name and see the full white moon on every container, but they weren't stacked on a Hudson River dock. They were dumped haphazardly among muddy puddles, weeds, and a familiar-looking faded white van—tires missing, windshield smashed, plates removed.

In the distance, I saw (and somehow *heard*) a horse clip-clopping along. The van and horse made me realize what I was looking at—Mike's crime scene!

Disturbed, I backed away from the magic telescope, unable to comprehend how I could be facing the *west* side of Manhattan, yet peering at the Hole, a plot of land over ten miles *east* of where I stood.

"Clare!"

"Bea?" I whirled at the sound of Mrs. Hastings's voice. It was no longer weak and distant. This time it was loud and desperate.

"Help me, Clare!"

"Where are you, Bea?"

"I'm on the balcony, below you! I'm hurt. Help me, Clare!"

I raced for the end of the roof—and nearly went over. Just in time I caught myself, suddenly aware of how high I was, over twelve stories up with the skyscrapers of Midtown soaring in the distance.

Desperately, I looked for something to lower me down. But there was nothing to grab on to! Then Bea's shouts went quiet.

Fearing the worst, I swiped at tears of fear and frustration, until I heard footsteps behind me.

Thank goodness!

Believing help was here at last, I began to turn, hoping to greet Suzie or Matt or even Nellie—but before I could see who had come, I was body-slammed so hard I lost my footing and flew off the roof.

Arms and legs flailing, I felt like a swimmer cast into water. But there was no water to buoy me, just thin air. Then the gravity did its bit, and down I went. Down, down, down . . .

I was beyond helpless now, a silent scream wedged in my throat as I fell into the gray fog, terror gripping me in the darkness, until I saw—

A bright light.

I opened my eyes.

Sunlight was streaming through the cracks between my drawn curtains. I was still in bed. Mike's big, warm body was still lying next to me, sleeping soundly.

Despite waking in my own serene bedroom, my heart was pounding, my breath labored. For a minute, I had trouble pulling my actual memories from the strange web of dream images.

Did any of it have meaning?

Seeing the Hole through that telescope on Bea's roof gave me chills, even now.

Were the two crime scenes connected? Or was my mind just mashing images together as it tried to process the stressful things I'd experienced last night?

Mike often mentioned he had bad dreams when he was under pressure.

I looked at his tall, powerful form stretched out next to me and wondered if he was having a dream like mine right now.

I wanted to hug him awake, tell him about my nightmare. But he was sleeping so deeply, I just couldn't. Instead, I let him get the rest he so badly needed and took a giant breath to help calm my nerves.

Sitting up, I reached for my mobile phone on the nightstand, wondering why the alarm didn't go off. But there was no phone. I'd left it downstairs, in the kitchen speaker dock with my Sinatra playlist on pause, and my morning alarm (obviously) useless!

Grabbing my digital watch, I checked the time. From the light through the windows, I suspected I was late, but not *this* late. I'd completely missed our pastry delivery.

Throwing off my covers, I careened out of bed. It was time—strike that, *way past time*—to start my day.

Twenty-two

⟨decorative border⟩

OPENING the Village Blend was usually a breeze.

Since I lived in the duplex apartment, right on top of my coffeehouse, I frequently scheduled myself to get the task done. Not that I didn't trust my staff to do it, but as the manager, I felt a sense of control in getting those doors opened on time for my first customers. And (for me, anyway) control equaled peace of mind.

Typically, I'd roll out of bed at 5:40 AM, step into clothes, tie back my hair into a kitchen-ready ponytail, and open the back door to usher in the bakery delivery by six. Then I'd fill the pastry case, calibrate the daily espresso (by dose and grind), and start brewing our Breakfast blend.

Two of my staff would arrive by seven to help with the morning crush. By eleven, I'd let them take over completely while I turned my attention to doing paperwork in my office, or roasting Matt's green beans in the basement, or (depending on how late I worked the night before) taking a well-earned nap.

There would be no napping for me today. I didn't deserve it.

Mentally kicking myself, I hurried down to the kitchen. Grabbing my traitorous phone, I saw multiple text messages from my ex.

Sorry, Matt, I don't have time to answer you!

Instead, I descended the back stairs, tying my hair as I went, wondering why our baker didn't leave a single text message. If Janelle's delivery wasn't accepted and signed for, she should have checked in with me!

I got my answer the moment I burst into the shop.

Someone was already here.

The rich aroma of freshly brewing coffee filled the place—and the bakery delivery was successful. Empty boxes on the counter and a full pastry case were testaments to that.

Expelling a breath, I looked around to thank whoever my savior was. I guessed it was Tucker, though it could have been Nancy, who was often conscientiously early for her morning shifts.

But it wasn't Tucker or Nancy who greeted me.

"Good morning, sleepyhead."

"Matt?"

"Clare, you look awful."

"Gee, thanks."

"Don't mention it."

He grinned as he said it, white teeth flashing once again in that dark beard, which I could see he'd finally tamed with a trim this morning. Then he turned his attention back to the hearth, where he'd already set up the logs and fired the kindling. While he coaxed the flames higher, I retied my sloppy ponytail and stifled a yawn.

Matt noticed. "You ready for a cup of coffee?"

"Are you kidding? Start pouring."

Twenty-three

"I'M really worried about Bea," I told Matt as he filled two large mugs with hot coffee. "I even had a dream about her . . ."

I sat down at the coffee bar and checked my watch. We had a good twenty minutes before our doors opened, so I pulled out my phone.

"Who are you calling?"

"The hospital. I want to check on her."

"I already did that. She's the same. Stable, but unconscious."

"Still in the medically induced—"

"Yes."

"Should we call your mother? I hate to interrupt her vacation, but I think she'd want to know what happened to Bea."

"I already tried to call this morning. Can't reach her. A big storm front has entered the Caribbean—"

"How bad is it? Is she in any danger?"

"She's not in danger. It's just a tropical storm. They'll batten down the hatches at the resort. But I can't get a call through. It may delay her return—or she might cut the trip short. We'll have to wait and see."

We fell silent after that, sipping black coffee in our own morose thoughts. Then I spoke up.

"After we left the hospital last night, I told Mike what happened to Bea Hastings. And what I thought."

"And what is that exactly?"

"That someone clearly attacked her. And whether they meant to kill her or not, they certainly left her for dead."

"Really? You think so?" Matt scratched his beard. "The police weren't so sure. I mean, look at that bee swarm that came through our basement exhaust vent. They were pretty scary. Don't you think her bees *could* have swarmed around her like that and drove her off the roof?"

"No. I don't. Mrs. Hastings is an expert beekeeper. And the cops on the scene weren't detectives. Once they're assigned, Mike thinks the security cameras will give them all the leads they need."

"Yeah, and you and I will be on those cameras, too," Matt pointed out.

"We're already in the police report, so that won't be news to the detectives, but you've got to stick around, okay? You can't go back to globetrotting until they do their follow-up interviews with us."

"I know, I remember. And anyway, if the perp is on candid camera, they should be in handcuffs pretty quick. What's your guess? Twenty-four hours?"

I nodded. "Unless the guilty party is on a plane to another state or country. Then it will take time to track them down."

"Well, if the bees didn't attack Mrs. Hastings, I'd like to know who did it. And why. Wouldn't you?"

"Of course, but that's not our job. The police will get us answers soon enough. Right now, I'm more concerned with the promise I made to Bea about taking care of her little lost souls—the ones the NYPD rescued from our roof and any other bees that survived the ordeal in the greenhouse. I'll be heading there later to get an update from her IT guy, Todd. He said he'd be working all night to fix the place up and get the systems working again. You don't mind keeping an eye on things here, do you?"

"Don't worry, Clare. I've got your back."

"I know you do . . ."

My business partner deserved thanks for showing up this morning like he did and saving the day, or at least the pastry delivery, and I told him so. Only one thing puzzled me.

"Matt, how did you guess that I'd need backup this morning?"

"When you didn't answer my texts, I assumed you were sleeping in, so I came over to open for you."

"Yes, but how did you even know to *text* me?"

"You're forgetting you confided in me last night about the problems you and Quinn were having in—" He rolled his eyes toward the ceiling. "You know—"

"The bedroom?"

"Hey, I'm trying to be discreet here."

"That's a first."

"Fine, I'll be blunt. Did you and your fiancé *finally* hook up? You two looked pretty cozy leaving the hospital together, which is why I set my alarm and texted you. I figured you might need the shut-eye—"

"You figured wrong."

"Is that right?" Matt refilled our cups. "Then spill it."

"The coffee?"

He looked outraged. "Are you kidding? These are my beautiful Peruvian beans that I sourced on the ground from Cajamarca. The only spilling of this excellent coffee should be into your yawning mouth. You know what I'm asking, Clare. So?"

"So . . . he fell asleep."

"Really?"

I shrugged. "We started out well enough. Very well, actually. I mean, as soon as we shut the door to my apartment, we were stuck to each other like we were coated in honey. But then Mike broke off—and I don't understand it, not really. I mean, he *claimed* he wanted to clean up and shave and have a romantic dinner first, so while he was showering, I warmed the stuffed shells and lit candles. I even brought him a glass of sangria in the shower."

"And he fell asleep?"

"Passed out would be more accurate."

Matt's eyebrows rose at that. "He passed out while he was showering with you?"

"No! I was not showering with him! I just brought him the glass of wine. He passed out on the bed *after* the shower."

Matt nodded. "I get the picture. I just don't understand why you served him alcohol so late at night?"

"It was *your* idea to give the man wine! You said his stress level was a heart attack waiting to happen. That I should try wine to relax him, help take the edge off."

Matt frowned a moment in thought. "Well, *after* he fell asleep, why didn't you just wake him that sexy way you used to wake me?"

"Let's change the subject."

"Listen, Clare, you don't have to be embarrassed with me. You obviously need someone to talk to. Think of me as a brother."

"I would never tell my brother any of this!"

"You don't even have a brother."

"That's beside the point!"

"All I'm saying is, as your ex-husband I'm also an ex-lover, so you shouldn't feel embarrassed. We've been there, done that, you know?"

"Believe me, I know."

"Look, I don't want to upset you. The flatfoot and I have had our differences, but I know he's a good guy, despite being a cop."

"Let's quit this subject while we're ahead, shall we?"

"Can I say one more thing?"

"No."

"As a man, I have some insight into Quinn's behavior. You want it?"

"I'm skeptical."

"Just hear me out. I would bet the coffee farm—if I had one—that the good lieutenant was ready and willing to get down and dirty with you right there in front of your umbrella stand and coatrack."

"Matt—"

"I'm not kidding. The reason he broke it off was guilt."

"Guilt?"

"Yeah, Quinn clearly feels guilty about neglecting your relationship, and he didn't want you to feel shortchanged by some brief encounter in a chilly apartment vestibule. The shower and shave and dinner were kind of sweet, actually. The guy probably would have been completely happy jumping your bones on the hardwood floor before passing out in your four-poster."

"You know, I might feel offended if I didn't think you were right."

"I know I'm right."

"And what am I supposed to do about it?"

"I told you already. Wake him up—you know, that sexy way you used to when you and I were—"

"I remember!"

"Good."

"But . . ."

"But what?"

"What if he pushes me away? That was one of the reasons I didn't try to wake him last night. I knew he needed the rest. But I also worried about his state of mind, and I didn't think I could handle rejection on top of frustration."

"Welcome to my world."

"What do you mean?"

"Clare, men wrestle with that dilemma all the time. We want to show our affection, but fear rejection."

I processed that for a minute, along with more of Matt's eye-opening Peruvian beans.

"You're right," I admitted. "I never truly considered that particular view of things, and I do see your point, though I'm not sure what your insight gets me."

"It's simple. If you have wants and needs, stop tying yourself in knots and *act* on them. The guy's crazy about you. If he's too stressed-out to show you, then *you* show him. Be aggressive. Take control. This may sound odd, but I need to put an idea in your head."

"What idea?"

"Don't be the honey. Be the bear."

"Be the bear?" I thought about that, trying not to laugh. The phrase certainly did sound odd, but I understood what he meant.

"Can you be aggressive, Clare? Go after what you want?"

"Yes, I can do that."

He smiled again. "I know you can."

A moment later, I was saved by the bell—the one over our shop's front door.

Raven-haired Esther and farm-fresh Nancy boisterously burst in, bickering over some crazy story in the local news—and (thankfully) putting an end to Matteo Allegro's "couples therapy" session.

Twenty-Four

"ALL I'm saying is that we have a real live superhero on the front page," Nancy exclaimed, tossing her braids as she waved a newspaper. "Maybe it's time for Tucker and Punch to revive their old superhero children's hospital charity show."

"Superheroes are so last year," Esther declared, pushing up her black-framed glasses. "And Tucker doesn't need a reason to wear tights." Just over the threshold, she paused. "Who cares about superheroes anyway? I want to know if we're entering a bee-free environment."

"No worries, Esther," I called from the coffee bar. "The police hauled those bees off to the pokey last night."

"Fresh-brewed small-lot Peruvian, anyone?" Matt announced from behind the pastry case.

The baristas instantly flocked to my ex.

"Mr. Boss, you're here so early. And you're being so sweet," Nancy cooed flirtatiously. "Did the bakery deliver you?"

Matt laughed. "Sorry, this tart is not for sale."

Esther moved past her roommate. "Caffeinate me, boss. Boris and I were up all hours—and, no, it was not for romantic reasons. I need a new theme for a poetry slam fundraiser and everything we brainstormed was either lame or done already."

Matt handed her a steaming mug. "The coffee doctor is in. Clare's excellent Vienna roast of my Andes-grown beans offers a cup that makes life worth living. Smooth body, eye-opening lemon-lime top notes, with honey and chocolate on the backbeat."

"Just what I need!" Esther declared.

"Bad news, though," Matt said. "If you want a second cup, we need more beans from the basement."

Esther raised an index finger as she plopped down on a stool. "One cup. Then I'll go down."

"Did you two see the headlines?" Nancy asked me and Matt, displaying the *New York Post*.

WALL-CRAWLER RESCUES ACCIDENT VICTIM

I was, in a word, *flabbergasted*.

The entire front page of the tabloid was a black-and-white photo of our Matt climbing down the side of the Hastings! Obviously taken from street level, the photo editor added an attention-grabbing inset with a blowup of Matt's bearded profile and the caption:

Who is this mystery hero?

The picture was so blurry that if I didn't know it was my ex, I wouldn't have recognized him. Obviously no one in my staff had made the connection—yet.

I pulled a stunned Matt aside. "Who took that photograph and how? You were on that wall all of twenty seconds."

He shrugged. "Read the article and let me know."

I borrowed Nancy's paper and scanned the story, plastered across pages two and three—mostly photographs, anonymously credited to "iPeeper," a new app that turned anyone with a camera into a crime reporter.

The story itself was two meager paragraphs about "an accident victim" in Chelsea who had received "critical first aid" after "a selfless hero" climbed down to her balcony from the roof.

The identity of the victim had not been released "pending notification of the next of kin," which I was relieved to hear. That meant the police were looking for Suzie Hastings, too—if they hadn't found her already.

"I wonder who he is?" Nancy said with a swoony sigh.

"A grandstanding jerk, that's who," Esther declared. "Just wait. This so-called selfless hero will step forward any second to wallow in public acclaim and hold his hand out for a fat financial reward—which he probably doesn't need—that some rich dude will offer. An offer that will further exploit the event to make the rich dude look virtuous *and* give his business a convenient media boost."

"That's pretty cynical, Esther," I said.

"Maybe. Or maybe I'm overly bitter right now because funding cuts are jeopardizing my city-kids poetry outreach program. Anyway . . ." She gulped more coffee and sighed. "I've seen what I've seen, and I know what I know. In this day and age, public displays of virtue should always be suspect."

Spoken like an under-caffeinated New Yorker, I thought.

I was sad to hear Esther's outreach program was in financial jeopardy. The program had done great things for at-risk kids. And I didn't entirely disagree with her on questioning the motives of people, especially in this town. But she was wrong in Matt's case. He had risked his life to help Bea. And he had no idea someone was taking his picture.

Silently sipping my own coffee, I glanced at my ex-husband. When the baristas first came in, I thought he would blurt out the truth—that he was the hero on that wall. But he stayed quiet. And now that Esther delivered her harsh assessment of the "hero's" motives, Matt's expression turned from amused to reserved.

"Well, I believe he's a hero," Nancy insisted forcefully.

"Spoken like a Disney Princess," Esther said then drained her mug and rose. "Time for more Peruvian!"

As Esther headed off to the basement, Matt sipped his coffee, deep in silent thought. I touched his arm.

"A penny for your—"

Esther's bloodcurdling scream suddenly rose up from the roasting room.

Matt snapped out of his funk. "Oops! I forgot—"

"To clean up the dead bees?" I presumed.

A laughing Nancy ambled over to the cellar door. "Hey, roomie! Do you need help down there?"

"There are still bee corpses on the floor!" came her harrowing reply.

"I'll get you a broom and a dustpan," Nancy sang. "Just like Cinderella."

"NO!!" Esther shouted.

"Why not? Are you *afraid*?" Nancy teased. "Do you need a hero prince to come to your rescue?"

"Absolutely not!" Esther insisted.

A minute later she appeared at the top of the stairs with a twenty-five-pound bag of beans and kicked the basement door closed with her foot.

"I've got a fresh bag of Peruvian, boss. But I am *not* sweeping up dead bugs. You can fire me first."

"No one's getting fired," I assured her. "And, anyway, I'm sure Matt won't mind sweeping them up for us."

"Bugs don't bug me," Matt said, heading for the back stairs. "You couldn't go where I go if they did."

But Nancy cut him off. "You're already our coffee hunter hero. I'll be your Cinderella and clean the basement floor. I don't mind."

As Matt sweetly thanked her, I checked the time and clapped my hands.

"Okay, team, I'm turning the *Welcome* sign around. As of now the Village Blend is open for business!"

Twenty-Five

≈≈≈≈≈≈≈≈≈≈≈≈≈≈≈≈≈≈≈≈≈≈

A few hours (and a hundred lattes) later, I was standing in the massive greenhouse on top of Bea Hastings's building. Things appeared to be looking up. But then, the world always looked better in the bright light of a sunny morning.

The cold darkness of the night before—the shattered hives, murdered bees, and battered body of Mrs. Hastings—made her glorious greenhouse seem like a nightmarish place. Not even my sleep could dispel the disturbing feelings. But on this radiant autumn morning, I only felt awe at the grandeur and ingenuity of this amazing botanical palace.

Steel support beams sparkled in the golden sunlight that poured through the vaulted glass ceiling. The all-pervasive scent of lavender rose from row upon row of dazzling purple blossoms that ran on several levels, the entire length of the toasty warm greenhouse.

So, what was I doing here?

A few hours earlier, when Esther had screamed about the corpses in our basement, I was reminded of my newly minted beekeeping responsibilities, along with something officer Darius Greene said last night—

"Returning the bees to their original home is the best thing for them. And that's what we'd like to do, if it's possible . . ."

To keep my promise to Bea *and* fulfill Officer Greene's mission, I placed a call first to Bea's tech guru, Todd Duncan, to confirm that her computerized greenhouse was back online, and then to the NYPD.

Officer Greene was delighted to hear that I'd found the swarm's home and was appalled at the situation with Bea in the hospital. He told me that he and his young partner would not only return the bees to Bea's greenhouse but would help restore the hives.

Officer Buzz Banner of the beekeeping unit beat me here by an hour and got as busy as his namesake. He'd already righted four hives and reinserted the drawers after replacing the shattered honeycombs with commercially bought ones.

I left the intensely focused policeman to his tasks, and went down to the eleventh floor, where Bea kept her business offices.

With Todd Duncan's all-nighter in mind, before I left the Village Blend, I filled a thermal mug with this week's featured coffee, that high-grown Peruvian, the one Matt had poured for me. I planned to have a long talk with Todd, and I wanted him awake for it!

I wandered the floor for a few minutes before I found Bea's redheaded tech wizard in a corner office. He wore a different tropical shirt today, but his pudgy, elfin, ginger-bearded face looked as youthful as ever, his manner admirably calm and unflappable—despite the four computer screens and four keyboards surrounding him, which he appeared to be working simultaneously.

"I didn't know you'd arrived already, Ms. Cosi, or I would have met you at the elevator," Todd said apologetically, his eyes barely glancing my way before returning to the screen as his fingers did a conga on the keyboard. "I already cleared you with our doorman, and I'm glad he remembered to let you right up."

As I moved to a chair, I was startled to see that Todd was not alone. The other man rose from a corner seat and flashed an NYPD detective shield.

I was immediately struck by the officer's lofty height—approaching seven feet, he was more than half a foot taller than Quinn, though the ebony-haired giant was much bulkier. I noticed the detective wore a little gold basketball for a tie clip, and (at his height) I figured him for a former college player.

"Detective Roger Novak," he said, shaking my hand. His expression was open and friendly, but his brown eyes narrowed as he studied me.

"I read your statement, Ms. Cosi. You and your business partner, Mr. Allegro, discovered Bea Hastings last night. I'm sorry I missed you. A uniform named Healey cut you and your friend loose before I got here."

"We went to the hospital to look after Beatrice Hastings. But I'm happy to answer any questions you have about her assault."

"I appreciate your cooperation, but most of my questions have already been answered. And for the record, it wasn't an assault."

"Not an assault? Surely you're not buying into the theory that Bea was attacked by her own bees?"

"Not at all. We've determined that Beatrice Hastings attempted to take her own life and failed."

"What?!" I couldn't believe my own ears. "That's preposterous!"

Detective Novak's eyes widened in surprise at my outburst. The room went quiet a moment and so did his voice—

"I know it can be upsetting to learn that a friend is suffering from mental illness or depression, but—"

"Bea didn't suffer from those things," I countered. "She was pragmatic, even hard-nosed at times, and she always had her wits about her."

Frowning, Novak reached for a file on the chair beside him. He tugged a single sheet of paper from the bundle and handed it to me.

"We found that posted on Bea Hastings's Instagram account."

I read with increasing disbelief:

Everything I tried failed.
And now this.
Better to end it now.
I cannot endure another disappointment.
I must destroy it all.

"The same message was posted on her Facebook page. Both were logged last evening, around the time of the incident, given the bee swarm that ended up at your coffeehouse."

I read the suicide note three more times, then shook my head.

"No, this is wrong," I insisted. "Last night, before the doctors put her in a medically induced coma, Bea pleaded with me to take care of her bees. Why would she try to destroy her own hives, shut down her own greenhouse?"

"What Mrs. Hastings said in the hospital last night may have no bearing on her state of mind before she jumped," Novak said. "I've seen more than one attempted suicide plead for their life in the ER. In Mrs. Hastings's case, I'd call it jumper's remorse."

"Are you *sure* it wasn't an assault? Did you review the security camera footage?"

Todd, who'd been banging at one keyboard or another during our conversation, jumped in.

"Bea erased the camera footage, Ms. Cosi. All of it. Right before she shut down the greenhouse and deleted my computer programs that ran the place."

I stood flabbergasted.

"The evidence is clear," Novak said, awkwardly adjusting his tie. "Crime Scene found no indication of foul play or of a bee attack. I believe the messages on social media mirror Bea Hastings's state of mind. Our digital forensics show that her accounts were not hacked. The messages were posted from Mrs. Hastings's personal computer."

"I can't believe it," I said. "And where is her computer?"

Novak shook his head. "Completely destroyed. Pieces were found in the alley below. We believe she flung it off the roof before jumping herself. I'm sorry to bear such bad news, and I hope Mrs. Hastings pulls through her ordeal and gets the help she needs."

He paused. If he was waiting for a reply, I had none.

"Attempted suicide is no longer illegal in New York," Novak finally added. "The NYPD won't be pressing any charges. I thank you both for your cooperation. If I have any further questions, I'll contact you."

Since Todd Duncan had returned to his digital trance, I followed Detective Novak into the hall.

"Excuse me, may I ask one more question?"

"Of course."

"Have you spoken with Susan Hastings, Bea's niece? She is the next of kin."

"We've contacted Ms. Hastings's mobile phone. But she hasn't responded yet. We understand she's traveling."

"What about her workmates? Can they reach her?"

"Ms. Hastings is self-employed. She has clients, not workmates."

"I see. Have you tried to *locate* her through her phone? Or search her financial transactions, credit card usage?"

Novak frowned. "If contacting her was part of a criminal investigation, we would seek a warrant. But invading the young woman's privacy is not something we would consider at this stage."

"But you are going to speak with her, right? Interview her? And what about Bea's housekeeper, Ella? Don't you want a statement from her?"

"Mrs. Hastings's housekeeper Ella Strobl has been in Austria for over a week. We spoke with Ms. Strobl by phone. She told us her sister suffered a stroke after her husband's sudden death. Mrs. Hastings was moved by the terrible news and immediately gave her housekeeper paid leave for a month, so that Ms. Strobl could return to Austria and help her sister and the woman's young children to cope."

"That's tragic. Or at least it *sounds* tragic. Did you confirm Ella Strobl's story?"

"Ms. Cosi—" Detective Novak started with a sharp tone before stopping himself. With a deep breath, he continued more calmly. "If you don't mind my saying, you seem to be searching for someone to blame for what happened. I understand your feelings, but you spoke with Beatrice Hastings yourself at the hospital. Did she state someone assaulted her?"

"No, but—"

"Did she mention anyone else who was with her last night?"

"No," I repeated. "But the doctors told me she's probably lost her short-term memory due to trauma."

"I hope that Mrs. Hastings makes a full recovery, both mentally and physically. And if she does name an assailant, we'll investigate. In the meantime, I think it's best to wait a day or two and give Susan Hastings time to turn up."

"What about Todd Duncan?"

"He doesn't know where Susan is, either."

"No, *where* was Todd Duncan when Bea Hastings supposedly tried to do herself in?"

"From seven to midnight, Mr. Duncan attended dinner with friends and Karaoke Night at the—" The detective paused to consult his smartphone. "Mynah Bird hookah lounge in Brooklyn. The lounge confirmed the event. There are photos of him at the get-together on the lounge's social media site and on his social media, and on his friends' social media— all dated and time-stamped. There's also an uploaded livestream video of Todd singing 'Hooked on a Feeling' in tribute to . . ." He squinted at the screen. "*Guardians of the Galaxy.*"

"I see. Well, thank you, Detective Novak. And please, do what you can to find Susan."

Twenty-six

~~~~~~

WHEN I returned to Todd's office. I wasn't sure he'd noticed I'd left until he spoke.

"Give me a minute, Ms. Cosi. I have to finish this," he said, tapping more keys after draining a can of Monster Energy.

"As you can see, I'm kind of a one-man show today. With Ella away, this place doesn't even have a receptionist. It's mental, right?"

While waiting for Todd to finish, I scanned his office. The space was small, the décor business standard, but Todd Duncan made the place his own. Plastic superheroes waged war with transforming robots across his desk, and I felt a tiny pang of nostalgia when I spied a Rubik's Cube among the combatants.

Todd Duncan's just-earned law degree was taped—frameless—on a beige wall. Hung nearby was his information technology degree from Berkeley, that one neatly framed.

A potted marijuana plant spread its leaves beside the window.

"Okay, execute." Todd swung his chair to face me. "That program has got to run for twenty minutes. Now, how can I help you?"

As he groped for a fresh can of energy drink, I stopped him and reached into my handbag for the Village Blend thermal cup I'd brought along.

"Try this," I said, unscrewing the top. "This Peruvian coffee has a silky body, bright citrus acidity, a touch of honey sweetness—and it's caffeinated, which you seem to appreciate."

"Sounds great!" Todd declared, accepting the mug. I winced when he reached into his drawer and dumped powdered coffee creamer into our premium brew.

After clearing my throat, I reminded Todd that Officer Banner of the NYPD beekeeping unit was already working on the roof, and Officer Greene would soon be here to return Bea's little lost souls to their palatial home.

Between appreciative sips of coffee, Todd assured me the computerized greenhouse wasn't likely to fail again. He also confessed that he knew nothing about hive maintenance.

"Bea was very territorial about her greenhouse and her bees," he said. "She wouldn't allow anyone else to get near them except Ella." Todd took another slurpy sip. "That tells me that Bea Hastings must really trust you, Ms. Cosi."

It was more likely Bea was desperate, I thought. I was at the right place at the right time. And given my close relationship with Madame, her most trustworthy friend, she clearly felt she could extend that trust to me.

Unfortunately, I was struggling to extend that same trust to Detective Novak—or at least his "attempted suicide" theory.

"Todd, tell me about Ella Strobl. Did Bea trust her?"

"Sure, why not?"

"And what reason did Bea give you for Ella leaving New York?"

"The only thing Bea said about Ella was that she would be going back to Austria for a month or more. I assumed she was taking a vacation to visit family. She's done it before."

"Do you know how to contact the woman?"

"Not a clue."

"What about the greenhouse? Was there any physical damage besides the broken door and the knocked-down hives?"

"Just the hives. Detective Novak believes a strong gust of wind broke the door."

"Why is a door there, anyway?" I asked. "It only leads to a narrow ledge that's too dangerous to stand on."

"Mrs. Hastings used to have an exterior staircase there. It led from her greenhouse down to her balcony, but she didn't like the size of the footprint, so she had it taken out. A spiral staircase was supposed to replace it, but she couldn't decide on the design and color."

"Okay. And how did the electrical power and heating systems fail?"

"I set up a master computer in the greenhouse that controls everything. Bea erased the program, which shut all the systems down."

"But you have it up and running now."

"I back up the system regularly." He pointed to the rectangular bauble, hanging like a charm on his chain-link necklace. "I always keep a copy on this external micro drive."

"I see. That's very clever of you."

"Thanks, it took me a while to upload the program and kick-start the system, but I did it in time to save the flowers. The thermometer dropped below forty degrees, but not long enough to do permanent damage to the plants. It did kill some of the bees."

"I take it Detective Novak came to speak to you to collect the greenhouse's security camera footage?"

He nodded, nose in the thermal cup. After a noisy gulp, he spoke.

"Yeah, that's when I found out the entire building's security footage got wiped, along with everything else."

Once again, I was flabbergasted. "The entire building?!"

Todd shrugged. "Bea knew how to do it. She owns the Hastings. And Novak was not happy."

"Tell me the truth, Todd. Does this add up to you? Do you really believe your boss had some sort of mental breakdown?"

"I don't know what to believe." Todd shrugged. "She certainly seemed bothered for the past few days. Paranoid and snappish, you know? She chewed out the guy who makes her jars because a shipment was late. She had to call up later and apologize before the guy canceled the contract."

"You know what I think? I think Detective Novak is wrong. And if he is, you can help me prove it. Do you know of anyone who had a serious grudge against Bea? Or maybe even threatened her?"

Todd expelled a breath. "The Ice Cream Man."

"Who?"

"His name is Felix Foxe."

"And he sells ice cream?"

"No. I call him the Ice Cream Man because he wears white suits, like all the time. But he doesn't sell ice cream. He's one of Bea's competitors in the honey trade."

"I remember Bea mentioned something to me about a gourmet honey vendor she exposed for selling adulterated product. Is that the man?"

"Yep. That's him."

"What else do you know about Mr. Foxe?"

"Only that Mrs. Hastings really hated the dude. Trash-talked him all the time. And she played the gotcha game with him when she figured out he was passing off artificially flavored honey as premium organic stuff."

He drained the last of the Peruvian from the mug, dribbling a bit.

"Good coffee!" he exclaimed. Grabbing a napkin, he wiped his mouth and tossed it at a garbage bin shaped like R2-D2. Todd missed, which he clearly did often. A half dozen energy drink cans lay scattered around the nearly empty droid.

Suddenly, the ceiling lights flickered, then went dark. Todd's computers kept on running, but everything else lost power.

"What's going on?" I asked.

"Wait for it," Todd replied. "Three . . . two . . . one . . . Lift off!"

And just like that, the power returned, and the lights came back on.

"Did you know that would happen?"

"Yep," Todd replied. "That's why I'm running these computers on battery power. When I first load my software to a new system, there's a brief blackout every eleven hours and eleven minutes."

"Eleven eleven? Why?"

"It's an auto-reboot with system checks. Once the program cycles through a few times, the blackouts stop. That takes a couple of days. No worries. There's no danger to the greenhouse or the bees."

Todd's fingers returned to dancing a rumba on one keyboard. But I didn't want to lose his attention. I still had questions.

"You told me last night that you know Bea's niece?"

"Suzie?" Todd nodded. "Of course."

"Do you have *any* clue where she might be? Or why she would ignore a message from the NYPD?"

"She likes to go off the grid, Ms. Cosi. She could be traveling, Zenning out at a yoga retreat or hiking beyond the reach of a cell tower. Like I told Novak, it's not unusual. I'm sure she'll turn up at some point."

"Does she have a boyfriend we can reach? A girlfriend? A BFF? Could Suzie be with any of them now?"

"Maybe her boyfriend, or maybe not," Todd said. "She has an on-again, off-again thing with some chef."

"Is she on or off, do you think?"

Todd's expression soured. "I would say off. Suzie came in a few weeks ago, crying to her aunt about how her boyfriend took a swipe at her. Now, she can be a real diva sometimes, and she's fought, broken up, and gotten back together with this loser before, so I kind of tuned out when I heard it . . ."

"I sense a 'but' coming."

"Yeah." Todd shrugged. "The guy really did come looking for Suzie a couple of hours later. He was agitated and threatening, so Freddie the doorman and I stepped in and sent him packing."

"You didn't call the police?"

Todd threw up his hands. "I would have. He's a scary guy, and—as you can see—I'm no Mike Tyson. But old Freddie, he flashed a Taser and that changed the chef's mind about sticking around."

"Who is this on-and-off boyfriend, the chef? What's his name?"

"Tyler . . . Tyler La Something. He's from New Orleans." Todd's tone turned bitter. He practically spit out his next words: "Year-round beach tan, six-pack abs, black curly hair, pretentious tattoos. Suzie dreamily told me Tyler was an Instagram model." He rolled his eyes. "He's also a caveman. I don't get why Suzie keeps going back to him. Maybe she likes his cooking."

"Where can I find him? What restaurant?"

"I don't know." Todd began tapping his keyboard again. "Once he was the big shot head chef at Armando's. But that was before the restaurant went belly-up."

"And you have no idea what this head chef is doing now?"

"I'm sure he's cooked something up, and I'll bet it fails. The guy's bad news. A real jerk."

From somewhere among the battling plastic figures, the intercom buzzed.

"Yeah, Freddie," Todd replied, hands free.

"There's a big cop here with a bunch of bees. Should I send him up?"

Twenty-seven

◎◎◎◎◎◎◎◎◎◎◎◎◎◎◎◎◎◎◎◎◎

Within an hour after Officer Darius Greene arrived with Bea's bees in two plastic containers, he and Buzz Banner wrapped up work on the final, most heavily damaged beehives.

Officer Banner surprised me with the news that there were a lot more surviving bees than just those who made it to my coffeehouse's venting stack. Four queens and their worker bees never even left the greenhouse. Instead, they found hot spots in and around the machinery where they clustered with their queen for warmth.

"As soon as we restored the hives, those bees began to return home," Officer Banner said.

"That's because I added a tray of sugar water to entice them," Officer Greene interjected proudly. "Just like my mother showed me when we raised our own bees on our roof in Brooklyn."

With silver linings breaking out all over the greenhouse, I should have known there would be a dark cloud looming.

"Mrs. Hastings had six hives and six queens," Greene told me. "Only that isn't the case anymore. One queen is missing."

"She wasn't among the debris of the broken hive?"

Greene shook his head. "She's likely dead, I'm afraid. Here in this greenhouse, inside your coffeehouse, or somewhere along the way."

"What does that mean, exactly?"

"Well, for the health of the hive, we usually try to replace the queen. Bees become aggressive and difficult to control without one. However, this particular type that Mrs. Hastings kept is unfamiliar to me—and I wouldn't presume to buy a queen from another species or sub-species and introduce it into Mrs. Hastings's colony—"

"I thought you said these were Carniolan bees?"

"I *guessed* they were last night. But we took a closer look this morning, and they're not. They're not Italian bees, either. We can't identify it."

"Then how do we solve the missing queen problem? Is there anything we can do?"

Officer Greene nodded. "Dr. Wanda advised me to try dividing up the queenless worker bees and integrating them into the other hives."

"Dr. Wanda?"

"Wanda Clay, PhD. When it comes to bees, that woman is an expert. She's also a professor at Columbia University and a staunch advocate for responsible beekeeping. She even hosts a regular podcast, aimed at our tristate beekeeping community. That's why I called her for advice. When she heard about our situation, she thought a swarm in autumn was news and reported the details on her morning podcast—where it came from and where it ended up."

"You mean my coffeehouse?"

"That's right." He smiled. "Thanks to Dr. Wanda, your coffeehouse might get a boost in business from curious beekeepers."

Officer Banner came around the corner in time to hear his partner's last remark. "Did I just hear you mention Wacky Wanda? I can't believe you got *her* involved."

Greene frowned. "Please don't mock a valuable civilian asset who voluntarily assists the police department with no thought of remuneration."

"Come on, Darius, you know Wanda is wacky."

"Don't let things get personal, Buzz."

"Hey, you two," I interrupted. "This back-and-forth is not instilling confidence in *this* valuable civilian asset."

"Wanda's okay," Officer Banner backtracked. "She is smart as a whip. And she's passionate about bees—a little too passionate in my opinion."

Greene laughed. "Just because she turned you down for a date?"

"Don't get personal, Darius."

(I was beginning to get the picture.)

"All kidding aside, Ms. Cosi," Greene said, "if you ever need to know something about bees, the person to see is Dr. Wanda Clay."

"And if you ever *do* meet Wanda, don't mention her hair," Officer Banner warned.

"Her hair?" I said. "What's her hair got to do with anything?"

Officer Banner just shook his head cryptically. Then, all business, he addressed his partner.

"The bees have returned to their hives. I divided the queenless worker bees among the other hives, and I hope they'll stay put. Otherwise, the bees seem healthy and calm, even happy. I'll bet the bees start gathering pollen in a day or two, like nothing ever happened."

"After all the excitement," I said, "you'd think those poor bees would just hibernate."

"Normally, they would, Ms. Cosi," Banner replied. "Bees routinely collect pollen in the spring and summer, their nectar is harvested in the early fall, and the bees sleep through the long winter. But the way Mrs. Hastings set up this massive place with flowers and climate control, well, the bees can work year-round. It's pretty amazing."

Something else pretty amazing happened a moment later.

Before I left for the Hastings, I'd posted a request to my staff on the activity board in the kitchen. I asked for anyone who was willing to care for Bea's bees to let me know because I was willing to pay them double their regular barista hourly rate.

"No experience necessary," I wrote in the posting. "Members of the NYPD beekeeping unit will give you all the training you'll need."

I figured my pleas had fallen on deaf ears. Unbelievably, I ended up with two volunteers.

Nancy Kelly, my youngest barista, happily jumped at the chance. She said she learned a lot about beekeeping from her aunt, when she spent a year on her farm in the Midwest.

More unbelievably (okay, shockingly), my second barista beekeeping volunteer was none other than my terminally bee-phobic senior barista, Esther Best.

Twenty-eight

⟨∿∿∿∿∿∿∿∿∿∿∿∿∿∿∿∿∿∿∿∿∿⟩

A tense Esther and her much calmer roommate watched the bee-keeping unit from what my nervous senior barista described as "a safe distance."

Officer Banner had prepared lunch for the hungry bees. Now he demonstrated the proper method to open a hive and feed them.

"We're giving them a sugar solution to replace the honey they lost when the hives were wrecked," Darius Greene explained.

"I hope those bees aren't too hungry," Esther replied. "Hunger turns to hanger real fast when you're dealing with dangerous wild animals."

"Don't be silly," Nancy countered. "Bees are domesticated livestock, just like cows, pigs, ducks, and chickens."

Esther's reply—something about Old MacDonald not mentioning venomous stingers in that song about his farm—was muffled by her heavily netted bee bonnet. For her first lesson in bee maintenance, Esther had borrowed Officer Greene's spare bee suit.

As Buzz Banner opened a hive and filled a small metal bowl with sugar solution, Esther watched, an expression of borderline panic barely visible behind the bee veil.

"Don't worry," Nancy insisted. "We'll work in shifts to babysit these sweet things night and day, until their mom comes home from the hospital. It'll be easy—and fun."

Esther shook her head. "Fun is going to a poetry reading. Fun is a pilgrimage to Emily Dickinson's Homestead. Fun is the Coney Island Mermaid Parade or blintzes and caviar with Boris pouring iced vodka in

Brighton Beach. But nothing—absolutely *nothing*—that requires protective gear can be classified as *fun*."

Nancy seemed baffled. "If you don't think this is going to be fun, why do it?"

Esther let loose with a long, painful sigh. "It's all because of Boris. He told me I was letting down one of my personal heroes."

"Queen Latifah?"

"Her too. But he was talking about Eleanor Roosevelt, a fellow cool New York chick who famously said: 'You gain strength, courage and confidence by every experience in which you really stop to look fear in the face . . . You must do the thing you think you cannot do.'"

"One of my favorite quotes," I noted.

"Well, I obviously forgot it!" Esther's mesh veil got caught between her lips, and she angrily spit it out. "When I called Boris on my break today to complain about the dead bees in the basement, he'd had enough listening to me and my fear of bees, especially after my rants last night. He's the one who reminded me of the quote—and he was right. Fear is the enemy, and I wasn't bravely facing it. I was just griping about it. That's when I came up with my absolutely brilliant idea!"

As Esther took a deep breath, we all waited pensively for her to tell us.

"Well? What is it?!" Nancy finally demanded. "What's your idea?"

Esther cleared her throat and announced—

"Boris and I are going to throw a citywide FACE YOUR FEARS Poetry Slam! We're staging it as a fundraiser for my city-kids outreach. With entries and covers we might even clear one thousand dollars—though my kids need closer to ten. But this will be a great start. Boris is already getting the word out. Everyone who participates will have to face a fear and rap about it. Starting with me. I'm going to face those bees!"

"Awesome!" Nancy said. "Let us hear one of your beekeeping raps right now."

Esther put her hands on her generous hips. "I can't rap about beekeeping until I've done it, now can I?"

"Okay then, Esther," Officer Banner said. "Do you want to feed the bees first?"

Esther visibly gulped. Then she adjusted her bonnet and hesitantly approached the busy hives, one cautious step at a time. When she finally reached the hive, a bee rose up to greet her. Esther flinched—but she didn't bolt, which I took as progress.

"What do these things eat?" she asked. "Just sugar water?"

"They need the same things we do," Banner replied. "Protein for building and repairing cells, and carbohydrates to fuel them. The sugar provides the carbs, pollen the protein."

With shaky hands, Esther opened the top compartment of a boxy hive. Several bees buzzed her head and I feared she would run.

"Remember, Ms. Best. Purposeful but relaxed," Greene coached. "Show no fear and the bees will respect you."

As the bee cops taught her, Esther used a blast of harmless smoke from a smoke pot to calm the bees. Then she filled the shallow metal pan inside the hive, using a long rubber tube connected to a squeeze bottle of sugar solution.

"Does that little bowl hold enough solution to feed a whole hungry honeybee hive?" Esther asked.

"You don't want to overfeed them," Officer Greene replied. "Bees naturally rid their hives of unproductive or overly aggressive members. And when food is too plentiful, bees get fat and lazy and they won't collect pollen or create nectar."

"I get it," Esther said with a nod. "Too many goodies and you end up with hive potatoes."

Officer Greene laughed. "Exactly!"

Immediately, hungry bees clustered around the sugar pan. Before Esther gently closed the box, I swore I detected a smile of motherly affection behind her bee veil.

"Great job!" Officer Banner slapped Esther on the back hard enough to knock her bonnet askew. "How did that feel?"

Esther stood thoughtfully a moment, then answered (in rap):

> *"The pedigree of honey*
> *does not concern the bee;*
> *A clover, any time, to him*
> *is aristocracy."*
> *So wrote Emily the great,*
> *Dickinson of late,*

inspired by her garden's state.
Like her, I felt no hate
when I stopped my fear of stings
long enough to feed
little souls with wings.

We all heartily applauded. Esther theatrically bowed, and Buzz Banner threw an encouraging wink at the cheeky grin and wheat-colored braids of my junior barista.

"Grab a bee suit, Miss Kelly. You're up next!"

While Nancy prepared for her lesson—a tad flirtatiously with Officer Buzz—Darius Greene pulled me aside. "I think your volunteers are going to work."

I released a breath that I didn't know I was holding and profusely thanked Officers Greene and Banner for all their help.

This trip to the greenhouse had been full of emotional ups and downs: Todd's dedication (and ingenuity) was uplifting. Novak's conclusions depressing. But the kindness of the beekeeping unit—and Esther's change of heart—gave my own little spirit wings again.

Twenty-nine

I still had a coffeehouse to manage, but I wanted to check on Bea at the hospital first.

I snagged one of the fancy new cabs with plenty of legroom and a tiny television in the back seat. As I sat down, a news segment began running.

"New York City is abuzz about the dramatic rescue of entrepreneur Beatrice Hastings," a local anchor reported. "After an apparent fall from her rooftop greenhouse to a balcony below, Mrs. Hastings was rescued by this mysterious wall-crawling daredevil—"

I'd heard enough about Matt's prowess this morning and switched it off. If this town really was "abuzz" with curiosity, then Matt's secret identity would not remain secret for long. But that wasn't the part of the broadcast that concerned me—

Bea's name was out now. Did that mean the police had located Susan Hastings?

I texted Todd:

Any luck finding Suzie?

He immediately replied:

Not yet.

I was puzzled and said so:

Bea's name is in the papers. How did that happen?
Freddie the doorman let it slip to a pair of indie journalists.

Impatiently, I tucked away my phone. It looked like I was going to have to find Suzie myself.

At the hospital, I learned there was no improvement in Bea's condition, but I visited her bedside anyway.

Seeing a friend in a hospital bed, let alone an ICU, was never easy.

Bea's vibrant form looked almost lifeless. But I knew she was still in there, and I held out hope she'd pull through.

I told her unconscious body all about the NYPD beekeeping unit coming to our rescue. About Nancy and Esther pitching in to help. About her greenhouse being back online and gloriously warm and sunny again. And I assured her that we would all do our best to keep her bees safe.

Finally, I whispered heartfelt prayers to Heaven, swiping away a few tears as I recited them. Bea was one of Madame's oldest friends. When my mentor was down, Bea lifted her up, even found a way to keep Madame going financially.

Bea didn't deserve this, I thought, as I gazed at her ghostly pale skin and motionless body. And she didn't do this to herself, either.

Despite so much evidence to the contrary, I couldn't bring myself to believe Detective Novak's attempted suicide theory. Not Bea Hastings.

If someone had done this to her—brutally pushed Bea off her own beloved greenhouse roof in an attempt to kill her. Well . . .

I promised Bea right then and there that I would discover the identity of this dark soul, hiding in the shadows from this awful act, and drag it—kicking and screaming, if need be—into the light.

THIRTY

CHECKING the time, I stepped up the pace of my day.

Leaving the hospital, I cabbed it back to the coffeehouse to help with the afternoon rush. This time, on Taxi-TV, the weather report included news on the storm front hitting the Caribbean—and Madame's island resort. The meteorologists expressed concern on the stalling of the storm front, which they said was gaining strength in the warm waters.

Pulling out my phone, I tried to reach Madame again, but the call still wouldn't go through. Were the cell towers down?

I texted her anyway.

Miss you and love you.

Wish I could talk to you.

Need you more than ever . . .

As I expected, at this time of day, my coffeehouse was packed, but my assistant manager Tucker Burton had the situation well in hand. I was happy to see things running smoothly because there was a newbie on duty.

Punch—Tucker's exclusive romantic partner for the past few years—was a fellow thespian, which was how they met. A near-legendary female impersonator on the local cabaret scene, Punch also worked part-time for the catering arm of our Village Blend. Over the past several months, Punch had worked side by side with my staff so often he'd become a skilled barista himself.

Now, with Esther and Nancy working part-time as beekeepers, Punch's presence was a gift from the theatrical gods—or more accurately, the gods of musical theater, for when I entered the coffeehouse, Punch and Tuck were regaling our customers with the "Work Song" from *Les Misérables*.

"Nice of you to entertain our clientele," I said as I put on my Village Blend apron. "But you might have chosen a more upbeat song than one sung by condemned prisoners."

"I wanted to sing 'Working in the Coal Mine,' but Punch nixed that snappy little number," Tuck replied.

Punch shuddered. "I can't help it, Ms. Cosi. Coal mines give me the creeps. A movie I once saw had scenes in a coal mine and I still have nightmares about it. The cold. The dark. All those soot-covered faces."

"Did people get trapped?" Tuck asked.

"Nothing like that," Punch replied. "It was just a tragic story about a handsome, talented young man who was forced to give up his dreams and work the coal pits. I had to turn it off, it was so disturbing!"

"Was it *How Green Was My Valley*?" Tuck asked. "I love those Welsh accents."

"Or maybe *October Sky*," I threw out. "That's the true story of a coal miner's son who becomes a rocket scientist."

"No, no, no!" Punch shook his head. "The movie I'm talking about is *Zoolander*!"

Right.

Song stylings (and male model coal mining nightmares) over, we went back to work.

The rush was heavier than usual today, as nearby offices emptied, and their worker bees buzzed by the Village Blend for a little caffeinated fortification before winging their way home. With the frantic hours flying by, it wasn't until after seven PM that my penchant for punning slowed considerably, along with the day's crush of customer orders.

Scanning the main floor from behind our Italian marble–topped coffee bar, I counted three tables occupied by university students, their noses buried in laptops. Near the hearth, a pair of regulars sipped espressos after their evening stroll through the Village.

The takeout line was now short and manageable, so I left my on-duty staff to handle the remaining hours before closing.

With an Americano in one hand and a plate of honey cookies in the other, I headed up to my cozy office on the second floor. To the relaxing sounds of hissing espresso machines, coffee talk, and smooth jazz on our sound system, I opened the computer and began my search for Bea's niece.

Thirty-one

~~~~~~

I quickly discovered Susan Hastings's public relations company was called Amplify, and I jumped right to its website. Her bio listed work for several Fortune 500 corporations: She helped launch a new line of pharmaceuticals and pushed wind power for an alternative energy company in Nebraska.

A *Forbes* article mentioned an aggressive campaign that Suzie waged in defense of an investment bank that had run afoul of regulators. And this year she began working for UrbanGro, a high-tech agricultural start-up that was "pioneering urban farming."

As far as I could tell, Suzie ran her operation without any full-time staff—which meant there was no one I could turn to for information about her whereabouts. I found a *Contact* page and wrote a short but intense message under the headline URGENT. If she were working remotely, I hoped she would check her site's page and find my note.

The only other lead Todd gave me was her on-and-off boyfriend. But Tyler "La Something" was as elusive as Suzie. Todd said he'd been the head chef at Armando's, but when the restaurant went down, its website went dark. After a long and frustrating search, I did find a maddeningly useless reference to the mysterious chef on another website.

"Our sympathies to the staff who lost their jobs when Armando's lost its lease," commented the online culinary journal *Eating the City* in an obit for the defunct business. "The honey-inspired dishes, both savory and sweet, creatively crafted by young head chef Tyler will be sorely missed, including his Honey-Glazed Baby Carrots, Spiked Honey Candy Apples (with cinnamon schnapps), and *especially* the boy's signature Honey Ginger Sesame Beef."

No surname, which meant the chef must have gone mononymous like Cher, Prince, the Rock, and a host of other celebrities.

But even a mononymous Tyler couldn't make the A-list. When I Googled the word "Tyler" by itself, all I got were references to rock star Steven Tyler; his actress daughter, Liv; and Tyler Florence, a much more famous chef.

I switched over to UrbanGro's home page to see if there was a reference to Suzie anywhere, and quickly recognized that I'd been hearing bits and pieces about this shiny new tech company for months now—on TV, online, even on subway posters. Not everything was good, but the positive stuff had been orchestrated by Susan as part of an elaborate PR campaign.

I went to the *About* page and saw a smiling face I recognized—Matt's cosmopolitan friend, Nellie Atwood, posing with the current mayor of New York.

Nellie, it seems, was on UrbanGro's financial board. Well, no surprise there. Matt did call her the Start-up Queen. But Nellie's presence at the Hastings, on the very night we found Bea's unconscious body on her balcony, seemed suspicious to me.

Sure, it *could* have been a coincidence. One of Quinn's little quips came to mind: *"Two and two always add up to four in mathematics, Clare, but motive and opportunity don't always add up to guilt."*

At this point, I couldn't imagine what "motive" Nellie would have for attempting to murder Bea Hastings. And the residents of Bea's beautiful building were all wealthy and well-connected. Nellie very well could have been there to visit another member of New York's one percent.

But it seemed to me Nellie Atwood should at least be questioned.

Matt could do it, I thought.

In the meantime, I tucked my suspicions away and resolved to bring them up once I found Suzie. If Nellie and Bea had a relationship, good or bad, Suzie would know—and we could go from there.

Scanning the screen, I returned my focus to UrbanGro.

Founded just eleven years ago by CEO Lukas Wyatt, "a descendant of five generations of American farmers and planters who survived being suddenly orphaned at an early age," UrbanGro's mission was to use innovative new technology to pioneer urban farming, repurposing skyscrapers, warehouses, and other structures to grow food crops right in the heart of urban centers.

I was so absorbed by Suzie's public relations prose that when my phone alarm chirped, I nearly spilled the dregs of my coffee.

It was time to head upstairs to my apartment and finish preparing dinner.

I was looking forward to seeing Mike Quinn tonight, for more than one reason. I knew he had his own caseload and plenty on his mind, but I was hoping to discuss Bea's situation with him, along with my thoughts and concerns.

As for any romance between us, I didn't expect a Hollywood movie. I didn't even want that. But Mike and I were both under stress and neither of us would be helped by worrying the night away.

When we were actually able to connect, what he and I shared gave us both the comfort and renewal we needed in our high-pressure lives. And we hadn't given that gift to each other in some time.

I just hoped tonight we would finally make things right—and find some relief in each other's arms.

Thirty-two

〜〜〜〜〜〜〜〜〜〜〜〜〜〜〜〜〜〜〜〜〜

I lit the candles the moment I heard Mike's heavy tread on the stairs. When his key hit the lock, I dimmed the lights. By the time he reached the kitchen, I was waiting at the table.

Mike wore his usual stoic expression, but his face brightened considerably when he saw the candles, the chilled wine, and dinner waiting.

"Nice," he said.

But Mike wasn't admiring the glistening sheen on my Honey Orange Glazed Chicken, and the perfect little orange peel garnish I'd placed on top. He was staring at the short, Pacific blue silk robe I'd stopped wearing years ago because I'd become so "curvy" it defied modesty—which was *precisely* why I put it on tonight.

That was only one of the "nice" things I'd done to prepare for this evening . . .

Earlier in the day I'd set aside two squares of our shop's delectable Honey Apple Cake (before they sold out). Then I'd whipped up my favorite Honey-Dijon Vinaigrette for our spinach and cashew salads. Next I marinated whole chicken thighs in orange juice, raw apple cider vinegar, and a host of seasonings. I added an Orange Blossom honey Bea had suggested from a vendor in Florida. Heavenly sweet with a mild citrus tang, it was perfect for this dish.

In a small saucepan I combined more orange juice, honey, and vinegar, along with cumin and brown sugar, and brought it to a simmer. As the glaze cooked down, the kitchen filled with a pleasurably sweet, citrus-honey scent.

Finally, I removed the chicken thighs from the marinade and sautéed them *slowly* in olive oil until the skin turned golden brown. The scent alone was a swoon-worthy experience—one I hoped would be repeated in many other ways this evening. With the sauce ready and the chicken holding in the oven, I jumped into the shower.

All through the cooking process I had listened for news on the worsening storm front in the Caribbean via my small flat-screen TV on the kitchen wall. My anxiety increased with the latest update. The tropical storm not only stalled over an area that included Madame's island resort, it also had been upgraded to a hurricane.

I texted Matt to see if he had heard from his mother.

Troublingly, he had not.

More than ever, I needed Mike Quinn's comfort tonight.

With nothing to do but wait, I popped the cork on the wine and sampled half a glass. Then I poured the warm, luscious glaze over the chicken, until it glistened in the candlelight.

By the time Mike reached my kitchen, his jacket was already off, his tie loose and collar unbuttoned. He tossed the coat and tie on an empty chair and draped his shoulder holster and service weapon over the back.

I poured him some wine and stepped closer than I needed to as I handed off the glass. I wanted Mike to feel a little of my body heat and smell the vanilla-scented soap, still lingering from my shower.

"So, how did it go today?" I asked.

"Some of the lab results came in for that body last night," he said, sinking into a chair. "The victim had the same tar oil on his shoes and clothes, the same food stains, and when toxicology comes in, I just know he'll be pumped full of the same drug, too." He sighed heavily. "No ID yet, but it's only a matter of time."

Mike rolled up his sleeves. "On top of that, I got a call from a friend at One Police Plaza. The funding cuts are giving the brass sleepless nights. They're strategizing cutbacks now, weighing which elite units to either trim or completely eliminate, including mine. And the OD Squad is far from a shining beacon of accomplishment right now. Not with homeless bodies piling up, all dead from XS12, a drug we *claimed* to have taken off the street but is obviously still on. And—"

"And?"

"Nothing."

When the silence stretched too long, I heard Matt's advice echo through my head: *Don't be the honey. Be the bear.*

Time to step up, I thought, as I moved behind Mike.

Bending low, I put my hands on his broad shoulders and began to massage the tension out of the knots in his hard muscles. When he sighed, I pressed closer.

"I'm sorry this is happening . . . I know it's tough," I whispered breathily into his ear. "But you've got to eat, right? And I promise, if you agree to set your troubles aside for a little while, give your worries a rest, this beautiful dish will help you do it. Joy came up with it for our Jazz Space kitchen in DC. She told me Franco loves it."

"Franco?" Mike grunted. "That's not a discerning endorsement, Clare. That shaved-headed punk will eat anything."

I frowned at his tone. "Where did that come from? You sound like Matt."

"Franco's been a pain all day, and I'm a little peeved at him, that's all. Your ex-husband's hate for Franco is on a whole other level."

"Matt doesn't hate Franco."

Quinn sat up, disengaging himself from my caresses. "Let's not talk about your ex. Not unless you want to drive me from the premises. How about a little music instead?"

"I left my phone in the bedroom. Turn on the flat-screen. Cable channel 1460 plays that ambient music you like. Very relaxing."

As I went to the fridge to grab our salads, I heard the television go on, but instead of music, Quinn landed on the local news—and kept it there.

The young anchorwoman was delivering a human-interest story.

"More than a day later, the identity of the concerned citizen who lowered himself onto a balcony to save a woman's life remains a mystery," she said. "But he may not remain anonymous for long . . ."

I rejoined Mike in time to see the now-familiar twenty-second descent to the balcony—so brief it was almost always broadcast in slow motion.

"Lukas Wyatt, CEO of UrbanGro, has offered the anonymous hero ten thousand dollars if he comes forward," the anchor continued. "Money he can keep or donate to the charity of his choice."

They ran the CEO's remarks, but I was more surprised by Wyatt's appearance than his words. The tech wizard looked like a log cabin pioneer with a buttoned-up flannel shirt and a bolo tie almost hidden behind a long, bark-brown lumberjack beard.

The announcer teased the sports segment next, and Quinn switched over to music.

"I have to admit that guy earned the ten thousand bucks," he said. "What he did some first responders would balk at trying. It was pretty heroic."

"Matt will be happy to hear that, especially coming from you."

Quinn blinked. "I'm sorry? Did I miss something?"

"No. But the city is—*missing* something, I mean."

I smiled, figuring it was okay to talk about my ex since Mike himself brought up his heroic act. "Matt was the man who lowered himself from the Hastings's roof to reach Bea's balcony."

Quinn stared blankly.

"It's funny," I went on. "Matt is usually a grandstander. But now he's really being humble about the whole thing. He's even embarrassed the photo got out, and he refuses to come forward with the truth, even to our baristas."

I finished my wine and poured a little more.

"Nancy was sure impressed. She doesn't have a clue it's her boss, but she never lost her crush on him. He's a real hero, she says."

"I see. Sounds like Matt's your hero, too."

I froze at Quinn's tone. I'd been watching the wine pour into my glass when I should have been watching my fiancé's expression. A terrible pall fell over the room, so cold it felt physical. I suddenly regretted the thinness of my robe and hugged myself for warmth.

"Mike, don't get the wrong idea," I said quickly. "I admire what my ex-husband did because he helped save Bea Hastings's life."

"So *obviously* Matt's your hero."

Now I was getting angry. "Look, I'm sure there will always be friction between you two, but you have to admit what he did was brave, even admirable."

"Admirable and Allegro are two words I never thought I'd hear *you* use in the same sentence."

Quinn was prodding me, that's what it felt like, trying to get some emotional reaction. Well, he finally got one—

"*Or* maybe you're just annoyed because Matt Allegro saved someone's life while apparently all your OD Squad can do lately is pick up corpses."

Immediately, I regretted my words, wished I could take them back. Seeing Mike's face fall nearly killed me. The man I loved had come to me at a new low in his life. And I'd completely crushed him.

I blamed the wine and my own stress. I tried to apologize, but when Quinn's phone rang, he instantly checked the number and stepped out of the kitchen to take the call. I didn't even have to get up from the table to hear his half of the conversation.

"I *told* you, no one else is going in. I *won't* lose another man."

Pause.

"I don't care if you're volunteering. I make the call and I say no."

Pause.

"That's not it and you know it."

Pause.

"What do you mean you're waiting to see the deputy commissioner? Right now? Are you trying to go over my head?"

Pause.

"Stay where you are. I'm coming downtown."

Quinn returned to the kitchen in a fury, strapped on his holster, and threw his coat and tie over his broad shoulder.

"Something's come up. I've got to go," he said, without even looking at me.

"Mike, stop. Please don't leave like this—"

He shut me down with a raised hand. "We'll talk later."

I'd arrived at a new low tonight, too. And Mike's raised hand practically crushed *me*. I knew I was wrong. I knew I'd hurt him, but we both needed so badly to connect tonight. I could see it. Why couldn't he?

Whatever his reasons, Quinn didn't stick around to tell me—or give us a chance to reconcile. Before I could even blow out my candles, he was out the door, down the steps, and gone.

Thirty-Three

I climbed out of a lonely bed the next morning with a slight headache and plenty of regrets over what happened between Mike and me the night before.

My toes barely touched the bedroom rug before I texted Mike again, without much hope he would reply. He had already ignored three other messages. Why should this one be any different?

Oh, I supposed he *could* have been busy all night. That phone call he received sounded like serious business. But it was more likely he was giving me the silent treatment because he was still angry about what I said. Maybe he had a right to be. Or maybe he was just too steamed to talk and wanted to spare me from words that would only make our situation worse.

As I tied my robe around me, Java and Frothy noticed I was up and jumped off the two armchairs near the fireplace. Their coffee bean brown and milk foam white forms yawned and stretched and wasted no time making their feline needs known—

Merrooow!

Translation: Breakfast, please!

"Okay, girls. Let's go . . ."

As I trailed two straight-as-flagpole tails to my apartment kitchen and fed their little furball faces, I waited for a text that never came.

I brushed my teeth, washed my face, dressed for the day, and time was up. Duty called, even if Mike didn't, so I put my sadness aside, pulled my hair into a ponytail, and set my mind to opening my coffeehouse.

Before I descended the service stairs, I did send out one *final* text.

But this one wasn't to Mike.

Twenty minutes later I was filling the pastry case when I heard a knock on the still-locked front door. Through the glass I spied a young man with a weight lifter's build in jeans and motorcycle boots, a worn leather jacket pulled snug over immense shoulders, and a shaved head with a street-tough face, partially obscured by tinted shooting glasses.

When I opened the door, a deep rumble greeted me.

"Hey, Coffee Lady."

"Good morning, Sergeant. It's nice to know not *everyone* in the Sixth Precinct is ghosting me."

"Not me. When you text, I come running."

"That's because you know I'll give you a bottomless cup of coffee and a key to our pastry case."

The tough guy suddenly looked sheepish. "I guess my tank *could* use a refill."

Sergeant Emmanuel "Manny" Franco, a member of Quinn's OD Squad, was the closest thing Mike had to a second-in-command since his longtime partner, Sully Sullivan, retired from the force.

Despite Franco's lack of tattoos (to my knowledge) he looked more like a member of a street gang than a police officer, which was why he started his law enforcement career in a unit that infiltrated and policed dangerous criminal gangs. It was courageous work, and Franco was an outstanding officer. Over the years, he had also been a sweet and devoted partner to my daughter, Joy—and a good friend to me.

"I haven't done the espresso calibration yet," I told him, "but I just brewed up a pot of my Breakfast blend."

I noticed that Franco had removed his tinted glasses and was eyeing two new items in our pastry case. Mini crostatas, the golden color of morning sun, bursting with glistening Honey-Glazed Peaches. And our outstanding new Chocolate Swirl Blondies.

"The baked goods are all fresh," I offered. "Take your pick."

He rubbed his hands together and grinned like a kid at a candy store.

"Now you're talkin'!"

THIRTY-FOUR

On this cold autumn morning, the shop still felt a little chilly, so we brought our coffee and Franco's loaded plate to a table next to the already-crackling hearth.

"Man, these fruit tarts are tasty," Franco raved after his first bite. "The peaches and honey are crazy good together."

"I agree. They're a happy pairing." I paused. "Like you and Joy."

He returned my little smile as I watched him inhale the rest of the mini crostata—and began to wonder if the two left on his plate, along with the three blondies, were going to be enough.

"Okay, Coffee Lady," Franco said, pausing to wash down crostata crumbs with a happy swig from his mug. "I'm guessing you didn't ask me here to feed me breakfast."

I got right to the point. "I understand there's some friction in and around Mike Quinn's OD Squad."

"Friction?" Franco grunted as he reached for his second pastry. "Yeah, I guess 'friction' is the right word if you call the Chicago Fire a little spark."

"It's as bad as Mike thinks it is, then?"

"Worse than you can imagine. I can't really talk about it. But I *can* tell you that a lot is on the line, including a few hundred lives." He took another gulp of coffee. "From your crack about ghosting, I take it you and Mike aren't talking?"

"We had a fight last night over . . . something stupid. It was terrible timing and exactly the opposite of what I wanted to happen."

"Well, what did you want to happen?"

"Let me put it this way. I cooked Joy's special Honey Orange Glazed Chicken—"

"Oh, boy. Good stuff."

"I set the mood with candles and wine, a *romantic* mood. You know what I mean."

"I get your drift."

"And before I knew it, my ex-husband came up in the conversation."

"Allegro?" Franco's jaw literally dropped. He stared at me as if I'd pulled the pin on a hand grenade. "After all that's happened? What the devil made you bring *him* up?"

"Never mind, Sergeant. You only have to know that Mike and I got into it after that. He implied some unfair things. I thought he was deliberately goading me, and I stupidly took the bait. I regretted lashing out at him the instant it happened and tried to apologize, but Mike got a work phone call in the middle of our disagreement and used that as an excuse to leave. I haven't heard from him since."

Franco grimaced. "Sorry. That phone call last night is on me."

"I got the feeling it was you, even though I only heard Mike's half of the conversation."

"I'm glad you didn't hear *my* half."

"I heard enough. I deduced the rest."

The bell over the door jingled as Nancy arrived. She was immediately followed by Tucker, who took Esther's morning shift because she was taking care of the bees.

With his honey-kissed peach pastries polished off, Franco drained his coffee mug. Sitting back in the wrought iron chair, he folded his muscular arms over his weight lifter's chest and stretched out his denim-covered legs.

"Impress me, Coffee Lady. Let's hear what you *deduced* about that phone call last night."

"Someone in your OD Squad is missing—"

"Not our unit," Franco corrected me. "It's a man from the Gun Violence Suppression Division. He was undercover. Deep dive. Mike wanted him to do a little side snooping since we figured the homeless OD victims being moved postmortem were coming from somewhere in the boroughs—Queens, or more likely Brooklyn. Anyway, this guy knew Brooklyn, but as soon as he joined our case, he went AWOL and hasn't reported in three days."

"Now you want to go undercover and find this missing officer, don't you?"

Franco shifted in his chair but said nothing. So, I continued my deduction.

"I'm assuming Mike nixed that idea. And you think he stopped you because my daughter loves you, and he refused to put your life on the line because of her—and me."

"He was wrong. That decision was wrong. Personal relationships shouldn't enter into command decisions."

"So you went over his head. Which caused even more sparks to fly. And I'm guessing even though Mike went downtown to object, you got your wish, didn't you?"

"Okay—" Franco raised a hand in surrender. "I'm impressed. You got it all right. Just do me one solid. Do *not* tell Joy. I don't want her to worry."

"Why does it have to be you?" I asked. I couldn't help it. For my daughter's sake and my own, I didn't want Franco to put himself in harm's way, either. "There are thousands of officers in the NYPD. Can't you let someone else go into the hornet's nest?"

"Nobody who's still on the force has dealt with this gang before. I have. As far as our suspects know, I was one of them until I had to become a fugitive a decade ago. That's how deep I was in with them. Mike *should* have sent me in *first*. If he had, the poor guy from GVSD might be back home with his family now, instead of—"

When he saw the look on my face, Franco abruptly stopped his bitter complaints. Suddenly, he was all confident and reassuring. "Anyway, there's nothing to worry about. I know what I'm doing."

Famous last words, I thought with a frustrated sigh. "Mike told me he was peeved at you. Now I see why."

"Peeved?" Franco gave a bitter laugh. "Trust me. He's more furious with me than he is with you. I never saw him like this. Worst part is, I can't convince Lieutenant Quinn that what I want to do is the right thing. I'm trying to save lives, not to mention our OD Squad—and my job."

"Mike told me there was a possibility the OD Squad could be reduced or even disbanded, but I didn't know you were in some kind of jeopardy."

"Nah, you misunderstand me. I'm in good with the PD right now, but if our unit gets cut . . ." His voice faded. "What I'm saying is that

Lieutenant Quinn's the best cop I ever knew, and he's the best command-ing officer I ever had. The man taught me more—and believed in me more—than anyone else on the force. If they reassign me—" He shook his shaved head. "I may leave the NYPD. I don't want to but—"

Franco's declaration was cut short by a startled scream from our alley. My body went cold.

"That's Nancy!"

Thirty-Five

❧❧❧❧❧❧❧❧❧❧❧❧❧❧❧❧❧❧❧❧❧❧❧

Franco's cop instincts kicked in immediately. He was off his chair and through the back door before I got to my feet.

Tucker came running and we both nearly collided with a shaken Nancy.

"Are you okay?" Tuck cried.

"I'm fine," Nancy said, face flushed. "I was surprised, that's all. I was taking the recyclables out for pickup, and I ran right into some man ripping open our garbage bags."

"Was he looking for food?" Tuck asked. "Do you think he was homeless?"

"He didn't look homeless to me," Nancy replied. "He was wearing a clean white suit."

Tuck shuddered. "If not homeless, then styleless. I mean, who wears white after Labor Day? Besides Colonel Sanders or maybe the Good Humor ice cream man."

"Ice cream man!" Pushing past Nancy, I rushed out to the alley.

The dumpster diver was gone, and so was Franco. But he returned a minute later with a staccato cop description—

"Heavyset guy. Caucasian. Late sixties. Short silver hair. Trimmed goatee. Wearing a white suit. He had one of your Village Blend cups in his hand, but you aren't open so he must have picked it up in the trash."

"Where did he go?" I asked.

"He had a car waiting. New Jersey license. It's probably a car service, easy to trace."

"It's okay," I said. "I know who it was. The proof is right in front of us."

Franco followed my pointing finger to the four garbage bags that had been torn open. They lay on the oily pavement, their contents half-spilled, including the bag that the Man in White was no doubt searching for—I knew because a mound of dead honeybees lay among the trash inside.

"I don't understand," Franco said. "What do you know that I don't? Spill it, Coffee Lady."

I brought Franco up to speed on the tragic events surrounding Bea Hastings, the swarm at our coffeehouse that led me to her greenhouse, and my disagreement with the NYPD's official "attempted suicide" theory. Finally, I confessed—

"Since the NYPD wasn't pursuing the investigation, I decided to ask my own questions. I started by grilling her IT guy, Todd Duncan, on anyone who might have had a serious grudge against his employer. Right away, he mentioned one of Bea's competitors in the honey trade, a man named Felix Foxe. Todd called him the 'Ice Cream Man' because he wears *white suits* all the time."

Franco frowned. "What exactly was the bad blood between this guy Foxe and your beekeeping friend?"

"Bea discovered Foxe was passing off artificially flavored honey as premium organic gourmet product. I don't know all the details, but I know she exposed him—and that must have cost him plenty. I have no doubt Foxe was the man in our alley."

"I follow what you're saying, but how would this honey peddler even know to look in your trash for dead bees?"

"Foxe obviously heard the podcast."

"What podcast?"

"The beekeeping officers told me about a podcaster who puts out news to the local beekeeping community. This week her news included our late-season coffeehouse swarm from Bea Hastings's hives."

"All right, that explains how he knew about your trash. But it also suggests something else. Unstable individuals are sometimes triggered into acting out in response to media broadcasts. I mean, what use would anyone have with a bunch of worthless dead bees? Sounds like crackpot behavior to me. Maybe the guy's touched . . ."

I considered the sergeant's words as I stood there, gazing at the dead honeybees. If Foxe was mentally unstable, that would certainly explain the vicious attack on Bea and her hives. Or . . .

"Maybe the dead bees aren't so worthless."

"How so?"

"The officers in the beekeeping unit said they weren't familiar with the type Mrs. Hastings was keeping. What if this is some kind of new species? A highly valuable species?"

"Interesting . . ." Franco rubbed his jaw. "But I'm not sure where you go from there."

"You know what? I am."

Just then, Tucker came through the back door.

"Is everything okay, CC? Can I help?"

"Yes! Wrap the sergeant's blondies to go. And bring me a pair of rubber gloves, an empty takeout cup, and a lid—make that a *large* cup, please. I need to collect all these dead bees."

"What on earth for?" Tucker asked with a horrified stare. "Are you going to give them a decent burial? Build a Tomb for the Unknown Drones?"

"I need to show them to someone . . ."

I knew the beekeeping unit couldn't help me with my questions. But Officer Darius Greene already gave me the name of a woman who could—

"Ms. Cosi, if you ever need to know something about bees, the person to see is Dr. Wanda Clay."

Thirty-Six

~~~~~~~~~~~~~~~~~~~~~~~~~~~~~~~~~~~~~~

A few hours later, when our morning crush finally slowed, I took a ride uptown to the Science Center building on Columbia University's Manhattanville campus.

My destination was a ninth-floor lecture hall, where Dr. Wanda Clay, renowned "apiarist" (a fancy word for beekeeper), distinguished "melittologist" (an entomologist who specializes in bees), and "earth advocate" (your guess is as good as mine), had just wrapped up her latest lesson in a course called Bees and Humans: Codependence Means Coexistence.

The moment I entered the auditorium, I recognized the doctor. Even if I hadn't seen her staff picture on the Columbia website, I would have guessed her identity based on Officer Buzz Banner's reference to the woman as "wacky," along with his cryptic warning—

"If you ever do meet Wanda, don't mention her hair."

She wore it in a retro beehive. Not so uncommon, really. Our Esther used to beehive her hair as a tribute to the late recording artist Amy Winehouse.

Dr. Wanda's beehive hairdo appeared to be a tribute, too, but not to a tortured torch singer. Hers was colored in stripes to mimic a honeybee's abdomen.

The hairdo wasn't the only offbeat aspect of Dr. Wanda's appearance. With her calf-length tiger-print dress, platform heels, and an absurdly long string of pearls, she more resembled June Cleaver—if you can imagine the *Leave It to Beaver* mom with a PhD and a punk-rock attitude.

Although the lecture had ended, the renowned bee specialist wasn't through lecturing. Several students had gathered around the podium to speak with her, and one undergraduate naively asked Wanda about her hair.

"It's amazing," the girl marveled. "Those stripes aren't sprayed on or anything! I can't imagine how you keep them aligned so perfectly."

"Never mind the 'how,' my young tutee; it's the 'why' that's important."

As she spoke, the professor's gestures emphasized her salient points, a habit likely acquired in large lecture halls like this one.

"I wear this hair"—she touched her head-hive with both hands—"in order to increase people's awareness of the plight of the humble bee, a species facing threats from pesticides, pollution, predators, profiteering, and poachers."

"Wow," the student replied earnestly. "That's a lot of *p*'s."

"And don't forget disease and deforestation," Wanda went on. "The very existence of the honeybee is being threatened. Do you have any idea what that means?"

The young woman took a nervous step backward. "Will this be on the test?"

"*Beep*. Wrong answer!" Dr. Wanda replied. "The test you *should* be worried about is the one taking place outside these lecture halls, because the bee is one of the most important animals on Earth. Without bees, pollination would be devastated. No pollination means no flowering plants. No plants, no crops. No crops, no us. Do you get it now, my young tutee?"

The student nodded like a bobblehead in an earthquake. "You're scaring me worse than your lecture did."

"Good. You *should* be scared."

The modest crowd scattered quickly after that. While Dr. Wanda gathered her notes—and drained the contents of a thermos bottle—I approached the podium.

"Excuse me, my name is Clare Cosi. I manage the Village Blend coffeehouse—"

"Ah, yes! You're the woman who discovered that off-season swarm the other night."

"It's more like they discovered me."

"How can I help you, Ms. Cosi?"

"Well, Doctor, I would like you to take a look at these."

I pulled the top off a Village Blend disposable cup and passed it to her. Dr. Wanda took a hard look. Her expression went from bland, to surprised, to alarmed—all in under five seconds.

"The bees. They're dying?"

"No, they're fine," I assured her. "The ones the beekeeping unit officers saved are back home. Except for this bunch. They perished the night we found them . . ."

I filled Dr. Wanda in on the rest of the story, including the tragic state in which I found Bea Hastings—along with her wrecked hives. I also told her about Bea's elaborate, computerized rooftop greenhouse and the premium floral honey she produced inside it.

Wanda listened quietly, asking no questions. When I was finished. she scooped up her papers and tucked the empty thermos under her arm.

"Follow me," she said.

Still clutching the Village Blend cup, the professor bolted for the exit so fast I had to hurry to catch up.

Thirty-seven

~~~~~~~~~~~~~~~~~~~~~~~~~~~~~~

Wanda Clay led me to a spacious but deserted lab and sat me down at a workstation. She opened a small refrigerator filled with metal thermos bottles—just like the empty one she had tossed in a sink.

Next, she set a new thermos on the counter in front of me, along with two plastic cups.

"Mead," she declared. "Made from alfalfa honey. Very traditional. Neat, clean, and sweet. About twelve percent alcohol, so there's a bit of a kick."

She poured a careful half cup for me and filled her own to the brim.

"Skoal!" She raised her cup.

I sipped the fermented brew. It tasted different. Sweeter than beer but thicker than wine. And with a lovely flavor of honey and subtle spices. Dr. Wanda drained her glass and poured a second.

"It's very good," I said. "Where did you get it?"

"I made it, at my home upstate," Wanda replied. "Sunshine in a glass! Did you know mead is mankind's first fermented beverage? Our hunter-gatherer ancestors drank mead before they domesticated animals or invented farming because they found ready-to-eat honey everywhere they roamed."

"Interesting. I remember a Polish neighbor from my childhood in Western Pennsylvania. She made her own honey liqueur—"

"*Krupnik*," Dr. Wanda said. "It dates back to the sixteenth century."

"And I've heard of a German version called *Bärenjäger*."

"That's a brand name, Ms. Cosi. The actual beverage is called *Bärenfang*, which means 'bear trap.' Eighteenth-century German hunters formulated it to lure bears out of hiding."

Dr. Wanda downed her second cup of mead. As she asked me if I'd ever tried a Gold Rush ("a gorgeous honey-sweetened whiskey cocktail"), she donned latex gloves and dumped the bee corpses into a glass lab tray. She selected a particularly plump specimen with tweezers, placed it on a slide, and tucked it under a microscope with double lenses.

"Officer Greene was unfamiliar with the species," I said. "He thought they might be a type of Carniolan bee."

"*Beep.* Wrong!" Dr. Wanda said without pulling her eyes away from the lenses.

"He didn't think it was an Italian bee, anyway," I said.

Wanda snorted. "They're not Great Danes, either!"

She lifted her head, moved the slide, and squinted through the microscope again.

"I don't want to sound rude, Ms. Cosi. As a responsible member of society, I try to accommodate the police. But the way things work best is when the police listen to *my* scientific opinion. Not when I listen to their ill-informed guesses."

"I understand. So, what is your scientific opinion, Dr. Clay?"

After a long moment, and another swig of mead, she swiveled on her stool and faced me. As she considered her words, Dr. Wanda began to spin her long string of pearls like Gypsy Rose Lee.

Suddenly, she stopped the pearl dance and spoke.

"From what I can discern, Bea Hastings has bred a previously unknown hybrid species. From everything you've described to me, I deduce she's done this for revolutionary commercial reasons."

I swallowed hard. "That's amazing."

"It's monstrous," Dr. Wanda proclaimed. "If I'm right, this hybrid was created to collect much more honey using far fewer flowers."

"You don't see it as an advancement?"

"For commercial purposes—producing honey—yes, it is. But from what you've described, I don't believe these bees could survive in this hemisphere's outdoor environment. Released in the wild, they would die."

"I'm sorry, but—how can you tell all that, just by looking at them?"

"Quite easily. Let's start with the evidence of their physical attributes.

Every one of these bees has a prodigiously long proboscis, which would allow them to probe deep into a blossom, catching much more pollen than any forager I've ever encountered. And, from the amount of pollen clinging to these worker bee corpses, this hybrid has the equivalent of Superman strength—or, in the worker bees' case, Superfemale."

"I don't follow."

"A typical Italian bee carries pollen to the tune of thirty-five percent of its body weight. This hybrid was designed to carry seventy-five percent."

"Like the spectacled bear," I mumbled.

"What's that?"

"Your mention of the pollen—and your concern for the environment and survival of the planet's bees—it reminded me of something my business partner mentioned about an endangered South American mountain bear. This spectacled bear has a powerful body, so as it moves through the brush, it clears the way for light to reach the forest floor, and its thick fur carries pollen to the flowers, trees—and the coffee plants—which is why the Peruvian coffee farmers fear losing it."

Dr. Wanda nodded as she prodded the bees in the tray with a thin metal rod.

"I deduce, Ms. Cosi, you are beginning to grasp what I try to teach my students. Taking for granted—or completely overlooking—the existence of the very creatures that help our ecosystem function is a crime. And that's my concern here. These bees weren't designed to help them survive in any natural ecosystem. You described a greenhouse with thousands of plants. But normal honeybees need far more flowers to fill their honeycombs with nectar. These hybrids require a fraction of the plants to create their honey harvests because of the copious amount of pollen each worker bee is capable of collecting."

Dr. Wanda frowned. "The drawback, however, is these creatures appear to be fragile. Like hothouse flowers. Exposure to relatively mild temperature drops turned out to be fatal for many of them. It was a miracle that swarm found your roasting room's ventilation stack—it must have given off a tremendous heat signature."

"It does. I was roasting for many hours and our stainless steel venting materials are rated to handle over one thousand degrees Fahrenheit."

"That explains the attraction to your coffeehouse."

"Do you believe these bees are valuable?"

"Immensely so—if you're in the business of creating and selling designer honeys."

"Officer Greene told me your podcast included news about my swarm. Is that right?"

"Yes. The beekeeping unit's activities are always of great interest to my audience."

"Do you know if a man named Felix Foxe heard that podcast?"

"I know Mr. Foxe is a beekeeper and an entrepreneur. He's posted comments on my Facebook page, but I have no idea how often he listens to my podcasts." Dr. Wanda paused, suddenly suspicious. "Why exactly are you asking about Felix Foxe, Ms. Cosi?"

"Because one of my baristas caught him tearing through the garbage in the alley behind my coffeehouse. Some of Mrs. Hastings's bee casualties were dumped there, and circumstantial evidence strongly suggests that he was searching for specimens."

"Yes, that's highly likely what Felix Foxe was doing. And I doubt he'll be the only one who will try to take possession of those bees."

"Is that a warning, Doctor?"

"No, Ms. Cosi, a prediction. But if you desire a warning, I can give you one."

She leaned forward on her stool and lowered her voice.

"There's a group operating in the city who call themselves BAG, the Bee Advocacy Group, though they are anything but. You see, when beekeeping was an underground hobby in New York, they helped beekeepers skirt the law. Then the movement toward legalization got underway, and BAG helped draft the regulations that are enforced in the city today. Unfortunately"—frowning, she spun those pearls again—"ever since beekeeping's been legalized, BAG has used the laws they wrote to seize the hives of struggling beekeepers for the slightest infraction. And once those hives are seized, the beekeeper never gets them back."

"They sound more like hive pirates than an advocacy group. Why don't the authorities do something?"

"You don't understand, Ms. Cosi. For all intents and purposes, BAG has taken on the role of the authorities. With more than six hundred hives and a mass of rules and regulations piled on top of recent funding cuts, the

Department of Health and Mental Hygiene lacks the resources and man-power for large-scale enforcement."

Dr. Wanda shook her beehived head.

"BAG jumped in to fill the gap and ever since the Seas brothers—the pair who runs the Bee Advocacy Group—have been personally profiting from their so-called enforcement."

The pearls suddenly stopped spinning.

"If Sean Seas or his twin brother get wind of the unique nature of Bea Hastings's bees, they will find some pretext in the law to seize them and neither you nor Beatrice Hastings will ever see those hives again. That, Ms. Cosi, is my warning."

She tugged off her gloves and poured another glass of mead for us both.

After that pronouncement, I needed it.

"Well, Dr. Clay, I appreciate the warning. But the Seas brothers were not in my alley this morning. Felix Foxe was. So now I ask you. Of what use are dead bees?"

The professor shrugged. "DNA extraction is possible. But it's more likely he was searching for a queen."

"A queen?"

"If a bee colony absconds—abandons its hive—the worker bees would fiercely protect their queen wherever she flew. And a heathy, well-fed queen is *always* pregnant. She'll lay up to twenty thousand honeybee eggs a day, so it's quite possible Foxe could harvest thousands of living eggs, even if the queen is already dead."

"Then he would—"

"He would be poaching, Ms. Cosi. Stealing Bea's honeybee hybrid away from her. I'm sure Mrs. Hastings spent a great deal of time and money developing these creatures. I assume their loss to a competitor would be a devastating blow."

Thirty-Eight

A devastating blow.

Dr. Wanda's words stuck like honey on my mead-buzzed brain as I made my way down to the Science Center's lobby and out to the sunny sidewalks of the Upper West Side.

Was a *devastating blow* what Felix Foxe intended to deliver to Bea Hastings? Or had he already delivered it on the night that Matt and I found the poor woman half-dead on her balcony?

Fury was rising in me, and I wanted nothing more than to track down Foxe and demand he return what he'd taken from my shop's garbage, as well as explain *how* he knew Bea Hastings's bees were so valuable, and *where* he was on the night of the coffeehouse swarm.

Maybe it was the mead, maybe the revelations about Bea's hives, but as I walked toward the corner of 130th and Broadway, I felt as if my heart was beating faster than worker bee wings.

Taking deep breaths, I tried to calm down and talk sense to myself—

A direct confrontation with Felix Foxe wouldn't be the smartest move to make. Yes, I wanted answers from Felix. But questioning him wouldn't be easy. Not like grilling Todd Duncan.

Todd was a happy-go-lucky employee.

Felix Foxe, by all accounts, was a bitter and ruthless rival.

From the way Todd described Bea's relationship with Foxe, it sounded almost personal. Like she had a real hate for him. It made me wonder—

Could they have been friends in the past? Was that how Foxe knew about Bea's hybrid honeybees?

I doubted Todd could shed any further light on their relationship since he hadn't been acquainted with Bea for very long. Unlike Madame, who'd known the woman for decades.

If anyone could help me fill in the blanks on Bea Hastings's history, *and* give me advice on what to do next, my beloved mentor could—which was why, after using my mobile phone to call for a car service, I checked for any response to the many messages I'd sent to her.

She still hadn't replied to a single one.

It seemed the hurricane had destroyed every phone service tower in its path—and I prayed that was the only harm it did.

Mike Quinn, on the other hand, didn't have the excuse of a tropical storm. After all this time, and all my texts, I couldn't believe he was still ignoring me.

Oh, sure, there might have been a reasonable excuse for his screaming silence. But it was more likely he was just being stubborn. In which case, one of Esther's saltier epithets (*"pigheaded jerk!"*) would certainly apply.

With my emotions swinging from fury to frustration to almost painful concern, I decided to swallow what was left of my pride and text Lieutenant Too-Quiet Quinn again. I was about to begin when a ding alerted me to an incoming message, not from my current fiancé, but my former husband—

Mother arriving at LGA tonight.

Am meeting her plane at 7PM.

Want 2 come?

I texted back:

U Bet!

Good news at last. Madame was safe!

I nearly shouted with joy. Then my happy smile faded as I typed the next words—

Did U tell her about Bea?

No. Talk 2 night.

I hated the idea of my former mother-in-law coming home to such horrible news about her old friend. Good thing her son and I would be giving her a warm welcome at the airport.

By the time my hired car pulled up, my worries subsided—at least about breaking the bad news to Madame, because Matt and I would be doing it together.

Thirty-nine

⟨⟨⟨⟨⟨⟨⟨⟨⟨⟨⟨⟨⟨⟨⟨⟨⟨⟨⟨⟨⟨⟨⟨⟨⟨⟨

That evening, I recognized Matt's furry face pulling up to the Village Blend. His rented SUV was new to me, but his pirate beard and athletic build were more than familiar.

Wishing my staff a good night, I pushed open the front door, and climbed into the passenger seat with two takeout cups, still toasty warm with freshly brewed caffeination.

Matt smiled his thanks through his bushy whiskers as I handed him the intoxicating joy of our prized honey-processed Costa Rican, the lively notes of peach and rose petal tasting almost as sweet as young love.

After a satisfying hit, we hit the road for Queens.

"How did you know what plane your mother would be on?" I asked. "She never replied to any of my texts or messages. Yet she managed to get a call through to you?"

"She didn't. It was her friend Babka who called, and not from the island. She called me from her flight to Vegas—"

"Vegas?!"

"She's overdue for some management meeting at one of her bakery-restaurants, the one in the MGM Grand, I think, so she took a separate plane to Nevada and called me from her flight."

"Did she tell you what happened?"

"Yeah. It was a vacation disaster. No one from the resort informed the guests that a hurricane was coming. They woke up to rain and wind and found the hotel completely abandoned by the local staff. Within a few hours the storm knocked out electricity, phones, everything."

"And to think I helped Babka convince Madame to go on this trip. Some vacation!"

"What *were* you thinking, Clare?"

"I was thinking they'd have a good time. Babka told her they'd have the run of the resort since it was off season."

Matt snorted. "Not off *hurricane* season. Something to keep in mind when you're planning that 'perfect' honeymoon getaway with Quinn."

"Uh-huh," I pitifully replied, wondering if there *would* be a honeymoon. Or even a wedding, which would be a tad difficult to pull off with the groom ghosting the bride.

"It's a miracle the guests made it to the airport," Matt went on, not noticing my crestfallen state. "Babka told me she jumped on the first flight available to the States and was working out a three-stop connecting path to her destination. Mother elected to wait a few hours for a direct ticket to New York."

"Listen, Matt, given what you've described, your mother is probably in a miserable, shaken-up frame of mind. We better tread lightly with the bad news about Bea . . ."

Which was the last thing I wanted since Madame was the only one I knew who could shed some light on Bea's personal life. But right was right, even though Matt saw it differently.

"She'd want to know, Clare. Wouldn't you?"

"I'm not your mother's age."

He fell silent after that, focusing on the traffic for a few minutes. "Maybe you have a point. Why don't we see what state she's in. Then we can decide whether or not to share the news."

"I think that's best."

A long red light allowed Matt to take a few more hits of the honey coffee. The caffeination appeared to redirect his focus.

"Speaking of sharing," he said, tossing me a wink. "How did that romantic evening go with your fiancé? What's the news?"

I groaned. "The *news* was the problem."

"Problem?" Matt looked stricken. "Why would there be a problem? My scheme was perfect. You served him low-alcohol wine like I said, right?"

"Right."

"And you made a nice meal, didn't you?"

"I did."

"Finally, and most importantly, you made the first move. You were the bear."

"No, Matt. *You* were."

"What?"

"We caught a news report about the CEO of UrbanGro offering the 'hero wall-crawler' a reward. I mentioned the hero was you."

Matt blew out air. "Clare, what is the matter with you? Who starts a romantic evening with the nightly news?"

"It just happened, okay. And it wasn't the news, anyway. The evening fell apart because after Mike told me he was worried about the NYPD brass disbanding his squad, I mentioned what you did was admirable."

I thought my ex-husband would be flattered. He wasn't.

"Are you telling me that while your fiancé is on the ropes with his job, you declare *me* admirable? How could you do that to him? You don't kick a man when he's down!"

"I didn't *think* I was doing that. I didn't think the two were *related*, at least not until Mike made me angry enough to say . . ."

An awkwardly long silence followed, until Matt tore his gaze away from the traffic jam on the Grand Central Parkway and cried—

"*What*, Clare? *What* did you say?"

"I can't repeat it. It was awful enough the first time."

Matt looked ready to throw me out of the car. "So how did this *romantic* evening end?"

"Mike got an emergency call and had to leave. I guess it was fate. Your plan was doomed from the start, and I haven't heard from him since."

The front seat fell silent again. For a long time.

Finally, I cleared my throat. "So, you wouldn't happen to have any more advice for me, would you?"

"I'm sorry. There's nothing more I can do," Matt said with the finality of a physician pronouncing a patient terminal. "I think you should speak to my mother."

Forty

꒰ᵕ꒱꒰ᵕ꒱꒰ᵕ꒱꒰ᵕ꒱꒰ᵕ꒱꒰ᵕ꒱꒰ᵕ꒱꒰ᵕ꒱꒰ᵕ꒱꒰ᵕ꒱꒰ᵕ꒱

We arrived at LaGuardia Airport just as Madame's plane was touching down, so we headed directly to baggage claim.

The vast room of luggage carousels looked daunting, but we soon located the correct conveyor belt. Standing back, we watched the knots of bedraggled passengers from Madame's Caribbean flight wearily trudge toward their circling suitcases.

Amid wailing children and exhausted adults, we witnessed many tearful reunions with concerned relatives. One young woman sniffled to her mother that the "hurricane honeymoon" had "destroyed her marriage!"

"Oh, Matt. These people look like they've been through—"

"Hell?" he said.

"A *hurricane*. I hope your mother is okay. After what she's endured, maybe we should get her right home and tuck her into bed. This news about Bea is bound to be too much."

More disheveled passengers and bawling babies followed the first group. But there was still no sign of Madame.

"Is this the wrong flight?" I wondered aloud.

"Not according to Babka."

And then I heard something incomprehensible, given the unhappiness around us—laughter.

Laughter?

It erupted several times from a single tight group of chattering people as they leisurely ambled toward the luggage carousel.

In the very center of the group, like the queen of the colony, I spied

Madame, stylish in a colorfully printed tropical pantsuit, a wide-brimmed hat topping her sleek, silver pageboy, and Jackie O sunglasses dangling from a seashell necklace.

"I'm still dreaming of that Sticky Bourbon-Glazed Chicken you barbe-cued for us the day after the terrible storm," remarked a young woman walking beside Madame.

A portly gentleman agreed. "It was mouthwatering manna from heaven after we'd gone all day without food!"

"I haven't cooked in years," a middle-aged woman confessed. "I still can't believe you took it upon yourself to raid the hotel kitchen and cook for us all!"

"We all came for a vacation, didn't we?" Madame replied. "Not to eat peanut butter sandwiches on stale bread."

"And you made all that amazing food with no electricity!" the younger woman marveled.

"My dear, you don't need electricity for a barbecue. As I demonstrated, all you need is a bit of charcoal, a small stack of guest stationery for kin-dling, a match. And the occasional sprinkling of island rum to keep the flames happy."

"Along with the cook!" the portly man reminded her.

"Yes, we all imbibed that first night, didn't we!"

"Yo, ho, ho, and a bottle of rum!" the portly man sang out and the group joined in. More laughter ensued.

Beside me, Matt said, "I don't know, Clare. Mother seems pretty re-laxed to me."

"And she's even got a suntan," I marveled.

My ex nodded. "Yep. That's a suntan."

Madame finally noticed Matt and me waiting in the wings. After throwing us a quick wave, she hugged all her new friends. With lots of goodbyes—and a few farewell tears—Madame detached herself from the crowd and hurried to embrace us both.

"It's sweet that you came to meet me," she said with a suspicious gleam in her violet eyes. "But the fact that *two* of you came suggests this is more than a simple ride from the airport."

When Matt and I failed to take the bait, Madame laughed and grabbed us both by the arms.

"Let's have a bite to eat and catch up, shall we? I've had nothing but watery coffee on that long flight—"

I stifled my own laugh. After surviving the winds and rain of a tropical hurricane, my mentor had only one complaint. The quality of her airline's brew.

"What's your pleasure, Mother?" Matt asked. "Upscale or down? You want to go local or all the way back to Manhattan?"

"How about a place that serves all-day breakfast?" Madame suggested. "We're in the borough of Queens, after all. There must be a good, old-fashioned diner close by, and I've been dreaming of a buttery omelet oozing with cheese and a slice of toast as thick as a Russian novel!"

Matt waved his phone. "I've got an app for that."

"Of course, you do," I muttered. (Since my ex-husband had discovered "swipe-to-meet" dating, *app* was practically his middle name.)

"Got one!" he declared. "Let's go, ladies. My treat."

Forty-one

꩜꩜꩜꩜꩜꩜꩜꩜꩜꩜꩜꩜꩜꩜꩜

Though Matt had found the Jackson Hole "Air Line" Diner with his foodie app, the place would have been easy enough to spot from the Grand Central Parkway.

Lit up like a glowing 1950s time capsule with shiny aluminum walls and Art Deco décor, it sported a retro neon sign (complete with a glowing jet plane) that was impossible to miss.

Like most New York diners, Matt's find featured an all-day breakfast menu. I counted thirty types of egg dishes; Belgian waffles crowned with balls of whipped butter or scoops of ice cream; and pancakes piled high with fresh fruit and whipped cream—not for the faint of heart (or low-carb enthusiast).

The charbroiled grill aroma got to Matt. He went for a juicy cheese-burger. My appetite was off, so I hung back with a simple toasted bagel with a schmear.

Madame put us both to shame, polishing off an absurdly overstuffed omelet oozing with cheddar cheese, grilled onions, and bell peppers. Plus a side of home fries and toast.

When Madame was finished regaling us with tales of her tropical adventure, Matt ordered a fresh round of coffee (a quaffable medium roast), and we finally broke the news about Bea Hastings.

"That's ridiculous!" Madame proclaimed, loud enough to cause the other diners to turn their heads. "There is no way Beatrice Hastings would ever attempt suicide!"

"Take it easy, Mother," Matt soothed.

She pursed her lips. "Tell me more. I want to know everything."

I did my best to fill her in, concluding with my frank opinion about the NYPD's view of things.

"Detective Novak accepted Bea's suicide posts on social media as genuine. I can't explain her posts, but I believe the detective ignored other leads, like the fact that Suzie has been completely out of touch through all of this—*conveniently*, I'm beginning to think."

"Oh, no, Clare. You can't suspect Suzie of harming her aunt," Madame insisted. "That girl loves Bea. And she *is* a nomad. Everyone knows it. She travels more than she's at home. I'm sure she'll turn up in a day or two. You'll see."

"I hope so," I countered. "Because if Suzie is innocent of harming her aunt, then I'm expecting her to help us push the police into investigating what really happened."

"I'm sure she will. And it's vital that she be notified," Madame agreed. "Suzie is Bea's heir."

"Wait," Matt said. "You mean if Bea passes, Suzie stands to inherit everything—the Hastings building, the greenhouse, the bees, not to mention the Hastings fortune?"

"That's right. Beatrice is a widow who never had children. Suzie is Bea's closest living relative."

Matt leaned forward. "That's a pretty big inheritance for one young woman."

He and I exchanged glances.

"I see what you two are thinking. But you're wrong. When Bea's sister was diagnosed with terminal cancer, never having married, Bea adopted Suzie as her own. And Suzie would never harm Bea. Certainly not for money! Bea gives that girl everything and anything she wants. She has all the privileges of money and none of the responsibilities—and knowing Suzie's vagabond personality, that's exactly how she likes it."

"What if there was something Suzie *really* wanted, and Bea denied it?" I proposed. "Could they have argued? Gotten into a fight that ended with Bea going off the edge of the roof?"

"That sounds far-fetched to me. Like I said, Suzie loves Bea like a mother. And Bea wouldn't deny her anything. She even invested in that new urban farm company Suzie started working for."

"UrbanGro?" I assumed. "Okay, now it makes sense."

"What does, dear?"

"UrbanGro's CEO was all over the local news last night, offering a reward to the 'hero wall-crawler' who saved Bea. Now I know why. She's an investor in his company."

"What's this about a hero wall-crawler?" Madame asked.

"Forget it," Matt said, waving his hand.

"Don't be modest," I said and turned to Madame. "Your son is the hero . . ."

I filled her in on the daring details.

"My boy!" Madame beamed. "I'm so proud of you. Why don't you accept the reward?"

He shrugged. "I don't need the money. And I don't want the publicity. Hey, what about Bea's housekeeper?" Quick to change the subject, Matt turned to me. "What do you know, Clare? Have the police spoken to her?"

"Yes," I said. "Novak spoke to Ella Strobl by phone. She's been in Austria for over a week. The thing is . . ."

"What?"

I shrugged. "Novak obviously took her story of a family tragedy at face value. When I asked if he'd confirmed the details, he deflected. *Defensively*, I thought."

"Because he wants to close the case on the circumstantial evidence of Bea's attempted suicide," Matt said.

"I agree. And I don't doubt Ella *is* in Austria. I'm sure Novak confirmed *that*. Which would make it the perfect alibi, wouldn't it?"

"Alibi for what?" Madame asked. "You can't think Ella would harm Bea? The two have been close for years!"

"Answer me this," I countered. "What happens if Suzie isn't around to inherit Bea's fortune?"

"You mean if something happened to Suzie?" Madame grimaced at the thought.

"Yes," I pressed. "Who gets the money then?"

"I remember Bea saying, quite seriously, that other than Suzie, her only other children were her honeybees."

"Her bees? Really?" Now I felt a grimace coming on.

"What is it?" Matt asked.

"Todd told me *Ella* was the only one Bea allowed to help her with her bees. It seems to me, Ella Strobl would be the beneficiary in that case, wouldn't she? The bees can't exactly cash checks or run the greenhouse by themselves."

"What are you thinking, Clare?" Madame demanded. "You said it yourself. Ella was almost certainly in Austria at the time of Bea's fall."

"Yes, but she could have been in league with someone else. Someone here in New York. Someone who could be paid off after Bea was dead and Ella inherited her fortune."

"But that would only work if Suzie were—"

"Out of the way," I finished for her. "In which case, Suzie wouldn't be guilty of anything. Just like her aunt, she would be a victim. And unlike her aunt, she could already be dead."

Forty-two

Madame went quiet for several minutes, thinking everything through as she sipped her coffee. Finally, she spoke—

"These possible explanations for why my old friend is lying unconscious in the hospital, they're mere *theories* at this point, are they not? Do either of you have a shred of evidence that Suzie is in danger? Or that Ella is in cahoots with a dastardly partner?"

Matt and I shared looks again.

"We have no evidence," I conceded. "But you *do* agree that the suicide note and the other peculiar things—the damage to the computerized greenhouse, Bea's own laptop, and especially her precious hives—they don't add up to something Mrs. Hastings would ever do."

Madame instantly nodded. "That's correct. I don't believe Bea, in her right mind or out of it, would have done any of that."

"Well, there *is* someone who has a strong financial motive for hurting Bea Hastings. And a personal grudge. His name is—"

"Felix Foxe," Madame finished for me with a sigh.

Matt leaned forward again. "You know him, Mother?"

She set down her cup. "I met him a few times. Long ago. He was well-mannered and charming. Wore white suits more often than Tom Wolfe. I doubt he'd remember me. It was another lifetime."

"Do you think it's possible Foxe was behind the attack on Bea and her greenhouse and hives?"

"I don't know if he's capable of attempted murder, dear, especially of Bea."

"Well, he's certainly capable of stealing from her."

"Money?" Matt assumed.

"No, bees. Dead ones, out of our garbage."

"What?!" Madame and Matt exclaimed together.

I locked eyes with Matt. "I didn't want to tell you because I didn't want you doing anything rash."

"You better tell me *now*, Clare."

I went through the whole story (leaving out Sergeant Franco for the good of Matt's digestion). I told them all about Dr. Wanda and the possible priceless value of Bea's hybrid bees.

"I see." Madame's head dropped with sadness. "Given all that, I would have to say it is quite possible Foxe is the man responsible for all this chaos, even considering the way Bea and Felix used to be."

"What do you mean?" Matt asked. "How did they *used to be*?"

Madame paused to sip her coffee. Matt impatiently rapped his fingers on the booth's tabletop.

"Come on, Mother," he pressed. "Share the honey."

"I will," Madame began. "But first I want you both to understand that Bea is not a combative person by nature, nor is she competitive with other beekeepers. She values her friendship with Martha Stewart, for instance. And just last year Bea visited Morgan Freeman in Mississippi, where the actor maintains his hives."

"So, Bea gets along famously with famous people," Matt said, "but not Felix Foxe?"

"That's right. Over the years Bea's feud with Felix has become almost obsessive. Which suggests what I always believed: The opposite of love isn't hate, but indifference."

"I don't follow." Matt folded his arms. "To quote the song, '*What's love got to do with it?*'"

"Beatrice Hastings and Felix Foxe met twenty-five years ago when she began buying flowers and plants from his New Jersey farm and nursery. The relationship progressed rapidly after that."

"Are you saying Beatrice Hastings and Felix Foxe were *lovers*?" Matt looked stunned.

Madame nodded. "I believe Bea's anger with him over the years has been a form of inside-out passion."

Forty-three

~~~~~~

MADAME'S revelation may have shocked Matt, but not me.

"Somehow, I'm not surprised," I admitted. "I sensed there was something more between Bea and Foxe than business. The animosity seemed so raw."

"Things were different decades ago," Madame said regretfully. "Foxe and Bea were happy, probably because they had their shared love of flowers and fascination with beekeeping to unite them. That's what happens with couples. Shared experiences can bond them—and break them. It can go either way . . ."

As Madame paused to drain her cup, I shifted uncomfortably under Matt's lingering stare. He and I were all too familiar with the roller coaster rides passionate relationships gave us all.

"Bea was already on her way to being a self-made millionaire when they met," Madame continued. "She had dozens of flower shop locations around the city, with thoughts of taking her brand national."

"And Foxe?" Matt asked.

"A moderately successful entrepreneur who took over his father's business and wanted more—*much* more according to Bea. It wasn't long before he tried to insinuate himself into her business."

"How so?" Matt asked.

"A deep recession settled over the economy. Bea's businesses faltered. Foxe strongly suggested cost-cutting measures that, according to Bea, gave the customers much less quality for the same amount of money. Bea would have none of it. She confided in me that Foxe's schemes revealed the man's true nature."

The waitress returned and filled our cups.

"Thank you, dear." Madame smiled.

"No problem, ma'am. Dessert?"

I caught Madame frowning at my half-eaten bagel. "Bring us two fat slices of New York cheesecake, won't you—and three forks?"

"You got it, honey."

"Mother, I have to say, what you're describing is sickly ironic. Bea looked down on Foxe for suggesting the kind of cost-cutting crap that's happening *right now* with Hastings Florists."

"I know. And what's happened to her company has deeply troubled Bea. She's spoken to me about it, but there's nothing she can do. They're still using her name, but it's no longer her business. I think that's why she's turned her attention so passionately to her greenhouse and bees. She's been shutting out the world, creating her own."

"Your friend has always been a difficult woman," Matt said. "You have to admit that."

"And *you* have to admit that Bea went through untold trials and tribulations in her life and business. When she started out as a little, powerless shop owner, she continually suffered financially at the hands of a crooked landlord who found fraudulent ways to circumvent the law and continually jack up her rent."

"Matt told me all about that," I said.

"Then you know why her view of frauds and cheats is dyed in the wool. And when Foxe started showing signs of it by pushing his cut-rate ideas and thinking they were ingenious business suggestions, things soured badly between them. She even came to doubt Foxe's affection for her. She couldn't stop questioning whether the man ever really cared for her, or simply wished to get his hands on her business."

"'*Heroes Are Hard to Find*,'" Matt said. "And that's my second song title of the evening."

"In any case, she's kept an eagle eye on Felix Foxe ever since. And when she caught him peddling artificially flavored honey to New York restaurants, she exposed him, gleefully, I'm afraid."

"Is that enough for a man to attempt murder?" Matt asked. "Or do you think it was just an argument that went too far?"

"Whether he intended it or not, if Foxe hurt Bea, he must be caught and prosecuted."

At that point, I reminded Matt and Madame of Felix Foxe turning up in our Village Blend's back alley, searching our garbage for Bea's dead bees, which he almost certainly found and stole.

Matt began simmering again. "I'm going to solve this. Tomorrow, I'm going to track down this man and confront him."

I tensed at the look of fury on Matt's face. "I can see you're upset, but that's not a good plan."

"Why not? I'll get Bea's bees back."

"But you'll ruin *my* plan. I already have a strategy to make Foxe return what he stole—*and* come clean about what happened between him and Bea on the roof the other night."

"What are you going to do, Clare? Use your fiancé to intimidate him? Quinn's position with the NYPD should be good for something, I guess."

"I wouldn't do that. And even if I could, Foxe lives in New Jersey. He's out of Mike's jurisdiction."

"So, what *are* you going to do? Visit him with a lawyer? That kid Todd Duncan? You said he has a law degree."

"Just trust me. My plan will work."

Matt sat back and refolded his arms.

"I'll give you one day. Then *I'm* going to see him."

Forty-Four

〜〜〜〜〜〜〜〜〜〜〜〜〜〜〜〜〜〜〜〜〜

"You don't really have a plan to deal with Felix Foxe, do you, dear?"

"No. But I didn't want Matt knowing that . . ."

Madame's slender form was lounging like an imperial feline on her antique couch. Wrapped in white silk pajamas, she sampled sips of our new honey-processed Costa Rican from a century-old demitasse. A half-empty French press rested beside her on a sterling silver tray embossed with interlocking fleurs-de-lis.

After the three of us left the diner, Madame wanted to see Bea Hastings before she went home. But visiting hours were over in the ICU, and she was forced to postpone her trip till morning.

It was after nine o'clock when Matt finally dropped us off in front of Madame's stately building on Fifth Avenue. As a welcome-home surprise, I pulled a pound of our new honey coffee out of my shoulder bag.

Delighted, she prepared it herself (and raved over her first cup) before we settled down for a long talk in the living room of her penthouse apartment.

Originally purchased by her late second husband, the French-born importer, the expansive suite of rooms used to feel heavy and dark with brocade drapes and Gallic statuary. Since Pierre's passing, Madame had redecorated several times.

The space felt much lighter now, with cream-colored walls, and modern art astutely selected to complement rather than clash with her treasured French provincial antiques. The heavy drapes were long gone, replaced with filmy sheers, pulled back to reveal the room's tall windows. As a longtime Village resident, I couldn't help but be enchanted by the magical nighttime view of Washington Square Park's gleaming arch, its central fountain, and NYU's twin libraries beyond.

"I do understand why you . . . *dissembled* to my son. He can be a hot-head," she admitted.

"He's overly protective, that's what he is," I replied. "And I don't blame Matt. I'm furious, too. Mr. Foxe violated our business and stole something valuable from your friend. Unfortunately, if your son tracks the man down in that state, I wouldn't put it past him to—"

"Punch Felix in the nose?"

"Yes, which would accomplish exactly nothing. Mr. Foxe would certainly call the police and—"

"We'd be bailing my son out of a New Jersey jail."

"Worse. With the wrong judge, he could get his passport revoked. Which means his sourcing business would be hurt."

"You're right, of course. My boy's direct approach would likely end in disaster and yield us nothing. It's up to us, then. We women must put our heads together and solve this problem!"

I nodded, ready to brainstorm.

"But not tonight," Madame said resolutely.

"Oh?" That disappointed me. "Are you tired?"

"No, Clare. What I am is *curious*. And worried."

"About Bea and Suzie?"

"About you, my dear."

"Me?"

"Back at that adorable diner, when you stepped away to use the powder room, my son spoke privately to me. He said you and I should talk because you are 'in dire need of a mature woman's advice'—that's how he put it."

I squeezed my eyes shut in embarrassment. "He told you about my love life problems with Mike?"

"Mike?" Madame's violet eyes went wide with surprise. "Matteo didn't mention a thing about your fiancé. I would never have guessed that you'd have a problem with that lovely man. He's crazy about you."

"Matt said the same thing—not that he's a lovely man. But that Mike is . . . well, passionate about me. About us."

"Because it's true."

"I think it *was* true. I don't know that it still is . . ."

Forty-Five

∾∾∾∾∾∾∾∾∾∾∾∾∾∾∾∾∾∾∾∾∾∾∾∾∾

I managed to get my story out without too much emotion, but when I saw the sweet compassion in Madame's gaze, I broke down.

"I said such terrible things to him last night . . . and I haven't heard from him since. I've texted him and left voice messages, but he's ignored every single one."

Madame shook her head. "I believe the invention of these amazing phones was a blessing for your generation—and a curse."

"You think using the phone is a cop-out?"

"Those are the perfect words, dear, considering the man's profession."

"What do you mean?"

"A man like Michael Quinn, trained to keep his private thoughts and emotions in check, is not going to open up to you easily, and certainly not over a phone."

"So, you think I should just *wait* until he decides to show up at my door?"

"I didn't say that. But I am certain you two won't resolve a thing until you're in the same room together."

"How are we ever going to be in the same room together? He doesn't answer my calls. It's obvious he doesn't want to see me!"

The tears came again. I felt so stupid, crying like a teenager. Madame grasped my hand. Pulling me next to her on the sofa, she hugged me close.

"My darling girl, Michael wants to see you. Trust me, he loves you. *You* aren't the problem."

"Then what is?" I sniffled. "His job?"

"Not his job. His work."

"Aren't they the same things?"

"No. They're not. Michael Quinn's identity is almost certainly tied up with what he does. That's nothing new. Human beings have egos. All of us do."

"But Mike isn't egotistical. He thinks of everyone *but* himself."

"You misunderstand. Your fiancé's *ego* problem isn't about pride. It's about identity. He's struggling with a fear that he will lose his work. And down very deep, an unspoken question is certainly torturing him: If he isn't doing the work of a police officer, who is he?"

"I'll tell you. He's an intelligent, heroic, loving, and selfless man—"

"And *that's* what you need to tell him, in no uncertain terms. Help him face that existential fear that he will lose all that he is. Prove to him that he's more than his work. To the world. To his colleagues. To his children. And most of all to *you*."

I swiped the last tear away and took final soothing sips of the honey coffee. "You sound so sure in your advice. Did something like this happen to you?"

"Twice." Madame smiled. "With two different men. And I dealt with the problem two completely different ways."

"There is no one way to solve this?"

"There's no *easy* way, but I'll share both stories and you can decide what's the better course for you with your fiancé."

Madame reached for the French press and found it empty. She went to the kitchen and returned moments later with a chilled bottle of Riesling and two crystal wineglasses. She poured and proposed a toast.

"In vino veritas!"

After savoring her first sip, she smacked her lips and began her story.

Forty-six

∾∾∾∾∾∾∾∾∾∾∾∾∾∾∾∾∾∾∾∾∾∾∾∾

"What I'm about to tell you took place decades ago. Before Matteo was even born. His father and I ran the coffeehouse and business was good. Then came a disastrous frost that struck South America."

I nodded, vaguely recalling the history.

"The coffee crops in Brazil and a lot of other countries were wiped out," Madame continued. "Coffee prices surged to five times their original cost. And we soon discovered it wasn't going to be a short-term problem. Not only was the harvest destroyed, but the coffee plants themselves had been killed. A war in Angola, troubles in Uganda and Ethiopia all added to the coffee shortage. It would be three years until production reached normal levels again."

"How did the Village Blend survive?"

"We almost didn't. Many coffeehouses failed. Others resorted to coffee extenders like chicory, but Matt's father wouldn't have it. Day after day, Antonio would call suppliers all over the country. All of them were either out of beans or charging exorbitant prices for the stock they had. The situation became so dire, we were forced to reduce our hours."

Madame drained her glass and poured another.

"Antonio suffered. The coffeehouse was everything to him. But I suffered, too. From the same lack of affection that you're going through. Nothing I said could break his obsession with saving the business."

"What did you do?"

"I fixed the problem."

"How? Did you buy a coffee plantation?"

"No, my dear. I became a coffee *detective*." She tossed me a cheeky wink. "I began investigating coffee shops and vendors in the tristate area, traveling to locations I had never before visited—Chinatown's warehouse district; Middlesex County, New Jersey; Flushing, Queens, which was only beginning to gain the huge Asian population it has now. I discovered places where the coffee prices were still low, and the green beans were plentiful."

"How could that be?"

"They imported from the Asia-Pacific region. The coffee industry there was in its infancy, as far as exporting went. But I found distributors in New York and New Jersey who were importing their crop. I made deals. I placed orders. After that, we were able to keep prices stable while the restaurants, diners, bodegas, and coffeehouses around us had to raise theirs. And that's how we weathered the storm.

"With our problems solved, Antonio's worries subsided, and our married life returned to normal. Better than normal." Madame smiled with the memory. "Not long after that, we felt happy and settled enough to start our family, and Matt was born."

"That's a wonderful story," I said and finished my wine. "But I don't see how that can be an example for me. I can't solve Mike's PD problems. Or the crimes that are stumping his elite squad of detectives."

"I see your point. Well, there is my other remedy."

"I'm all ears."

Madame refilled my glass and began another story.

"As you know, years after I lost Antonio, I married my second husband, Pierre. He worked for his family's business. Though the Dubois were French, their headquarters was in Switzerland and their business culture was all about efficiency and excellence.

"Pierre's father encouraged all three of his sons to compete with one another. Pierre was the oldest and never liked the rivalries. The three were continually trying to top each other, which was good for their business, but put constant strains on their relationships."

With a sigh, Madame polished off her second glass.

"Pierre's youngest brother, Rene, was rather an obnoxious fellow. But out of sheer luck he landed a lucrative contract to export Bleu de Gex to the United States."

"Bleu de Gex?"

"It's a creamy blue cheese from the Jura region. In any case, my second husband's confidence was shattered as two major deals he had lined up both fell through."

"Was he ruined?"

"Oh, no. Pierre was rich and could live off his fortune, even if he never worked another day. His ego was bruised, and he made me suffer for it. Months before his troubles, we had agreed to spend our fall in Paris. And it should have been glorious, but the first week was miserable because Pierre was such a terrible ogre to me and everyone else. Every outing I arranged, he declined to attend, until I'd had enough."

"What did you do?"

"For one thing, I made a firm decision. No more tiptoeing around the man. I refused to be mistreated or neglected any longer. So, I used a bit of Pierre's money to make a grand gesture. I bought off the gendarmes guarding the Eiffel Tower overnight."

"You didn't."

"Oh, yes, I did. I explained to the gendarmes what I planned to do." Madame shrugged. "They were French. They understood."

"What did you do, exactly?"

"After the tower closed, I lured Pierre to the very top."

"Lured? How?"

"I sent him a written note with an ultimatum. Show up to see me tonight or you may never see me again. He showed my note to the bribed gendarmes, and they let him through. When the elevator opened and he climbed the final stairs to the observation deck, he found me up there, all alone, waiting with a picnic. And with the lights of Paris spread out before us, we shared champagne and caviar. I seduced him on the spot. We made love on a pile of blankets, which I brought for that very reason . . ."

With a wistful smile, Madame gazed out the window, at the lights of the park. I refilled her glass, emptying the bottle.

"It worked," she informed me, blinking herself back from the past. "Pierre stopped brooding and neglecting our relationship. We had a splendid time after that."

"And what came of his brother Rene's cheese deal?"

Madame laughed. "That November our government changed their

import regulations so that all cheese had to be made with pasteurized milk. And since Bleu de Gex is made with unpasteurized milk, his entire deal collapsed."

While I thought about her tale and the twinkling lights of Paris, I downed another glass of the sweet, crisp wine. Madame rose and fetched a second bottle. She popped the cork and refilled my glass.

"I enjoyed your story!" I said, feeling more than a little giddy from the Riesling's buoyant effects (not to mention its jaunty hints of lemon peel and honeyed fruit). "And I'm sure Tucker would be thrilled to see Mike and me take his honeymoon suggestion to escape to the Paris Ritz. I wouldn't mind it either but—"

"You miss my point, Clare. It doesn't have to be Paris. Or the Eiffel Tower. Or the Ritz. But it does have to be somewhere else. Somewhere unexpected. Somewhere surprising and preferably beautiful. And most of all, somewhere neutral."

"What do you mean neutral?"

"Neutral territory. Your duplex and his apartment are both crowded with memories good and bad, things that should be put aside if you're to rediscover one another. Remember, he isn't the enemy. And neither are you. But you do have one."

I knew what she meant. And so did Esther Best. Of all people, Esther in her bee bonnet suddenly came to mind.

"Fear is our enemy," I said. "And we must always stand up to our enemies."

"That's right, dear. Your fears and especially *his* are what's keeping you apart." Madame nodded her encouragement. "Don't be afraid to shock the fear out of him. While you're doing it, you may surprise yourself. I certainly did, with both of my husbands. And, like them, I believe Mike will surprise you, as well."

Forty-seven

◧◧◧◧◧◧◧◧◧◧◧◧◧◧◧

I'm not sure whether Madame and I finished that second bottle of wine, or the wine finished us. Either way, by midnight I was far too woozy to return home alone.

While Madame went off to check the guest room, I phoned Matt and asked him to open the Village Blend in the morning.

"I'm crashing at your mother's."

He was glad to hear it. "Take the whole day off, Clare. You deserve it. You two should have time to catch up."

"Ooooh, aren't you nice, Matty. O-kay, but would you please go upstairs and feed my kitties in the morning? My sweet little furry babies will be lonely by sunup without their mummy there to rub their ears and give them oodles and oodles of kisses . . ."

"Hmm," my ex grunted suspiciously. "Have you been drinking?"

"Why, yes. I had a little drink-y or two of some sexellent wine, but I ashuuur you I am sur-fectly po-ber."

Then I hung up and immediately passed out on Madame's antique sofa.

Eight hours later, I woke to the sun screaming through the penthouse windows. I squinted at my surroundings, trying to get my bearings.

One of the tall windows was opened slightly for fresh air, and the room felt cool, but I was snug and warm under the softest of cashmere throws that Madame had draped over me.

Sounds echoed up from the street below: chattering students heading off to class; the beeping of horns and revving engines from the traffic on Fifth Avenue.

My eyes felt sticky, my mouth like a rustic village had spent the night mashing a bushel of sour grapes in it—with their feet!

I couldn't begin to guess what my hair and face looked like. Yet Madame was already up and dressed, fresh as a French lily as she waved a steaming cup of my own Breakfast blend under my nose.

"Wake up, sleepyhead," she cooed—with a far too sunny smile for someone supposed to be recovering from a drinking jag.

I sat up and thanked her for the coffee.

"Get yourself caffeinated," Madame insisted. "Then have a nice hot shower to refresh yourself."

"My clothes?" I muttered, frowning at the wrinkled duds I'd slept in.

"Not to worry. I had my son send over clean things for you—jeans, a nice sweater, and undies, of course!"

She winked, and I tried not to die of embarrassment.

"Visiting hours start in a short while, my dear, and I want to see Bea as soon as possible. Shake your tail feathers!"

Forty-eight

꩜꩜꩜꩜꩜꩜꩜꩜꩜꩜꩜꩜꩜꩜꩜꩜꩜꩜꩜꩜꩜

I don't know what Madame expected. Did she think Bea would be improving? Conscious? Speaking, perhaps? Whatever her expectations, they weren't met.

When we were finally ushered to Bea's bedside, Madame seemed genuinely unnerved to see her once vigorous friend now attached to tubes and monitors and not even cognizant of her surroundings.

Seeing Bea this way upset me, too. She seemed so tiny and frail in that giant bed, her skin so waxy it looked like the morticians had already worked on her.

I had to look away—in time to catch sight of the quiver in Madame's lips and the single tear rolling down her gently wrinkled cheek. I thought she would break down, but within a minute, her jaw firmed up and her mouth tightened with resolve.

I touched her arm. "Are you okay?"

"Let's go, Clare."

Madame didn't speak again until we reached the sidewalk.

"If Felix Foxe did this, we must make him pay," she said in a cold, flat tone I rarely heard her use.

I agreed with her, of course, but had to point out, "We need evidence."

"Then we must obtain it. What about the dead bees you believe he took from our Village Blend garbage? You say they're valuable?"

"Immensely so, according to Dr. Wanda Clay."

"Then we must get them back. If we do nothing else, we can accomplish that. This man must not profit from Bea's misery."

Forty-nine

We returned to Madame's Fifth Avenue penthouse by way of our Village Blend's pastry case. When we first came into the shop, Matt greeted us with a warm smile, but his dark gaze burned with a warning before we left.

"You have one day," he mouthed to me, index finger raised. "Then I'm paying him a visit."

Back at Madame's penthouse, she and I debated our next move over a fresh pot of my Vienna roast and samples of our new Iced Apple Pie Scones and Peach Muffins with Honey Butter.

As we talked—and licked our sticky lips clean of the delectable honey-cinnamon icing—Madame's violet eyes burned as hotly as her son's. Hating injustice, she was furious with Foxe. She also knew Matt as well as I did. If he took matters into his own hands (or fists), the consequences could be dire.

Fueled by bites of spiced apple scones, honeyed peach muffins, and sips of my boldly roasted coffee, we used our mobile phones to aggressively research Foxe and his company. "Foxe Farms Enterprises" sold a variety of items, primarily flowers and an array of honeys, which he harvested from his private farms in New Jersey, Pennsylvania, South Carolina, and Georgia.

After ten minutes, no ideas were hitting us, beyond *direct confrontation.*

"Then let's simply do that!" Madame exclaimed. "We cannot allow this pirate to get away with stealing Bea's legacy and perhaps her life."

"You know he'll just deny it. And there's no calling the police, although we could try."

"And report that Felix Foxe stole garbage from our back alley?" Madame waved her hand. "Take it from my years of experience, the police will do nothing to Foxe, and we'll have wasted valuable time. Once you discard something, Clare, it's no longer in your possession, and no longer yours legally. Neither the alley nor the dumpster are owned by the Village Blend. And, from your account, no one witnessed him actually taking the dead bees."

"That's true. Legally, the evidence is circumstantial."

"Then we'll have to take our chances on pressuring him to confess."

"Unless we can find . . . Wait a second, what's this—"

"What's what?"

"Foxe's company website includes a link to the architecture and design firm that built his New Jersey headquarters. According to their specs, Foxe's facility includes a bee lab. That's got to be where he took those valuable specimens. Hmm . . ."

"What are you thinking?"

"If I could find a way to get in there, I could steal back Bea's bees."

"Is that possible? How will you be able to see which bee specimens are his and which are the ones he took?"

"Not see. Smell. Bea cultivates designer honeys by changing the flowers in her greenhouse. Her latest honey project is lavender. And the dead bees are reeking of it."

"Brilliant, dear!" Madame snapped her fingers. "And I know a way in. It's so simple. Foxe is a merchant. We'll simply represent ourselves as potential new customers of his flowers and honey."

"I'm game. Let's give it a try right now."

Fifty

The phone number was right there on his website, and I quickly dialed it. With Madame listening, I called as the representative of the Village Blend and asked to speak with someone about a distribution contract.

"You may talk to me, Ms. Cosi. I am Mr. Foxe's personal assistant, Darla."

"Hello, Darla. I'd like to purchase your honey and flowers to supply my coffeehouses in New York and Washington, DC."

"I see. Exactly how many coffeehouses do you own in New York and Washington?"

"One in each city."

"No, no, Ms. Cosi," Darla chirped condescendingly, "Mr. Foxe is only looking for large distribution partners, not a small concern like yours. I advise you to check our website for vendors who will sell you our products at retail."

Without even a goodbye, the woman hung up.

Madame sighed. "Well, when honesty fails, dear, we sometimes must fall back on . . . dissembling."

"Fine, what are we going to lie about?"

Madame's expression turned sly. "I wonder how Mr. Foxe and that assistant of his would respond to the chance to make an international deal with a major French import company willing to place his unique American honeys throughout the European Union?"

I laughed. "I doubt Darla would hang up on them."

Madame rose, went to her antique desk, and began rummaging through its drawers.

"Ah, here they are!"

With a look of triumph, Madame handed me a stack of vellum business cards, embossed in gold.

Blanche Dreyfus Dubois

International Representative, Dubois Imports

*New York * Bern * Paris*

"Pierre had these printed after we were married. He wanted me to travel to trade shows and business meetings with him, but he also wanted to declare my presence as a business expense to the appropriate tax agencies. So, he made me a 'representative' of his export company."

"How do you intend to use these cards?"

"I shall return to my role as Blanche Dreyfus Dubois, International Representative of Dubois Imports, of course."

"But won't Foxe remember you? Last night you mentioned meeting him—"

"Many years ago! If Felix remembered me at all, it would be as a much younger American coffeehouse manager named Mrs. Allegro, not a silver-haired French citizen representing a major import/export firm."

"You're going to pretend you're French."

"I am French! And I shall speak French with a smattering of English. You will act as my assistant and translator. Call Mr. Foxe's Darla again, this time talk the deal up as potentially worth a fortune in a multiyear import contract, and I'm *sure* he'll agree to meet us."

"I hope Darla doesn't recognize my voice."

"Speak formally, with a slight French accent, and in short sentences. And make up a name for yourself. I've always been fond of Josette."

"I can do that. But what if Foxe puts us off long enough to check our story?"

"Dubois Imports is a going concern. Why should he doubt us?"

"Time isn't on our side, either. Foxe has had those dead bees for almost twenty-four hours. If there's a queen in there, he could be harvesting her eggs as we speak."

"Then we shall inform Mr. Foxe that I am returning to Paris this evening, with or without recommending his product to our board of directors. We'll see if a running time clock makes the Bee Pilferer hop to it."

I thought of another ugly wrinkle. "What if Mr. Foxe speaks French?"

Madame smiled with confidence. "That will be even easier. In that case I shall divert him with conversation while *you* look around."

"Just be aware, I can speak French, but I'm not fluent."

"Oh, pooh. I shall prattle on at length, and you can translate my words anyway you choose, asking any question you choose."

"All right," I said, "though I'm not sure what we're getting ourselves into."

Madame's violet eyes danced. "Why, a *hive* of scum and villainy, of course!"

I was not amused. "You do realize this plan is so shaky it's likely to fail?"

Madame placed a firm hand on my shoulder. "But it *will* succeed, my dear, because it *must*."

"O-kay," I said, clearing my throat to call Darla again.

At least now I remembered where Matt got his streak of fearless optimism.

Fifty-one

❧ ❧ ❧ ❧ ❧ ❧ ❧ ❧ ❧ ❧ ❧ ❧ ❧ ❧ ❧ ❧

"THEY call New Jersey "the Garden State" for good reason. Once through the Lincoln Tunnel, and past the industrial facilities and warehouses that service New York, the state turns very green, very fast.

An hour's drive west from Manhattan takes you to Hunterdon County. Jump off the main highway around picturesque towns like Clinton, Phillipsburg, and Lamberton and you'll encounter miles of narrow, winding blacktop with rolling hills, horse and cattle farms, plowed and planted fields, working barns, and busy farmhouses.

That was our view from the back seat of a sleek luxury limousine Madame had leased—along with the driver—for this little adventure. Though we were well into October and the summer bloom was off the trees, nature's spectacle brought back memories of a time in my life not so very long ago.

"It's so peaceful," Madame said. "I can see why you raised Joy here."

"I lived closer to New York City," I reminded her. "And my neighborhood was suburban, not rural. But I was happy to raise my daughter here. There's a lot to be said for New Jersey."

Madame smiled slyly. "But not enough to keep you there."

"Not after someone made an offer I couldn't refuse."

We didn't speak much after that. Madame and I had run through our parts several times. Though Madame seemed cool and relaxed, I felt a rush of apprehension when we drove through the open gate and along a winding driveway that led up to Foxe Farms headquarters.

The architect took great pains to give the facility a country feel, but the result seemed oddly out of place in such a rustic environment. Foxe's offices more resembled a short row of brand-new town houses than a corporate headquarters, with four stories of red brick, neat white trim, and a peaked roof. The structure had picture windows on the top three floors, but the ground level had only an entranceway tucked between two huge loading docks. A trio of Foxe Farms delivery vans were parked inside.

We arrived a little after noon—lunch hour, which aligned with our plan. Fewer employees on duty would give me an easier shot at snooping.

As we pulled into the parking lot, several employees were already hopping into cars for their meal trips. A half dozen others brought lunch and gathered at a cluster of umbrella-shaded picnic tables behind the facility.

Inside the reception area, a stout blonde in low heels and a beige dress introduced herself as Darla. Her cool gray eyes passed over quiet Josette's plain skirt and blazer with the practical shoes and shoulder bag and homed right in on her splendidly dressed boss.

Madame had donned a custom-fitted pin-striped suit from her business travel years with Pierre, and (Madame being Madame) couldn't resist adding a splash of shocking color with a violet scarf that matched her eyes. With French-tipped fingers, she presented her business card. Darla barely glanced at it. She only needed to see two words: *Dubois Imports.*

"Madame Dubois, what a pleasure to meet you."

Madame let fly with a string of platitudes (in French). When Darla turned to me for a translation, I knew we were in the clear, and did my best to deliver my reply with a pronounced French accent—

"Madame Dubois says she is very honored to be here, and she very much looks forward to meeting the head of this fine company."

"Mr. Foxe seldom allows himself to get pulled away from research, but for you, Madame, he's made an exception."

Behind the reception desk, a door opened. "Here is Mr. Foxe now."

I recognized the man from Sergeant Franco's cop description—

"Heavyset guy. Caucasian. Late sixties. Short silver hair. Trimmed goatee. Wearing a white suit."

Only two things were different. He'd swapped his signature white suit for a spotless lab coat, and he was wearing glasses.

As he shook Madame's hand and completely ignored "Josette," I studied the man who was once Bea's lover. His close-set eyes were veiled behind the huge horn-rimmed glasses, and he constantly wet his thin lips as he launched into his sales pitch.

"My English is . . . tee-nee," Madame replied after Foxe's spiel. "But my *secretaire* Josette will 'elp wis ze big words."

"Shall we proceed to the tasting room, Madame Dubois?"

"*Non, non,*" Madame insisted, followed by an avalanche of French. Foxe looked to me for an answer.

"Madame would like to tour your facility first," I said. "She has heard you do research right here in an on-site laboratory."

Foxe frowned. "I'm sorry. The lab is off-limits to all visitors. I hope you won't think me rude. It must be so because my research is ground-breaking. My competitors would love to learn what I am up to. I fear such security is tedious but necessary."

"*Non, non,*" Madame said, sounding the way I felt—hugely disappointed.

Did we make this trip for nothing? I wondered. If so, I was determined to go confrontational rather than leave this place empty-handed—or let Matt take over where I left off.

"It's on to the tasting, then." Foxe smiled and offered Madame his arm. "Shall we?"

Fifty-two

❧❧❧❧❧❧❧❧❧❧❧❧❧❧❧❧❧❧❧❧❧❧❧

"I have a captivating array of honey varietals for you to sample, Madame Dubois, many of which aren't available in the European Union."

With his pudgy arm wrapped around Madame's—and me trailing behind—Foxe led us to a small, mirror-walled elevator that took us to the fourth floor.

We exited into a deserted hallway with restrooms and a water cooler at one end. On the other end were two doors standing opposite each other. One solid wooden door was opened wide. The other, a metal door with a small round window, was clearly marked *Laboratory*.

"My company markets many honey varieties," Foxe said. "We also cultivate and sell flowers—only locally, of course. I was a florist before I became an apiarist."

Foxe led us down another hall to a small, cozy room with lounge chairs and a polished oak coffee table set with a dozen small jars, a pitcher of water, and a dish of tiny disposable spoons.

"Please, make yourselves comfortable."

Foxe poured tumblers of water and set them in front of us. "To clear your palate," he explained.

He indicated the tiny jars. All bore the Foxe Farms label.

"I thought we'd start with honey varieties unique to North and South America. You'll find that Buckwheat, Black Mangrove, Avocado, and Kudzu are wonderfully complex honeys. Though these may taste unfamiliar to you, I'm sure you'll find them enchanting."

For the next ten minutes, we sampled several honeys—all of them produced by Foxe Farms. Like coffee, tea, and wine, each possessed unique flavor profiles that varied wildly.

We began with Cranberry Blossom: light, fruity, tart, and tangy. Avocado Blossom honey was next. Creamy with the smoky taste of chili pepper and stewed plums, it was surprisingly complex.

Black Mangrove was the first green honey I'd ever seen. It was thinner than the others and had a sweet-and-salty taste I could only describe as *swampy*. The Buckwheat almost knocked me over with pungent notes of leather and an earthy undertone that was not particularly pleasant when it first hit my tongue. Fortunately, the flavor profile quickly morphed into hints of cocoa and coffee.

Foxe ended his honeyed tour of this hemisphere with Kudzu honey.

"Kudzu is a plant that originated in Japan and was transplanted in this country over a century ago to help reduce soil erosion," he informed us. "Alas, it is often referred to as 'the vine that ate the South' because of its aggressive nature."

"*Sacrebleu.*" Madame opened her eyes wide. "How aggressive?"

"If not controlled, it can swallow up entire buildings and foul electric wires."

Madame and I reacted with appropriate gasps. The Kudzu honey, however, was perhaps the sweetest (and strangest) I'd ever tasted—almost like grape bubble gum.

Our appreciative comments during the tasting were genuine. Foxe's honeys seemed so pure and clean, I doubted any of them had been adulterated with added flavors or ingredients, as Bea had so outspokenly alleged.

Foxe produced a second tray with more jars. "Now let's try some honeys you'll be more familiar with . . ."

Seeing my chance, I cleared my throat. "May I freshen up? The American water . . . It does not seem to agree with me."

"Of course," Foxe replied. "You'll find the room down the hall, near the elevators."

"Please, do not wait for me. I know how valuable your time is, *Monsieur* Foxe."

I hurried back toward the elevators and past the water cooler. As I approached the lab, I saw the office across from it was no longer a problem. The wooden door was now firmly closed.

I peered through the small round window of the lab's metal door and was elated to see no one inside. The technicians were most likely at lunch, which meant we timed our visit perfectly. But just as I was about to test the lock, that wooden office door opened, and Darla appeared.

"Can I help you, miss?" she asked sharply.

"Oh, *excusez-moi*. I am looking for the ladies' room?"

"Wrong door," Darla replied as she moved toward the elevator and pressed the button. "The ladies' room is over *there*." She pointed.

"I see, thank you."

As I slowly made my way toward the restroom, the elevator arrived, and Darla stepped inside. When the double doors closed, I made a speedy U-turn back to the lab and pushed through the door.

I'd entered an honest-to-goodness research facility, not some sham show lab to adulterate honey. The windowed walls were lined with workstations. There was also a refrigerator, an electronic scale, a centrifuge, and an incinerator to dispose of biological waste.

In the center of the lab, a translucent floor-to-ceiling column as thick as a barrel held an active beehive. Its captive occupants futilely bumped their little bee heads against the plexiglass prison.

I spied a workstation that seemed to be in use. On the cluttered surface I found a dead bee pinned to a specimen pad. Beside it, a pile of handwritten papers sat beside a foam box the size of a pound of butter. The box was labeled *Fragile/Frozen Eggs*.

Beside that box lay a small plastic bag filled with deceased bees. I unsealed it and the scent of lavender filled my nose. These were the bees Foxe took from our shop's back alley; I was sure of it, and I had no doubt the foam box held the missing queen and her eggs.

I gathered up all the bees—including the one pinned to the specimen pad—then I grabbed the foam box and stuffed them all inside my shoulder bag.

Now it was time to get out of Dodge. But before I exited the lab, I peeked through the window to make sure the hall was empty.

It wasn't. At that moment Darla stepped out of the elevator and headed into her office. This time she left the door wide open.

I was trapped!

Fifty-three

〰〰〰〰〰〰〰〰〰〰〰〰〰〰〰〰〰〰〰〰〰

Maybe Darla went back to her office to grab something, I told myself, and she'd be gone in a moment.

Cracking the lab door to listen, I hoped to hear her leaving. Instead, there was a tired sigh followed by a rattly squeak as the woman plopped down on her chair. Then I heard her lift the phone. Within a minute she was chatting to a friend.

I had to get out soon. I'd accomplished the impossible, but if I got caught now it would all be for nothing. And I had no doubt Darla and her boss would be searching my bag—and calling the police.

Take a breath, Clare. Once you get past Darla's office and down the hall, you're home free. Foxe will never know what happened until you and Madame are gone.

But I'd been missing for many minutes already. Foxe was sure to come looking for me soon. What should I do?

I couldn't help thinking of my ex-husband and his fearless stunts.

What about a window exit, Clare? Matt's voice seemed to taunt. *How much of a climb down could it be? Find a rope and try it.*

"That's crazy," I whispered.

Still, I couldn't help myself from taking a look.

I chose a window on a side of the building that I knew wouldn't be visible from the company's picnic benches. Looking down, I saw three dumpsters parked on a concrete patio four stories below.

Come on, Clare, you can do this. The ground is less than forty feet below where you're standing—

"It's also a long drop to hard and unforgiving concrete if I slip."

But the annoying Matt voice had a point. It *was* only four stories between me and discovery. And I (theoretically) knew how to execute the South African abseil technique I'd seen Matt use to rappel down the wall of the Hastings.

I searched for a rope—with no luck. But the bottom of a supply closet held three coils of Day-Glo orange extension cords piled one on top of the other.

Summoning my Girl Scout merit badge memories, I bound the electric cords together with secure knots and looped the cord around a sturdy building column. I then wrapped the opposite ends around my torso and through my legs—exactly the way Matt did—to create a makeshift harness.

I looked darned foolish with my skirt tucked around my waist and my pantyhose showing, but appearances were the least of my worries.

I'd removed my shoes and stuffed them into my shoulder bag with the bees. They were sensible flats, but I certainly wasn't doing anything sensible.

"Wish me luck," I muttered to the voice in my head.

All of a sudden, my loquacious ex had nothing to say.

Great.

My first move was to get out the window. But as I climbed onto the ledge, I made the mistake of glancing at the concrete below, which nearly brought on a panic attack.

No more looking down, Clare. This time I didn't know if it was Matt talking in my head or me scolding myself.

Moments later, I was out the window, my near-naked toes resting on the white trim, my back to the four-story abyss. With white knuckles gripping the plastic cord, I leaned backward a little at a time, settling my weight into the makeshift rope before I began my descent.

For a comparison of what that felt like, remember the first time you floated in deep water? Before you could learn how to swim, you had to trust that you wouldn't sink.

Well, when I propped my feet against the side of the building and leaned my full weight on the rope, I had to trust my own half-remembered Girl Scout knot skills—which meant I had nobody to blame but myself for what happened next.

With a jolt, the knot slipped, and I dropped like a rock.

They say your life flashes before your eyes during that final moment before the curtain falls. But only a single, powerful memory flooded my mind—my first ride on the Thunderbolt, an old wooden roller coaster in Kennywood Park.

I never forgot the moment the coaster crested the incline, then took that sudden downward plunge, making me feel as if the seat under me had fallen away. That's how it felt now, only much worse!

Suddenly, the knot caught, and I halted as abruptly as the initial plunge—only now I was hanging upside down from my waist, spinning helplessly, twenty feet above the pavement. There was no way for me to go up or down. And there was nothing for me to do but cry—

"HELP! SOMEBODY HELP!"

God, this was humiliating. But I'd take red-faced embarrassment and a burglary charge over a cracked skull any day—

"I'M UP HERE! WOULD SOMEBODY PLEASE HELP?!"

Fifty-four

~~~~~~~~~~~~~~~~~~~~~~~~~~~~~~~~~~~~~~~

The Hunterdon County Volunteer Fire Department was amazingly efficient, or maybe they were just closer. In any case, they arrived minutes before the police.

Meanwhile, Foxe's staff interrupted their lunch break to gawk at me dangling like a lewd Christmas ornament with its unmentionables showing.

Fortunately, the volunteers were quick to do their job. I'd already been lowered to the ground—and ready to kiss it—when the cops slapped the cuffs on me. There was little doubt of my guilt. During my upside-down circus act, my shoulder bag had slipped, spilling its contents on the concrete.

That's where a spitting-mad Felix Foxe found the pilfered bees.

"Who are you?" he cried, shaking the bag in front of my face. "Why did you steal these? Are you a corporate spy?"

"You shouldn't be asking these questions, Mr. Foxe," one of the county cops said timidly. "We haven't Mirandized her yet."

"Mirandize her, then!" Foxe demanded. "And arrest her accomplice, while you're at it. Unless that old—"

"Felix Foxe! Let me remind you *who* I am and tell you *why* I'm here."

Madame's sharp voice bounced off the redbrick wall, her tone so rich in authority it froze everyone within earshot.

"My name is Blanche Dreyfus Allegro Dubois, but many decades ago you knew me simply as Mrs. Blanche Allegro, the widow who ran a coffeehouse in Greenwich Village, and Beatrice Hastings's trusted friend."

His dark expression of rage was suddenly replaced by the shock of remembrance. His thin lips moved, but nothing came out. Then he noticed his staff watching the show.

"Go!" he cried. "Get back to work, all of you. Lunch is over!"

Then he faced Madame. When he spoke again, his voice was shaky.

"Why did you come?"

"Because *you stole* something that belongs to Bea Hastings." Madame's lips curled contemptuously. "And for all I know, that's the least of your transgressions against that poor woman."

"What?" Foxe sputtered. "What are you saying?"

"Excuse me, Mr. Foxe," the policeman holding my elbow interrupted. "We've got to move on. Are you going to press charges or not?"

"No, no!" Foxe declared. "It's all a misunderstanding. Go about your business."

A few moments later, the firemen and the police were gone, and I was rubbing my sore wrists (and wondering why it never hurt when Mike did it).

With Bea's bees and queen back in his hands, Fox directed us toward the front door.

"Come inside," he said. "We'll speak in private."

Fifty-five

～～～～～～～～～～～～～～～～～～～～～～～～

Felix Foxe took us to his corner office on the fourth floor. The space was right out of the Marie Kondo stylebook—a cherrywood desk, a chair, a phone, a computer, a box of Kleenex, and a pen.

A single framed picture hung on the wall, a color photograph of a group of people posing in a field of clover in front of dozens of beehives.

Madame took a long look at that picture but made no comment.

"Please sit," Foxe said before settling in behind the desk. He mopped his forehead with a tissue, then locked eyes with Madame.

"I do remember you, Blanche—though you look very different now. Believe it or not, I'm happy to see you again. But I demand to know what this charade you pulled is all about."

"It's about protecting Bea's legacy," Madame replied. "Those hybrid bees represent many years of work and great expense. I don't want that stolen while Bea hovers in a coma between life and death."

Foxe leaned across his desk. "You've seen Bea? What's the prognosis? I tried to find out, but the hospital refused to answer my questions. I'm not a member of the family, you see, or even what she'd consider a friend."

Madame blinked. "You pretend as if you care. Or are you afraid Bea will awaken and reveal who did this to her?"

Foxe flinched as if Madame had delivered a blow.

"I . . . I would never . . . Never . . ."

Suddenly, Foxe broke down. Sobbing into his hands, his glasses fell to the ground, his broad shoulders convulsed. The sight of a grown man emotionally disintegrating was a terrible thing. I looked at Madame, who seemed as shocked as I. We were both at a loss about what to do. Fortunately, Foxe quickly pulled himself together.

"Forgive me," he said, swiping at tears with the sleeve of his lab coat. "So much has happened between Bea and me. So many misunderstandings. It's difficult to endure yet another."

He slid the bees and the queen across the desk.

"Take them. With the promise that you will be on your guard. Others will come for those hybrids, and their motives will not be as altruistic as mine."

Madame lifted an eyebrow. "Altruistic, you say?"

"I only went after those specimens because I didn't want to see our dream unfulfilled. I wanted Bea's legacy—*our* legacy—to endure."

"You said *our* dream, *our* legacy?" I noted.

"Yes, Ms. Cosi. Because it was *our* dream." Foxe rubbed the last of his tears away with a tissue.

"I suspect you already know Bea and I were once lovers. We had a shared passion as well. It was our goal to create such creatures as these. Breeding hybrid bees that can produce more honey with less pollen was my idea to begin with. Bea, with all her money and resources, made it happen."

"When was this?" I asked.

"Long ago. Bea and I were making progress when a horrible recession nearly destroyed Bea's business. I tried to help, suggested solutions to her financial plight. She rejected them, then accused me of trying to co-opt her business and her fortune."

Foxe's expression hardened.

"She willfully misunderstood me," he said. "Bea used that as an excuse to push me away. And I let it happen. My pride stopped me from fighting to change her mind, and we both let our fears of rejection erode our affections. The result was decades of *what could have been*. A lost life together, and endless regret . . ."

Foxe shook off the memories. "A few weeks ago, when Bea accused me of adulterating my honey before the entire culinary community, she called me privately to gloat.

"Bea told me she had succeeded in creating the hybrids. She boasted that *she* achieved what *we* could not. She plunged the knife in deeper when she suggested I had stooped so low as to adulterate honey."

Foxe sighed. "It wasn't true. I did not adulterate anything, I simply blended three types of pure, natural honey to achieve a certain flavor profile. Once again, Bea willfully misunderstood me. I suspect that will never change."

"There is one thing I would like to understand," I said. "You claim you didn't hurt Bea. But can you prove it? Where were you the night Bea was harmed?"

Foxe opened a desk drawer, pulled out a newspaper, and slid it across the desk—a copy of yesterday's *Hunterdon County Journal*.

LOCAL BUSINESSMEN HONORED AT TRENTON BANQUET

"I was with the governor and a dozen other New Jersey entrepreneurs. You can check for yourselves. Now, please go."

As we rose, Foxe snatched the newspaper, tossed it into the drawer, and slammed it shut.

"One more thing, Blanche," Foxe said. "I want you to send Beatrice my *dearest* wish that she fully recovers. She won't believe it coming from me, and she may not care, even if it comes from you. But it must be said, and Bea should hear it."

Fifty-six

MADAME and I sat in thoughtful silence for a time, watching Jersey's hills and fields roll by as our driver followed the winding road back to New York.

Finally, I spoke—

"Do you believe everything Foxe told us?"

Madame's violet eyes remained contemplative as she gazed out the car window. "Foxe always had a silver tongue, and before today I would have said it was all an act. But he could not have anticipated our arrival or strategically placed that photo on his wall for us to see."

"I saw you studying the picture."

"Yes. A photo of the original staff of Foxe Farms, Felix himself, and a smiling Beatrice Hastings in his arms. The picture was inscribed, and signed, 'Love, Bea.'"

"That picture was the only personal item in his office."

"Yes, Clare, and that's why I believe him."

With a deep breath, Madame shook off her sad musings and squeezed my hand. "Let's remember the bright side. Thanks to your daring, we recovered those bees!"

"Yes, we did. And now we can tell your son to stand down."

"I can't wait to tell him what we accomplished! Though he's sure to scold us both. But it *was* rather exciting, wasn't it? It's a shame our career as cat burglars had to end so abruptly."

"And what a joke that turned out to be. My ex-husband climbs down the side of a building, and everyone wants to crown him the town hero. I do it and nearly get arrested."

"But you didn't, my dear. We return triumphant!"

"Only for the moment." Checking my messages, I sighed. "There's still no word from Suzie Hastings. That girl is a ghost." (And so was Mike Quinn. Still no word.)

As I considered my options (on both ghosts), Madame proposed an idea.

"What about Suzie's boyfriend? That chef . . . Taylor."

"Tyler," I corrected. "But I don't have a last name, and I can't locate him."

Madame clutched my arm. "Not long ago, Suzie threw a party to attract investors for her chef boyfriend. I declined the invitation. But I know someone who did attend. Perhaps he can tell us where this mystery chef has disappeared to. Are you hungry?"

"Starving."

"Good!"

Madame pulled out her phone and hit speed dial.

"Hello, my dear, it's Blanche. Oh, I'm the berries, and you? Tell me, are you in your restaurant right now? . . . Which one? . . . Splendid, I'm dropping by for an early supper with a guest. Would you have a drink with us? . . . Marvelous, see you soon!"

After giving a street address to our driver, Madame flashed me an excited smile.

"We're on our way!"

Fifty-seven

My next question was inevitable.

"On our way to *where* exactly?"

Madame blinked at me, as if the answer were obvious. "Why, Dennis Murphy's newest restaurant, of course."

"You *know* Dennis Murphy?"

Everyone in the New York food and beverage business knew that name. Though I'd never met him personally, I'd always wanted to. "How many restaurants does he have now?"

"I've lost count. It seems he opens a new one every few years."

"When did you meet him? And how?"

"Oh, my goodness . . . Denny and I became friends decades ago, after I became a young widow. I was managing the Village Blend alone, and Matt was still a boy. Denny opened a restaurant in the Village, a little bistro."

"Good food?"

"Excellent. Little Fishes, it was called. He used our beans for his coffee service. I dined there many times, always with pleasure. Critics gave the place high marks, and Denny had ambitious plans." Madame frowned. "Of course, I lost touch with him for a few years when he went to prison—"

"Prison! I never knew that!"

"For three years. The judge only sentenced him to two, but Denny got into a few scrapes behind bars that extended his stay."

"What did he do to land him in prison in the first place?"

"Assault and battery, but it could have been worse. The charges were reduced from attempted murder with a deadly weapon."

"This is a chef and restauranteur we're discussing, right? And not a gang member?"

"Well, my dear, you have to understand Denny's background. He had an Italian mother and a mid-level Irish mobster for a father, and he was raised in Hell's Kitchen . . ."

Madame didn't need to elaborate further.

These days "Hell's Kitchen" was an upscale neighborhood chiefly known for providing a "restaurant row" to Manhattan's Theater District. But decades ago, things were much different. An Irish American gang called the Westies ruled its streets. Their reputation for violence was extreme, their body count high. Mike Quinn once joked that the Westies made the old-school Italian mobsters look like a bunch of grumpy uncles.

"What exactly happened that sent him to prison?" I asked, not sure I was ready for the answer.

"Dennis was a perfectionist, as most good chefs are. He was also volatile. When his sous-chef at Little Fishes repeatedly oversalted the bouillabaisse to the point it was spiteful sabotage, Denny should have simply fired him. Instead, he got so angry he plunged the man's head into the soup pot."

I winced. "Seafood stew as a deadly weapon? I hope he isn't serving any now."

"Oh, no. Denny has a new foodie passion. You'll see . . ."

And I soon did.

As we pulled up to the curb on Second Avenue, just a few blocks from Baruch College's ultramodern skyscraper campus, NYU's College of Dentistry, and the affluent residents of Gramercy Park, I saw the tasteful sign that simply read—

Grandma's Pizza

We entered the restaurant through a shallow arch façade that reminded me of the Doge's Palace in Venice.

After years of New York living, I'd entered enough pizzerias to expect plastic booths and dinky tables, a counter to place orders, and a trash can to dump out your orange plastic tray. But this wasn't that kind of pizza shop.

Dennis Murphy had created an upscale haven with polished wood, virgin white Gothic arches, and modern art on the walls. A magnificent marble-topped bar, serving specialty cocktails, ran the length of the restaurant. At the rear, an open kitchen displayed the beautiful brick pizza oven that allowed the yeasty aroma of baking crust to suffuse the high-ceilinged dining room, along with the smell of Italian herbs and the sweet umami scent of simmering tomatoes and sautéed garlic.

The airy, relaxed space was filled with happy customers, young and old, sipping drinks and conversing.

Madame told the hostess we were expected, and she led us to a cushioned banquette, where a bottle of sparkling water and spotless glasses awaited.

"Mr. Murphy will be with you shortly," she assured us as a busboy set down a basket of warm garlic knots, glistening temptingly with melted herbed butter.

The menu was inventive with an emphasis on quality. The mozzarella cheese and ricotta were "made fresh daily, on the premises." But Grandma's also used imported provolone, Asiago, and even Gorgonzola on their specialty pizzas.

Along with traditional toppings, there were vegetarian options and creative fusion pies: chorizo; tandoori chicken; a French onion flatbread with a creamy white sauce; and a Thai-inspired pizza topped with satay sauce.

As we perused the menu, Madame touched my arm.

"I'm confused, dear. Some of these choices are listed as 'Grandma Style,' which is described as a square pizza with a thicker crust. But isn't that a *Sicilian* pizza?"

"Ah, but there's a difference, Blanche," a sharply dressed gentleman declared as he approached our table. "Would you like me to explain it?"

Fifty-Eight

꩜꩜꩜꩜꩜꩜꩜꩜꩜꩜꩜꩜꩜꩜꩜꩜꩜꩜꩜꩜꩜꩜

"Dennis Falco Murphy! You look marvelous!" Madame's face instantly lit up.

I felt mine freeze in shock.

Honestly, the way Madame had described Dennis Murphy, I'd been expecting a hard-faced ex-con in a stained tank top with muscular arms and prison tattoos—you know, "love" on one hand and "hate" on the other.

Instead, I found myself gaping at a charming, bespectacled man in a yacht club blazer and pressed pants. As he bent low to gently peck the back of Madame's hand, I noticed he held her violet eyes in his dark gaze much longer than necessary. (Hmmm . . .)

"You look better than ever, Blanche," his deep voice purred. "Retirement suits you."

"Like hard work always suited you," she teased. "Dennis, I'd like you to meet my protégé and the Village Blend's master roaster, Ms. Clare Cosi."

It was only when he sat beside me that I realized the restauranteur was older than he initially appeared. His profile was more Falco than Murphy, his curly black hair heavily salted with gray. With his stocky build and deep brown eyes, he could have passed as a member of any Italian-American family in New York.

After joining us, he immediately ordered a round of cold Manhattan Specials. And I was instantly impressed—for two reasons.

The Manhattan Special was a delightful coffee soda, made with espresso beans, seltzer water, and pure cane sugar. A part of New York's culinary history since 1895, the sweet, fizzy espresso drink was sold in bottles—which was the only way I'd ever sampled it.

Mr. Murphy treated us to his own version, mixed fresh at his bar.

I was doubly impressed because Mr. Murphy knew very well that Madame was a harsh judge of coffee quality. And he'd just learned I was her master roaster.

So, this drink wasn't just a drink. It was a test. Not for us, but for his own bartender and coffee bean supplier.

"How do you ladies like your espresso sodas? Be honest, would you?"

"Excellent," Madame pronounced. "Clare?"

"Very nice, Mr. Murphy," I said, feeling the sweet crema foam clinging to my lips. "No complaints."

He nodded, appearing pleased to see me happily licking my lips clean.

Clearly, this man had no insecurities about criticism (something I understood completely). He cared enough about the quality of his work to welcome expert opinions—be they positive or negative.

"So, my old friend?" Madame playfully teased. "Are you going to educate us on the difference between Sicilian and Grandma pizzas?"

Denny's dark eyes sparkled as he sipped his drink. "Why don't you let me show you?"

With the slightest lift of his chin, a waiter appeared at this side. And soon after, our dinner arrived. A Sicilian *and* a Grandma pie, side by side. He began by gesturing to the latter version.

"Now, think of a real Italian grandma, and how she would bake a pizza. Grandma's a busy woman with no time to waste, so that pizza goes into the oven as soon as the dough is stretched over the pan.

"That's not true of a Sicilian pizza, where the dough is given time to rise. The result is a fluffier crust with tiny air bubbles. But Granny, she likes a denser crust with a little crunch to it. Lots of olive oil in the pan ensures a crispiness to her crust. Notice that fried bread flavor as you chew while the fluffier Sicilian has a mouthfeel more like focaccia."

Denny invited us to dig in and try it for ourselves.

"And then there's the sauce," he continued. "The Sicilians prefer a sweet sauce from a tomato grown in volcanic soil. Grandma isn't so picky. She wants a little tang in her sauce. A New Jersey red is fine." He paused.

"Now I want you to take a deep breath, open your mouth a little, and inhale."

Denny led us. "You can smell the difference. Granny uses enough garlic to scare Dracula. Our Grandma pizzas are infused with garlic, and we use garlic olive oil, too. If you don't like garlic, honey, you're in the wrong pizzeria."

Madame laughed at that. "Tell Clare how you began your career. You have such a fascinating background."

He seemed almost embarrassed as he began to speak. And as he did, I found there was a surprising serenity about Dennis Murphy that I seldom encountered in our eager, ambitious, overstimulated town.

Like Madame, he displayed the wisdom of maturity with a youthful energy. But beneath it all was a calming sense of acceptance, a natural state of relaxed confidence that emerges after years of living out successes and failures. A peace that comes from knowing.

"I learned to cook from my mother," he began, "even though cooking wasn't high on my father's list of 'manly' virtues. My pop wanted me to be a wiseguy like him. My burning desire was to run my own restaurant kitchen. At fourteen, I left home, nailed down a job as a busboy at Grand Central's Oyster Bar, and never looked back."

"You did have one detour," Madame prodded gently.

"Prison?" Denny nodded. "Best thing that ever happened to me. I was over two years into my sentence before I took a class in transcendental meditation. Meditation worked where rage, booze, coke, and even running a kitchen didn't. I became centered and felt tranquility for the first time in my life."

He laughed. "I felt like that philosopher guy Viktor Frankl. I was in prison, yet I was finally happy. It's crazy, right? When I got out of jail, I traveled to India to learn more from a real guru. But I still had to earn a living. I could cook, but I didn't know a thing about Indian food. So, I learned all I could and made my own contribution. With the help of some local investors, I brought 'Denny's American Fried Chicken and Waffles' to Mumbai."

Denny shrugged. "Five years later I sold the business to a restauranteur on Altamount Road. With that money, I returned to New York and saw a niche in the quality comfort food market. I opened Buttermilk Kitchen.

From there I started Shake & Burger, Lobster Shack, Off the Hook Seafood Market, the Welshman's Steakhouse, Green Fields, and now Grandma's Pizza."

"You invest in other restaurants, too, don't you?" I asked.

"Sure. The right chef with the right plan."

"I understand you recently went to an investor party for a chef named Tyler?"

Denny frowned. "You mean Tyler LaFontaine? Yes, I went, but I didn't bite."

"His food was not to your liking?"

"His dishes were fine, Ms. Cosi. A few of them were outstanding."

"Then what was your objection?"

Denny sat back. "The young man wasn't ready to take on the responsibility of running his own restaurant. From what I heard, even before I *personally* observed his immaturity, Tyler couldn't even control his kitchen at Armando's. One of his former sous-chefs works for me at the Welshman now. He referred to his former boss as '*the cutthroat chef.*'"

Fifty-nine

～～～～～～～～～～～～～～～～～～～～～～～～～

"Cutthroat," I rasped, thinking of all those razor-sharp knives in a professional kitchen.

Madame and I shared an uneasy glance.

"Can you tell us more, Mr. Murphy?" I asked. "Did Tyler actually try to . . . you know?" I drew my hand across my neck.

"No, no," Murphy said with a laugh. "He would have done hard time like me if he'd tried something like that. Tyler's problem is immaturity and inexperience. You have to *earn* the respect of a kitchen staff. You can't bully them into respecting you. And when you undercut their efforts, they remember—and spread the word to their colleagues about how you treated them. That's a hard lesson I learned early. And I paid for it, believe me. Tyler is still learning and still paying."

"So, he has a hot temper?" Madame pressed. "What more can you tell us?"

"Tyler never climbed the ladder; he jumped on halfway up. Kids like him have Michelin stars in their eyes—and they can almost taste that TV show. But a fancy degree does not a chef make."

He sat back and sipped his drink. "I never had the opportunity to earn a culinary degree. But I learned how to survive and thrive in this business—and recognize people who have that stamina."

"You said you started out bussing tables?"

"That's right, Ms. Cosi. I washed dishes, mopped floors, then I learned how to do prep work, short-order cooking, and on to the big leagues. In my business, you have to run like the devil just to keep in place, eyes always open for consumer trends. Front-of-house mistreatment of customers is just as damaging as kitchen crews who slack off. Either one will ruin your rep faster than you can say Yelp Reviews."

Madame and I exchanged glances. We knew exactly what he meant.

Denny shrugged. "I can still perform every job in the places I own. And I learned every reason a restaurant succeeds or fails." He shook his head. "Boys like Tyler, they come and go. Unless they learn how to master the heat of these kitchens, they melt down."

"Do you have any idea where Tyler is now? I ask because I'm trying to locate his girlfriend, Susan Hastings—"

"I know Ms. Hastings. Just met her. Smart young woman. Too bad she falls for pretty faces."

Madame blinked. "What do you mean?"

"Susan is the one who set up the investment party for Tyler. Nice party, too, but no one bit. It wasn't her fault. Tyler didn't see it that way. I saw him lashing out at her at the end of the evening. For a second there, the boy lifted his fist. I thought he was going to belt her. If he did, I would have stepped in, believe me."

"How many people saw this?" I asked.

"Me and maybe one or two of the other guest investors. Most were gone at that point. I stayed behind to have a private talk with him, give him some helpful advice about the drawbacks of his proposed project— but after seeing how he treated that nice girl, I changed my mind."

I shifted uneasily. The incident Murphy described certainly validated Todd Duncan's claim that Tyler had taken *a swipe* at Suzie.

Mr. Murphy leaned forward. "Why are you having trouble finding Susan Hastings? Is she all right?"

"Suzie's aunt had a terrible accident," I quickly explained, "and she hasn't been notified yet. I thought Suzie might be with Tyler. I'm told she's a traveler, so I'm wondering if Tyler went to another city or country to find work. Suzie might be visiting him."

Denny shook his head. "Tyler never left New York. He's managing a ghost kitchen in some resi-dustrial backwater neighborhood in Queens."

Sixty

~~~~~~~~~~~~~~~~~~~~~~~~~~~~~~~~~~~~~

MADAME and I left Dennis Murphy's restaurant happily stuffed yet far from happy—not after what we learned.

Night descends quickly in autumn. By now, the sun was setting behind Manhattan's buildings, its dying rays gilding the highest surfaces of the city's towers, lighting them up against the darkening sky. The streetlamps were flickering on, and shopwindows glowed around us as throngs of commuters crowded the shadowy sidewalks, jostling their way home.

It felt too late to go off chasing ghost kitchens on the other side of the East River. And anyway, I knew Madame and I wouldn't find Susan there.

The young Ms. Hastings was a wealthy butterfly—emphasis on *wealthy*—and while I believed she'd fly off to Paris, Singapore, or Dubai to visit her volatile chef boyfriend, I couldn't imagine her spending even one hour in a *"resi-dustrial backwater neighborhood in Queens."*

Madame came to the same conclusion as we drove away.

"As of now, I can only deduce two possible reasons Susan has been out of touch for days. The first is that she's 'off the grid,' as my son often is—though not in the African outback, sourcing coffee. Rather, she might have flown to some faraway place for a retreat or short vacation."

"It's possible," I conceded. "Go on."

"The other reason for her silence could be that she *knows* who assaulted her aunt, felt threatened herself, and went into hiding—or, God forbid, is herself in harm's way, perhaps kidnapped."

"Could be," I agreed again. "But, Madame, you are missing an obvious third reason. Suzie may be involved in the attempt on her aunt's life."

"As I've told you, Clare, Suzie loves Bea like a mother and would never hurt her."

"Maybe not. But hear me out. What if she witnessed someone else arguing with her aunt? A handsome boy with whom she's infatuated? What if—after Tyler's investment party failed—Suzie suggested they approach her wealthy aunt for the money to back his restaurant concept? What if Bea said no and Tyler became upset with her? Angry words could have been said, and he might have raised a fist—just as he did with Suzie after his failed party. Bea backs away, falls over the roof edge. Tyler believes she's dead and convinces Suzie it's a terrible accident and what's done is done."

"Oh, Clare, that would be awful, *criminal.*"

"Yes, it would. Suzie would be in a shocked and suggestive state. And Tyler is a strong personality. He appears to have Suzie in his spell. What if he convinced a confused and panicked Suzie to wipe the evidence of his guilt, make the scene look like Bea was unbalanced and committed suicide? Then he instructs her to run away and hide until it all blows over?"

Madame frowned deeply. "And when it all blows over—meaning Bea is pronounced dead—Suzie would inherit everything, and if Tyler marries Suzie—"

"All his financial problems are solved," I finished.

And when I did, my quest came full circle, because to discover which of our theories was correct, we would have to *find* Suzie, dead or alive. And the only living lead we had was her volatile boyfriend, Chef Tyler LaFontaine.

On the car seat beside me, Madame sighed as she gazed out the window. I noticed she stifled a yawn.

"Would you like me to take you home?" I asked gently. "I'm going to the greenhouse to return the bee bodies to their final resting place. But we can stop—"

"The greenhouse!" Madame exclaimed, suddenly animated. "Why, I haven't seen the greenhouse since Bea first opened it. Take me with you, Clare. I'd love to see it again."

Sixty-one

∽∽∽∽∽∽∽∽∽∽∽∽∽∽∽∽∽∽∽∽∽∽∽∽∽

SHINING like a crystal palace in the Manhattan night, Bea's greenhouse was a stunning sight. Madame and I paused on the lighted walkway of the Hastings rooftop, admiring its splendor before going inside.

Once through the door, Madame was completely captivated. She watched the bees buzz around the hives, then wandered down the center aisle, running her fingers along row upon row of purple lavender blossoms while inhaling their intoxicating floral scent.

I joined Esther and Nancy in the work area, where they were discussing a bee. Not bees, mind you. The topic was one bee in particular.

"Are you sure you haven't seen Spot today?" Nancy asked.

Esther rolled her eyes. "I didn't see your precious Spot, but there *are* thousands of bees. One particular drone is easy to miss."

"Not Spot!" Nancy countered. "He's special. He's really big for a little drone, he lives in the last hive on the left, and he has a distinctive white mark on his abdomen—"

"Hence the name Spot," Esther sighed. "You really reached for that name, didn't you?"

Esther went off to hang up her bee suit for the day.

Nancy had just come off her afternoon shift at the Village Blend and I asked how things went. She said Matt was a great boss, and he worked all day, until about an hour ago when he got a visitor.

"A visitor?"

"A runway model type with a designer bag and witch-toed boots. Tall and thin with long, blond, shampoo-commercial hair. Acted kinda stuck-up," Nancy said, making a face. "Snapped her fingers at us. I didn't like her."

"Did you catch her name?"

"No, but she was talking Italian to Dante and nonstop flipping her hair and wetting her lips. Maybe *he* knows who she is."

"Never mind, I already know."

It was Nellie Atwood, Queen of Start-ups. As far as I knew, the last time she and Matt spoke was the night Bea was assaulted.

I supposed she could be making a play for my ex-husband. Heaven knew, Nellie wouldn't be the first. But I hadn't stopped thinking about her presence at the Hastings the same night we discovered Bea's broken body on her balcony.

My thoughts were interrupted when the workroom phone buzzed.

Nancy answered with a big "Hello!" Then she went quiet, nodding several times. Finally, she dropped the receiver and faced me, expression panicked.

"Freddie says two men are on their way up here right now. He said a whole bunch of guys showed, but he only let two on the elevator. He says he's sorry, but he had to let them in because they had a court order!"

"A court order?"

My spirits soared with hope. Had Bea woken from her coma and named an assailant? Had they come to collect evidence?

"Are they uniformed officers or detectives?" I asked.

"They're not police. Freddie says they're wearing vests that say 'bag' on them."

"Bag?" I blanked for a moment, until I remembered the warning Dr. Wanda gave me about the *Bee Advocacy Group*—and the men who ran it.

"If Sean Seas or his twin brother get wind of the unique nature of Bea Hastings's bees, they will find some pretext in the law to seize them and neither you nor Beatrice Hastings will ever see those hives again."

"Good grief!" Bolting out of the workroom, I left Nancy perplexed.

"Boss? What's wrong?"

"Esther!" I screamed. "Lock the door. Now! These men are here to steal Bea's hives!"

Sixty-two

~~~~~~

Esther ran to lock the greenhouse, but my warning had come too late. Already, a pair of bodybuilding supermen in canary yellow vests were at the door. As she groped for the latch, the interlopers tried to push through.

An outraged Esther pushed back.

"Watch it, jackboots," she cried. "Or you'll feel the business end of my Doc Martens where no shoe belongs."

Nancy and I rushed to her aid. But before we reached the door, the pair in yellow knocked Esther back and stormed across the threshold.

The broad-shouldered frost giants faced us, legs braced, mugging defiantly. The platinum-haired pair were identical in features, manner, and dress, though only one wore glasses. I deduced "Spectacles" must have been the alpha because he did the talking.

"We have a legal right to enter these premises," he announced.

"The hell you say," came Esther's reply.

"You better back off," Nancy warned.

Like guardian worker bees, Esther, Nancy, Madame, and I made a female wall to block the hives.

"Who are you?" I demanded. "What *right* do you have to be here?"

Spectacles took two steps forward, to loom over me. He looked me right in the eye and I lifted my chin to stare him down.

"I'm Sean Seas and this is my brother Kevin," he said. "We represent the Bee Advocacy Group, an organization that supports the interest of responsible hive owners in New York City's urban environment."

"Nice speech," I replied. "Why are you *really* here?"

"I have a court order to confiscate these hives." Spectacles could barely suppress a sneer as he said it.

"Not *my* bees you won't!" Esther cried.

"These aren't your bees, honey. And they don't belong to Mrs. Hastings, either. She's committed far too many violations to retain ownership. We're taking charge of the hives now."

"Violations?" I challenged. "These hives are *legally* registered. You can see the certificate posted on the wall behind you."

"This isn't about registration—"

"No," I interrupted. "It's about you and your conniving brother twisting the law to grab what doesn't belong to you."

"We're protecting the urban beekeeping community," Sean countered. "Some of these bees escaped this greenhouse. Who knows what damage was done to the local ecosystem, or what other hives they may have infected?"

"Infected?" Nancy cried, outraged.

"It's possible some of these bees infiltrated local hives, carrying any number of diseases or parasites," Sean maintained.

"That's crazy!" Nancy exclaimed.

The spectacles-free brother spoke for the first time.

"American foulbrood, nosema, acarine disease, sacbrood." As his fingers ticked them off, his nose crinkled in disgust. "Any or all of these illnesses could be spread by rogue bees like this swarm."

"They aren't rogue, and they aren't swarming," Esther countered. "They are right here where they belong."

"The NYPD beekeeping unit already checked them out for diseases," Nancy declared. "There is *nothing* wrong with these bees. They're perfect!"

Spectacles spoke into his smartphone. "Robby, send up the rest of the guys with the packing boxes. We're moving these hives now."

"Why are you doing this?" Nancy demanded.

"It's only recently that bee farming became legal in New York," Spectacles explained. "We want to make sure beekeeping stays legal. That's why BAG goes after rogue keepers like Mrs. Hastings."

"BAG is the perfect name for you," Esther said with a scowl. "Like all thieves and pirates, you want to *bag* everything in sight."

"Enough," Spectacles declared. "Bea Hastings's mutant bees are a danger to the entire ecosystem, and they have to go."

Mutant bees?

Nancy grabbed a broom and jumped in front of the yellow vests. Braids flying, she wielded the long handle like Little John's staff.

"Stay back," she hissed, baring her teeth. "My babies are staying right here with me."

I stepped in front of Nancy. "You're not taking these bees without a fight."

Kevin Seas flashed me an angry glare. "Don't make me do something you'll regret," he warned.

Madame stepped forward, hands on hips. "Do something about *me*, you strutting popinjay!"

Next she addressed us. "Clare, Esther, Nancy. Camera phones, please!"

Within seconds three phones were trained on the yellow vests, ready to video record whatever happened next. Faced with a stubborn, elegant elderly woman and a battery of cameras, the twins glanced at each other uncertainly.

"Now," Madame declared, folding her arms. "I'm an octogenarian who means business. To get to those hives, you're going to have to knock me down and run me over. That should make for interesting viewing on New York One."

For a moment I could have cut the tension inside the greenhouse with garden shears. Then, to my horrified surprise, the yellow vests moved toward my mentor!

Sixty-three

With a shrill warrior-woman cry of her fighting Irish ancestors, Nancy Kelly jumped between the brothers and swung the broom like a bat, nearly cracking Spectacles in the nose.

To dodge the blow he reared back, stumbling over his own feet. He regained his balance with the help of his twin. Then he scowled at the angry, wild-eyed barista.

Esther curled her fingers into cat claws and made ready to charge the pair. Figuring a fight was inevitable, I searched for a weapon and came up with an empty bee smoker, which I shook futilely like a crazed old lady with a teapot.

In the middle of the melee, Madame stood her ground like a human statue.

To our surprise, the twins paused, with Kevin Seas face-to-face with my defiant employer. In a burst of rage, Kevin began to lunge, but his spectacled twin thrust out his muscled arm in a "mommy block" that effectively halted his infuriated brother. "Robby! Where the hell are you guys?" Spectacles shouted into his phone. "We've got a situation up here!"

A moment later, the young man's arrogant demeanor was wiped away.

"What do you mean 'turned off'?" he bellowed. "Who turned the elevators off?"

"I did."

The declaration was made by an impressively loud and happily familiar voice. Sean Seas groaned in angry frustration.

"Who's the buttinsky?" asked Kevin.

"Me? I'm the guy holding a cease-and-desist order," replied a grinning Todd Duncan.

Standing in the greenhouse door, his tiki shirt fluttering in the breeze like Superman's cape, Todd displayed a legal-size document.

Stepping through the door and right up to the much bigger twins, Todd waved the paper in the Seas brothers' faces.

"Read it and weep," he said.

Sean Seas knocked Todd's arm aside.

"Fine," Todd said calmly. "I didn't think you two gorillas could actually read. But I think you know how to walk, so get the heck out."

The twins glowered.

"Now, gentlemen, no long faces," Todd continued, almost jovially. "You're trespassing on private property, and we can't allow that."

Freddie the doorman appeared next.

"Come on, let's go," he ordered the twins. "I'll turn on the elevator so you can join your friends downstairs. Unless you'd rather walk."

When they hesitated, I stepped up.

"Violate that cease-and-desist order and bother us again, and I *swear* I'll round up other beekeepers you've ripped off and we'll file a class action suit against you. Have fun spending money on lawyers to defend yourselves. We already have our legal eagle, as you can see."

That did it.

The Seas brothers finally stopped staring bullets at Todd. After a quick exchange of worried looks—and a few gentle shoves from the elderly doorman—they departed.

I don't think any of us breathed until Esther locked the greenhouse door behind them.

"That was fun," she quipped.

Todd Duncan immediately began to apologize. "Look, I'm really sorry I didn't get here sooner and that you had to face those goons alone."

"It's a miracle you got here as fast as you did," I said. "And with court order in hand."

"A miracle indeed," Madame declared.

"I call it buffalo chips," Todd replied.

"What do you mean?" I asked.

"In law, Ms. Cosi, sometimes a bluff can be a powerful tool, especially when you're dealing with hustlers."

"I don't understand. How did you bluff them?"

Todd shrugged. "I printed out a sample cease-and-desist order from one of my law e-textbooks. Then I scribbled a bunch of signatures on it with different color pens and ran up here."

Todd paused to take a breath. "Those stupid clowns would have figured out it was a fraud if they actually read it. But their own legal paperwork was flimsy and probably wouldn't hold up in court, either, so—"

"My hero!" Nancy cried, wrapping her arms around Todd, and raining kisses on his face. "You're amazing!"

"I'm really not," he replied, blushing. "Those guys from BAG, they're just bullies."

"You're too modest," Madame declared. "What you did was clever and brave, young man."

Nancy hugged Todd again.

Beside me, Esther shook her head. "Looks like Nancy's got a new crush."

"That's okay," I replied. "After tonight, I think we all do."

Sixty-Four

∽∽∽∽∽∽∽∽∽∽∽∽∽∽∽∽∽∽∽∽∽∽∽∽∽∽∽∽∽

Feeling victorious (for once), I headed home.

With hugs and promises to call, Madame dropped me at the Village Blend. By now, Matt was done for the day, and the coffeehouse was winding down in the capable hands of Tucker and Punch.

After wishing them a good night, I trudged upstairs, kicked off my shoes, and greeted my feline roommates. They had a thing or two to say about my being away so long.

"Yes, girls, I know. Time for dinner."

After silencing the cat chorus with a can of their favorite Fancy Feast flavor, I went to the living room and sank into the sofa. Unlike Java and Frothy, I wasn't hungry. Still stuffed with Dennis Murphy's pizza, I considered that bottle of sangria in the fridge. With a slight shiver, I also considered starting a fire.

Mike usually did that.

Remembering made the room feel colder.

Wrapping my arms around me, I took a breath. "Come on, Clare, pull yourself together."

While I was eating dinner with Madame, I purposely stopped checking my messages. Alone now, I had nothing to distract me from another night of being ghosted by my own fiancé.

Steeling myself, I reached for the phone to check, yet again. And there it was, the name I'd been waiting for—

MIKE QUINN

My spirits instantly lifted. Until I read his reply.

SORRY. CAN'T TALK.

I didn't expect Mike would text me a sonnet with an outpouring of affection. But I *did* expect an explanation for his forty-eight hours of silence, or at least a plan to get together soon.

You'd think his ice-cold reply would have increased my shivering. Instead, those three terse words made my blood begin to boil.

I tried to understand. (I really did.) I reminded myself what Franco had confided about everything Mike was going through at work—*except* this didn't feel like work. It felt like old-fashioned stonewalling. Or petulant evasion.

Of all people, Felix Foxe suddenly came to mind. Sad Felix and his choked-up confession.

He and Bea Hastings had been happy once. And they could have spent many contented years together if they had worked at it. But they hadn't. I could still hear Felix's agonized words—

"She willfully misunderstood me. Bea used that as an excuse to push me away. And I let it happen. My pride stopped me from fighting to change her mind, and we both let our fears of rejection erode our affections. The result was decades of 'what could have been.' A lost life together, and endless regret . . ."

Was I destined to be Felix one day? Regretting the loss of a cherished love?

No, I decided, I'd be damned if I was going to sit here and let Mike Quinn push me away.

I found my shoes and shoved them back on.

"Remember, he isn't the enemy," Madame's voice had warned me last evening. *"Your fears and especially his are what's keeping you apart . . . Don't be afraid to shock the fear out of him."*

Fine, I thought, because I was done trying my ex-husband's fifty shades of honey remedies. Esther was right. We all needed to face our fears. And it was time Mike Quinn got a bracing dose of *shock* therapy.

Sixty-five

⟋⟍⟋⟍⟋⟍⟋⟍⟋⟍⟋⟍⟋⟍⟋⟍⟋⟍⟋⟍⟋⟍⟋⟍⟋⟍⟋⟍

My "Shock Mike" plan wasn't complicated, but it required a little recon.

First, I texted Franco. No response came.

That worried me—because it likely meant he was already working undercover—but it didn't deter me.

With a quick phone call to another young detective on Mike's OD Squad, I got what I needed.

Grabbing my jacket, I promised Java and Frothy I'd be back and snuggling with them soon. Then I headed downstairs to place a coffee order.

In no time, I was marching up Hudson, toward the NYPD's Sixth Precinct. The squat Bauhaus structure was bright with light and activity. I nodded to the desk sergeant (who recognized me) and handed off my first complimentary latte of the night. Then I headed upstairs where the detectives worked.

Their desks clustered in one corner of the second floor, Mike's squad was a tight-knit group, presumably still working the case of the homeless ODs.

"Coffee, anyone?" I announced.

Mike's detectives looked up; their grim faces immediately brightened. I'd packed a delivery tote with stacked trays of steaming-hot lattes and swiftly passed them out.

"Thanks, Coffee Lady!"

"Just what I needed."

"You're a caffeine angel, Clare."

"Oh, this is good!"

"One more thing," I said. "Do any of you have an interest in taking this box of Honey Cupcakes with Honey Buttercream Frosting off my hands?"

Did they ever. The group made our shop's new melt-in-your-mouth cupcakes disappear faster than a wizard with a magic wand.

Licking a layer of honey buttercream from his lips, Tony DeMarco sidled up to me and tipped his curly, dark head toward the corner office.

"He's in there, Clare, like I told you."

Mike's glass office had a view of the squad room. The blinds were open, but he hadn't noticed my arrival. Facing the exterior windows, he appeared to be absorbed in a phone call.

"Do me a favor?" I asked DeMarco, handing him a paper sack. "I saved two cupcakes for your boss, along with his favorite latte. Give it to him after I leave, okay?"

"Ah, sure," said DeMarco, taking it with hesitation.

"What's the matter?"

"You'll see." He tipped his head toward Mike again. "Proceed with caution."

"It's that bad?"

"Never seen him like this."

"Thanks."

As I slowly moved toward Mike's half-closed door, I felt like Esther approaching a beehive for the first time. Was I about to save my engagement? Or destroy it? Would I ultimately get stung?

There was still time for me to change my mind and turn around. Should I?

The answer came to me in three simple words—

SORRY. CAN'T TALK.

That infuriating text message obliterated any remaining "proceed with caution" qualms, and I strode forward with renewed determination, into the heart of the lieutenant's hive.

Mike was currently burning the ear off the party at the other end of his phone line. "Then you GET the information. Do you UNDERSTAND?!"

The bang of the slamming door was loud enough to spark speculative murmuring in the squad room behind me. It also prompted Mike to whip his chair around. I thought he was going to bite my head off, until he saw it was me who'd slammed his door.

"Hold on," he barked into the receiver. "What are you doing here, Clare? Are you okay?"

"I'm fine. I came here to see for myself."

"See *what*?"

"That you *can* talk. It's just *me* you refuse to talk to."

"Clare, I can't—"

"Yes, you *can*." Folding my arms, I stared him down. "And when you're done with that call, you *will*."

Mike was a seasoned pro at displaying a poker face, but even he couldn't hide his stunned reaction to my "shock therapy" stunt. He was also acutely aware of all those eyes in the squad room, curiously looking our way.

"Shall I close the blinds?" I asked.

Mike shook his head. "You remember where the interview rooms are?"

"Of course."

"Find an empty one and wait for me inside. I'll be there in five minutes."

Sixty-six

~~~~~~

FIVE minutes was a long time to sit alone in an NYPD interview room, especially one with (as crazy as it sounded) romantic memories.

Not so long ago, I was standing in this very space when Mike shut the door, crossed the floor, and took me in his arms. Our relationship was still brand-new back then. We'd just made that precarious bridge from being friends to lovers, and we were completely intoxicated with each other.

His lips would often find mine before I could finish a sentence. That's how hot his passion burned. He'd catch me by surprise, and I never minded. My arms would drift north to circle his neck, and he'd back me against the wall to get serious.

When he wanted to, Mike could dissolve the world with his kisses. He liked to take his time with his lips and tongue, until there was no coming up for air. Just a dizzying need for more.

When we finally parted that day, in this very room, he'd smiled down at me. Stray locks of chestnut hair had drifted across my cheek. The touch of his fingers sent sweet shivers through me as he brushed the hairs aside and curled them around my ear.

"*Tonight, sweetheart,*" he'd rasped. "*My place.*"

I swallowed hard at that memory, recalling the love we used to make, all night long. Would we ever get there again?

Mike's quick, heavy steps were approaching now. And as much as I cared about him, I knew this was no time to go soft.

Drawing myself up, I set my chin as I watched his tall, powerful body stride into the small room and shut the door.

"Sit down," I said. "This won't take long."

Sixty-seven

~~~~~~~~~~~~~~~~~~~~~~~~~~~~~~~~~~~

"Look, Clare, before you start in on me, you should know: I didn't want to ignore you. But it's obvious I'm disappointing you. And the way I'm feeling, I knew we would just end up arguing, like we are now."

"I'm not arguing. I'm listening . . ."

Mike and I were now facing each other across the dented metal table inside the claustrophobic box that served as a precinct interview room. No exterior windows, just a one-way observation glass with the blinds pulled down for privacy. It was warm in here, airless and unpleasant, but at least Mike was talking. Or he *started* to, anyway.

Rubbing the back of his neck, he studied the scuffed tabletop. "What do you want me to say?"

"More," I insisted. "What's going on with you? What are you afraid of? I mean with us?"

"Here we go." Mike shook his head. "You know, I went through all this in my first marriage. The very same pattern. I disappointed my wife. My work got in the way, and we ended up in terrible fights. I could see the same thing happening with us, so I pulled away. I didn't want us saying things to each other that could destroy our relationship."

"Wait. So, you actually *care* about our relationship?"

His gaze quickly returned to mine. "Of course I do."

"Well, let me tell you something, Lieutenant, we're not *having* a relationship. Your solution to our problems is to keep us apart, effectively turn us back into single people. You've been shutting me out. And not just in the last two days. It's a red flag that you are *not* ready for a second marriage."

Mike's poker face suddenly cracked. A flash of dread twisted his expression and his body tensed, as if I'd given him a punch and he was bracing for another.

"You're breaking up with me?"

"No! If I'd wanted that, I wouldn't have bothered coming here. I would have stayed away until you ghosted our relationship into oblivion!"

Mike sat back a little, but the wary tension remained. "So why are you here? What do you want, Clare?"

"You should know by this time that I am *not* your first wife. Unlike Leila, I care very much about your work. And I know you're in a workaholic fog right now and probably can't see anything clearly. You told me yourself: Tunnel vision can set in when you focus too hard and too long without a break."

"Target fixation," he muttered, mouth turned down. He didn't like being reminded of his own advice. Well, too bad, he needed to hear it.

"Believe me, I know what's on the line for you and your team. I quizzed Franco at the coffeehouse yesterday morning. I know he's doing undercover work with a dangerous street gang—at your objection."

Mike drew back in surprise. "He volunteered that?"

"No, I deduced it. He just confirmed it."

"Really?" He sounded impressed.

"I know you're on the cross about Franco. I'm worried about him, too. And I know the future of your squad and command are hanging in the balance. But no matter what the downtown brass decide about your job, or the universe dishes out for the lives of your detectives, *you alone* cannot control everything by sheer force of will or hours worked."

Mike rubbed his jaw, bristling with stubble. "Anything else?"

"Yes, it's easy to lose perspective when you're under pressure—you told me that yourself once, too. So, I'm here to remind you that you are *not* just your work. You're a human being who is dearly loved. Are you hearing this? I need you to. No matter what you do, Mike Quinn, I will always love you for the exceptional man you are."

Mike's arctic blue gaze melted—just a little—at my words.

"And by the way, for the record, I am not 'disappointed' in you. At least I wasn't until you stopped communicating with me. Which means if I'm going to be a cop's wife, it can't be like this. With you shutting down for weeks and then shutting me out entirely. You want to bring up first-marriage baggage? Fine. I'll remind you of mine.

"*My* fear is that you'll turn into another Matteo Allegro. Sure, Matt can be a good guy—for a while. But then he's *gone*. That's his nature. To be happy he's got to feed the adrenaline monster. Ship off to another continent, jump off another cliff, or into another bed. I don't want that. I never did. I want a *steady* partner, someone who's not only there for me, but gives *me* the chance to be there for him."

I stood up and shouldered my bag.

Mike and I had plenty more to talk about, but this airless sweatbox was intolerable, and he had important work to do. I knew that. I also knew he desperately needed a break, which was why I had a second shock ready for him.

"Here—"

"What's this?" He took the paper from my hand.

"It's an invitation. Midnight tomorrow. A commitment requires an active sign. That's what a wedding ceremony is for—to *show* commitment."

"I don't understand."

"Just follow the instructions I wrote. I'll be waiting at that address. If you come, we'll keep talking. For better or worse. In good times and bad. If you don't come, I won't stop loving you, Michael Ryan Francis Quinn. I promise our relationship will continue. But I *will not* marry you."

Quinn remained speechless as I headed for the door.

"I'll see you tomorrow, Mike. Or I won't. The decision is yours."

Sixty-eight

I slept restlessly that night. No fire in the hearth. No strong, loving arms to keep me warm. Only Java and Frothy. At least my cats were happy. They also had more room than usual to stretch out in the four-poster.

Quinn, however, remained out of touch, which didn't bode well for our future—at least as a married couple.

"It's better this way," I told Matt at the Blend the next day.

"Better for who?"

"Both of us. Either Mike enters a *real* partnership with me or . . ."

"Or what? You break up?"

"No! We care for each other too much for that. But I won't continue to plan a wedding under these strained circumstances. And I don't want to get my hopes up that Mike will decide to meet me tonight."

"Where exactly is this big rendezvous supposed to happen?"

"Someplace special. Your mother gave me the idea. Apparently, she once seduced Pierre on top of the Eiffel Tower."

"Won't it be chilly up there at this time of year?"

"Very funny. I'm not meeting him in Paris."

"No. I didn't think so."

"And I don't intend to seduce him. I just want him to have a break from all the stress. I want us to reconnect somewhere beautiful—and neutral. Which was also your mother's advice. You want another espresso before we hit the road?"

Matt checked his watch. "Naw, let's get going. Lunchtime rush should be letting up by now . . ."

* * *

Matt was soon driving us out of Manhattan. Our destination was the Queens address of a "ghost kitchen," where Madame's friend, restauranteur Dennis Murphy, reported Chef Tyler LaFontaine was now working.

By all accounts, Tyler was an unpredictable young man. Which was why I asked Madame to sit this one out and instead let her son accompany me to the borough of Queens. She agreed and said having the day free would allow her to sit with her old friend at the hospital.

"Would you keep me informed, Clare?" she asked at the end of our phone call. "I'm going to worry until you check in."

"No problem. I'll let you know what we find out. And try not to worry too much. You know Matt. When it comes to protecting the people he cares about, there's nobody better."

"I agree, my dear. And nobody more experienced . . ."

Madame was right. Matteo Allegro had faced almost every dangerous man and beast on this planet—and survived. I was confident whatever tantrum the Cutthroat Chef threw our way, Matt would be able to handle him. Or at least help me dodge any permanent damage.

"**S**o, what the heck is a ghost kitchen?" Matt asked as we crossed the Queensboro Bridge.

"Basically, it's a restaurant with all the equipment needed for food preparation but with no dining area or walk-in service."

"Deliveries only?"

"Sometimes it's more than that. But it's usually attached to a delivery app, an invention that's led to what the industry calls a *digital brand*. Pete's Pizza or Harry's Hot Dogs no longer has to pay for a brick-and-mortar location. With a ghost kitchen, they can fulfill orders and essentially exist only in the digital domain."

Matt nodded, impressed. "That's certainly an economical way to start a food business."

"Or more than one. Some ghost kitchens run two digital brands out of the same space, so one cook can be broiling Harry's Hot Dogs, while five feet away another cook is sliding a Pete's Pizza into the oven."

Matt whistled. "No dining area and no waitstaff is a real cost cutter."

"Remember that adage: *Location, location, location*? You and I know restaurants that rely on heavy traffic pay for that exposure with higher rents. Ghost kitchens can locate themselves far from urban centers, where the rent is dirt cheap. That's why some of these kitchens find income through contracts with those high-end restaurants, making food for the catering or delivery ends of their businesses."

"So, does Tyler want investment money to start his own digital brand? Or is the money supposed to get him out of this ghost kitchen and into his own brick-and-mortar restaurant?"

"I think it's the latter. Either way, we're about to find out."

Sixty-nine

~~~~~~

Matt turned the van off Northern Boulevard, one of Queens's main thoroughfares, and rolled us up to a sprawling single-story industrial building on 62nd Street.

Across the road a ratty warehouse squatted beside P.S. 152, a redbrick school surrounded by a black wrought iron fence. Our destination was redbrick, too, but its façade was beautifully restored, and fronted by tall casement windows facing the street. A neat row of shrubbery decorated the entranceway with landscape lighting that likely looked lovely after sunset.

A parking sign warned us this space was *Delivery Only*, but we were driving the shop's van with the Village Blend logo prominently displayed, so Matt decided to live dangerously.

As soon as we opened the door to the ultramodern facility, my ears picked up the muted clanging of pots and pans while my nose was assaulted by clashing hot-oil smells—everything from sizzling beef tallow to simmering peanut oil. Yet the long bank of spotlessly clean silver ovens and refrigerators appeared inactive. The cooking was going on deeper inside the building, beyond a huge pair of pastel blue doors.

We approached a small counter in front of the facility. A young woman in her mid-twenties stood behind it, wearing an apron the same shade of blue as the double doors. She greeted us enthusiastically—well, actually, she greeted *Matt*.

"How can I help you?" she said, grinning widely. (Yes, definitely meant for Matt.)

I cleared my throat, mostly to draw her attention away from my ex.

"We're looking for Chef Tyler LaFontaine. We understand he works in this facility."

"Tyler?" The young woman froze, chewed her bottom lip, then bolted like a startled deer. "Let me get someone who can help!" she called over her shoulder.

"Hmmm," Matt muttered. "I get the feeling Tyler may have been exorcised from this particular ghost kitchen—"

I silenced my ex with an elbow jab as a *very* young man approached. He couldn't have been more than twenty-one. The woman in blue trailed behind him. His eyes were dark and intense, but his smile was open and friendly.

"Hi, I'm Nazim. I manage this facility."

After introductions, Nazim steered us to one of several glass enclosed spaces, each with a large central table.

"This is our tasting area," he explained. "We're mainly a catering company and serve samples to clients here."

Matt's eyes lit up with feigned excitement. "A catering company! What perfect synchronicity! I know of a wedding coming up that's sorely in need of good catering." He glanced pointedly my way (very funny). "Is there anyone I can speak with?"

"Colleen can help you." Nazim indicated the woman who first greeted us (as Matt, no doubt, expected).

"Excuse me." Matt headed off to talk with Colleen, leaving me to interrogate Nazim.

"If you have time, would you mind answering a few questions about Tyler LaFontaine?" I asked. "It's important I know his background—anything you can tell me."

"Oh, of course, Ms. Cosi." Nazim slipped into the seat across from me. "You can't be too careful when you're considering who to hire, and I'm *more than happy* to provide you with background on that man."

The way he said "that man" gave me a clue this wasn't going to be a very positive recommendation.

Seventy

"**Y**ou said you were *primarily* a catering company?" I began, trying to get the lay of the land.

"We have twenty-two full kitchens," Nazim informed me, "and we lease eight in the rear of the building to entrepreneurs like Tyler LaFontaine."

"You say he's an entrepreneur?"

"He was starting a brand, I believe. A digital bakery that supplied French pastries to restaurants and other eateries in Manhattan. He seemed successful . . . *moderately* so, anyway."

Yes, there was absolutely an undercurrent of disdain, bordering on contempt, in Nazim's view of Tyler. I wanted to know the cause of it. Pressing on, I asked—

"Were you surprised to find the former head chef at Armando's leasing a ghost kitchen? It seems like quite a comedown, doesn't it?"

"Not at all. Tyler isn't the only prominent chef to begin a digital brand in our kitchens. Another, whose name and restaurant affiliation shall remain anonymous, sells empanadas with a small staff from eleven AM until four PM daily."

"You said there are eight kitchens. I suspect there are more than eight digital brands, then?"

"More like a dozen. Some of the kitchens are shared by two or three brands. It's a good arrangement and things usually run smoothly. We clean and maintain the equipment, and the chefs bring in their own staff, specialty utensils, and ingredients. Each kitchen hires its own delivery people, as well."

"Is Tyler here now? Will he be in later?" I asked, sensing the answer.

"As I said, things *usually* run smoothly." Nazim folded his arms. "They didn't when Chef Tyler LaFontaine was around."

"Was?"

"Tyler recently lost his lease, Ms. Cosi. When he was around, things tended to go wrong."

"What sorts of things?"

Nazim shrugged. "He exploded one morning when he discovered his canelé batter, which he'd left to cure in the refrigerator, was completely spilled. Maintenance moved the refrigerator for cleaning the night before . . . a regrettable accident."

Nazim didn't sound all that regretful.

"And a perfectly understandable response," I argued. "Canelé batter takes at least twenty-four hours to cure."

"True," Nazim said with a shrug. "But then there was the Jonagold incident."

"Jonagold? As in apples?"

"An apple with a short harvest period and one that holds up well in a rustic French apple tart, according to Tyler. He had several bushels shipped especially from a specific upstate orchard. They were delivered here, but to the wrong kitchen. Those expensive apples ended up minced and fried in De-Lite Donuts."

Nazim sighed. "We've had a few heated arguments break out between sous-chefs. It's a kitchen, it's crowded and hot, it happens."

He leaned across the desk and lowered his voice. "But we never had two kitchen managers go at it. Then the sous-chefs jumped in, and it became a riot. That was too much for the owners and they cancelled both men's leases that very afternoon."

"One more question," I said. "Do you have any idea where Tyler is right now?"

"Not a clue," Nazim replied with a slick smile.

Seventy-one

~~~

BACK in the van, I struggled with the shoulder strap in a frenzy of frustration.

"What a waste of time!"

"Not for me." Matt waved a pink sticky note and grinned behind his wild-man beard.

"How nice. You cajoled Colleen's phone number out of her."

"Not quite."

"Just drive us back to the Village Blend, okay?"

"One more stop first," Matt said, turning the ignition.

"Where to now?"

"Another ghost kitchen. You do want to talk to Tyler LaFontaine, don't you?"

"Yes, but we don't know where he is."

"Now we do."

Matt slapped the pink sticky note on the dashboard in front of me. "That address isn't far from here. Tyler is working for a local business-man. Colleen recommended him for the job—apparently, she felt sorry for the poor pathetic slob. She thought he got a raw deal from Nazim and company. Or maybe she felt something more."

"Why do you think that?"

"Just the way she talked about him."

"Well, Tyler is supposedly very handsome—a former Instagram model. So, a young crush on Colleen's part makes sense, along with some rooster jealousy from Nazim. Tyler obviously rubbed that manager the wrong way. Those 'mistakes' sounded suspiciously malicious to me."

Matt shrugged. "Are you all that surprised? After what you heard about Tyler's volatility, you didn't expect him to be a guy with a ready smile and a sunny disposition, did you?"

"You're right. Let's find him."

Matt pulled away from the curb, passed the school, and turned left on Northern. "Colleen gave me the exact address. But the way she described the place, we can't miss it."

Matt drove us to a railcar diner on busy Northern Boulevard, squeezed between a gas station and a Best Buy parking lot. Probably built in the postwar boom of the late 1940s, this railcar was shaped like its namesake. And like a train (and that Jackson Hole "Air Line" Diner we'd stopped at with Madame), it was wrapped with an exterior layer of stainless steel siding, only this exterior had lost its shine.

There was a sign over the front door.

BOULEVARD DINER

But the red neon was dim, the windows were papered over, and the glass door was covered with signs for DoorDash, Grubhub, and Uber Eats. Several electric scooters and bicycles leaned against the diner's faded steel façade.

As Matt reached for the handle, the door burst open and a stocky man in a black hoodie stormed out. He stamped his sneakered foot while cursing profusely in Spanish. (I didn't understand most of what he said, but I sure do know when someone's cussing.) He tugged a Mets cap over his crew cut, climbed onto a scooter, and sped off against traffic.

Three more young men spilled out of the diner, much faster this time. I watched as they grabbed their rides and zoomed away in all directions.

"Clare, watch out!"

Matt's shout came a split second before he literally yanked me off my feet and swung me out of the way.

Just in time, too.

The door burst open again, slamming against the jamb so hard the glass cracked. Two men in white tumbled onto the pavement. Locked in a fighting ball of fury, they nearly rolled across the narrow sidewalk into oncoming traffic. The flailing men spat curses (English this time) as they fought, but despite all the wild swings, few of the punches connected.

Matt stood by for a moment, hands on his hips, shaking his head.

"Aren't you going to do something?" I asked, outraged at this barbaric display.

He shrugged. "If you want."

Matt watched the pair scuffle for a few more seconds. When he spotted an opening, he grabbed both men by the scruff of their chef's jackets and hauled them to their feet.

With arms spread wide to keep the two apart, Matt spoke.

"Okay, boys, what happened? Did someone get butter in the jam jar again?"

The tall one, thirtysomething with dark curly hair and a peeling bandage on his handsome face, threw off Matt's grip. Still full of fight, he stood erect, on widespread legs, jabbing his index finger at the other.

"This—lazy, incompetent jackass—can't even grill a simple hamburger. With him it's three ways. Raw, medium well, or burnt to a crisp!"

The other, a spindly youth barely out of high school, shook a steel spatula at his accuser. Ignoring the blood that poured from his nose and over his wispy blond beard, he answered back—

"I've been making Quik Burgers for six months, man. Six months! And not one customer ever complained."

"They complain with their feet, you moron," the dark-haired man spat back. "How many repeat customers do you have? The business is dying. That's why I was hired!"

The blond youth waved his spatula dismissively. "Ah, what do they want for five bucks?"

"They want the best meal that five dollars can buy, that's what! And it's your job to provide it. Do your job or lose it."

The youth slammed the spatula to the concrete. "I quit."

He stripped off his chef's jacket and tossed it on ground beside the bent utensil.

"Take your stupid coat back, too, Tyler. I don't know why you made me wear it. Before you came, Uncle Theo didn't even give me an apron!"

As the kid stormed off, Matt and I exchanged glances.

We finally found Tyler LaFontaine.

Seventy-two

THE Cutthroat Chef winced as I covered the growing lump on his noggin with an ice pack. The wound, he claimed, was caused by the doorjamb.

"That little jackass never laid a hand on me," he insisted.

Tyler was sprawled across the only open booth, which sported a Formica tabletop and worn vinyl seats. It was used as a break area by the delivery people, and in their frenzied retreat they left empty beer cans, paper cups, and a half-eaten burger.

I found a first aid kit behind the counter and grabbed a large bandage to replace the one dangling off Tyler's sweating cheek. I tugged away the old dressing, which masked three ugly parallel scratches.

I cleaned his cheek with a damp paper towel.

Were these defensive wounds the result of the fight Nazim described at the other ghost kitchen? Or did he get them somewhere else? From *someone* else?

Once he was bandaged and ice packed, Tyler settled back in the booth while I looked around. Though the late-afternoon sun shone brightly, the brown paper on the windows gave the interior the sepia tone of an old frontier photograph.

The space was typical railcar diner: a short-order kitchen along one wall, a long counter with stools, and booths lining the opposite wall. The grill was sizzling hot and smelled of grease, and a fan hummed quietly.

The fan was the only sign of activity. Instead of customers, the booths were crowded with takeout boxes, plastic utensils, and other delivery supplies.

From behind the idle cash register, a phone rang. Then another one chimed in. Soon there were three.

Tyler knocked beer cans aside as he pulled himself out of the booth. He limped across the narrow aisle, reached behind the counter, and ripped the phone line out of the wall. That stopped the ringing, and the place fell silent again—except for the fan.

Clutching the ice pack to his head, he faced us. "Who are you and why are you here?"

"I'm Clare Cosi and this is my business partner, Matt. We're looking for someone who is missing, and we hope you can help us find her."

He visibly winced. "Her?"

"Suzie Hastings. I understand you and she have a relationship?"

"Had. We parted on . . . bad terms."

"Was that when she went off on her trip?"

Tyler stared at me through darkly hooded eyes. "How do you know about that?" he spat angrily. "Are you police? Are you following me?"

Matt immediately jumped in with conciliatory words.

"We've been trying to find you, Chef. You know Ms. Hastings. We can't find her. And we hoped you could help. It's that simple."

"Why are you looking for Suzie?"

"Suzie needs to be notified that something happened to her aunt," I explained. "Please, can you help us locate her?"

He frowned and looked away. "I'm not the one you should be talking to."

"We don't know where else to turn."

The chef grunted in disgust. "Try Lukas Wyatt."

"Lukas Wyatt?" Matt's brow wrinkled. "I know that name, don't I? Where have I heard it?"

"He's the CEO of UrbanGro," I said. "The one who's offering a *reward* for the hero wall-crawler." (I shot a pointed glance Matt's way.) "Is that who you mean, Tyler?"

"The genius with a vision," the young chef spat. "The man Suzie's been working for. Or should I say working *under*?"

"You sound bitter," I said.

"Ms. Cosi, in the past three months, I lost my position as head chef of a top-tier restaurant. Because of financial hardship, I lost my apartment.

Because of professional jealousy, I lost my chance at a fresh start baking pastries. Now I lost this lousy, stinking job working for a man who's better off selling pipe fittings."

He tossed the ice pack on the counter.

"And I lost Suzie, too."

He stepped away and stripped off his own chef jacket. Under it, he wore a worn T-shirt with a hole near the collar.

"When was the last time you spoke with Suzie face-to-face?" I asked.

"About ten days ago—she said she was leaving on a trip, which you already know. I'm sure it was another business trip with Lukas Wyatt. He's launching the same urban growing program in Portland that he did here. Suzie's running his publicity. She didn't come back to New York until this week."

"This week?" I asked skeptically. "How do you know she's back?"

"I got a message from her four days ago," he claimed. "Suzie texted me that she just arrived home and she wanted to meet me."

"She has her own apartment in the city?"

Tyler shook his head. "She lives with that aunt of hers at the Hastings."

"What you told me sounds like a lie," I bluntly replied. "That's the same evening Bea Hastings suffered a near-fatal accident. She fell or was pushed off her roof. I was there, in that penthouse. The police were there, too. But Suzie was nowhere to be found."

"I . . . I don't . . ." His voice faded. Tyler seemed as baffled as I.

"Are you sure it was that day?" Matt jumped in. "What time was it?"

"Just before six PM," Tyler replied. "I know the date and time are right because that was the evening I got mugged."

Matt raised his hands. "Whoa! You better back up and start from the beginning."

Tyler took a breath. "I was on my way to this job. The evening shift starts at six. I live in a one-room walk-up in Jackson Heights these days. From here, it's a twenty-minute walk. Along the way, I had to go under the Brooklyn-Queens Expressway. It's a lighted underpass, kind of creepy, almost always deserted.

"Just as I got to the underpass, Suzie texted me. I stopped to open my phone and read her text. Like I said, she was back home and wanted to meet up. I was about to reply when I saw movement. Some guy was rushing me, and I almost got body-slammed. I moved out of the way, but the guy's arm caught me. I stumbled and hit the concrete wall."

Tyler winced at the memory.

"The mugger tried to bash my head against the wall. I guess that's how my face got gashed."

He touched the fresh Band-Aid.

"Anyway, I was out cold for a minute. When I came to, he was gone. He got my phone because it flew out of my hand. He didn't take my wallet or anything else. Just my phone."

"What did he look like?"

Tyler shrugged. "Couldn't tell you. I remember a black jacket with a hoodie underneath, ski mask, gloves. The hood was up, the underpass was dark, I wouldn't know him if he walked through that door right now."

"But you're sure it was a 'him'?" Matt asked.

"I guess," he replied. "It was a mugger. They're guys, right?"

"Did you call the police?" I asked. "File a report?"

"What's the point? Nothing would come of it. It was a prepaid phone, anyway, a piece of crap. I went home, took aspirin, and called off sick."

"You didn't have time to text Suzie back?" Matt asked.

"I only had the one phone and no landline. I couldn't even get a new phone until I got paid yesterday. As soon as I did, I called Suzie a dozen times and left voice mails, and texted her plenty. But she never called back and never replied to my texts."

"You believe it's over between you and Suzie?" Matt asked.

"What do you think? She's with Wyatt now. I'm sure she only wanted to meet me that night to break up. I doubt I'll ever see her again."

Tyler balled up his chef's jacket and stuffed it into a worn Equator gym bag.

"Now, if you'll excuse me, I've got to lock this place up and register for unemployment."

Seventy-three

〜〜〜〜〜〜〜〜〜〜〜〜〜〜〜〜〜

"Do you think Tyler really received a text from Suzie?" I asked Matt. "Because I think he's lying."

Matt didn't respond. He was too busy keeping a wary eye on traffic. We were heading toward Manhattan while most commuters were fleeing, but that didn't guarantee an easy trip.

When I pressed him for an answer, Matt finally shrugged. "Tyler's phone was stolen, so there's no proof he did or didn't."

"Convenient. Wouldn't you say?"

"What do you mean by that?" he asked.

"Did you see the scratches on his face? They looked like they were made by fingernails—"

"They were. The mugger's."

"Tyler said the mugger wore gloves. And what kind of mugger scratches a guy?"

"I've seen far more mano a mano fights than you have, Clare. All sorts of things can happen. Tyler was lucky, because it sounds like the mugger was trying to finish him off for good."

"Well, I thought those cuts looked more like they were made by a woman."

"What are you saying?" Matt asked. "You think that chef kid assaulted Suzie? Murdered her?"

"He could have attacked Bea four nights ago. Those could be defensive wounds from the night she went off the roof."

"That seems like a stretch."

"I don't think so. He certainly is desperate for investment money. And

Suzie could have helped him cover it all up. If she inherits Bea's fortune, Tyler's money problems are presumably solved."

"What's your evidence of this dastardly scheme?"

"I have none, obviously."

"We should have gotten the kid's alibi," Matt fretted.

"He doesn't have one. Didn't you hear? He said he went home the night we found Bea. He called off sick."

"He *might* have an alibi. A friend or neighbor here in Queens."

"Tyler's story doesn't add up. If Suzie really is back, then where is she? Why is she hiding out and not answering the police or anyone else?"

"Why indeed?"

"What does that mean? You think Suzie is guilty? And Tyler is completely innocent?"

"I don't know what to think."

"Okay, this speculation is officially pointless," I said. "And it's not getting us any closer to finding Suzie. I think we have to dial it back to that trip she supposedly took ten days ago with Lukas Wyatt. We have to know if Suzie came back to the city—as Tyler claimed—or if she's still working in Portland. Or somewhere else."

"Staying in Portland sounds logical," Matt said. "If she's working publicity like Tyler said, then Suzie has to be an available spokesperson, doesn't she?" He snapped his fingers. "Hey! Check Google News. If she gave a press conference or issued a statement on UrbanGro's behalf, you'll find it there."

"And if I don't find anything, we'll have to do what Tyler told us to do and ask Lukas Wyatt ourselves."

Matt snorted. "Just how easy do you think it will be to personally quiz a CEO of a billion-dollar tech company?"

"Easy as pie if you agree to accept Lukas Wyatt's award and admit to the public that you're the hero wall-crawler."

"Oh, no you don't." Matt looked incensed. "I am perfectly willing to help you play *Desperately Seeking Suzie*, but I am not—repeat *not*—willing to become the center of a media freak show."

"Freak show or not, there's a nice monetary award."

"I don't want Lukas Wyatt's damn money."

"Why not? Use it to find a real apartment and stop sleeping illegally in your own warehouse."

Matt scowled in silence, eyes on the road—which was plain stubbornness on his part since we were so snarled in traffic we weren't even moving.

"Just think about it, okay?"

Matt made a noncommittal noise I knew well. He'd put up a brick wall and no amount of huffing and puffing by me was going to blow that house down.

With a sigh, I sat back and stared out the window. If I wanted to speak with Lukas Wyatt, I would have to figure out how to get to him myself.

After five minutes of silence, Matt tuned the radio to 1010 WINS, hoping to learn the reason for all the traffic. "You give us twenty-two minutes, we'll give you the world" was their tagline, but that meant pretty much the same news (plus eight minutes of commercials) repeated every half hour—and so we listened to Lukas Wyatt's sound bite about the wall-crawler reward (sponsored by UrbanGro, of course) twice before we crossed the bridge to Manhattan.

When we finally did hit the mile-long span, I took in the skyline of towers in front of us, hundreds of them, side by side, with tens of thousands of windows flashing gold as honey in the afternoon sun. The stunning sight reminded me of something I'd learned recently.

Officer Darius Greene had mentioned that bees purged their hives regularly. They tossed out the dead weight: the weak, the sick, the lazy, the drones who were overly aggressive or stopped cooperating.

Once exiled, those bees were never allowed back into the hive. Other bees instinctively blocked their way until the exiles flew off alone, to wither and die. A cruel example of natural selection. And one that happened regularly to humans in New York. It certainly appeared to be happening to Chef Tyler LaFontaine.

He came to the hive of the city, a new drone full of ambition and hubris, but not enough discipline or maturity to balance things out. So, instead of the success he craved, Tyler stumbled from one self-inflicted failure to another, until there was no place left for him.

Now I couldn't help wondering—

If Tyler was a misfit drone, cast out into the cold, how far would he go to reclaim his cushy place inside that hive? Wouldn't someone that desperate be capable of anything? Even attempted murder?

Seventy-Four

~~~~~~

After we returned to the Village Blend, Matt jumped behind the counter to help service the after-work crowd. I joined in at the espresso machines, but as soon as the crush eased, I went to my second-floor office and fired up my laptop.

With Matt being less than cooperative about accepting that wall-crawler reward, I was determined to find another way to get to Lukas Wyatt.

Matt's suggestion of an Internet search yielded no sign of Suzie in Portland or anywhere else. No press conferences, no press statements, no new stories on UrbanGro whatsoever—and (still) no answer to the message I sent to Suzie's PR company website.

Before we left Chef Tyler in Queens, I pressured him for Suzie's personal mobile phone number, and he gave it up. But just like Tyler's messages, my own voicemail and texts went unanswered.

Finally, I Googled "Lukas Wyatt," and struck gold.

The CEO was in the local news, and not just because of the reward he offered for finding Bea's savior. Wyatt was scheduled to appear at a local food festival. In fact, he was scheduled to deliver remarks at the opening ceremonies this very evening.

Though I'd never attended the "Alternative Edibles Organic and Natural" foods show (aka AEON), it was already in its fifth year in New York, though only its second at Hudson Yards, the newest and trendiest of upscale Manhattan neighborhoods.

The festival website gave a list of vendors, events, and attendees. The site also featured biographies of the festival founders, including the young supermarket heiress Salena Heath (now CEO of her own fledgling company, Heath's Health Foods), and Lukas Wyatt, CEO of UrbanGro.

Wyatt's history read like a Damon Runyon story. He was orphaned at an early age when his parents died. After living in a string of foster homes, he ended up with an affluent family in Long Island, where he attended an exclusive school, won a sports scholarship, and went on to Drexel University where he got a degree in software engineering and development.

Another revelation turned up on the food festival's *About Us* page.

I learned Beatrice Hastings was also a founding member and currently sat on its board of trustees. Armed with that knowledge, I called Todd Duncan.

"Yeah, Mrs. Hastings was involved with AEON from the beginning, but she hasn't attended since it moved from the Javits Center to Hudson Yards."

"Todd, I need two tickets to tonight's event. Can you help me?"

"Not a problem," he replied. "Mrs. Hastings always gets complimentary tickets. They're in the office somewhere. I'll scare up two and have someone hand deliver them within the hour."

Matt was in the back, restocking the pantry, when I approached him a few minutes later.

"So, do you want to join me on another expedition?"

His eyes narrowed suspiciously. "Where to?"

"An alternative foods festival in Hudson Yards."

"Why are we going there?"

"I want to talk to Lukas Wyatt. He's speaking there tonight, though how I'll get close to him at a busy convention, I don't know yet."

"It's that important, you think?"

"He's our best chance of getting answers about Suzie Hastings. And maybe finding out whether Tyler lied to us about their relationship. Either way, I can't stop worrying about that young woman. There may be a logical explanation for her dropping off the map. On the other hand, she may be an accomplice to what happened to her aunt, or—"

"A victim herself?"

"Or both."

"Get the tickets, Clare. I'll go with you. And don't worry. I'm sure we'll find a way to meet Lukas Wyatt."

Seventy-Five

∿∿∿∿∿∿∿∿∿∿∿∿∿∿∿∿∿∿∿∿∿∿

Some say New York is a city of "haves" and "have-nots." In those terms, Hudson Yards was built for the ones who have it all—or almost all, anyway.

The massive real estate development on the far West Side consisted of concave skyscrapers, luxury apartments, and a vertical mall filled with glittering shops—many of them far too exclusive for a mere coffeehouse manager.

Not that this current Hudson Yards wasn't an ingenious improvement over its previous incarnation. A century ago, railroad tracks ran side by side with narrow streets teeming with the poorest of the poor. Fatal accidents were so common the area became known as "Death Avenue."

In the brand-spanking-new Hudson Yards, lighted, tree-lined walkways led to upscale restaurants and ingenious architecture. And though the busy West Side rail yard still existed, the grit and grime of industrial machinery and manual labor were now hidden beneath buildings of shimmering steel and spotless glass.

Though I personally preferred the historic downtown neighborhoods of New York, I had to admit this new development was impressive. The golden beehive sculpture of Escher-like staircases known as "the Vessel" was my favorite attraction, but the gleaming, silver-white, telescoping walls of "the Shed" were lofty, imposing, and beautiful, too—especially when brilliantly lit on this clear autumn evening.

Our destination was the aforementioned Shed, a multipurpose performance and convention space. As Matt and I approached the entrance from the crowded plaza outside, vertical AEON banners fluttered wildly around us in wind gusts stirred by a brewing storm.

Arching high above was a sunny yellow banner, so large you could probably see it from space:

ALTERNATIVE EDIBLES ORGANIC AND NATURAL
AEON 5.0

I knew getting to Lukas Wyatt here and quizzing him about Suzie Hastings was a final Hail Mary pass on my part. The problem was: I had hoped for a quaint little convention populated by hard-core foodies, not a mob scene.

"How are we going to get near the CEO of UrbanGro—let alone grill him about Suzie—with this huge crowd around?"

"There must be thousands of people here," Matt agreed.

And there were rows upon rows of displays inside.

"By the way," he added, "I need to eat something."

"There should be lots of organic and natural foods to sample," I said. "Not to mention the alternative stuff."

"I'm all for organic and natural. It's the *alternative* food I'm worried about. What is that, anyway?"

"I guess we'll see."

When Matt and I reached the reception desk, we received our nifty name tags created on the spot by a 3D printer out of eco-friendly biodegradable plastic. The moment we'd finished registering, a full-figured young woman swathed in a burgundy pantsuit approached us with a ready smile. She paused to read Matt's name tag.

"Matteo Allegro! I've been waiting for you to arrive since your call. We've had a lot of cranks and pranksters contact us. But once you came forward, we verified your identity with the police, and it seems you truly are the hero who climbed down the side of a building to rescue Bea Hastings."

"Guilty as charged," Matt replied.

"Matt, what is going on?" I whispered in stunned surprise. "I thought you didn't want to come forward?"

Before my ex could explain why he did a complete one-eighty on accepting Lukas Wyatt's reward money—and suddenly didn't mind being the center of a media "freak show"—an official photographer slipped beside the Woman in Burgundy and began snapping photos of him. Meanwhile, my head felt as if it were turning completely around like that girl in *The Exorcist* movie.

Matt noticed my shock and threw me a wink.

Just then, a petite woman in a belted, bell-sleeved Valentino with a halo of bouncy brown curls extended her hand.

"Hello, I'm Salena Heath, one of the founders of AEON."

As Matt greeted her, she read his badge. "And what is the Village Blend?"

"The landmark New York coffeehouse owned by my mother." Matt pushed me forward. "And managed by our excellent master roaster, Ms. Clare Cosi."

"Honored to meet you," I said, pulling it together after my initial shock.

"I'm so glad you both decided to visit our festival." After a quick, nononsense shake, she waved her hand. "Come along. I'll escort you through security."

I followed Matt and our elfin executive escort through the final gate, held open by the security team.

"We've all heard what happened to Beatrice," Salena Heath said, "and we are so grateful to you, Mr. Allegro, for risking your life to help her. She's a member of our board of trustees."

As we entered the event space, the little socialite wrapped her arm around Matt's. "Mr. Wyatt wants to present you with an award personally."

Matt brushed that aside. "I'd just like to meet the man. Shake his hand for all the good work he's done."

"I'll be sure to arrange that," Salena promised, "right after Mr. Wyatt's opening remarks. Will that work for you, Matteo . . . May I call you Matteo?"

"My friends call me Matt." He smiled down at her, all charm.

Still locked arm in arm, she pulled him closer. "I'll call you Matt, then, because it feels like we're friends already. And please, call me Salena."

Oh, brother . . .

Thankfully, the flirt-fest ended when a young staffer appeared.

"Ms. Heath, the deputy mayor is here. You promised him a photo op."

Reluctantly, Salena released Matt's arm. "Duty calls and I must run, but we've partitioned off a space we call 'the Forum' for our opening ceremony.

It starts in an hour. I'll reserve you both a seat in front, and after the talk, I'll introduce you to Mr. Wyatt."

"I appreciate it," Matt said.

"My pleasure. Looking forward to seeing *you* soon." Salena was off, but not without a final glance at Matt over her shoulder.

I poked my ex. "So, what have you got to say? Why did you decide to come forward?"

He shrugged. "You wanted to meet Lukas Wyatt, didn't you?"

"But you objected so strongly before—"

"*Before* I thought of a good use for that reward, you mean?"

I nodded. "I hope you'll invite me to your homecoming party when you find your new place."

"Humm," Matt replied.

"Hey." I poked him again. "Good work. And thanks."

"Come on. We've got an hour. Let's check out the show."

Seventy-six

꩜꩜꩜꩜꩜꩜꩜꩜꩜꩜꩜꩜꩜꩜꩜꩜꩜꩜꩜꩜

THE Shed was an ingenious venue with a retractable roof that extended outward like a huge mobile tent to create a convention space called the McCourt. That's where we were now, strolling up and down the rows of exhibition booths.

Colorful signs, raucous video displays, and food samples assaulted our senses as we grazed our way through the show. We tried everything from "meat analogue" burgers and "fishless" fillets made from a portmanteau of vegetable proteins to surprisingly yummy Flourless Chocolate Brownies topped with decadent-tasting Chocolate Fudge Frosting (amazingly, made from avocados) and cleverly homey Oat Milk Oatmeal Cookies (miraculously made without flour or butter) and served with dunking glasses of (you guessed it) oat milk.

But Matt and I were the most impressed with the sweet corn bread made with a combination of organic cornmeal and spelt flour, an ancient grain that imparted a delicate, nutty taste to the finished product. I took the vendor's card and even snagged the Spelt Corn Bread recipe.

When we came upon a sign for *Alternative Coffee*, we glanced at each other and took the bait.

The young hostess read Matt's badge as we approached her booth.

"The Village Blend! You should be interested in our featured product. Castaneda Coffee is an environmentally friendly and sustainable coffee."

Matt raised an eyebrow. "But coffee is a crop that comes from a bush. It's already sustainable—"

"Our coffee is a caffeine-free organic product produced right here in the USA. It will delight the dedicated locavore because there is no need for costly international shipping. That's what makes Castaneda Coffee environmentally friendly."

"How do you grow coffee locally?" Matt asked, genuinely curious. "Coffee plants are equatorial. The best coffees are high grown on volcanic soil and cultivated by native cultures that have been doing it for generations."

"We repurposed abandoned coal mines in West Virginia, Mr. Allegro," she brightly replied. "Castaneda Coffee is made entirely from varieties of consumable mushrooms using our own proprietary process."

Matt reacted with a frozen smile.

"We're going to serve samples in a few minutes. You should try it! You'll be pleasantly surprised."

"I'm sure I'll be . . . *surprised*," Matt replied. "Unfortunately, I have pressing business at another booth."

Matt gripped my arm. "Keep moving, Clare, and don't look back."

Seventy-seven

ᘒᘎᘒᘎᘒᘎᘒᘎᘒᘎᘒᘎᘒᘎᘒᘎᘒᘎᘒᘎᘒᘎᘒᘎᘒᘎ

LUKAS Wyatt appeared on the Forum stage right on time.

Jacketless and tieless in denims and a flannel shirt, his lumberjack beard reached his lapels. He more resembled a lanky frontier pioneer (or maybe a young Abe Lincoln) than a tech industry leader—when he wasn't mimicking an earnest country preacher.

He had a habit of joining his hands and gazing skyward each time he made some point, almost as if in prayer. The man was so wide-eyed about his mission, he came off a little naive, or maybe just eccentric. But then, genius inventors were supposed to be eccentric, weren't they?

Genius or not, the UrbanGro CEO had drawn a packed crowd. Thankfully, Salena Heath reserved two seats for Matt and me in the front row among the VIPs, mostly city bureaucrats.

I was glad to hear Wyatt begin his talk by citing the tons of fresh fruits and vegetables that UrbanGro was giving freely to food pantries and charity kitchens across the five boroughs.

"All of that food was grown not far from where we are right now," he proclaimed. "Not outdoors, on expansive farmland that had to be irrigated and fertilized. It was grown inside a single converted warehouse I call UrbanGro One."

On cue, the giant television screens behind him displayed the image of a shabby, twenty-story industrial building that had long been an eyesore on the West Side skyline.

A video of the interior appeared next, featuring tier upon tier of green growing racks on a vast, brightly lit floor. In a time-lapse video those stacked decks shifted positions, just like the flower racks in Bea Hastings's greenhouse, but on an even more massive scale.

"With our revolutionary software system, we've been able to produce more than one hundred acres worth of crops in that single retrofitted, solar-powered warehouse, employing only a few computer technicians. We use hydroponics and grow lights, also powered by solar panels across the roof—"

New images appeared as Wyatt continued.

Suddenly, a booming voice with a New York attitude and a heavy Brooklyn accent erupted from our VIP section.

"That's a very pretty picture you paint, Mr. Wyatt, and you're a real smart guy. But I have something to say to you!"

The dissenter was a wizened man with an age-spotted head that seemed almost too large for his spindly body. His tailored evening suit was impeccable, and he leaned on an elegant gold-handled walking stick.

Next to Salena, I heard the deputy mayor whisper: "It's Henry Tilson, the head of urban planning."

Lukas Wyatt accepted the challenge. "Go on, Mr. Tilson."

"A city is not a farm, Mr. Wyatt. The expense of growing crops in an urban environment eats up any savings in shipping costs."

Wyatt answered back and soon the gist of their argument was lost as the two bandied about words like *vertical forest, entomology*, and *phytopathology.*

"Do you really think the city council will let you ruin the aesthetics of New York with your ultimate goal? To control valuable city-owned real estate and capture billions of dollars in public funds to build ugly farming towers that we don't need." Tilson pounded his stick on the floor to emphasize his point.

The bearded CEO fired back, "They will, because it's an investment in the city's future. When the city council realizes the benefit of my sustainable food source, they will have no choice but to vote *yes*, even if it means changing zoning laws."

Just then, a shout came from the audience. "But your food isn't naturally sustainable!"

"It's artificial food," another cried.

"It's wrong!" a woman called.

Suddenly, a young man rushed in front of the podium and directed sections of the crowd like a conductor. In places strategically located all along the Forum's benches, protestors jumped to their feet and unrolled the banners they'd smuggled in.

They immediately began to chant the message painted on their signs—"UrbanGro must go! UrbanGro must go!"

Lukas Wyatt stood his ground. "We grow natural crops hydroponically," he shouted over the crowd. "UrbanGro is dedicated to food purity—"

Some members of the audience were on Wyatt's side and challenged the protestors. Now disputes were breaking out all over. Suddenly, leaflets were flying. I grabbed one and read the title:

THE TERRIBLE TRUTH ABOUT URBANGRO

I shoved it into my jacket for perusal later.

Meanwhile, the youth orchestrating the protest was so frustrated by audience interference that he grabbed a folding chair and hurled it.

Wyatt dodged the flying furniture in an impressively athletic move. The chair struck one of the television screens, shattering it in an explosion of sparks. Not satisfied with this level of destruction, the angry protestor rushed the podium.

Matt was right behind him. My ex grabbed the youth by his collar and yanked him backward. In a smooth move Matt literally turned the troublemaker around and thrust him into the arms of a security detail who'd arrived (in not exactly the nick of time).

Then security cleared the scene of protestors, and Salena Heath took the stage. With a forced smile of sunny optimism, she resumed the opening ceremonies.

Seventy-eight

〜〜〜〜〜〜〜〜〜〜〜〜〜〜〜〜〜〜〜〜

WHEN the Forum crowd finally dispersed, an appreciative Lukas Wyatt took hold of Matt's hand. In a brotherly gesture, he covered it with his left—just as that official photographer reappeared to snap more photos.

"Thank you for the assist today," Wyatt said. "And thank you sincerely for what you did for Bea Hastings."

"Do all your talks end so dramatically?" Matt asked.

Wyatt's laugh was gentle. "If you think this was a riot, you should have been in Portland. There is always resistance to new ideas. If you kick the hive, the bees get angry."

"Interesting analogy," I quietly noted.

Wyatt regarded my ex. "I saw your picture on the front pages. That was the South African abseil you used, wasn't it?"

Matt brightened. "You've got sharp eyes. Are you a climber?"

"I've done a lot of rock climbing and mountaineering. Took on Everest, too. But I'm a business executive now, so my insurance policies don't allow for fun. I miss my rugby-playing days at Drexel more than anything."

"Rough game," Matt said, impressed.

Before the conversation degenerated into a hairy chest–beating contest between two danger-seeking daredevils, I jumped in with a question.

"You spoke about Portland, Mr. Wyatt. Did you recently return from Oregon?"

"No, Ms. Cosi. Our Portland initiative died months ago. Too much resistance."

"I guess I got bad information. Someone told me that Suzie Hastings traveled with you to Portland?"

"She did go to Portland with us. But like I said, that was months ago."

"Then Suzie hasn't gone on a business trip in the past week or so?"

Wyatt looked uncomfortable answering. "She opted to go on an off-the-grid vacation, ten days ago. We all need that—from time to time." His smile seemed strained. "We miss Suzie. I had hoped she'd be back in time to help publicize this festival, but we're getting by with Salena Heath's press team."

"I'm sorry to push. But you *must* have some kind of contact information for her, don't you?"

His smile looked brittle. "Off-the-grid is off-the-grid. She could be anywhere from a resort in the South Pacific to a mountain retreat in Nepal." He seemed to force a shrug. "That's our Suzie."

"Mr. Wyatt, Suzie still doesn't know what happened to her aunt. Do you mean to tell me that there's *no way* to get a message to her?"

"Yes, that's what I'm telling you. Her plans were *private*." He sounded irritated now, and clearly didn't want to show it. After a pause, his voice went back to gentle preacher. "She said she needed to decompress. That's all I can tell you. But I understand her aunt survived her fall and is under good care. Suzie will be back in touch soon. Give her a few more days, and I'm sure—"

Just then, one of Wyatt's assistants appeared and whispered in his ear.

The CEO looked almost relieved. "I'm afraid duty calls. But enjoy the festival. Both of you."

Wyatt swiftly exited with Salena Heath and several assistants in tow.

Matt turned to me. "Well, that was useless. But I'm still hungry and I'm sniffing something mighty good. Let's check out some more booths."

"Go. Eat for two of us. After that dead-end exchange with Wyatt, I lost my appetite. Meet me back here when you're done."

Off Matt went, following the scent of barbecue wafting from some distant booth. I sat down on a Forum bench and was about to pull out that protest leaflet, "The Terrible Truth about UrbanGro," when I spotted a familiar face—one who clearly did not want to be spotted.

Nellie Atwood.

Though her flowing blond hair was pinned up and her attire so casual as to be invisible, I recognized her from that night at the Hastings. She frowned when she saw the wreckage the protesters had left behind. She edged one of the fallen banners with her booted foot. She must have sensed she was being watched because she seemed to panic when she looked up and saw me staring at her.

Nellie immediately gave me her back, but I wasn't going to let her get away.

"Nellie Atwood!" I yelled. "It's Matt Allegro's business partner, Clare Cosi!"

When Nellie—and everyone within earshot—heard me loudly calling her name, she dropped the pretense that she hadn't noticed me.

"Oh, hello," she said, turning to face me. "I . . . I didn't recognize you."

"Understandable," I replied. "We only met the one time. At the Hastings. On the night Bea had her accident."

Nellie's smile seemed as forced as her comeback. "If I'd known Matt was going to play the hero, I would have stuck around to watch."

"You heard the news, then?"

"Salena Heath issued a statement to the press thirty minutes ago." Nellie held up her phone screen.

Nellie seemed skittish, ready to bolt at any moment, so I steered her back toward the VIP chairs near the empty Forum stage for privacy.

"I'm surprised you weren't here when Lukas Wyatt spoke, and for all the excitement he sparked." I pushed aside a fallen banner to make a seat for us. "You're on UrbanGro's board, aren't you? A financial officer, I believe."

"Chief financial officer," she corrected. "You're pretty informed for a barista."

"I'm also the manager of a successful landmark business," I fired back. "But I don't know everything. For instance, I don't know who you were visiting that night at the Hastings. Would you care to tell me?"

She bit her glossed lower lip. Then Nellie's expression melted into a frown. Finally, she lifted her perfectly sculpted chin in defiance.

"I've got nothing to hide, Ms. Cosi. I was visiting Susan Hastings."

Seventy-nine

~~~~~~

I stared at Nellie, speechless for a moment. "You saw Suzie that night, upstairs with her aunt?"

"No, I didn't see her. My *reason* for going to the Hastings was to visit her. I rang the penthouse bell a dozen times and even banged on the door. No one answered, so I left."

"And that's when you ran into me and Matt?"

"That's right. I remembered that tenth-floor access to the service elevator. Back on Labor Day, Suzie threw a party for UrbanGro—we had investors, staff, city officials. There were so many people coming and going up to her aunt's penthouse, we had to utilize the second elevator. Anyway, I had no idea what happened to her aunt until I saw it in the news the next day."

"And yet you obviously kept Matt's 'wall-crawler' identity to yourself?"

Nellie shrugged. "What can I say? Once that publicity train got rolling, I wasn't about to derail it. Matt's stunt and Lukas's reward bought us a fortune in media exposure. Besides, I didn't want to . . ."

Nellie hesitated. Her eyes looked a little glazed, as if she'd been drinking. I leaned closer and caught a whiff of whiskey on her breath.

"Go on," I coaxed. "What didn't you want?"

"I didn't want anyone at UrbanGro to know I was trying to conference privately with Suzie, okay? And I'd appreciate discretion from you and Matt."

"Discretion? Sure, but I don't get it. Why wouldn't you want anyone at

UrbanGro to know you were trying to meet privately with Suzie? She is head of PR for the company, isn't she?"

"Why do *you* care so much, Ms. Cosi?" Nellie snapped back. "Really, what business is it of yours?"

"I'll tell you. I consider Beatrice Hastings a friend—and she's a lifelong friend of my mentor. Neither of us believe she attempted suicide."

Nellie glanced around uneasily, clearly anxious about anyone overhearing our discussion. When she was sure we were alone, she lowered her voice.

"I don't believe that suicide story, either. But when I spoke to the police, that was their conclusion, and I didn't think there was anything more to be done—other than wait for Suzie Hastings to surface again."

"You spoke to the police?"

"Are you kidding? As much as I'm fond of Matteo, I don't know *you* at all. And I thought the police should know I saw you both at the Hastings that night. What were *you* doing there, Ms. Cosi?"

I explained what happened with the bee swarm at my coffeehouse and Nellie sat back. She appeared a bit less tense after that, but only a bit. In an effort to ease her paranoia—and encourage her to continue opening up—I told her about Mike.

"Ms. Atwood, my fiancé is a lieutenant with the NYPD. You can trust me. Please talk to me. You seem a little anxious." (That was putting it mildly.) "What are you afraid of?"

"Let's just say I'm not feeling very safe these days."

"Why not?"

Once again, Nellie glanced around. Her voice dropped even lower. "Apparently, I'm asking too many questions—that's what I've been told. Warned is more like it."

"Warned by who?"

"I don't know. The letter was anonymous. Plain white paper, standard printer ink—that's what the private investigator said, anyway."

"You hired a professional investigator?"

"I felt it was time."

"And what questions have you been asking? Are they about Bea?"

"No, Ms. Cosi. Whatever happened to Bea can be handled by the police. My questions have been about the business practices of UrbanGro."

"What practices?"

She sighed. "Look, I don't expect you to understand the technical details, so I'll boil it down to the big picture. On the night I went to see Suzie, I had drinks with a client I've known for a dozen years. Two years ago, I persuaded him to invest heavily in UrbanGro. As you've obviously seen tonight, there have been problems."

With disgust, Nellie gestured to the protest leaflets still littering the floor. "My client wanted answers that I didn't have about the city's financial commitment and our timetable for expansion, so I decided to circumvent Lukas Wyatt's continual evasions and go to Suzie with my questions. I wanted to know what Lukas was keeping from me."

"I still don't understand why you would go to Suzie. She's just a public relations manager. What would she know that you, as the CFO, wouldn't?"

"Suzie has gotten . . . close to Lukas."

"How close?"

Nellie rolled her eyes. "What do you think?"

"I don't know, you tell me."

"They're sleeping together, Ms. Cosi. Susan Hastings and Lukas Wyatt are lovers."

Eighty

꧁ ꧂꧁ ꧂꧁ ꧂꧁ ꧂꧁ ꧂꧁ ꧂꧁ ꧂꧁ ꧂꧁ ꧂꧁ ꧂꧁ ꧂꧁ ꧂꧁ ꧂

Nellie's revelation wasn't a surprise as much as a confirmation. Chef Tyler had alleged exactly that, but I didn't know whether to believe him. Now I did.

"Don't you see?" Nellie went on. "That's why I didn't simply phone Suzie the other night. I had to make sure she wasn't *with* Lukas when I spoke to her. Not to mention the added complication that everyone working at UrbanGro has been given a complimentary company phone, including Suzie. I couldn't risk surveillance of our conversation."

"But aren't you all working for the same goals?"

Nellie massaged her temples with manicured fingertips. "Ms. Cosi, do you know what a CFO typically does? They steer the financials of a company. They hold the reins on budgets, spending, planning. They usually know more about a company than the founder."

Her laugh was a bitter bark. "Do you know what I do as chief financial officer of UrbanGro? I bring in the money; that's been my role. Lukas Wyatt has insisted on controlling the budget, the planning, and everything else. But nothing gets done! He used to be ruthless about business, pushing the envelope, steamrolling problems, and all that—I assumed it was because of what happened to his parents—but his drive and focus have been off for months. Meanwhile, the start-up money is evaporating fast. New investors are wary, and the original investors aren't getting their questions answered."

"Wait, back up. What did you mean about Lukas Wyatt's parents? I read about his upbringing. Orphan makes good and all that."

"The orphan bit is true, but few people know the rest. Both of his biological parents committed suicide."

"Suicide?" I blanched. "Do you know the circumstances?"

"Lukas told me they ran a florist shop on the Upper East Side, poured their hearts into it, until some bigger competitor crushed their business. His dad hung himself. His mother purposely drank herself into an alcohol poisoning death within a year."

It was a tragic story, but I was too flabbergasted to react because the details were triggering a memory. The night of the bee swarm, when Matt and I took that chilly walk to Beatrice's greenhouse, he told me the ugly truth of how Bea made her fortune. She *crushed* mom-and-pop florist shops all over the city by buying the buildings they rented, kicking them out, and turning their shops into part of her chain.

"Ms. Atwood, do you know if that bigger competitor happened to be Hastings Florists?"

"Hastings?" Nellie stared blankly for a moment. "As in Bea Hastings?"

When I nodded, Nellie fell silent. Finally, she whispered, "That would be an odd coincidence, wouldn't it?"

I sat back, considering the possibility that it wasn't a "coincidence" at all. "Has Lukas Wyatt ever mentioned Suzie's aunt in negative terms?"

"No, never. Bea is an investor in his company; why would he?"

Why indeed? I thought, and since Nellie's tongue was good and loose at the moment (being a little tipsy certainly didn't hurt), I tried to keep her talking—

"Speaking of investors, Ms. Atwood, would you mind telling me why exactly the investors are so wary?"

"Once again, I'll put it in simple terms for you, Ms. Cosi," Nellie said with barely veiled condescension. "Suzie once told me she learned many things from her aunt. One of those things she called the *wisdom of the bee.* In a successful hive, the queen is in charge and everyone else follows her lead. But all that busy buzzing will come to an end if the queen runs a hive that can't make honey."

"Honey as in money?"

"What do you think?" She smirked. "It's not exactly a secret. If Urban-Gro ever wants to go public, Lukas has to start earning a profit."

Nellie checked her phone. "I've got to go. If I can help you with Bea Hastings, give me a call. Or better yet, tell Matteo to contact me—he has my number. And if you hear from Suzie, *please* let me know. I'm at the end of my rope with Lukas, including the way he coddles that girl."

"What do you mean 'coddles'?"

Nellie sighed. "I just found out *yesterday* that Lukas allowed Suzie to go on an *off-the-grid* vacation, which is unforgivable. Suzie has become an asset to our success, and this is the worst time for her to drop out of sight." She gestured to the stage and that shattered television screen. "This demonstration *never* would have happened if Suzie had been in charge of tonight's publicity."

"But I understand there was even more chaos in Portland. Wasn't Suzie in charge then?"

"Lukas's fault once more," Nellie whispered. "Suzie was turning the negative press around—and learning how to preempt protests, like this one. In another month Lukas would have gotten his Portland initiative passed. Instead, he walked away. You wouldn't believe the panicked investor revolt I had to quell *that* week."

She shook her head. "I can't fault Lukas for being the genius that he is. The technology behind UrbanGro One is a major achievement. The donations of what he's been growing to food banks and homeless shelters has been a smart PR move."

"Homeless shelters?" I repeated with a frown, remembering Mike's case of dead homeless men.

"The donation idea was Suzie's, too," Nellie went on. "Brilliant PR."

Just then, her phone rang. "Yes, Salena, I'm here," she cooed in a soothing voice while rolling her eyes to the ceiling. "I'm on my way . . ."

Without another word to me, Nellie gave me her back, and this time I let her go.

I remained on the bench for several long minutes, contemplating all the possibilities for Bea's hospitalized state and Suzie's suspicious absence, including one I didn't want to consider . . .

I had imagined a scenario where the volatile Chef Tyler had attacked Suzie's aunt and convinced Suzie to help him cover it up. What if that scenario were true—but the attacker was Lukas Wyatt?

Could Lukas have approached Bea for more investment money?

If she said no, and instead demanded answers, could he have argued with her, sent her over the edge, knowing that Suzie would inherit her huge fortune? With one strategic shove and a few gentle words in Suzie's ears, did Lukas Wyatt think he was solving UrbanGro's funding problems?

And what about the fate of his biological parents?

I flashed on that awful suicide note Detective Novak showed me that Beatrice supposedly wrote before "jumping" off her own roof.

Could Lukas have staged Bea's fall as a "suicide," as his own sick form of justice—or vengeance—for what her larger company did to his parents' small business, all those years ago? Down deep, was Lukas Wyatt really like Bea? Harboring his bitterness so long that it became an obsession, like Bea's obsession with Felix Foxe?

If he did attack her, it was brilliant timing.

Todd Duncan was otherwise engaged at that karaoke bar. Ella, the housekeeper, was in Austria. And the old night doorman was unreliable, at best.

There would be no one around to see Lukas Wyatt's confrontation with Bea. No one, it seemed, but Suzie. And she was currently nowhere to be found. Suspiciously so, given tonight's PR disaster.

Now even Nellie was playing the *Desperately Seeking Suzie* game.

When we did find her, we'd have to get her side of the story—and check the details thoroughly enough to judge whether she was telling the truth or covering up for herself or someone else.

Unless . . . she was too scared to show herself.

What if Suzie did cover up for Lukas Wyatt but now *regretted* it?

What if she was hiding out, scared and confused about what to do next? Her aunt couldn't help her. Not in the state she was in.

Madame and Matt and I would certainly do all we could to advise her—for Bea's sake. I was about to phone Matt and talk things over with him when I was interrupted by a shocking text.

I know you're looking for me, but I can't be seen talking with you. It will put us both in danger. Meet me at the top of the Vessel, ASAP. Please come alone.

I gawked at the name and checked the number to be sure. It was verified. The text came from Susan Hastings.

Eighty-one

～～～～～～～～～～～～～～～～～～～～～～～～

Tᴴᴱ moment I got Suzie's text, I headed for the exit as quickly as the crowd would permit. She'd asked me to come alone, but I wasn't going to honor that. No way.

As I swiftly walked along, I typed out a text to Matt, telling him I was going to the top of the Vessel to talk with Suzie, and finishing with a command to—

Meet us at the top ASAP!

I wanted Matt there as my witness to whatever Suzie admitted, but also as her protection, if we discovered she needed it. This text certainly implied that she did.

After hitting *Send* on the text, I pushed through the door and into the night. A stiff breeze stirred my ponytail, and sudden flashes of lightning whitened the clouds. The plaza around the Vessel was nearly deserted as I approached it.

To envision this climbable work of art, you have to imagine that someone turned a 150-foot steel beehive upside down, hollowed it out, kept the top open, and took the walls away, leaving a mazelike bowl-shaped circle of staircases and landings. The exterior of those stairways was covered with honey gold, reflective metal siding that completed the beehive theme. On a crowded day, the Vessel's mirrored surfaces even made the people moving on the stairs and landings look like bees swarming inside a hive.

When Matt and I first arrived at the food festival, the entrance to the

Vessel had been roped off and a uniformed security officer stood guard. Now the velvet rope lay on the concrete like a dark blue snake, and the guard was nowhere in sight.

After hurrying across the threshold, I was all alone in the imposing steel skeleton. I faced multiple staircases going up and then out in many different directions. I hoped they all led to the top, because when I pressed the button for the elevator, nothing happened.

With twenty-five hundred steps, sixteen stories, and eighty landings, I was facing a long climb. I hit the steps, counting on my regular trips to the Y's swimming pool for the stamina I needed.

The vast empty sculpture, the desolate stairs, and the night's blackness beyond the illuminated walkways left me feeling intimidated. The occasional rumble of thunder and bright flash of lightning didn't do much to soothe my nerves, either.

I climbed and climbed, the wind whistling around me, until I hit the tenth level. Then I leaned against the glass railing—probably the only thing holding me upright—and looked up. I still had six more stories to climb.

While I caught my breath, I checked my phone. Matt had responded to my text with a simple "on my way," but the chances of him finding me in this maze seemed pretty slim, at least until we got to the top, and I was counting on that.

I pulled out my phone to send Matt a "where are you" text when I heard footsteps. Was it Suzie? Matt? A second later I sensed movement behind me—too late!

I was body-slammed with enough force to knock me up and over the glass railing. I heard myself scream as I reached out in a blind panic and managed to snag the safety rail with my right hand.

When I bounced off the side of the structure, the impact was almost enough to break my grip. Thankfully, the fingers of my left hand closed on the rail, too. Now I was hanging a hundred feet over the plaza with both hands.

Instead of looking down, I had the presence of mind to look up, in time to see a masked figure in black dive down the stairs and out of sight. They were gone so quickly I could make out no details—not even a gender. The person who pushed me could have been anyone.

I tried to pull myself up, but the glass was slippery, and I lacked the strength. For the second time this week I screamed my head off for help.

My cries were answered a moment later, when a horrified Matt gripped my wrists and hauled me onto the landing.

"My God, Clare, are you all right?!"

"Now I am," I gasped between desperate gulps of air. Doubling over, I tried to catch my breath while simultaneously attempting to stop my knees from buckling.

"Thank you, Matt . . ."

"What *happened*?"

Studying the tops of my ankle boots, I shook my head, because I honestly didn't know.

Eighty-two

ꙮ

The police had an answer for what happened to me. They said I was "mugged."

A "snafu" by Salena Heath's people left the Vessel unguarded. Apparently, a VIP party had been scheduled to take place at the top of the sculpture. Salena had arranged for private security to clear the Vessel of tourists and keep the public out, which they did. But she abruptly dismissed them when the party was postponed, due to the approaching storm.

As the police saw it, when I foolishly went inside alone, I was "followed" and attacked "for my mobile phone."

Their narrative was completely logical and (in my opinion) completely wrong. I couldn't prove I'd gotten a text from Suzie Hastings. My phone was lost, knocked out of my hand, and snatched up by the assailant—which bolstered the "mugging" theory in the eyes of the uniformed officers who took my crime report.

As for Matt, he couldn't help, beyond what he'd already done, of course. When he heard my screaming, he came running, focused entirely on saving my neck. The assailant I'd glimpsed must have descended on a different staircase because Matt saw no one.

When the police were finally finished with all their questions, it was well after eleven, and I remembered Mike Quinn. I had little time left to get to a midnight date I *could not* miss.

As I dragged Matt toward the busy street in search of a cab, he loudly complained, "What's the rush, Clare? I just got done climbing a bajillion steps looking for you!"

I explained it to him.

A minute later, he practically threw himself in the path of an oncoming taxi. When the driver stopped, my ex shoved me into the back seat.

"Go straight to the Hastings. I'll catch another cab to the Blend. I have some overseas calls to make—"

"But the shop is closed by now. Do you have keys?"

"Yes, don't worry. I can take care of myself," Matt insisted. "You take care of Quinn."

"I can't believe this is happening," I moaned, close to tears. "I was going to put together a romantic picnic among the flowers with food and wine. Now there's no time."

"Quinn doesn't care about that. He only wants to see you. In the flesh, if you get my meaning."

"So *you* say. But Mike might not even show. Why should he? Just because I gave him some stupid ultimatum—"

"Quinn will be there. Or I don't know my apple-swiping, pension-padding flatfoots."

With that, Matt closed the door, and the driver sped off.

I arrived at the Hastings fifteen minutes later, relieved I was early enough to fix my face, at least. But when I got to the roof, I was shocked to discover the greenhouse was already glowing like a crystal palace.

I found an even bigger surprise inside.

Mike was there, waiting among the lavender blossoms, with a smile on his face and a dozen roses in hand. I spied a bottle of wine and two glasses on one of the greenhouse worktables. There might have been more, but I couldn't see it—my eyes were too blurred with tears.

"I guess these roses are pretty silly among all these beautiful blossoms. I never imagined a place like this could exist—"

Mike stopped talking when he saw my expression.

"Clare! What's wrong?"

I couldn't tell him. After all the awful events of these past few days, including the question of whether he would even be here, I was too choked up to speak.

It didn't matter. I didn't need words. A moment later, the roses were on the floor, and I was in Mike's arms.

Eighty-three

～∂✺∂✺∂✺∂✺∂✺∂✺∂✺∂✺∂✺∂✺∂✺∂✺∂✺∂✺✺～

Outside the greenhouse, the downpour finally came. Thunder rumbled and lightning flashed, but the deluge didn't touch us. In this idyllic glass house, we barely noticed the storm—for a little while, anyway.

Mike held me close. His body felt warm and strong. His cheeks were newly shaved, and his skin smelled faintly of a soapy shower, which meant he'd taken pains to clean up for our special meeting.

Me? I was a wreck. Thank goodness for the perfume of lavender blossoms around us because I was rank with sweat, while Quinn smelled fresher than the raindrops drumming against the greenhouse roof. He didn't seem to care, because when he kissed me, it felt as though he never wanted it to end.

When we finally did part, his eyes still looked bluer than an arctic lake, but there wasn't a trace of ice. The stone-cold cop had melted into a man in love. And, honestly, that was enough for me. A wedding didn't have to follow. All Mike had to do was admit that fact, and it would be done, over. Our plans to become husband and wife would simply end here. And that was okay, because our future as a couple would not, of that I was certain.

"So . . ." I began, hoping to make things easier for him. "You're here. And you still love me."

"Of course I love you, Clare."

"I can tell." I reached up and touched his lips. He kissed my fingers. "But, Mike, you have to be honest now. With me and yourself. Do you really believe you're ready for another marriage?"

Ever the reticent cop, he answered with four simple words.

"With *you*, I do."

I almost laughed. "Keep those last two words in mind. They'll come in handy if we ever get to the altar. But I'm not sure we should."

"Well, I am. I was sure the moment you walked into my office last night and slammed the door."

"Are you kidding?"

"I'm dead serious. There are seasoned detectives on my squad, men who'd dodged bullets and risked their lives undercover, who told me they were too afraid to do what you did yesterday."

"What? Stage an intervention?"

"Is that what you call it?"

"No. I call it shock couples therapy."

"Well, it worked."

"Worked how, exactly? I know we love each other. But for me to trust that you're ready for another marriage, I need to know more."

Mike paused to study my face. "How about a glass of wine first? You look like you can use it."

I wasn't going to argue, especially after what happened to me at the Vessel.

Mike steered me to the table, sat me on one of the stools, and uncorked the pinot noir. Then he brought out a treat that cost him a lot more than the wine—two magnificently overstuffed pastrami sandwiches from Katz's Deli on Houston.

The smoke-kissed meat was nestled between fresh-baked slices of rye with nothing more than a swipe of mustard and a pickle on the side—and that's all this famous New York sandwich ever needed.

"I feel better now," I said after my third bite. Sips of the fruity medium-bodied pinot complemented the sandwich perfectly, and I told him so.

"Wine pairings are a mystery to me," Mike confessed. "But I knew enough to ask the deli guy for a clue."

He smiled. "Anyway, Cosi, feel free to keep that mouth of yours busy chewing because last night you did most of the talking. Now it's my turn . . ."

EIGHTY-FOUR

~~~~~~

MIKE glanced down thoughtfully, as if he were a defense attorney preparing to address a jury. Finally, he looked up, gaze intense as he asked (in all seriousness)—

"Do you think there's such a thing as matrimonial PTSD?"

Mouth full, I answered with an all-too-knowing nod.

"Good," Mike said, "because post-traumatic stress is the closest comparison I can make to explain what was going on in my head. I was having—I don't know—flashbacks, I guess? To my first marriage."

Mike rubbed the back of his neck, as if he were experiencing that bad marriage tension all over again. "In Leila's eyes, I was a constant disappointment. I could never do anything right. And the *last* thing she wanted to hear about was my job."

Before I could say a word, Mike's hand went up.

"I *know* that's not you. And I know you're not Leila. But . . . over the past few weeks . . ." He shook his head. "I felt like I was failing at everything. And failing everyone. Disappointing *you* was the last straw."

"But that's not true!" This time I insisted on interrupting. "Yes, I was upset because I felt you drifting from me, and I didn't know how to reach you, but I was *never* disappointed in you, Mike."

"I know that now. When you had the guts to come to the squad room last night, and confront me like that . . ." He shook his head again, this time with a bemused smile. "That's something Leila never—*not in a million years*—would have dared to do. And the things you said. They never would have come out of my ex-wife's mouth."

He paused a moment. "After you left that interview room, I sat there for ten minutes, realizing that everything you said was true. I knew it. And more than that. You jolted me out of my fog. I went straight into the squad room and apologized to my detectives for acting like an ass for the last few days."

"Really?"

"Yes," Mike said. "And you know what they said to me? They all had the same advice. Do *not*, under any circumstances, screw things up with the Coffee Lady. But, honey, I'd already decided that."

He touched my cheek. "I would have called you last night, but I wanted to respect your wishes. Your written instructions stated that you wanted to see me here, tonight, at midnight. So, I waited until now to tell you what it is I want in my life."

"And what is that?" I whispered.

"I want a partner who'll talk sense into me when I need it. Someone who believes in me, and in what I do. Someone who has the nerve to dive into the dark chasm and drag me—kicking and screaming, if necessary—back up to the light. And that person is *you*, Clare . . . if you'll have me again. Because if you say yes, I know my life will be blessed."

By now, I had stopped eating because I couldn't swallow. Choked up with tears streaming down my cheeks, I couldn't speak, either.

All I could do was throw my arms around my fiancé's neck and shower him with kisses.

Eighty-Five

꩜꩜꩜꩜꩜꩜꩜꩜꩜꩜꩜꩜꩜꩜꩜꩜꩜꩜꩜꩜

If we could have, Mike and I would have stayed in that idyllic glass bubble forever. But all our storms had not yet passed.

When we finished reconciling, I pulled my arms from around his neck and told him I needed to talk. I wanted Mike to know everything that had happened to me over the last few days, including being body-slammed off the Vessel.

(I left out the part about my ex-husband saving me—we didn't need to go down the "Matt-as-hero" road again.) Fudging the details, I simply said I pulled myself up (with Wonder Woman strength, ha ha)—and that was the reason I looked a wreck and almost missed our date. I *did* inform him that Matt was the one who threw himself in front of a cab to get me here on time.

"He really does want us to be happy, Mike."

"If you say so," he replied tightly.

I wasn't going to argue, not tonight. And there were more important things to talk about, anyway.

"Sweetheart, let's get back to the fact that you were almost killed." Mike looked sick about it. "What was the PD response? Please tell me you reported the crime."

"Of course I did. Two uniformed officers came to the scene and concluded that I was 'mugged' for my phone."

"But you received a message, luring you in there."

"I did, and they took my statement. But Suzie's whereabouts remain a mystery. Her chef boyfriend claims she's in town and texted him four nights ago. But her tech boss, who is supposedly sleeping with Suzie on the side, claims she's on an 'off-the-grid' vacation at some exotic locale."

"What's your opinion? Do you think it really was Suzie who texted you?"

"I know the text came from her phone. I saw the number. But that doesn't prove a thing. Which means—yet again—I don't know if this girl is a criminal or a victim. Or both. Or neither. I've uncovered other suspicious things, too. But I have no evidence of anything."

"Forget the proof for now. In the morning, after you open the shop, go to Detective Novak. Tell him what happened at Hudson Yards, and what you know. He's familiar with the case. He'll listen."

"He didn't before."

"You made *me* listen, didn't you?" He smiled.

"That's true."

"So, give it a try. Sit down with him and lay out everything you learned and what you believe. Ask him to follow up with Lukas Wyatt. It's one thing for you, as a civilian, to question him. It's another if a detective starts pressuring him for answers on Susan's whereabouts. It's entirely possible the man does know where she is."

"Okay. I'll do it. And after that, I'll go to the hospital and check on Bea. Madame sat with her today, and we're hoping and praying she'll recover, though she may have permanent damage. We'll see . . ."

Just then, Mike's phone loudly vibrated.

"I have to answer, Clare. It might be about Franco."

I went cold when he mentioned the name of my favorite young sergeant, Mike's right-hand man, and the love of my daughter's life.

I knew Mike had been fighting Franco about going undercover. Now it sounded like something had gone wrong.

Mike stepped away before he answered—making sure I couldn't hear the conversation. He spoke for several minutes, then returned to me with determination in his step.

"Was that about Franco? Is Franco missing?"

"No word from him for twenty-six hours. But he's deep undercover, Clare; no need for alarm—not yet anyway."

"So, what was the call about?"

"A break in the case." Mike grinned, melting an ice age of worry off his face.

"The case of the homeless men?" I assumed.

When Mike nodded, I recalled the basic facts: How all the men had overdosed on the same synthetic opioid, XS12, which Mike's squad had worked so hard to take off the street. How they all had traces of tar oil on their shoes and similar food stains on their clothes.

"What's the break? Can you tell me?" (I was dying to know.)

"The body dumping in the Hole stopped," Mike explained. "But we continued to find homeless victims in the surrounding area. Then, last night, an off-duty paramedic, jogging after work, noticed two men dumping a body on Fountain Avenue in Brooklyn, just a ten-minute drive from the Hole. He took a phone photo of their van's license, and we lifted tire prints. Today our forensics people told us they matched the prints we got from the Hole."

"That's great. But what about the van?"

"That's why I've got to go," Mike said apologetically. "Two officers just spotted the vehicle on Linden Boulevard. Their patrol car was right behind it in a McDonald's drive-through. Two perps are being arrested as we speak."

"Wow. Done in by a Mac attack."

Mike's grin got even bigger, not that my joke was all that funny. But gallows humor was the way of his world, and my little quip reminded him I understood that—just another confirmation I was the right partner for him.

"So," I said, "I assume you have to leave this pretty place?"

Mike nodded. "When they bring them in, I've got to interrogate them."

"Go," I said. "We'll talk later."

"We'll do more than that." He brushed his lips across mine. "And you should stay. Finish your sandwich and wine. If this is a false lead, I'll be back in an hour."

Eighty-Six

~~~~~~

I sent Mike on his way with a loving look, doubting I would see him again tonight. But after my frantic day, I was relieved to have some quiet time, and reluctant to leave this jewel of tranquility.

Outside the storm had passed, and the moon made brief appearances between drifting clouds—a vista visible through the glass roof. A little while ago the lights dimmed, and the greenhouse echoed with the sound of a babbling brook—an audio illusion created by the irrigation system controlled by Todd Duncan's ingenious software design.

The bees in their hives, stimulated by the sound, hummed soothingly.

I found these magical surroundings far too pleasant to abandon just yet. I decided to relax at the table and give Mike his hour.

When I shrugged off my jacket, I felt something crinkle in the pocket and remembered the protest leaflet I'd picked up at the food festival. Now that I had some time on my hands, I took a look, starting with the screaming headline:

THE TERRIBLE TRUTH ABOUT URBANGRO

Packed with hyperbole, the leaflet mixed broad speculation with dire warnings of a future world *under the green thumb of corporate food giants who build farm towers when what cities really need is affordable housing.*

They also questioned UrbanGro's real estate activity.

Why have they leased a Hudson River dock? Are they planning to ship food? Make a profit on crops intended for the people of New York and paid for with tax breaks and subsidies?

The mention of the dock reminded me of Bea's telescope. She had locked it into place, pointing at a particular pier on the Hudson.

Was that pure coincidence? Or could she possibly be attempting to verify the charges being made by protestors—that UrbanGro was doing something shady with its warehouse-farmed food?

I went to the back of the greenhouse to investigate. The telescope was still locked in place, and I peered through the lens.

A barge was just docking at the brilliantly lit pier. I watched a man rope it off with the help of another hand on board. A moment later both vanished behind a warehouse that blocked some of the view.

I didn't know what was going to happen next. But, given the events of the past few days, I felt as though I should be taking pictures.

My mobile phone was gone. On the worktable beside the telescope, Bea had left a high-end video camera—most likely to film her flowers and bees and all the automated magic inside her greenhouse, because filming the activities on the pier would be impossible this far away.

The only other device nearby was the new laptop that Todd installed to replace the one hurled into the alley on the night we found Bea. It sat on the worktable, too, compiling away as one of the monitors to the network that ran this greenhouse, its screen displaying temperature, humidity levels, and a dozen other metrics automatically controlled by Todd's software.

I knew the next best thing to a photo would be another witness to the activity on the pier. So, I went to the greenhouse landline and phoned one.

"Matt, are you still at the Blend, making international calls?"

"Clare? What went wrong this time? Don't tell me. Let me guess. You and Quinn decided to start your romantic evening with Wolf Blitzer on CNN."

"No. But we may end up in one of his stories."

"What are you talking about?"

"Get over here, and I'll tell you."

Eighty-seven

～⌒⊙⌒⊙⌒⊙⌒⊙⌒⊙⌒⊙⌒⊙⌒⊙⌒⊙⌒⊙⌒⊙⌒⊙⌒⊙⌒⊙⌒⊙～

Matt was in a fine mood when he arrived. He discovered Quinn hadn't touched the other half of his pastrami on rye, and—after following me to the back of the greenhouse—he proceeded to dig in.

Meanwhile, I dragged a stool over to the telescope and kept watch.

The pier and the barge were still lighted, but there was no activity, and my patience was soon wearing thin.

"What's going on?" Matt asked.

"Nothing."

Matt puttered around Bea's worktable. He picked up one pair of binoculars, then the other.

"Are you bored?" I asked. "How about some karaoke? I can show you a killer rendition of 'Hooked on a Feeling.' Todd Duncan sang that song at a karaoke bar the other night—actually, it was the same night we found Bea on her balcony."

Matt looked skeptical. "Can he carry a tune?"

"It's cute. Let me borrow your phone and I'll show you."

"Shouldn't you be watching for UFOs?"

"Why don't you take over? Squinting gives me a headache."

Matt sat at the telescope and fiddled with the focus. "Fascinating view. Okay, I'm officially bored."

"Just a second . . ."

I went to Todd's Facebook page and expected to discover a treasure trove of funny karaoke bar videos from him. I didn't. Mostly, what I found were auto-posts about a video game called *Kick Squad*—

Todd Duncan is playing Kick Squad at home, or *Todd Duncan is playing Kick Squad at the office . . .*

I passed his "Hooked on a Feeling" karaoke performance and kept scrolling back through weeks and then months of posts. All were about *Kick Squad,* except two. One was a photo of Todd on Labor Day. The caption read, *Drunk as a skunk at the UrbanGro Labor Day party.* Todd wore an inebriated smile and was posing with Suzie Hastings and Nellie Atwood.

"I thought I was going to hear some karaoke," Matt said.

"This is strange."

"What is?"

"Todd's Facebook page. I can't find any other karaoke video posts. Only auto-updates on when and where Todd is playing his online game. Responses to his game updates are nonexistent, and so is his social life—except for an UrbanGro Labor Day party, which was held here, and the single karaoke bar outing on the night we found Bea."

"That's coincidental, isn't it?"

"Yes. And it *could* be a coincidence. Or . . ."

"Or what?"

I didn't like saying it, but: "If I were a suspicious type, I'd think Todd Duncan was setting up an alibi."

"Hold that thought, Clare." Matt was no longer bored. He was now intensely staring into the telescope. "A bunch of guys just showed up on the pier. Four, five . . . No, seven of them."

"Let me see."

A half dozen men in ragged clothes began to lower pallets of La Luna Farms produce with a mobile crane that had rolled into view. Matt and I soon came to the same conclusion.

These men weren't loading the barge; they were *unloading* it.

After the work was done, around two in the morning, the workers clustered together. First they ate food from plastic trays dished out by the supervisor. And when they were finished, that same man helped everybody light up—but it wasn't cigarettes, cigars, or even marijuana they were smoking. I knew because what I saw made my body go cold. Curling around these men was the distinctive blue smoke of the highly addictive street drug XS12.

That's when I told Matt about the case of the homeless OD victims that Quinn and his squad were working—

"The first victim had been a longshoreman. All of the dead men had tar oil on their shoes—just like the blacktop of this brightly lit pier. They also had traces of the same foods on their clothing, suggesting they shared a communal meal—which we just watched. Finally, all the victims were killed by XS12."

"You should call your boyfriend," Matt insisted.

"I can try, but I doubt I'll reach him. As we speak, Mike is trying to solve this case with a *real* lead, one with hard evidence attached to a Brooklyn crime scene, the borough where all the bodies were found. *This* is Manhattan. What we're seeing could be nothing more than a group of casual users on a dock. But I do think we should report this. I'm going to call 911—"

"No way." Matt grabbed back his phone. "If you call the police those men will scatter as soon as a patrol car pulls up. And what do we tell the police? Well, officer, we were too far away to make out any faces, but we're pretty sure they were smoking XS12."

"You're right," I said. "That would be no help at all."

"Put in a call to your flatfoot. Who knows? Quinn might *not* have a real lead. He could be staring at another dead end."

More likely he was in a cramped, airless interrogation room staring down a perp, I thought. But when Matt handed me his phone again, I punched in Quinn's number—and immediately got voice mail. I left him a message explaining what I'd seen and asked him to call as soon as he could.

Fifteen minutes later, Matt and I were still waiting for Quinn's call.

Restlessly, Matt peered through the telescope. "The action down on that pier is going to be over soon."

"What can we do?"

"We need evidence, Clare, a photo or video. Close ups of faces. Then we can hand your boyfriend the mug shots he needs to detain and question those men."

"We're too far away for that kind of close-up photography. We don't have the equipment."

"So, I'll go down there," Matt said. "I'll record them with my phone camera."

"I don't like it. It's too dangerous."

Matt waved me off. "The only danger from those guys on the pier is that they see me and scatter—or try to chase me off. But they won't even do that because they won't know they're being photographed. If you're worried you can watch through the telescope. Anything goes wrong, you can call in the cops with the greenhouse landline."

"No, Matt. There's no reason to take the risk. Tomorrow I'll tell Mike what we saw. He'll believe me. And if he thinks it's warranted, he can set up surveillance and a sting."

"Okay, fine . . ." Matt shrugged, about to accept my decision. Then he spotted Bea's video camera on the worktable.

"Wait, what about this?" He picked it up and tested it. "The zoom works, but it's not strong enough to get close-ups from here. Maybe Bea kept more powerful lenses in the worktable drawer . . ."

"What worktable drawer?"

Matt opened a drawer I hadn't noticed before. It was set inches back from the edge of the table—making it nearly impossible to spot.

"How did you know about that hidden drawer?"

"I have a table like this at my warehouse," he said. "If we're lucky it's unlocked."

We were lucky. The drawer opened easily, though Matt didn't find any video camera lenses. What he did find was something Bea apparently wanted to keep out of sight. In addition to pens, a digital clock (still running), and a pair of Bea's reading glasses, Matt pulled out a ledger.

"Let me see that . . ."

Only the first four pages of the ledger had entries—handwritten arrival dates of barges (with their serial numbers) and a notation about their cargo—things like Vidalia onions, blueberries, sugar snap peas, and lettuce. Each page represented a month, starting four months ago. Each shipment occurred between a week and ten days apart.

If I had any doubts about what I was reading, the top of each page dispelled them. Written in Bea's flowing cursive were four words:

Produce Shipments to UrbanGro

Eighty-Eight

ᘓᘓᘓᘓᘓᘓᘓᘓᘓᘓᘓᘓᘓᘓᘓᘓᘓᘓᘓᘓᘓ

"**WHY** would UrbanGro ship produce *into* New York?" Matt scratched his beard. "Isn't the purpose of urban farming to grow food locally, so you *don't* have to ship it?"

"I have a one-word answer to that paradox, and I don't like it."

"What's the word?"

"Fraud."

Matt blinked. "You think Lukas Wyatt is *pretending* to grow food?"

"I can't see many other explanations, can you? Before Suzie's text lured me into the Vessel, I had a talk with your friend Nellie Atwood. She said she hired a private investigator because someone anonymously told her to stop asking questions about UrbanGro."

"She was threatened?"

"Sounds like it. Nellie said her investors are wary. And Lukas Wyatt has been evading her questions about plans for expansion and profitability. Something's gone very wrong at UrbanGro."

"You believe they can't make it work, so they're secretly shipping food in to keep up appearances?"

"That's what it looks like. Listen, Bea Hastings is an investor in the company. And her ledger shows she's been gathering evidence against it, proving they've been shipping food *in* to the city and not out. Most likely, the same food they've been distributing as donations to food pantries and homeless shelters as a publicity ploy. Just like your wall-crawler reward. That was for publicity. Media exposure. Nellie confirmed it. She said Suzie came up with the idea for food donations—an idea that also conveniently shows the public *and* investors that the UrbanGro start-up is working."

Matt shook his head. "If you're right, this is a devastating scam to un-cover. Lukas Wyatt and Suzie Hastings would be shamelessly promoting a fake narrative."

"A good way to continue getting private investment and public money, isn't it? Nellie said the start-up funds were evaporating fast. Wyatt must be desperate."

"Too bad," Matt said. "He seemed like such a nice guy."

"Maybe he is. Maybe he tells himself he's simply buying time until he can fix whatever problems his urban farm is having."

"It's still fraud. And what about Nellie?" Matt said as a wayward bee buzzed by. "If what you're saying is true, the Queen of Start-ups could really get stung."

"Forget stung. Nellie could end up dead. She was already threatened. Look what happened to Bea." I pointed to the ledger. "She was doing more than asking questions. She was gathering evidence against Urban-Gro. It seems to me, someone found out what Bea was doing and tried to end her investigation—permanently."

"Which someone? Suzie?"

"I know your mother thinks Suzie would never harm Bea, but Lukas Wyatt had every reason to . . ." I told Matt what I'd learned from Nellie about his biological parents. "They killed themselves after their little florist business was ruined by Bea's expanding chain of Hastings shops."

"I buy your theory," Matt said, "but it's still all speculation."

"What's happening down there, *right now*, on that pier isn't. That's a fact. Something I can tell Mike about tomorrow."

"I think you're wrong to wait, Clare." He pointed to the ledger. "Ac-cording to Bea's own observations, there won't be another shipment for at least a week. Seven days before Mike's squad could even set up surveil-lance or a sting. From what we've seen down there, those workers are being given narcotics as a form of payment—or bribery to keep their mouths shut. If we don't act now, how many XS addicts will die in the meantime?"

I closed my eyes, considering the stakes, and decided Matt was right. The ledger itself wasn't evidence of wrongdoing. And the drug users at the pier could easily scatter if police moved in. I hated to admit it, but the best option we had was Matt's.

"Are you *sure* you can get pictures without being seen?"

Ever ready for an adrenaline rush, Matt grinned. "Piece of cake."

"Okay," I said, "but I'm going with you."

"Fine, come along." He picked up the video camera. "But nothing will go wrong. Trust me."

Eighty-nine

❧❧❧❧❧❧❧❧❧❧❧❧❧❧❧❧❧❧❧❧❧❧❧❧

Matt and I hit the street and headed west, toward the Hudson River.

There wasn't much foot traffic in Chelsea in the wee hours of the morning. Only the occasional dog walker mingled with barhopping college kids. And the farther west we walked, the more desolate the area became. Tall warehouses looming on either side made the narrow street seem claustrophobic. Traffic noise receded and walking became difficult as barriers directed us around great steam-belching pits in the roadway.

Beyond Eleventh, the asphalt was replaced by a narrow lane of ancient cobblestones that led to Twelfth Avenue and the river.

Soon the pier we'd watched through the telescope was in plain sight. We were a hundred feet away and could see the men working, but a tall chain-link fence and a stretch of empty concrete prevented us from getting closer. We crouched among some brush that grew around the fence and argued our next move.

"I have to get closer," Matt said. "I can't get sharp enough video from here."

"Are you kidding?"

Matt peered through the lens again. "This zoom is crap. Everything looks tiny or blurry. Sorry. There's no getting mug shots from this spot."

"What are you going to do?"

Matt curled his fingers through the chain links. "I'll hop this fence."

"Hop? It's eight feet high!"

I pointed to a section of the fence farther along the bike path. "What about those gates? You could drive a truck through there."

"Which is probably how they move the produce from the pier to UrbanGro. But those gates are locked. I can see the padlock from here."

Matt tucked the camera into his jacket. Then he pointed to a small structure on the other end of the stretch of concrete—

"See that shed?"

The building was the size of a van, fifty feet away, and for all I knew it was occupied. Matt dismissed my fears with a wave of his hand.

"I have my mobile phone. If I run into trouble, I'll speed dial 911. One tap and the cops will be on their way."

I didn't like it. Matt was about to depart with the only phone we had. If something went wrong, what could I do?

"Stop looking so worried," Matt teased. "I'll climb over the fence, run to the shed, and film. You keep out of sight until I'm back."

Before I could talk him out of it, Matt was climbing. When he landed on the other side he flashed me a thumbs-up, then took off running.

I held my breath until Matt reached that shed. His break-in plan worked; nobody spotted him. At least, that's what I thought—and he did, too. But just as my grinning ex flashed me a second thumbs-up, two men emerged from either side of the van-sized building.

Matt saw them coming—right for him—and ducked a punch. Going into a crouch, he tried pulling out his phone, but one of the men immediately kicked it out of his hand.

There would be no police to save us now.

In desperation, I tried to distract Matt's assailants, give him a chance to break free.

"THIS IS THE POLICE!" I bellowed as loudly and sternly as a street cop would. "FREEZE!"

They did. Even Matt stopped struggling and looked my way.

Unfortunately, so did a silent lookout somewhere behind me. Something struck my back, I fell to the ground, and a mocking voice laughed in my ear.

"Good night, Officer."

Then everything went dark.

Ninety

〰〰〰〰〰〰〰〰〰〰〰〰〰〰〰〰

I opened my eyes to the glare of a naked bulb dangling from a wire. My nose was immediately assaulted by the stink of old oil, burnt rubber, and other things I chose not to contemplate because a wave of gut-clutching nausea hit me like a hammer.

I rolled over—and fell off a narrow cot. I landed hard because my hands had been tied behind me. The memories of my capture came flooding back. Fighting panic, I scanned the shadowy space, hoping for some way out. But I couldn't even see a window—only a garage door–sized opening that had been boarded up.

Where's Matt?

A few feet away another cot lay on its side, facing the wall. I spied a third cot and felt a rush of relief. Matt was there—unconscious—and like me his hands and feet were tied. He was also lashed to the cot by coils of thick rope. I tried to call out to him, but my words morphed into a gagging cough.

"Are you a cop or a fed?"

The deep voice startled me. Someone was tied to the knocked-over cot. I couldn't see who.

"What?" I choked out. My tongue felt like it was wrapped in gauze. "What happened to me?"

"You got Tasered. Then they used ether on you to keep you knocked out," the deep voice informed me. "Are you NYPD? DEA?"

Oh, my gosh, I know this voice. "Franco!" I cried.

"No, I'm Franco."

"It's me! Clare! Joy's mother! Your Coffee Lady!"

"What the—" It was Sergeant Franco's turn to freak out. "What are *you* doing mixed up in this?!"

"It's a long story. And I'm not alone."

"You're with Lieutenant Quinn? That makes sense. The punks who brought you here were bragging about how the big cop put up a fight. It took two of them to beat him down."

"The big cop wasn't a cop. It was Joy's father."

"Allegro?"

"What?" Matt bellowed in response. My ex was suddenly awake and struggling against his bonds as if they were living opponents.

"Matt! Are you okay?"

"Clare? They got you, too? I told you to stay out of sight!"

"I did. They found me anyway."

"Where are the cops when you need them?" Matt groused.

"You got one right here."

"Franco?" Now Matt was groaning. "And I'll bet you're tied to a cot."

"No comment."

Matt cursed—in four different languages. "Isn't this just too perfect?"

"I'm not tied to a cot," I informed them. "I fell off it."

"That's good news, Coffee Lady. Now you can slither over here and untie me. If you can get me off this cot, I'll get my hands free."

Matt's laugh was bitter. "Then what, flatfoot? We're still locked in here. And where is here, anyway? I don't suppose *you* know?"

"It's an auto repair joint, maybe an old chop shop. But I was out when they brought me here, same as you." Franco coughed. "And I haven't seen anything but this wall since a jackass kicked my cot over."

"When was that?" I asked.

"I don't know. What day is it?"

Lying on my back, I searched for some clue that revealed where we were. Finally, I spotted an official notice.

DAN'S ALL-NITE IS A
REGISTERED AUTO REPAIR SHOP
IN THE STATE OF NEW YORK

Now, where did I see that sign before?

My still-fuzzy mind reached back, to the night Mike Quinn took me to a crime scene with a dumped body, near an old, abandoned garage.

"We're in the Hole!"

"Yeah," Matt said. "It's a deep one, too. And I don't know how the devil we're going to dig ourselves out."

Ninety-One

~~~~~~

I struggled for many minutes, inching across the floor, to reach Franco. Then I angled myself so I could work the knot that held him captive—and loosening a knot while your own hands are tied behind you is a frustrating job.

"What are they going to do with us, Franco?"

"They think you're law enforcement, so they'll probably work you over for information. The big boss wants to know what we know."

"Who's the big boss?"

"I don't know. I got made before I could find out."

"What *did* you find out?"

"I found the lab where they're cooking up brand-new batches of XS12. And the old street gang's got new corporate backing now. Some company sprang the guy out of prison who knew the formula. They called it job training, only his job consists of cooking up the same poison at a warehouse near the river on the West Side."

"A warehouse?"

"I don't know the address of the place. I was transported from Brooklyn in the back of a windowless van. They took me to a huge produce warehouse, where they told me to stand as a lookout. Pallets of vegetables were everywhere, and some homeless guys were unloading truckloads of La Luna Farms lettuce. I was snooping around, taking photos, and trying to learn more when they caught me. I never did figure out where I was."

"UrbanGro One. I'm certain of it."

I told Franco about the activities we witnessed on the pier: the secret food shipments and the addicts being used for manual labor. "I think the pier is where those dumped bodies are coming from."

"Makes sense," Franco agreed. "Plenty of junkies will work for three squares a day, a place to crash, and as much XS12 as they can inhale."

Abruptly, the rope slipped through my fingers as the knot came undone. Franco untangled himself, curled his legs under him, and slipped his bound arms under his feet.

"Where's the door?" I asked.

"When they leave I hear hammering. I think we're boarded up in here."

"Untie me and I'll *kick* that damn barrier down," proclaimed a spitting-mad Matt Allegro.

With his hands in front of him again, the sergeant found the sharp edge of a broken shelf and began to saw at the ropes on his wrist.

Meanwhile, Matt raged. "Look who's out of bed! Tell me, Franco. What kind of cop needs a coffee roaster to rescue him? A cop who's as dumb as a rock, that's who. You're lucky we showed up, you bald numbskull. Hey, maybe we should use your head as a battering ram to get us out of here."

Franco laughed. "That's funny."

"I'll tell you what isn't funny. If you die on this job and break my daughter's heart, I'll kill you!"

"I'll remember," Franco said, still sawing.

With a tearing sound, the ropes on Franco's wrists finally separated. He immediately untied me. Then Franco took my bloody and broken-nailed hands in his. "You okay, Coffee Lady?"

Absurdly, I channeled Madame. "Nothing a manicure wouldn't fix."

"Hey!" Matt bellowed. "Aren't you forgetting someone?"

"I'd like to," muttered Franco.

"I heard that!" roared Matt.

Dizzy and unsteady, I carefully stood. Every sudden move caused a wave of nausea to wash over me, but I doggedly put one foot in front of the other until I reached the boarded-up garage door.

"Wow," I heard Franco exclaim. "They sure hog-tied you, Allegro. No wonder they had no rope left for Clare."

Not even an enraged Matteo Allegro could possibly knock this barrier down. I couldn't even find a crack between the boards. I did find a knot at about eye level and poked it with my sore thumb. It moved, just a little.

I poked it again, then again. Despite my aching fingers I kept it up until the knot fell to the ground on the other side of the wall. Fresh, clean air streamed through an opening about the size of a baseball.

I took a deep, luxurious breath.

From what I could see, the area was deserted. Any cry for help would go unheard by human ears.

But what about *nonhuman* ears?

I put my mouth to the hole and called out in my best high-pitched cat-whisperer voice. "Missy! Missy! Here, Missy, Missy, Missy!"

The men stopped bickering.

"Who's Missy?" Matt asked.

"The ether hasn't worn off, that's all," Franco replied.

I called again, louder, "Missy! Missy girl! Come on, Missy!"

"It's PTSD or something," Franco continued. "The Coffee Lady's obviously lost it."

"Missy! Come here, Missy!"

Matt groaned. "If she keeps this up she's going to end up in a psychiatric clinic—again."

"Got it!" Franco cried, pulling the ropes off Matt.

"Keep quiet," I commanded the men. "I think it's working."

Matt rolled his eyes. "What's working? Certainly not your brain."

"Shh!"

Soon even Matt and Franco could hear the sound of hooves as they thundered closer and closer.

"Is that what I think it is?" Franco asked.

Peeking through the knothole, I informed my fellow inmates—

"The cavalry has arrived."

Ninety-two

⊶⊷⊶⊷⊶⊷⊶⊷⊶⊷⊶⊷⊶⊷⊶⊷⊶⊷⊶⊷⊶⊷⊶⊷⊶⊷⊶⊷⊶⊷

"Is someone there?" Wild Bill Moxley called.

"Help!" I put my mouth to the knothole. "It's me, Clare Cosi! Three of us are trapped in here. Would you call the fire department to free us?"

I heard Missy snort. Then the horse slammed against the wooden barrier so hard the vibration smacked me in the nose.

"I don't think Missy has the patience to wait, Ms. Cosi," said our urban cowboy savior. "You better stand back. She's rearing!"

A moment later the barrier was shaken again as the horse slammed her front hooves against the stout planks. Another slam and splinters were falling away. Finally, Missy smashed right through the barrier and the whole thing came tumbling down.

The fresh air felt like a spring shower as it washed over me. My head began to clear as breathable air dispelled the last of my brain fog.

I cried with joy. "Wild Bill Moxley, you saved the day!"

"Hey, there, Wild Bill. You got a phone?" Franco asked.

Moxley tossed Franco his smartphone. Inside of a minute the sergeant's call was patched through to Mike Quinn.

"Because of Clare's help, we can wrap up this case tonight," Franco told his boss. "Yeah, *your* Clare. She's here with me now . . . Relax, she's fine . . . Listen, Mike, I know where the XS12 lab is. We can get a warrant and move on the place within the hour."

Moxley watched everything from the back of his horse. Missy nudged me with her snout until Will Bill tossed me a carrot. I presented it to the heroic horse, and she gobbled it up.

I heard sirens. Missy snorted and backed away. Seconds later, two NYPD patrol cars and an EMS ambulance rolled into the cul-de-sac.

Franco thanked Moxley, then faced me.

"I've got to go, Coffee Lady," He jumped into the police car. "The EMS is here to check you out. Mike said he'll find you later to get your statement—among *other* things."

Franco winked and the patrol car raced away, siren blaring.

Moxley calmed Missy, who was clearly annoyed by the noise and activity. I patted her snout again. Meanwhile, the EMS team worked on Matt's cuts and bruises.

"If you don't mind, Mr. Moxley, I'd like to borrow your phone. I'll make sure you get it back tomorrow."

Moxley smiled as he tossed the device my way. "Keep it. It's a prepaid job. I can always buy another."

He tugged Missy's reins. As she swung around to leave, Moxley tipped his hat. And once again, the Last Cowboy in the Hole vanished into the night.

Ninety-three

꩜꩜꩜꩜꩜꩜꩜꩜꩜꩜꩜꩜꩜꩜꩜꩜꩜꩜꩜꩜

Not long after the sound of Missy's hoofbeats faded, the EMS team declared us fit. A lone uniformed officer drove Matt and me back to the Village Blend.

We were both too keyed up to go to bed. I decided to stay up and wait for Quinn. Matt insisted on waiting with me. So I pressed a pot of our special honey-processed beans (we earned it) while Matt started a fire in the hearth to dispel the chill.

I found four Honey Cupcakes, two Apple Pie Scones, and a few saved squares of our Honey Apple Cake in the refrigerator, and we ate like starving pigeons.

"Well," I said after a long silence. "I guess I helped solve Mike's case, but I still don't have any evidence on who assaulted Bea Hastings and made it look like a suicide."

Matt shrugged. "I'm ready to throw in the towel. Lukas Wyatt? Suzie Hastings? Her chef boyfriend? Or even that Karaoke Kid you mentioned? I don't know, Clare—"

"My gosh, I almost forgot!"

"What?"

"Something I found out before we attempted your brilliant plan to take mug shots."

I reminded Matt about Todd Duncan's nonexistent social life—no dinners or nights out with friends, just that Labor Day party thrown for UrbanGro and a single karaoke bar performance on the night Bea was attacked.

To prove my point, I called up Todd's Facebook page. Sure enough, an hour-old post informed me Todd was playing *Kick Squad* in the office all night.

"Don't you see, Matt? It's like Todd worked very hard to establish an alibi that night. One that Detective Novak completely bought."

"So, you actually suspect the Karaoke Kid? I don't get it. What would he gain?"

"Hear me out. We believe UrbanGro has a problem. And if it's true that UrbanGro One doesn't work, the company would need a solution—and fast. What if the solution was in Todd Duncan's software design? Suzie knew all about Todd's ingenious work. What if she and Todd confronted Bea that night?"

"About what?"

"Sharing Todd's software design with UrbanGro, maybe with a payoff to Todd. What if Bea objected? An argument leads to an accident. Suzie sees herself inheriting a fortune and solving Lukas Wyatt's problems. Todd sees himself gaining monetarily.

"To cover it up Todd erases all the surveillance camera footage. Then he and Suzie deactivate the greenhouse and wreck the hives to deflect from the real motive. And Suzie pretends to leave town—maybe because she doesn't trust herself to lie to the police."

"What about Todd's alibi?"

"I'm sure any young man smart enough to create this automated greenhouse could hack social media geotags and create a convincing evening out with posts that appeared to verify it."

"What about the Vessel?" Matt asked.

"I think that really was Suzie. Todd could have informed her how doggedly I've been trying to prove that Bea's 'suicide' was a setup. And she decided to kill my investigation—by killing me."

Matt groaned. "Which means this whole time we were desperately seeking an attempted murderer?"

I glanced at the phone screen still in my hand and my heart stilled.

"Or maybe an actual murderer. Look what just went viral."

I displayed Todd's Facebook page. In bold white letters on a black background, it read:

I tried to kill Bea Hastings and I can no longer live with the guilt. The criminal justice system can't punish me more than I've punished myself. The penalty for what I have done is death.

"I don't believe it! It's another setup," I said. "Just like Bea's phony suicide note."

"Let's go!" Matt cried.

We got lucky and caught a cab. Less than ten minutes later, Matt and I burst into Todd's office, where we found him slumped over a desk, a game controller clutched in his cold hands.

All the screens were operational. Most displayed surveillance footage— of the lobby, the sidewalk, the exterior of the greenhouse. But the largest screen was alive with *Kick Squad* action.

I wasn't so sure about Todd.

"He's still breathing," Matt said. "But barely."

When he sat the youth up, something tumbled to the floor. A hypodermic needle. There were two glass vials in Todd's lap. One was empty, the other half filled with a blue liquid.

Matt blanched. "That looks like XS12."

A rubber cord was wrapped around Todd's upper arm. Matt loosened it. Then he grabbed the phone off the cluttered desk and dialed 911.

While Matt was giving details to the emergency operator, I noticed a flicker on one of the display screens. Then words appeared on a black background.

ROOF CAMERA CONTENT SUCCESSFULLY DELETED

Seconds later the same thing happened to another screen.

ELEVATOR CAMERA CONTENT SUCCESSFULLY DELETED

I faced Matt, who was still dealing with the emergency operator.

"I think Suzie is upstairs. She's using the greenhouse computer to delete all the surveillance footage, just like the last time."

Matt nodded distractedly.

"I'm going up to stop her!" I cried.

As I ran to the elevator, Matt called for me to wait. But time was running out. Suzie had to be stopped before she completely destroyed the greenhouse—and the evidence of her crimes.

Ninety-Four

⟨≈⟩⟨≈⟩⟨≈⟩⟨≈⟩⟨≈⟩⟨≈⟩⟨≈⟩⟨≈⟩⟨≈⟩⟨≈⟩⟨≈⟩⟨≈⟩⟨≈⟩⟨≈⟩⟨≈⟩

THE roof lights had been extinguished and the greenhouse itself was a hulking black shadow framed by half-lit skyscrapers. Down on the street, sirens approached. In less than a minute the police and EMS would arrive.

Inside the greenhouse, I tried the light switch, but only the emergency lights were working. The rows of flowers and the mobile shelves brimming with plants were lost in shadows. The irrigation system was silent, and the bees ceased their contented humming. I felt a rush of relief to see the hives were untouched.

I padded all the way across the greenhouse as quietly as I could. As I approached the worktable near the telescope, I saw a slender blond woman bent over the laptop computer, her back to me.

"Suzie!" I cried. "It's over, Suzie—"

The woman turned just as I reached her. And I stopped dead.

I don't know what surprised me more. Nellie Atwood's smug face. Or the shiny gun in her hand.

"You again?" Nellie snapped. "You've really worn out your welcome, Ms. Cosi."

She was so sure of herself, so cool about her crimes that she held the weapon with her elbow crooked, as if she was lazing in the Hamptons propping up a gin martini. The other hand was poised over the keyboard, but she stopped typing the moment she spied me.

I would have smacked myself for being so wrong, but I didn't want to make any sudden moves while I faced a gun-wielding assassin.

Instead, I spoke, almost conversationally.

"I guess I *should* have known. That talk about the *wisdom of the bee* and bringing home the honey. You really wanted to be crowned queen bee of UrbanGro, didn't you?"

Nellie sighed. "Someone had to take charge. One strong leader was required, so I stepped up. I'd already been fixing Lukas Wyatt's mistakes for six months. There was no one better for the position."

"By fix, you mean the secret food shipments?"

Nellie smirked. "Among other things. I solved our manual labor problem through our homeless outreach. It's only fitting that we get *something* in return for all that donated food. A simple XS12 lab was all we needed to get a street gang watching our back. I even solved UrbanGro's technology problem."

"You mean acquiring Todd's software? What did you do? Buy off the poor kid and then turn on him?"

"Nothing so elaborate," she sniffed. "I simply stole the boy's software while he was passed out drunk at Suzie's Labor Day party. I took the little micro storage drive off his silly necklace, copied the program, and returned it to his pudgy body before he even woke up."

"How did you know about his software?"

"Suzie told me. She's a real asset, that girl. She told me lots of things. About her aunt's greenhouse and how it worked, about Todd's brilliant programming and software design, about that psycho chef boyfriend she can't seem to detach herself from."

"You mean she isn't in love with Lukas Wyatt?"

Nellie scoffed. "I wish. That would make things so much easier. Maybe once Tyler is six feet under, she'll give Lukas a chance."

"Then you—don't tell me *you* tried to kill Tyler LaFontaine."

"Of course I did. Well, not me exactly. I paid one of the gang members to do it. That worthless heap of nothing is why Suzie had to 'decompress' with an off-line vacation. I'm the one who convinced her to go and get her head clear of that jerk. Like drug rehab. I told her I would take care of things while she was gone. I even convinced Suzie to leave her phone with me, made her believe she would find no peace or serenity if she were bothered by Tyler's calls—or her own pathetic need to call him."

"You certainly put her phone to good use. A fake text to lure me up the Vessel, another to distract Tyler long enough for him to be ambushed."

"Yes, too bad the job wasn't complete on that stupid boy. But there's always another day—and another mugging."

It dawned on me while Nellie spoke that she wasn't aware that Matt was in the building. Nor did she notice the sirens in a city where there are always sirens—two strategic errors.

If I stalled for time, I had a chance of getting out of this mess alive.

"I erased all the evidence I was here, Ms. Cosi. What the police will find is Bea's attacker—dead, of course, but with a tidy social media confession to tie things up. Busy detectives like to close cases fast. And I've given them all they need to shut their book on Todd. Once I pay a visit to poor Bea in the hospital, her case will be closed, too."

"So, you fed me a load of baloney at the food festival."

"That's right. My clever little package of lies threw the scent off me and had *you* running to meet 'Suzie' at the top of the Vessel. I still don't know how you survived it, and I don't care. But you're not going to survive this."

Nellie lowered her arm until the gun was aimed at my heart.

With a backward thrust of her booted foot, she knocked the rear door open. Cold air rushed into the warm greenhouse. The wind immediately caught the door and it banged against the wall. Glass shattered and splinters tinkled far below.

"Out you go, Ms. Cosi," she said, waving the gun. "Jump, or I'll shoot you and throw you out. Either way, I'll make it appear that you're just another victim of 'crazy' Todd Duncan."

I remained frozen in place.

"Move," Nellie commanded. Then she smiled. "Who knows? You might get lucky and land on Bea's balcony."

I shook my head. "You'll have to shoot me, Nellie!" I said it loud enough for Matt to hear—if he were *anywhere* in the vicinity.

"Very well," Nellie said with a smirk.

At that moment, Matt's shout filled the greenhouse. "It's over, Nellie! The police are downstairs. Drop the—"

Nellie turned and fired in the direction of Matt's voice. That gave me the opening I needed to lunge at her. Seizing her arm, I struggled for the gun. She held on, and we became locked in a tug-of-war embrace.

Nellie was surprisingly strong, but I was angry, madder than I'd ever been.

"Let go!" I shouted.

"You let go, you stupid bit—"

I kicked Nellie's shin with the toe of my half boot. Her pained howl gave me a measure of satisfaction. Then she pulled away with such force that I couldn't hold her. As her gun bounced to the floor, Nellie's own momentum carried her through the door and right over the side of the building.

I met her horrified eyes just before she vanished from sight.

A short scream ended with a thump.

I jumped, startled, when my ex appeared by my side.

"God, Matt, I thought she shot you!"

"Not even close," he said. "Are you okay?"

I nodded. "I'm not so sure about Nellie, though."

Matt moved to the ledge and peered over it.

"Looks like she landed on Bea's balcony."

"Oh, no," I said.

"Oh, yeah," he replied.

Then the coffee hunter with the wild-man beard found more rope, wrapped it around his body, and dropped off the end of the building. Before he walked himself down the wall, I swore he winked at me and said—

"Here we go again!"

Epilogue

They whom truth and wisdom lead, can gather honey from a weed.

—WILLIAM COWPER

"THERE'S an awful lot of fear in the world," Esther proclaimed a few weeks later, at the start of her first annual Face Your Fears Poetry Slam. "But I'm excited to see so many of you are willing to express those fears and strive to overcome them."

The event was originally scheduled to take place in our second-floor lounge, but Esther sold so many advance tickets the entire Village Blend was filled to capacity. Even perennial pessimist Esther seemed pleased as she looked over the packed house.

Madame sat at a table with Dennis Murphy, who'd arrived with a bright twinkle in his eye for my mentor—and dozens of fresh pizzas, which he dished out by the slice for the price of a five-dollar donation to Esther's group.

Despite the pride Madame felt at receiving the Golden Demitasse the week before—not to mention the shower of sweetness heaped on her at her official honey roast by all of us who loved her—I'm convinced my employer had a lot more fun at Esther's event.

Italian pies and coffeehouse sweets flowed freely, along with Village Blend drinks and the spoken word.

One young woman rapped about her dread of losing Wi-Fi. She titled her piece "Severed" and began by bravely turning off her phone in front of everyone.

"Ant Hills and Sleeping Pills" was a slam about the fear of creepy-crawlies—including those found in most older New York City apartment buildings.

"Reflect Shun" was a powerful piece of performance art about a woman who feared the perceived imperfections she saw in the mirror.

People rapped about Facebook snubs and Tinder dates and riding the subway at night. Many were slyly satirical and most ended on an upbeat note of "fear conquered" or at least kept at bay.

Mike Quinn and I didn't rap. But we shared plenty of amused (and knowing) glances when performers brought up the fears we must conquer when they threaten to damage relationships.

And then Matteo Allegro walked onstage.

My barista staff was as stunned as I was to see Matt approach the microphone. My ex had never rapped before. He only ever waxed poetic over shade-grown arabica or heirloom cultivars harvested from ancient volcanic soil.

"I think Esther Best is owed a round of applause," he began. "She has successfully conquered her personal fear of bees, and I hope I can put her biggest fear to rest this evening."

Matt then presented a flabbergasted Esther with his ten-thousand-dollar UrbanGro "wall-crawler" reward check to fund her poetry program.

It was a check Matt clawed out of Lukas Wyatt before the CEO was arrested on a host of charges—all of which he would likely beat with a good lawyer. In the end, Nellie was the queen bee of the illicit operations inside UrbanGro. It was poor, naive, idealistic Lukas who was left completely out of the operations loop.

His only claim to CEO status, according to Nellie's own hospital-room confession to detectives, was *"buggy software and the ability to look like a young Abe Lincoln to sell the project nationwide."*

TODD Duncan didn't regain consciousness until the day after his assault. Before anyone was allowed to see him, Detective Novak took his statement.

After the detective's interview, Nancy Kelly and I visited Todd in the ICU. Hooked not on a feeling but to a heart monitor, he looked pale, but his spirit was strong, and he gamely offered us a wan smile. He also told us what he remembered about that night.

"Suzie texted me that she was home, the doorman was on his meal break, she said, and could I buzz her in? I did, and then forgot all about it. Detective Novak told me I should have checked the lobby camera because it was really Nellie Atwood who I'd admitted. I was playing the game when I got grabbed from behind and something covered my face. The next thing I knew I was here."

Novak told Todd he'd been set up by Nellie twice—the night she tried to kill him, and the night Nellie tried to kill Bea.

I had convinced myself that the karaoke night was an alibi set up by Todd. But it turned out that Todd had a habit of playing video games on his office supercomputer well into the night. For Nellie to catch Bea alone, she had to get Todd out of the way.

To that end, Nellie created a phony *Kick Squad* Karaoke Sweepstakes, then notified Todd and his online gaming buddies they had "won." The prize came with an open bar and free food, so of course Todd showed up in his best tiki shirt—the one he was wearing the night I met him inside this very ICU.

When I left Todd, Nancy stayed behind. And, like the bees, she visited him every day, feeding him sweet words to keep his spirits up until his release. To no one's surprise, she continued to remain friends with Todd long after he'd made a full recovery.

THE day after Todd's assault, Suzie Hastings stepped off a direct flight from Nepal to JFK, wondering why the car Nellie Atwood promised would meet her was a no-show—the first of many unhappy surprises that awaited young Suzie.

Returning from her off-the-grid vacation, she had no phone to order a car and was forced to wait in a long taxi line. When Suzie finally arrived at the Hastings, she was greeted by members of the Crime Scene Unit gathering evidence inside the duplex she shared with her aunt.

During her interrogation, Detective Novak informed Suzie about her aunt's condition—a shock that no doubt destroyed any mind/body serenity she achieved on her spiritual journey.

But at least Suzie was home now, and she was by her aunt's side when Beatrice Hastings, at long last, awoke from her coma.

Novak immediately took Bea's statement. Though her memory about the events of the night in question was wiped out, Bea remembered her logbook and the food that went into UrbanGro One in La Luna boxes and left bearing the UrbanGro logo.

Nellie Atwood's own hospital-room confession revealed the rest. It was Nellie who arranged the private meeting that night with Bea *"to review all the evidence"* she had gathered showing that *"Lukas Wyatt was keeping up appearances for a failed start-up and defrauding investors and taxpayers."* Poor Bea didn't realize until too late that Lukas was a front man, and the entire scam was being run by the woman she'd "alerted"—Nellie herself.

In fact, Nellie was full of strategic surprises.

The tale she told me about Lukas Wyatt's biological parents committing suicide was a complete fabrication. They were New Jersey farmers who'd died in a car crash.

We also learned that the XS12 cooker Nellie sprung from prison through a "work and rehabilitation" program was an old college lover—a genius chemist who'd dropped out of an Ivy League school, "broke bad," and made millions until he was busted. He was the one who helped Nellie get cozy with his old "associates," the dealers who originally distributed his product.

"The company some people keep," Matt said, shaking his head in astonishment when we all found out.

"What is *wrong* with that woman?" I asked Matt over coffee one morning. "You knew Nellie. Did you ever think she was capable of this?"

Matt shrugged. "She led a pretty charmed life, Clare. Nellie never lost at anything. And she had a big ego. Fear of failure and public humiliation can turn some people desperate, destroy their better judgment."

"Like a bad drug."

A former addict himself, Matt knew all too well what happens when you lose your grip and fall into a deep, dark chasm.

"Whenever I'm on rocky terrain," he once told me, "and descending a steep incline, I hold tight to that rope and keep my sights up. If you lose your nerve, look down in fear, you're lost."

I couldn't agree more.

And speaking of keeping your sights up . . .

We all closely followed the news stories about Wild Bill Moxley's crusade to stop the illegal dumping of garbage—and crime victims—inside that strange area of the city known as the Hole.

New York One assigned a dedicated reporter to the story, and within a month Wild Bill was a bona fide local hero, testifying before the city council. The result was an unprecedented interborough cleanup.

Emboldened by his civic success, Moxley threw his cowboy hat into the political arena and won a city council seat. The Village Blend was only too happy to support his candidacy and cater his victory party—a small measure of thanks for what he and Missy did for us.

UrbanGro, the top polluter of the Hole with its thousands of illegally dumped La Luna boxes, was handed a hefty fine they would never pay. The company collapsed into bankruptcy shortly after nefarious Nellie's misdeeds made national and international news headlines.

But there were a few silver linings.

A tech billionaire, fascinated by the in-depth story, contacted Todd Duncan with an offer to invest in the young man's ideas on automated greenhouse designs.

And with UrbanGro gone, Salena Heath took immediate action. The supermarket heiress marshaled several corporate food giants to step up to the dinner plate and replace the food that UrbanGro had been providing to food pantries and charity kitchens—but this time with a legit and sustainable nonprofit foundation. For the foreseeable future, many of New York's most needy would be cared for, and those XS12 addicts would get humane treatment instead of more deadly drugs.

As for young chef Tyler LaFontaine, last I heard, he sailed away from our New York hive with a chef's position on a cruise ship.

Tucker and Nancy were now following his Instagram page, where his modeling career also resumed with various poses of his toned and tanned body reclining on deck chairs, showing off his six-pack, wearing nothing but a Speedo and a chef's hat.

With any luck, the ocean breezes would chill the boy's hot temper. Otherwise, his fate was inevitable. If his coworkers didn't throw him overboard, they'd have him taken away in handcuffs.

Given Dennis Murphy's own journey from hotheaded cook to coolest restauranteur in the city, I held out hope that Tyler would learn life's lessons without a prison sentence.

Who knew? One day, in a decade or two, I could be sampling the latest foodie trend in one of Tyler's new restaurants.

Finally, one last ray of light graced these dark events.

When Madame first heard the news that Bea Hastings was conscious, she insisted on visiting her old friend as soon as possible—which turned out to be the same evening as the Tri-State Specialty Coffee Association meeting, where Madame was presented with that Golden Demitasse.

Madame and Bea had a long conversation, long enough for the guest of honor to be late for her own ceremony. But also long enough for Bea to hear the truth about what Felix Foxe did for her—and how he truly felt about her.

Madame believed the hospital room discussion she had with her old friend was more important than any award.

I agreed.

The result of the intense talk was the formation of the Hastings-Foxe Apis Project, a joint effort between Felix Foxe and Beatrice Hastings to improve the heartiness and survivability of Bea's hybrid bees—a species now dubbed *Alba Album* or "white bees," a subtle nod to the woman who inspired the merger, *Blanche* Dreyfus Allegro Dubois.

Dr. Wanda Clay accepted a position as scientific adviser for the project. And the NYPD's beekeeping unit happily attended the launch party—also catered by the Village Blend with Honey-Cinnamon Lattes for everyone.

It was at Bea and Foxe's party where I learned that willful misunderstandings weren't limited to romantic relationships.

That story Matt told me about Bea cruelly crushing mom-and-pop florist shops had been a twisted exaggeration. In truth, Bea had offered those family-owned businesses the option to become part of her growing chain. A few had turned her down and relocated, but most welcomed the opportunity. And some, who'd been operating on the margins, were even saved from bankruptcy.

In attendance at the party were several of those florist shop families who expressed continued gratitude to Bea for helping them make their fortunes.

From them I learned it was one of Bea's rivals who had planted hit pieces in several papers, twisting the facts of her business practices while leaving out the rest of the story, including Bea's cosigning of loans for many of those small business owners.

Such was life in the more ruthless quarters of New York. But this high-pressure hive wasn't always one of scum and villainy.

Sometimes there was honey . . .

$\mathcal{N}$ot long after our cases were closed, I issued Mike Quinn another ultimatum—actually it was more like an invitation with an instant RSVP. Like my first, I delivered it to the Sixth Precinct along with coffee and treats for the rest of Mike's team.

Everyone in the room visibly relaxed when I entered Mike's office and greeted him with a loving kiss instead of a slamming door, though my voice was firm when I commanded—

"Listen up, Quinn, because I have a new order. Now that your squad is in good standing in this department, and you've agreed to take a well-earned vacation, I want you to meet me at *this* address as soon as you go off duty tomorrow."

Mike glanced at the card, bemusement on his face. Then he nodded once. (I had my RSVP.)

Smiling, I left his office thinking about all the ups and downs we'd been through—and more (undoubtedly) that were yet to come.

The way I saw it, exhilarating inclines and heartbreaking drops were part of life on this precious planet Earth. At one time or another, we all find ourselves dangling on the end of a rope. All we can hope for is some-one on the other end who'll pull us back up. Someone who won't let go . . .

$\mathcal{M}$IKE showed up the next evening with wine this time, instead of roses. As he suspected, we didn't need more flowers.

After a lingering kiss hello, I took his hand and led him to Madame's penthouse sitting room. It was brimming with lavender blossoms, cour-tesy of Bea Hastings. The blaze in the marble fireplace and the candles I lit were the only illumination. The dancing flames bathed the space in a honey-gold glow.

With its panoramic view of Washington Square Park, the grand marble arch, and the lighted fountain sparkling in the purple twilight, the fabulous space felt like our own magical glass house.

I'd greeted Mike at the door, wearing something a lot more enticing than my oversize Pittsburgh Steelers nightshirt. The intense hunger burning in his eyes told me I'd whetted his appetite.

We sat down on a blanket I'd spread over the Persian throw near the hearth. Chilled champagne and a basket of tasty edibles were opened. After our first toast, we enjoyed a second spectacular kiss. When it ended, I sighed with contentment.

"We have this place to ourselves, complete privacy for an entire week," I informed him. "What would you like to do first?"

Mike swept me into his strong arms and stretched me out on the blanket.

"First?" He smiled. "That's easy. And I'll show you in a minute. But later on . . ."

"What?" I said. "What do you want to do later on?"

"It may sound crazy, but I hope you're up for it."

"Oh," I breathed into his ear. "Now that you've got me all hot and bothered, you have to come clean."

Mike shook his head. "I don't know if you're ready. But, honey, after all the fears you made me face, I absolutely am."

I squirmed under him. "Give it up, Lieutenant. By now you should know I'm always ready for anything. What are we going to do?"

He grinned like a happy bridegroom. "We're *finally* going to read your honeymoon brochures."

"Really?" I laughed. "How about a preview?"

Mike's reply involved his lips, but no more words were necessary.

Recipes & Tips
From the Village Blend

Visit Cleo Coyle's virtual Village Blend at
coffeehousemystery.com
for a free, illustrated guide to this section
and even more recipes, including:

Clare Cosi's Stuffed Shells
Clare Cosi's Homemade Ricotta (with step-by-step photos)
Peach Muffins with Honey Butter
Honey Candy Apples (No Corn Syrup!)
Spiked Honey Candy Apples (with cinnamon schnapps)
Honey-Roasted Almonds

Beatrice Hastings's Guide to Honey

Honey, a remarkable food that never spoils, is the sweet nectar bestowed on us by the magnificent honeybee. Bees make honey from sugars in plants by adding enzymes, evaporating the water, and storing it in honeycombs.

Pure honey contains many beneficial ingredients beyond its nutritional value. You'll find yeast in honey (which is good for your digestive system), along with antioxidant, anti-inflammatory, and antimicrobial properties. The consumption of pure honey that is both LOCAL and RAW can provide relief from seasonal allergy symptoms comparable to antihistamines.

We are speaking of pure honey, of course, not honey that has been adulterated with water, corn syrup, sugar, food coloring, or other additives that corrupt one of nature's purest and most ancient foods. Always purchase your honey from producers guaranteeing one hundred percent purity. Even better, look for producers in your area. It may be a bit more expensive, but the quality and health benefits, especially in helping your own body combat local allergens, are well worth it.

Queen Bea's Tips

Three ways to tell your honey is adulterated.

1) Take 1 cup of water, pour in 2 tablespoons of honey. If the honey settles at the bottom of the glass in a single clump it is pure. However, if it

begins to dissolve or break down it has been adulterated with corn syrup or other additives—a culinary crime!

2) Put a small dollop of honey on the tip of your index finger. Turn it over once or twice. If the honey drops it has been adulterated. If it sticks or falls off in a single clump it's quality honey. Very good!

3) Place a teaspoon of honey in the middle of a paper napkin. Fold once and press down. If you see wet spots around the honey it has been adulterated. If there are no wet spots it's pure—and that's what you want!

What Do Those Labels Mean?

All commercial brands of honey are EXTRACTED. This is the most common method of harvesting. Centrifuges spin the honey out of the combs, or the crush and drain method is used. Extracted honey can be processed in a variety of ways but most brands are BLENDED and PASTEURIZED (heat treated) which has both benefits and drawbacks.

BLENDED HONEY is the most common type sold. This is extracted honey processed from many regions, often many nations (seventy percent of the honey sold in the US is imported). The honeys are mixed, sometimes to improve the flavor profile but mostly out of expedience. It's pasteurized to eliminate particulates, bubbles, etc., BUT heating *also* kills the active enzymes and pollen, along with some of the honey's natural homeopathic goodness. Blended honey is also FILTERED, so the honey is clear, rich gold in color, and has no bubbles, pollen, or impurities.

STRAINED HONEY is pushed through a mesh to remove bits of wax and other particles, but no heat is applied so the honey retains its healthful pollen, minerals, and enzymes.

RAW HONEY is obtained by extraction, but no heat is applied, nor is it filtered or strained. Raw honey is often cloudy and may contain visible pollen, bubbles in suspension, and even particles of wax, but you can be sure it retains its healthful pollen, minerals, and enzymes.

COMB HONEY is raw unextracted honey in its original wax comb. This is the most natural way to consume honey; you get the benefits of pollen, minerals, enzymes, and, yes, a bit of wax in each spoonful.

ULTRASONICATED HONEY is made with an alternate process not involving pasteurization (heat). Ultrasonicated honey retains many of the qualities of unheated honey, but it should not be used to create honey liqueurs like mead because the yeast has been eliminated so the honey will not ferment.

WHIPPED HONEY is processed to control crystallization. Whipped honey contains small crystals that prevent the formation of larger crystals that occurs in non-heat-treated honey. But the main purpose of whipping is to create a thick, smooth, and consistently spreadable honey. Wonderful on warm muffins and fresh-baked bread!

CHUNK HONEY is jarred extracted honey with a chunk of honeycomb included. Usually, the extracted honey is heat treated, but the honeycomb is raw, so you will get a nice sampling of both.

DRIED HONEY is natural honey with the moisture extracted to create solid granules. Dried honey is used commercially in baked goods, or as a garnish. Dried honey will liquefy (melt) if gently heated.

Popular Honey Varietals

"Monofloral" honey has a distinctive flavor profile because it's made from the nectar of a single plant species. Monoflorals are labor intensive, which is why they're more expensive than blended honey. There are *hundreds* of varietals of monoflorals from all over the world, everything from Alfalfa to Wildflower. Here are some of the most popular in our North American hemisphere:

ACACIA honey is almost as clear as glass and resists crystallization, which prolongs its shelf life. Derived from the nectar of the black locust tree flowers, it has a light floral aroma, and a sweet flower-like flavor to match.

ALFALFA honey is amber in color with a mild floral aroma and a delicate grassy flavor with buttery notes, most likely because it's higher in protein than most honeys.

BUCKWHEAT honey is not as sweet as other varietals, and it is much darker in color because of the high-level of antioxidant compounds. This honey has the pungent flavor of molasses with malty notes and its taste lingers in the mouth. Generally, buckwheat honey is consumed for its vitamins, antioxidants, and other healthful qualities rather than its off-putting taste.

CLOVER honey comes from many types of clover, from white Dutch to yellow blossom. It varies in color from clear to amber to bright yellow depending on the type of clover used. Clover honey has that sweet, mild, flowery taste with which most of us are familiar because most domestic honey is produced from clover.

GOLDENROD honey is light amber to sunny yellow, with notes of raw sugar because it is often crystallized at purchase. You *may* notice a fermented scent, like pungent cheese, but your tongue will only detect this honey's sweet magnificence.

HONEYSUCKLE gets its name because of the old tradition of sucking nectar from its flowers. Honey made from this blossom has a floral, perfumed taste with underlying nutty notes.

KUDZU is a nuisance to many, seen as an invasive weed that swallows everything in its path. But the purple honey made from its pollen is sheer magic. Powerfully sweet, this unique nectar has the taste of (yes!) grape jelly and a scent not unlike Kool-Aid.

LAVENDER is the premium honey of all premium honeys. My favorite! This golden-amber nectar has a flavor that is well-rounded and perfectly balanced, with notes of grass, hay, and even peaches.

ORANGE BLOSSOM is a light amber honey with citrus notes and more than a hint of orange marmalade, with a lingering floral aftertaste. A beautiful honey for baking and mixing into drinks.

SUNFLOWER is sweet and floral like other honeys, with hints of apricot and grass. But the texture is quite different, firm and crystalline rather than fluid, which is why it tends to clump.

WILDFLOWER honey is produced when bees range freely, collecting a variety of nectars from many species of flowers, which they combine in the hive. Like wine, Wildflower honey differs from region to region and from season to season. Each possesses a one-of-a-kind color and flavor profile impossible to recreate.

And those are just a few of the countless reasons honey is the most glorious food on our precious planet.

Honey Coffee

While honey and tea are a classic culinary pairing, the sweetening of coffee with honey is becoming increasingly popular. The many types of coffees (from blends to single origins) that can be combined with the vast array of honey varieties will keep any coffee drinker happily sampling endless combinations. If this is your first time hooking up your java with a honey, start with your favorite coffee and a light, sweet raw nectar—such as Clover, Acacia, or Lavender honey. From there, you can experiment with different combinations of honey and coffee until you've found Honey Coffee nirvana.

Makes 1 cup

6 ounces brewed coffee
1 teaspoon honey
Cream, milk, or half-and-half

If you enjoy hot coffee, then fill your cup. Stir in the honey until dissolved and add your cream or milk to lighten. It's that simple (and delicious). The higher quality your coffee and honey, the better your Honey Coffee will taste.

TIP: If you're concerned about preserving all the benefits of raw honey and its nutrients and enzymes, be sure to allow the coffee to cool below 95°F. (Use an instant read kitchen thermometer.) Splashing in cold cream or milk will help speed up the cooling time. Then stir in the raw honey and enjoy your drink with all the raw honey health benefits intact.

Roasted Honey Coffee

Although Clare Cosi was correct in explaining to her youngest barista Nancy Kelly that no actual honey is involved in the making of honey-processed coffee, there is such a thing as Roasted Honey Coffee. The coffee beans are roasted and then coated in pure golden honey. Thanks to Savannah Bee Company for the inventive inspiration. Learn more, or purchase this outstanding coffee to sample for yourself, visiting this link: savannahbee.com/organic-honey-roasted-coffee.

Clare Cosi's Honey-Cinnamon Latte (3 Ways)

Espresso machine directions: (Serves 1) Pour **1 to 2 shots of hot espresso** into an 8-ounce mug and stir in **1 tablespoon of Clare's homemade honey-cinnamon syrup (recipe follows)**. Add ⅔ **cup steamed milk** and stir to distribute the syrup. Top with foamed milk. Garnish with a light sprinkling of ground cinnamon and serve with a cinnamon stick.

Stovetop or microwave directions: (Serves 1) Warm ⅔ **cup cold whole milk** on top of a double-boiler or in the microwave (do not allow milk to boil or scorch). Using a hand blender, hand mixer, or standard blender, beat the warmed milk for about 60 to 90 seconds until frothy (do not over-beat). Frothing the milk brings out its sweetness and creates the telltale latte foam. To create the latte, pour **4 tablespoons of double-strength coffee or stovetop espresso** into an 8-ounce mug. Stir in **1 tablespoon of Clare's homemade honey-cinnamon syrup** (recipe follows). Add the warmed and frothed milk, using a spoon to hold back some of the froth as you pour.

Stir the drink to distribute the syrup. Top with the reserved frothed milk. Garnish with a light sprinkling of ground cinnamon and serve with a cinnamon stick.

Simplest version: (Serves 2) Warm 1⅓ **cups cold whole milk** on the stove or microwave (do not allow to boil or scorch). Add the warmed milk to a blender with **8 tablespoons double-strength brewed coffee or espresso.** Add **1 to 2 tablespoons of your favorite honey** and ⅛ to ¼ **teaspoon ground cinnamon** (to your taste). Pulse the blender until the entire mixture appears frothy (about 20 seconds). Divide into two cups, using a spoon to hold back some of the froth. Spoon the reserved froth on top of each cup. Garnish with a light sprinkling of cinnamon.

Clare Cosi's Honey-Cinnamon Syrup

Makes 1 cup syrup

Place ⅔ **cup honey,** ⅓ **cup water,** and **2 to 3 cinnamon sticks** (***see note below**) into a saucepan. Bring to a simmer, stirring occasionally, until the honey completely dissolves. That's it! No need to over-cook. Now cover the pan with a lid and allow the cinnamon to continue to infuse the liquid as it cools. Store in an airtight container.

*Note on types of cinnamon: The amount of cinnamon sticks you'll want to use for this recipe will vary, depending on the kind of cinnamon sticks you're using, as well as their freshness. For example:

Cassia cinnamon (aka Chinese cinnamon) sticks are the most common type found in grocery stores. These are hard sticks with a single layer of curl. Because of their hardness, Clare suggests using 3 Cassia cinnamon sticks to make her syrup, rather than 2. Their time on store shelves also tends to make them less potent so that 3rd stick is usually needed to make a good cinnamon syrup.

Ceylon cinnamon sticks are softer and also of higher quality and potency. You can recognize them by their many layers. Because they are primarily sold by spice merchants at a higher price point, they tend to be fresher and more powerful. They truly do have amazing flavor, well worth the price! Clare suggests using 2 Ceylon cinnamon sticks for her recipe.

Clare Cosi's Honey Cookies with Honey-Roasted Almonds

These outstanding honey sugar cookies are delicately flavored with honey, vanilla, and lemon. (Don't leave out the lemon because its chemistry, along with the honey, adds a pleasant little chew to the cookie.) This complex flavor profile makes them satisfying treats to pair with coffee or tea. Clare makes these cookies two different ways, and so can you. The first is with a simple sugar coating. The second version amps up the flavor and crunch with honey-roasted almonds. You can save time by using store-bought honey-roasted almonds or you can make your own. To get an easy recipe for Honey-Roasted Almonds and see a photo of these Honey Cookies, visit Cleo Coyle's online coffeehouse at coffeehousemystery.com, where you can also download an illustrated guide to this recipe section.

Makes about 40 cookies

12 tablespoons (1½ sticks) unsalted butter, softened

½ cup white, granulated sugar

1 large egg and 1 egg yolk (whisked together)

¼ cup honey

½ teaspoon salt

1 teaspoon pure vanilla extract

1 teaspoon baking powder

½ teaspoon baking soda

½ teaspoon fresh lemon juice (do not omit)

2 cups all-purpose flour (spoon into cup and level off)

½ cup finely chopped honey-roasted almonds (optional, see note*)

1 cup white, granulated sugar (to coat before baking)

*Note: To make your own Honey-Roasted Almonds, visit coffeehouse mystery.com for the easy recipe. Or use a store-bought version.

Step 1—Make the dough: Using an electric mixer, cream the butter and white, granulated sugar in a large bowl. Add the egg and egg yolk (whisk together before adding), honey, salt, vanilla, baking powder, and baking soda, and beat well. Blend in the lemon juice (an important part of the flavor profile; do not omit). Next, turn the mixer to low and mix in the flour, ½ cup at a time, to create the silky dough. Do not overmix, but be sure all flour is incorporated and bowl is scraped clean. If using, now is the time to fold in the chopped honey-roasted almonds. Dough will be soft and sticky and hard to handle, which is why you need to be patient and chill it. If you sample the dough at this stage, don't worry about the lack of sweetness. This dough is designed to balance the addition of sugar before baking.

Step 2—Chill it, baby: Cover the bowl tightly with plastic wrap (to keep it from drying out) and chill the dough for 1 hour in the refrigerator to firm it up and allow the flavors to develop. If you'd like to store the dough longer than 1 hour, scrape it into an airtight plastic container and keep it chilled in the refrigerator. Do not store longer than 2 days before baking.

Step 3—Prep for baking: When you're ready to bake the cookies, preheat your oven to 350°F and line a cookie sheet pan with parchment paper or a silicone mat. Pour 1 cup of white, granulated sugar into a shallow bowl or pie plate. To form each cookie, dampen your hands and coat your fingers well with sugar (to prevent the dough from sticking to them). Break off a piece of dough and form a ball, about 1 inch in diameter. Roll the ball in the bowl of sugar, generously coating, and place it on your lined baking sheet, allowing room for spreading.

Step 4—Bake in your preheated 350°F oven for 10 to 12 minutes (the time will depend on your oven). Finished cookies should be creamy on top and golden brown around the edges. That golden brown caramelization is important for flavor, but do not allow the bottoms to turn overly brown or burn. Remove pan from oven and allow cookies to cool a few minutes to set before carefully sliding the parchment paper of baked cookies onto a rack to finish cooling. As the cookies cool, they will harden, becoming lightly crispy on the outside yet soft and chewy on the inside. Eat with joy!

The Village Blend's Apple Pie Scones with Honey-Cinnamon Icing

A fabulous breakfast or coffee-break treat, these amazing scones deliver the homey flavor of apple pie in a tender and flaky wedge of iced pastry. Clare and Madame ate them with lip-smacking joy while hatching their plot to catch a sly fox. The cream cheese in the recipe is one of the secrets to their tenderness. Be sure to follow the directions closely, paying special attention to keeping the ingredients cold as you work because the cold scones in your hot oven are the key to flaky success. To see a photo of these fantastic Apple Pie Scones, visit Cleo Coyle's online coffeehouse at coffeehousemystery.com, where you can also download an illustrated guide to this recipe section.

Makes 8 scones

For the apple pie part

2 cups shredded Golden Delicious or Granny Smith apples
1 tablespoon granulated white sugar
½ teaspoon apple pie spice (premade or use recipe on page 317)*

For the scones

3 tablespoons cold heavy cream, plus a little more for baking
1 large egg, lightly beaten with fork
1 teaspoon pure vanilla extract

2¼ cups all-purpose flour (spoon into cup and level off)
1 tablespoon baking powder
½ teaspoon apple pie spice (premade or use recipe below*)
½ teaspoon salt
½ cup very cold unsalted butter, cut into cubes
4 ounces very cold cream cheese (block not whipped), cut into cubes
⅓ cup granulated white sugar

*Make Your own Apple Pie Spice: For every 1 teaspoon, mix the following spices: ½ teaspoon ground cinnamon, ¼ teaspoon ground nutmeg, ⅛ teaspoon ground allspice, ⅛ teaspoon ground ginger.

Step 1—Prep the apples: Peel the apples and shred them into a bowl using a boxed grater. You want 2 cups of shredded apple (allow the bowl to capture any liquid). Toss the shreds well with 1 tablespoon sugar mixed with ½ teaspoon apple pie spice. Cover the bowl with plastic wrap and set aside on the counter for 60 minutes. As the apple shreds macerate, the sugar will draw out their liquid, which you should drain off and set aside for use in the scone glaze (recipe follows). After the apple shreds are well drained, measure out exactly 1½ cups of apple shreds, set this aside in the refrigerator to chill, and begin to make your scones.

Step 2—Make the dough: In a small bowl, whisk together these three wet ingredients: 3 tablespoons cold heavy cream, egg, and vanilla extract. Set aside in refrigerator. (Keeping things cold is key in this process.) In a large bowl, whisk together your 2¼ cups flour, baking powder, apple pie spice, and salt. Using clean hands, work the very cold cubes of butter and cream cheese into the flour mixture. Rub and squeeze until all the mixture resembles coarse crumbs—there should be no large "lumps" of butter or cream cheese left. All crumbs should be no larger than a pea. Now stir in the sugar with hands, combining well, and gently fold in the 1½ cups of seasoned and drained apple shreds from Step 1. Finally, pour in the chilled wet ingredients. Gently mix with hands until dough forms.

Step 3—Form and chill: Generously flour a flat surface and flour your hands, as well. Turn the dough out onto the surface and gently form it into a ball. Pat the ball into an even circle of about 7 or 8 inches in diameter and ¾ inch in thickness. Use a sharp knife to slice the circle into eight wedges—do not fuss with the wedges or try to perfect the edges, handle very little. Chill the wedges in the refrigerator for a full 30 minutes while preheating your oven to 425°F. (The cold dough going into the hot oven will help give you nice, flaky scones.)

Step 4—Brush and bake: Line a baking sheet with parchment paper and place it into the oven to heat it. After the dough has chilled, brush the tops lightly with cold heavy cream and transfer the wedges onto the hot pan, allow space between the wedges for rising. Bake 20 minutes at 425°F, rotate the pan, reduce the temperature to 375°F, and continue baking for a final 5 minutes. Cool and top with Honey-Cinnamon Icing (recipe follows).

Honey-Cinnamon Icing

1½ cups (or so) confectioners' sugar
5 tablespoons heavy cream (do not substitute)
1 tablespoon honey
¼ teaspoon apple pie spice (premade or see recipe on page 317)
1 to 3 teaspoons apple juice or apple cider (for thinning the glaze)

Sift 1½ cups of confectioners' sugar into a mixing bowl. Add heavy cream, honey, and apple pie spice. Whisk well to create a glaze. If the glaze is too thick, whisk in apple juice or apple cider, 1 teaspoon at a time, until you have your desired consistency. Test the glaze by drizzling on a plate. If the glaze is still too thick, add more apple juice (or cider). If it becomes too thin, whisk in more confectioners' sugar. Finally, finish the scones by drizzling the glaze on with a fork. Or, if you create a glaze with a thinner consistency, you can simply dip the top edges of your scones into the glaze. Be sure to quickly set the scones upright on wax or parchment paper, allowing any excess glaze to drip decadently over the sides before setting.

Easy Honey-Glazed Peach Crostata
with Ginger Whipped Cream

A crostata is a rustic, free-form Italian baked dessert tart, usually filled with jam or fruit. Clare serves a mini version of this light and lovely pastry at the Village Blend. When she summoned Sergeant Franco to her shop for a stealth interrogation about Quinn and his problems, this pastry helped loosen the young man's tongue. Honey and peaches are a perfect pairing, and this tart, with its healthful, shimmering filling of honey-glazed peaches, is like a crust filled with sunshine. Clare adapted this version years ago when she was still writing her In the Kitchen with Clare column while raising her daughter in New Jersey. If you're a pro at mixing and rolling crusts, Clare invites you to use your favorite recipe. For everyone else, a good-quality premade crust makes this a snap to throw together. To see step-by-step photos of this recipe, visit Cleo Coyle's online coffeehouse at coffeehousemystery.com, where you can download an illustrated guide to this recipe section.

Makes 8 servings

1 tablespoon butter

1½ tablespoons honey

2 tablespoons flour (for thickening)

Pinch of sea salt

5 large, ripe yellow peaches skinned and diced (or 6 small)

1 premade refrigerated pie crust

1 egg, lightly beaten with fork (for brushing crust)

2 tablespoons coarse sugar for dusting (try turbinado sugar aka "Sugar in the Raw")

Fresh Ginger Whipped Cream (recipe follows)

Step 1—Prepare filling: In a large saucepan, melt butter over low heat; add honey, flour, salt, and diced peaches. Gently stir for about 3 to 5 minutes to coat the peaches with the glaze and soften them up. Before the next step, allow filling to cool. Use a slotted spoon to drain some of the excess liquid, but not all. This crostata bakes quickly in the oven, and the butter and honey will create a more succulent crostata than baking the fruit without this honey glaze.

Step 2—Fill tart: Line a baking sheet with parchment paper. (The parchment paper lining on your baking sheet makes it easier to transfer the tart to a serving platter.) Take 1 roll of your boxed pie crust out of the refrigerator and allow it to come to room temperature. Gently unroll it on the parchment paper. Now fill the tart. Using a slotted spoon to drain some (but not all) of the fruit filling's excess liquid, mound diced peaches in the center, leaving a 2-inch border.

Step 3—Brush with egg and fold: Mix 1 lightly beaten egg with a splash of water and brush this egg wash along the exposed border of dough around your crust. Next create a pretty rustic edge to your crust. Using clean fingers, lift up the border a bit and pinch a small section of the dough together; continue pinching every inch or so around the tart. Finally, fold down each pinched peak over the fruit. (To see step-by-step photos of this process, come to coffeehousemystery.com.)

Step 4—Brush and sprinkle: Lightly brush the crust again with egg wash and sprinkle with coarse sugar.

Step 5—Bake: Place baking sheet on lowest rack of an oven that's been very well preheated to 400°F. The crostata will be done in 15 to 20 minutes. Allow to cool a bit before slicing and serving right from the baking sheet. Want to move the tart to a serving plate? See Clare's note below.

*Crust Note: In this tart, the fruit is the star, not the crust, which is too thin to move without breaking. That's why the baking sheet should be lined with parchment paper. When the baking is done, use the paper to slide the crostata onto the platter then pull the paper out from under the crostata or trim around the edges before serving.

SERVING SUGGESTIONS: This dessert is delicious served with ice cream or whipped cream. The Ginger Whipped Cream (recipe below) pairs very well with the flavors in this rustic tart.

Ginger Whipped Cream

Place 1 cup heavy cream, 3 to 4 tablespoons sugar, and ½ teaspoon ground ginger into a well-chilled bowl and beat with an electric mixer. The cream will thicken as you beat it. When it forms stiff peaks, you're done. Do not overbeat. Makes 4 servings.

The Village Blend's Chocolate Swirl Blondies

The texture of these tasty blondies will not be crunchy or cake-like but moist and chewy like fudge brownies. Instead of chocolate, your canvas is a buttery vanilla-caramel blondie batter into which you'll creatively swirl melted chocolate before baking, producing your own culinary version of an abstract expressionist masterpiece. Even better than a painting, after it's baked, you get to eat it. To see a photo of these finished blondies, visit Cleo Coyle's online coffeehouse at coffeehousemystery.com, where you can also download an illustrated guide to this recipe section.

Makes 1 13-by-9-inch pan of blondies (12 squares)

For the batter

10 tablespoons (1 stick plus 2 tablespoons) unsalted butter, softened

1 cup packed light brown sugar

½ cup white, granulated sugar

2 eggs, room temperature

1 teaspoon brewed coffee

1 tablespoon vanilla

½ teaspoon finely ground sea salt

1½ teaspoons baking powder

¼ teaspoon baking soda

2 cups all-purpose flour (spoon into cup and level off)

For the chocolate swirl

¼ cup chocolate chips (semisweet or dark/bittersweet)
1 teaspoon brewed coffee
1 teaspoon butter

Step 1—Prep the oven and pan: First preheat your oven to 350°F. Butter a 13-by-9-inch baking pan (the butter will act as glue) and line it with parchment paper, allowing the excess to hang over the 2 long ends. This allows you to lift your final baked product out of the pan to cool and easily slice into squares.

Step 2—Mix the blondie batter: Using an electric mixer, cream the softened butter and brown and white sugars. Add eggs, coffee, vanilla, salt, baking powder, and baking soda. Beat well until the batter is smooth. Finally, blend in the flour, but do not overmix. Batter will be thick. Scrape it into the pan and use the back of a spoon to spread it evenly and smooth the top. Set aside.

Step 3—Make the chocolate swirl: Place the chocolate chips in a microwave-safe bowl. Toss chips well with 1 tablespoon brewed coffee. Chop in a small amount of butter (½ tablespoon). Stir again. Now zap in a microwave for 15 seconds. Stir. Zap again. This method ensures you will not burn the chocolate, which cannot be saved once ruined. You can also melt it all in a double boiler.

Step 4—Finish and bake: Using a spoon, dollop very small mounds of the warm chocolate ganache (in polka dot fashion) over the entire top surface of the blondie batter. Using a wooden skewer, chopstick, or knife, swirl these dollops through the batter well, creating your own abstract expressionist masterpiece. Bake until a toothpick inserted comes out clean, about 20 to 25 minutes. Do not overbake. Remove and allow to cool in the pan for at least 30 minutes. The blondies will deflate, and ridges will appear. The cooler they become, the easier they will be to handle. When completely cool, slice into squares, and eat with joy!

Clare Cosi's Honey Cupcakes
with Honey Buttercream Frosting

The natural sweetness and abundant varieties of honey make it a marvelous ingredient to use in baking. It blends well, brings a warm golden color to your baked goods, and helps them stay fresher longer. These moist and tender little cakes carry notes of honey and vanilla. They're the perfect canvas for Clare's Honey Buttercream Frosting. Like the officers of Mike's OD Squad, one taste of these honey-kissed cakes and you'll be licking your lips and begging for more.

Makes 10 cupcakes

1 cup self-rising flour (use fresh, check expiration date)
8 tablespoons unsalted butter (1 stick), softened to room temperature
¼ cup granulated white sugar
2 large eggs, room temperature, fork-whisked (*see tip below)
1 teaspoon pure vanilla extract
½ teaspoon baking soda
¼ teaspoon baking powder
½ cup whole milk
2 tablespoons honey
Honey Buttercream Frosting (recipe follows)

Step 1—Prep oven and flour: First preheat your oven to 350°F. Next measure the self-rising flour by spooning it into a cup and leveling it off. Set aside.

Step 2—Make the batter: In a large mixing bowl, beat the butter and sugar with an electric mixer until light and fluffy. Add the (room temperature) fork-whisked eggs, pure vanilla extract, baking soda, and baking powder. Whip everything on high speed about one minute, scraping down the bowl, until well blended. Turn the mixer to low and add about half the flour, along with the whole milk and honey. Slowly and gently blend in the remaining flour, scraping down the bowl, until completely incorporated, but do not overmix or your cupcakes will be tough instead of tender.

Step 3—Bake: Line 10 cups of your cupcake pan with paper liners. Divide this batter evenly among the cups (each should be a little over half full). Bake at 350°F. in center of oven for about 18 minutes. Cupcakes are done when the top springs back after a light touching and a test toothpick comes out free of wet batter. Allow the cupcakes to cool in the pan for about 5 minutes. Gently remove from pan and finish cooling on a rack. When completely cool, frost with Honey Buttercream Frosting (recipe follows).

Note: Clare uses self-rising flour because it gives you a lower protein flour for a more tender cake and includes some of your leavening as well as salt. In other words, for best results, use the ingredients listed and do not substitute all-purpose flour. Also be sure to use fresh self-rising flour that has not gone beyond the expiration date; otherwise, the leavening agent may not be potent enough to give you good results.

*TIP: To warm cold eggs quickly, place them (still in their shells, of course!) in a bowl of warm tap water. Warming the eggs and pre-whisking them with a fork is important for proper blending into the batter.

Clare Cosi's Honey Buttercream Frosting

Makes about 1½ cups frosting

> 8 tablespoons (1 stick) unsalted butter, room temperature
> 2 tablespoons cream cheese, room temperature
> 3 tablespoons honey
> ¼ teaspoon vanilla
> Pinch of finely ground sea salt (or to taste)
> 2 to 2½ cups powdered sugar

In a large mixing bowl beat the butter, cream cheese, honey, vanilla, and salt until well blended. Add the powdered sugar, ½ cup at a time, beating between additions until you see a smooth frosting form. If the frosting seems too thin, beat in more powdered sugar. If it feels too stiff, add a bit more honey. Taste test and add a pinch more of salt, if needed for balance.

Clare Cosi's Rooftop Picnic Buttermilk Fried Chicken

On a sultry midsummer night Clare and Mike celebrated the Fourth of July with a picnic high over the city streets, on the roof of the Village Blend. For the occasion, Clare made her tender and juicy buttermilk fried chicken with a twist. One little change of ingredients—using self-rising flour instead of all-purpose—made Clare's spectacular fried chicken juicier and crispier, with a batter-like coating that was achieved without preparing a batter. The result is perfect fried chicken, served hot or cold.

Serves 4

3 pounds of fresh chicken wings and/or drumsticks, skin on

1 quart buttermilk, regular or light

3 cups self-rising flour (be sure it's fresh!)

2 tablespoons McCormick Poultry Seasoning (or your favorite chicken spice blend)

1 tablespoon salt

1 tablespoon white pepper, ground very fine

2 tablespoons sweet paprika

1 teaspoon cayenne pepper (optional)

Dash of MSG (optional)

Shortening or vegetable oil for frying

Step 1—Marinate: Cut the wings into 3 pieces and discard the tips. Place wings and/or drumsticks in a large glass or plastic container and pour the buttermilk over the chicken. Marinate in the refrigerator for 1 to 3 hours, but no more.

Step 2—Create coating: In a large plastic or paper bag, combine the self-rising flour, poultry seasoning, salt, finely ground white pepper, sweet paprika, and optional cayenne pepper and MSG. Shake until well blended.

Step 3—Shake it, baby: After marination, remove chicken from buttermilk and shake off excess liquid (do NOT rinse). Drop chicken into the bag, 2 or 3 pieces at a time. Shake well, until each piece is evenly coated.

Step 4—Fry them up: Heat your oil or shortening in pan deep enough to allow your chicken to be submerged in hot oil (at least 2 inches). Add your coated chicken pieces to the hot oil one at a time. Add the chicken slowly and don't crowd the pan, or the oil temperature will drop, and your chicken will be greasy. Fry each batch for 8 to 10 minutes, turning occasionally until chicken is cooked evenly and is golden brown.

Step 5—Finish and hold in oven: Put the finished pieces on a rack over a foil-covered baking sheet and place in a 220°F oven to dry out excess grease and keep the chicken warm until all the pieces are fried.

Note: Self-rising flour has a finer texture than all-purpose flour and includes a leavening agent. That's why you'll get good results with this recipe, BUT be sure to use *fresh* flour that has not gone beyond its expiration date. If the self-rising flour is stale, the leavening agent will no longer be active, and your results will be disappointing.

Clare Cosi's Creamy Pasta Salad

This cool and creamy pasta salad pairs wonderfully with Clare's fried chicken, which is why she served it as a side at her intimate July Fourth rooftop picnic with Mike Quinn. Formerly prepared by Clare's nonna and sold in her family's Italian grocery store in Western Pennsylvania, this recipe makes a satisfying salad any time of year.

Serves 4

1 16-ounce box elbow macaroni
1 cup large black olives (pitted)
1 red, orange, or yellow bell pepper

4 scallions
¼ cup mayonnaise
Salt and pepper to taste

Step 1—Prep the ingredients: Cook the pasta until al dente, as per label instructions. When the pasta is done, drain it in a colander and rinse with cold water. While the pasta is cooling and draining completely, slice the black olives into rings, dice the bell pepper, and peel and chop the scallions.

Step 2—Finish the salad: In a large bowl, mix the cooled pasta with the sliced olives, diced peppers, and chopped scallions. Add mayonnaise, salt and pepper, and blend thoroughly. Place in an airtight container (or cover bowl tightly with cling wrap) and chill in the refrigerator for at least an hour. Before serving, if the salad seems dry, stir in a bit more mayonnaise and eat with joy!

Tyler LaFontaine's Honey Ginger Sesame Beef

In Tyler LaFontaine's better days, the handsome Instagram model turned head chef was the culinary genius at Manhattan's tony bistro Armando's. Specializing in dishes using honey, the young Chef Tyler met Suzie Hastings when he came looking for Bea's gourmet varieties. Tyler and Suzie had a sweet affair until the chef's world turned sour. Nevertheless, when Tyler exited the New York restaurant scene, he left diners with the memory of some delicious dishes, including this beef feast, where honey and ginger combine with sesame seeds to create savory-sweet magic on your plate. To see a photo of Tyler's signature Honey Ginger Sesame Beef, visit Cleo Coyle's online coffeehouse at coffeehousemystery.com, where you can also download an illustrated guide to this recipe section.

Serves 3–4

1½ pounds flank steak
Salt and pepper to taste

For the marinade

1 tablespoon rice vinegar (or white vinegar)
2 tablespoons sesame oil
1 tablespoon Worcestershire sauce

For the glaze

1 tablespoon rice vinegar (or white vinegar)
2 tablespoons Worcestershire sauce
1 tablespoon grated ginger
6 cloves of garlic, minced
½ cup honey
¼ teaspoon red pepper flakes (optional)
3 tablespoons sesame oil
2 tablespoons sesame seeds (for cooking)
3 scallions, diced

Step 1—Marinate the beef: Slice the flank steak into 1½ to 2-inch pieces, cutting across the grain for tenderness. Salt and pepper the meat. In a flat glass, plastic, or ceramic container, combine the rice vinegar, sesame oil, and Worcestershire sauce. Blend well. Add the beef pieces, rolling in the marinade until well coated. Cover container with plastic wrap (or seal with a lid) and marinate in the refrigerator for one to three hours.

Step 2—Prepare the sauce: In a large bowl combine rice vinegar, Worcestershire sauce, grated ginger, minced garlic, honey, and optional red pepper flakes. Whisk ingredients together, blending well. Set mixture aside.

Step 3—Sauté the beef: Remove the steak pieces from the marinade and discard the liquid (do not rinse the meat). Place a nonstick pan over medium-high heat and add the sesame oil. When the oil is hot enough for a drop of water to dance across its surface, arrange the steak pieces in a single layer in the sizzling oil. Cook for 2 to 3 minutes, then flip the pieces and sear for another 3 minutes.

Step 4—Add the sauce: Reduce the heat to medium-low and add the sauce mixture from step 2 to the pan of meat. Toss well and simmer until the liquid is reduced by half and forms a sticky glaze (10–12 minutes).

Step 5—Add the sesame seeds and garnish: During the final minute of cooking, add the sesame seeds and stir. Plate the dish and garnish with a sprinkling of scallions and more sesame seeds before serving. This dish goes well over rice (white or seasoned). For a complementary side dish idea, see **Tyler's Honey-Glazed Baby Carrots** recipe, which follows this one.

TIP: Before cutting, place the flank steak in the freezer for 20 to 30 minutes. Chilled but not frozen, the meat will be easier to slice without tearing.

Tyler LaFontaine's Honey-Glazed Baby Carrots

Caramelized baby carrots with a kiss of honey, butter, and thyme—a simple and beautiful side dish. Serve it with roast beef or chicken or keep the honey theme going and try it with Tyler's signature Honey Ginger Sesame Beef, the recipe that precedes this one.

Serves 4

3 tablespoons olive oil, divided

1 pound peeled baby carrots

3 tablespoons butter

⅓ cup honey

1 teaspoon balsamic vinegar

½ teaspoon fresh or dried thyme

Sea salt

Coarsely ground black pepper

2 sprigs fresh thyme (optional for garnish)

Step 1—Bake the carrots: Preheat oven to 375°F. Line a large baking pan with foil and grease with 1 tablespoon of olive oil. Place the remaining 2 tablespoons of olive oil in a large bowl and toss in the carrots until they are evenly coated. Arrange the carrots in a single layer in the prepared pan. Bake 25 to 30 minutes, until the carrots are fork tender. Stir once or twice so the carrots do not stick.

Step 2—Make the glaze: Gently melt the butter in a small saucepan over low heat, then stir in the honey. When well blended, add the vinegar, thyme, sea salt, and ground black pepper. Heat slowly and do not let the mixture boil (about 2 minutes). Remove from heat, cover, and reserve.

Step 3—Combine, bake, and serve: When the carrots are fork tender, remove the pan from the oven and drizzle the glaze over the carrots. Toss gently and return the pan to the oven for about 15 minutes, stirring every 5 minutes to prevent burning. If the carrots have not yet caramelized, toss again and roast for another 5 minutes or until a nice glaze forms. That's when you know the carrots are done. Place in a serving dish and garnish with a few sprigs of fresh thyme.

Joy Allegro's Honey Orange Glazed Chicken

Clare's daughter, Joy, is the manager of the Village Blend's second shop in Washington, DC, operating as a coffeehouse on the first floor and a relaxed jazz supper club on the second. The menu has become the talk of Georgetown. (Read all about it in Cleo Coyle's Dead to the Last Drop.)

For this outstanding recipe, Clare adapted her daughter's professional kitchen version into a one-pot delight that's easy to make at home. In fact, Clare made it for her special evening with Mike that didn't end so special—but don't blame it on the food. A certain news story and emergency work phone call sent Mike out the door before he even had a chance to sample this lusciously flavorful dish. Don't worry. Clare and Mike are bound to have better luck next time.

Serves 4

1 cup orange juice (no pulp, freshly squeezed is best)
¼ cup raw apple cider vinegar
½ cup dark brown sugar, packed
⅓ cup Orange Blossom honey
1 tablespoon coriander
1 tablespoon cumin
2 cloves of peeled garlic, whole
2 pounds chicken thighs, skin on
¼ teaspoon sea salt
¼ teaspoon white pepper
2 tablespoons olive oil

Note: To boost flavor, Joy and Clare highly recommend that you take the time to marinate your chicken before starting the recipe. Combine 1 cup orange juice, ¼ cup raw apple cider vinegar, and 2 tablespoons Orange Blossom honey and marinate the chicken pieces for 2 to 3 hours. Discard the marinade (do not rinse chicken) and begin the recipe below.

Step 1—Prepare the glaze: Combine orange juice, raw apple cider vinegar, dark brown sugar, honey, coriander, cumin, and garlic in a saucepan and bring to a boil. Reduce heat and simmer for 40 minutes or until sauce has reduced to about 1 cup. Remove the garlic.

Step 2—Sauté the chicken: Season the chicken thighs with the salt and white pepper and let them reach room temperature, about 15 minutes. Add the olive oil to a large saucepan. (Size does matter. You don't want to crowd the chicken!) Over medium-high heat, slowly cook the thighs until 165°F in center and the skin is a nice golden brown.

Step 3—Glaze and serve: Drizzle the glaze on top and allow to simmer for 1 to 2 minutes, making sure the chicken is coated well in the glaze. Serve immediately. If you like, garnish with thin slices of orange or twists of orange peel.

Clare Cosi's Honey-Dijon Vinaigrette

Clare prepared this bright and lively dressing for a spinach and cashew salad the night of her special dinner with Mike, but this versatile dressing goes well on almost any type of salad. It even makes a honey of a dressing for coleslaw. Enjoy!

Yields ¼ cup dressing, enough for 4 small or 1 large salad

2 teaspoons Dijon mustard
1 teaspoon white or rice vinegar
2 tablespoons honey (Clare likes Clover honey)
1 tablespoon fresh lemon juice (do not use bottled)
2 tablespoons olive oil
Sea salt and ground pepper, to taste

In a bowl, whisk together the Dijon mustard, white or rice vinegar, honey, and lemon juice. Vigorously whisk in the olive oil until the oil is completely blended into the dressing. Add sea salt and ground pepper, to taste. Clare suggests taste-testing the dressing on a lettuce leaf. If too sweet, whisk in a bit more vinegar or mustard. If too tart, add honey. Pour over fresh greens or try as a dressing for coleslaw.

Madame's Sticky Bourbon-Glazed Barbecued Chicken (For Oven or Grill)

This mouthwatering glaze brings many flavors together. The sharp woodiness of the bourbon blends beautifully with the smokiness of the charcoal and the sweetness of the molasses and brown sugar. The lemon brings buoyant brightness. It was Clare who created the option of preparing this glistening sticky chicken into an easy one-pan dish you can make in your kitchen, but her beloved mentor was the one who delighted a hapless group of tourists after a hurricane struck their Caribbean resort.

When the powerful storm finally passed, Madame and her starving resort-mates emerged from their basement bunker to find no hotel staff, no transportation, no power, and no phones. But thanks to the intrepid owner of the Village Blend, dinner was served. Madame whipped up this delectable dish from the stores she found in the kitchen and bar—the latter is where the bourbon came from, along with plenty of good Caribbean rum to toast their resilient host.

Servings: About 10 pieces of chicken

Note: Chicken thighs and drumsticks are good with this recipe because dark meat tends to remain juicier during grilling, but it works equally well with breasts and wings.

For the Bourbon Glaze

½ cup bourbon whiskey
½ cup molasses (unsulfured, and not blackstrap)
½ cup light brown sugar, packed
3 teaspoons freshly squeezed lemon juice
3 tablespoons plus 1 teaspoon cornstarch (for thickening)

To make the Bourbon Glaze—Combine the bourbon, molasses, brown sugar, and lemon juice in a medium nonstick saucepan. Stir for a minute over medium heat until the sugar dissolves. Whisk in the cornstarch, one tablespoon at a time until it disappears. While continuing to stir the glaze, increase the heat and bring the glaze to a simmer for 5 to 7 minutes. When glaze thickens enough to coat the back of a spoon (about the consistency of honey), it's done.

Troubleshooting: If the glaze seems too thin, increase the heat and bring it to a full boil while continuing to whisk. This should do the trick. If it doesn't, whisk in a little extra cornstarch (1 teaspoon at a time) and it should thicken up fast. If the glaze becomes too thick, simply whisk more bourbon into the saucepan, a little at a time, and continue to heat and whisk until the glaze loosens to the right consistency for brushing.

TO COOK IN YOUR OVEN:

Step 1—Prepare chicken and pan: Rinse your chicken parts, pat dry. Prepare a shallow baking or roasting pan by lining with aluminum foil. (You'll want to do this for easy cleanup.) Now coat the foil with a nonstick cooking spray. Place chicken in the pan, skin side up.

Step 2—Bake and baste: Preheat oven to 350°F. Place your pan of chicken pieces in the middle rack of your oven. After cooking for 15 minutes, remove the pan and generously brush your Bourbon Glaze on top of each chicken piece. After another 15 minutes (at the 30-minute mark), flip each piece (so that the skin side is down) and glaze the unglazed side of the chicken. Bake for another 15 minutes. Flip the chicken pieces one last time so that skin side is up again and generously brush on a final coat of glaze. Return the chicken to your oven for another 20 to 25 minutes. Total cooking time is a little over 60 minutes.

Note on cooking time: If you are baking chicken breasts, which are bigger and thicker than thighs, you will need to add 10 to 15 minutes to the cooking time. For smaller pieces, such as wings, the cooking time should be shortened by 10 to 15 minutes.

TO COOK ON YOUR GRILL:

Step 1—Roll chicken pieces in vegetable oil and shake off excess. You want a nice, light coating. Sprinkle salt on all sides. If you are using a charcoal grill, you must create a cool area where there are fewer coals.

Step 2—Lay the chicken pieces skin side down on the hot side and grill for 5 to 10 minutes, depending on how hot the grill is (you do not want the chicken to burn). Once you have a good sear on one side, move the chicken pieces to the cool part of the grill (if you are using a gas grill, lower the heat to medium-low). Cover and cook for 20 to 30 minutes.

Step 3—Turn the chicken pieces over and baste them with the Bourbon Glaze. Cover again and allow to cook for another 20 to 30 minutes. Repeat, turning the chicken pieces over, basting them with sauce, covering, and cooking for another 20 to 30 minutes.

Finishing zap: Here's a quick and easy cheat to make sure your chicken is cooked through. Remove cooked and glazed chicken from the grill and place in a microwave on high for 1 to 2 minutes. Then return the chicken to the hot part of the grill for another 3 minutes. This should take the meat to 165°F and keep the seared skin nice and crispy.

Honey Syrup and Honey Cocktails

Honey-based cocktails have been getting all the buzz in recent years. The complex sweetness, rich texture, and depth of flavor make honey a dazzling and distinctive replacement for simple syrup. But adding honey to a drink just won't work—you will end up with a gluey mess at the bottom of your cold cocktail.

To prepare a great honey cocktail you must first prepare a honey syrup. Relax, it's easy—far easier than making simple syrup out of white sugar. Honey syrup keeps longer than sugar syrup and won't crystalize on you.

And FYI: Honey syrup is also great for topping ice cream, yogurt, fruit, cereal, pancakes, and even for baking.

How to Make Honey Syrup

Simmer **1 part water** to **2 parts honey**, stirring occasionally, until the honey completely dissolves. That's it! No need to over-cook. Let cool and place in an airtight container or bottle with a tight cap. Honey syrup can stay fresh in the refrigerator for 2 to 3 weeks. Feel free to experiment with honey varieties to create a taste profile that mixes great with your favorite spirits. Here are three easy cocktail recipes that all use honey syrup.

Traditional Bee's Knees

One of the most popular honey cocktails in the world, this delightful gin drink is both sweet and refreshing. Dating back to Prohibition, the Bee's Knees was a clever way to make inferior "bathtub" gin more palatable. Clare discovered how wonderful it can be when Bea Hastings served it to her with superior honey and premium gin. You can be creative with both. Between the wide varieties of honey and artfully crafted gins on the market today, the potential taste profiles for this cocktail are limitless.

Makes 1 cocktail

1.5 ounces (a traditional shot) of your favorite gin
¾ ounce fresh-squeezed lemon juice
½ ounce honey syrup (see recipe above)

Mix ingredients in a container with ice, shake well, and pour.

Clare Cosi's Honeybee's Knees

A bubblier, lighter take on Bee's Knees, this sweeter version of the traditional Bee's Knees cocktail cuts back on the citrus and even adds a touch of ginger.

Makes 1 cocktail

1.5 ounces gin
5 ounces ginger ale
1 ounce honey syrup (see recipe on page 336)

Mix in a glass with ice and stir.

Gold Rush

A *"gorgeous honey-sweetened whiskey cocktail" is how Dr. Wanda Clay described one of her favorite drinks (besides her homemade mead, of course). Honey and whiskey pair beautifully together—so much so that several distillers are now marketing their own bottled honey whiskey. The honey in this sweet kiss of a cocktail enhances the nutty, woody complexity of the whiskey.*

Makes 1 cocktail

1.5 ounces scotch whiskey
1 ounce honey syrup (see recipe on page 336)
½ ounce lemon juice

Shake with ice and pour.

Krupnik (Honey Liqueur)

Krupnik *is a sweet alcoholic liqueur made from vodka and honey and laced with aromatic spices. According to legend,* krupnik *was created by Benedictine monks in the sixteenth century, and today it's popular in Poland, Belarus, and Lithuania. Clover honey is the main ingredient, but dozens of different herbs are used, depending on re-*

gion and tradition. Home recipes have been passed down through generations.

Yields 4 cups

> *2 cups honey*
> *1 whole clove*
> *1 cinnamon stick*
> *10 black peppercorns*
> *Zest of ½ lemon*
> *¼ vanilla bean pod, sliced down the middle*
> *5 allspice berries*
> *2 cups vodka*

Step 1—Combine honey, clove, cinnamon stick, peppercorns, lemon zest, vanilla, and allspice berries in a saucepan. Warm enough to thin the honey but do NOT boil. Let steep for 10 to 15 minutes.

Step 2—Add vodka and stir. Remove from heat, cover, and let the mixture steep for a couple of hours. When cool, strain the liquid, and pour into a bottle or airtight container. This beverage can be served warm, at room temperature, or chilled over ice.

Spelt Corn Bread
(Ancient Grain Quick Bread)

Clare was so impressed with this delicious corn bread at the Alternative Edibles Organic and Natural (AEON) food festival that she asked for the recipe. Spelt is an ancient grain that lends a beautiful, nutty flavor to baked goods. It's also a good source of protein and has more dietary fiber than all-purpose flour. This Spelt Corn Bread will have a more rustic, darker look than traditional corn bread and a slightly nutty flavor that's perfect for slathering with butter and drizzling with honey. To see a photo of this alternative corn bread, visit Cleo Coyle's online coffeehouse at coffeehousemystery.com, where you can also download an illustrated guide to this recipe section.

Makes 1 8-inch square pan

1 large egg

½ cup milk (whole, 2 percent, or skim)

½ cup sour cream (drain off any visible liquid)

½ cup white, granulated sugar (for savory corn bread reduce to 2 tablespoons)

½ teaspoon kosher salt or ¼ teaspoon fine table salt

¼ cup canola (or vegetable) oil

2 teaspoons baking powder

½ teaspoon baking soda

1 cup spelt flour

¾ cup yellow cornmeal

Step 1—One-bowl mixing method: First preheat the oven to 350°F. In a mixing bowl, whisk together egg, milk, sour cream, sugar, salt, and oil. When the mixture is well blended *and the sour cream smoothly incorporated*, whisk in the baking powder and baking soda. Finally, measure in spelt flour and cornmeal. Switch to a spoon or spatula and stir until all the dry ingredients are incorporated into a loose, lumpy batter, but do not overmix or you will develop the gluten in the flour and your corn bread will be tough instead of tender.

Step 2—Bake: Prep an 8-inch square nonstick baking pan by coating the bottom and sides of the pan with cooking spray or generously buttering or lining with parchment paper. Pour your batter into the pan and tilt it back and forth to even it out. Bake in your preheated 350°F oven for 20 to 25 minutes. When a toothpick inserted in the center comes out with no wet batter clinging to it, remove from oven.

SAVORY CORN BREAD—For savory corn bread, consider adding ½ to ¾ cup sweet corn kernels (fresh or thawed frozen; if using canned, drain well). You might also add 1 finely chopped jalapeño pepper (remove seeds) and/or ½ cup shredded cheddar cheese.

Flourless Chocolate Brownies (Gluten-free)

Another delightful discovery of Clare's from the AEON food festival. Clare was amazed to learn this recipe contained no flour. The gluten-free structure comes from the superfood black beans, which add nutrition, fiber, and protein. Most impressive of all, there was no taste of the beans; only rich, luscious chocolate drenched her taste buds. To see a photo of these finished brownies, visit Cleo Coyle's online coffeehouse at coffeehousemystery.com, where you can also download an illustrated guide to this recipe section.

Makes 1 9-by-9-inch pan (12 squares)

8 ounces semisweet chocolate, roughly chopped (do not use chips)

2 tablespoons canola oil (or coconut, avocado, vegetable, or corn oil)

1 (15.5-ounce) can black beans (low sodium or no salt), rinsed, soaked, and drained

¼ cup brewed coffee or espresso (deepens the chocolate flavor)

4 large eggs, lightly beaten with fork

½ cup light brown sugar, packed

½ cup white, granulated sugar

1 teaspoon pure vanilla extract

⅛ teaspoon table salt or finely ground sea salt (if using coarse salt, increase amount to ¼ teaspoon)

1 teaspoon baking powder

Optional additions: ½ cup toasted and chopped nuts (walnuts, almonds, or hazelnuts) and/or ¾ cup chocolate chips

Frost with the next recipe!

Step 1—Prep oven and pan: Preheat your oven to 350°F. Create a sling with parchment paper and lightly coat the paper and sides of the pan with nonstick cooking spray. Set aside.

Step 2—Melt the chocolate: Place the chopped chocolate into a microwave-safe bowl. Pour the canola oil into the mixture. IMPORTANT: Chocolate burns very easily, and once that scorched taste is in your chocolate, your brownies are ruined. To prevent burning, heat the oil and chocolate in 20- to 30-second increments in your microwave. Stir between each session until everything is melted and smooth. Once melted, place the bowl on top of the preheating oven to keep the chocolate warm.

Step 3—Prep the beans: Drain the canned beans (see tip below), place them in a bowl, and cover them with water. Allow them to soak for 5 minutes, then drain well.

Step 4—Make the batter: Combine the beans, coffee, and eggs in a food processor or blender/processor. Process until smooth. The mixture will look like a chocolate milkshake. Add the brown and white sugars, vanilla extract, salt, and baking powder. Finally, add the melted chocolate and mix well until smooth. (If adding optional chopped nuts and/or chocolate chips, *stir* them in now with a large spoon.)

Step 5—Bake: Pour the batter into your prepared 9-by-9-inch square pan and bake for around 20 to 25 minutes, depending on your oven. When the top surface is set (spongy but firm to the touch and no longer liquid) and a toothpick inserted near the center comes out with no wet batter clinging to it, the brownies are ready. Allow the hot pan to cool for a few minutes, then run a knife on the unpapered edges to loosen sticky bits. Gently lift the parchment paper handles, transferring the brownie cake to a wire rack. Allow the brownies to cool (and set) before cutting into large or small squares and frost with the Chocolate Fudge Frosting (no butter, no dairy).

Quick tips for this recipe . . .

The black beans should be low sodium (or salt-free). Be sure you rinse the beans well by soaking them for 5 minutes in cold water and then draining well.

Use chopped block chocolate. Chips won't give you the same quality brownie. Do not attempt to make this recipe with chocolate chips. You can, however, tart the recipe up by stirring in chips and/or toasted, chopped nuts just before baking.

Be careful when melting the chocolate. Once chocolate is burned, there's no saving it. Be sure to follow the directions in the recipe.

Don't overbake the brownies. All brownie recipes are better if they're slightly underbaked. This one is no exception.

Alternative Chocolate Fudge Frosting (No Butter, No Dairy)

At the AEON festival, Clare was intrigued by this "buttercream" frosting which had no butter or cream, yet it tasted like a chocolate fudge dream. In the end, Clare decided there are some good reasons to consider replacing the butter in your chocolate frosting with avocados: less calories, for one. Avocados will lighten up your frosting by reducing those calories. And you'll find 20 essential nutrients in avocados, including fiber, potassium, Vitamin E, B vitamins, and folic acid. A healthier chocolate frosting. Who knew?

Yield: This recipe will make 1 cup of icing, which will frost 1 pan of brownies, 12 cupcakes, or the top of a 13-by-9-inch sheet cake. To frost a 2-layer cake, double or even triple this recipe. If you prefer a glaze, see the next recipe.

½ cup mashed Hass (aka Haas) avocado (1 medium or 2 small)
½ cup natural, unsweetened cocoa powder
1½ cups powdered sugar (aka confectioners' sugar)
1 teaspoon pure vanilla extract
Pinch of salt

Step 1—Cut, pit, and scoop the flesh out of a ripe avocado. Mash the avocado with a fork or puree it in a blender or food processor until the flesh is completely smooth and without even small chunks or lumps. It's important to be sure you've pureed it well. You'll need ½ cup of this, so measure it out.

Step 2—Place the avocado, cocoa powder, powdered sugar, vanilla extract, and salt into a bowl. Using an electric mixer, beat the ingredients. At first, the mixture will seem very dry and powdery, but continue beating the ingredients. DO NOT ADD LIQUID. As you beat the mixture, the avocado will penetrate and moisten the dry ingredients until a smooth chocolate frosting forms.

Note: If you live in a very dry climate, and the frosting is too dry after a reasonable amount of beating, then add a very small amount of liquid (1 teaspoon at a time). What liquid you use is your choice, milk or coffee or you can add a touch more vanilla and even complement the vanilla by using another extract such as almond, hazelnut, or rum.

TIP: Your avocado should not be overripe. Do not use avocado flesh that is brown, bruised, or mottled. Conversely, do not use flesh that is under-ripe and hard.

Chocolate Glaze

For a looser chocolate glaze simply add more liquid to the frosting until you get the consistency you like. Start with 1 tablespoon of milk or coffee or rum or a liqueur (e.g., Kahlúa, Amaretto, or a chocolate liqueur). Add more if needed to reach the glazing consistency you like.

Oat Milk Oatmeal Cookies
(No Flour, No Butter, No Kidding!)

Here is another "alternative" cookie idea that impressed Clare at the AEON festival. The easy technique for this recipe is this: You soak the oats in a mixture that includes oat milk for 6 hours or overnight. This hydrates the oats, allowing the mixture to develop great flavor and the proper texture for the recipe. Then you simply stir in a few more ingredients and create drop cookies that bake up fairly flat, resembling pralines. Amazingly easy with remarkable results: no flour, no butter, yet with good chewy texture and yummy notes of caramel. Serve with oat milk to complete the perfect pairing. To see a photo of these finished cookies, visit Cleo Coyle's online coffeehouse at coffeehousemystery.com, where you can also download an illustrated guide to this recipe section.

Makes about 2½ dozen drop cookies

For the oat milk soak mix:

2¼ cups "quick-cooking" oats (not instant, not rolled, not "old-fashioned")
1 cup light brown sugar, packed (and lump-free)
⅓ cup oat milk
⅓ cup vegetable, canola, or coconut oil
1½ teaspoons apple pie spice (premade or use recipe below*)

For stir-in additions:

1 large egg, lightly beaten with fork
½ teaspoon pure vanilla extract
¼ teaspoon finely ground sea salt
½ cup finely chopped walnuts (chop first, and then measure)
⅓ cup raisins

Step 1—Oat milk soak: Into a plastic container, stir together the quick-cooking oats, light brown sugar, oat milk, oil, and apple pie spice. Mix until well combined with all oats thoroughly dampened. Seal the plastic container and place in the refrigerator for 6 hours or overnight. Do not skip this step. You must allow the oats to hydrate and the flavors to develop. (Do not soak longer than 48 hours.)

Step 2—Create the dough: After the oat mixture has soaked, transfer it to a mixing bowl. In a separate bowl, whisk the egg, combining with vanilla and salt. Pour the egg mixture over the oats and stir well. Fold in the finely chopped walnuts, and raisins. Mix well. (If adding optional extras, fold them in now.)

Step 3—Line your pan: Preheat oven to 350°F. Very important: You must line a baking sheet with parchment paper or a silicone sheet.

Step 4—Drop and flatten the dough: Using the tablespoon utensil from your measuring set, scoop out heaping rounds of the oat batter and create little mounds on your baking sheet, allowing space between for spreading. With the prongs of a fork, crisscross each mound to flatten, much as you would a traditional peanut butter cookie. Bake about 15 minutes. Allow to cool at least 5 minutes on the pan before transferring. Cookies will set up and harden as they cool. They will appear flat, resembling pralines, but give them a taste and enjoy!

*Make Your own Apple Pie Spice: For every 1 teaspoon, mix the following spices: ½ teaspoon ground cinnamon, ¼ teaspoon ground nutmeg, ⅛ teaspoon ground allspice, ⅛ teaspoon ground ginger.

Tasty variations: Replace raisins with Craisins or dried cranberries; replace walnuts with finely chopped pecans or hazelnuts.

Extra add-ins: ½ cup toffee bits (such as Heath brand Bits O' Brickle). In addition, try adding ½ cup butterscotch chips; OR ½ cup white chocolate chips; OR split the amount, adding ¼ cup of butterscotch chips and ¼ cup of white chocolate chips.

The Village Blend's Honey Apple Cake
(Dairy-free: No Milk, No Butter)

This superb sheet cake is a unique showcase for the happy pairing of honey and apples. The cake batter is spread across the pan and topped with spiced, shredded apple, then drizzled with honey before baking. Out of the oven, the golden canvas of tender baked cake carries the crowning caramelized sweetness of honey-kissed fruit.

Enjoy this cake on your coffee break, as an after-dinner dessert, or (as Clare and Matt discovered) a way-past-midnight snack. As far as honey, use a good-quality raw, sweet honey for amazing flavor. And the best apple for this recipe is Golden Delicious—not to be confused with Red Delicious. Golden Delicious apples are slightly sweet and buttery and an excellent apple for baking. To see a photo of this finished cake, visit Cleo Coyle's online coffeehouse at coffeehousemystery.com, where you can also download an illustrated guide to this recipe section.

Makes one 9-by-13-inch sheet cake

3 medium Golden Delicious apples, peeled

¼ cup honey (for outstanding flavor use raw honey)

1 teaspoon ground cinnamon

½ teaspoon ground ginger (do not use fresh)

½ teaspoon nutmeg

4 large eggs

¾ cup light brown sugar

½ cup white, granulated sugar

¾ cup canola oil (or vegetable or coconut oil)

½ teaspoon kosher salt (or ¼ teaspoon finely ground sea salt)

1½ teaspoons baking powder

1½ cups all-purpose flour

1 to 2 tablespoons honey (to drizzle before baking)

Pan prep: Fit a 9-by-13-inch pan with a parchment paper sling. The excess paper hanging over the longer sides of the pan will act as handles, allowing you to lift the cooled cake onto a serving platter. *(Tip: Spray the pan lightly with nonstick spray before adding the paper, which will help the paper stick better to the pan's bottom and sides.)* Also coat the sides without paper with nonstick spray.

Step 1—Make the honey-apple topping: Shred *peeled* apples with a box grater or food processor. Put the shredded apples in a saucepan and toss well with honey, cinnamon, ginger, and nutmeg. Cook and *gently stir* over medium-high heat for 10 to 15 minutes. This precooking will evaporate the excess moisture from the apples and soften and caramelize them for great flavor. When finished cooking, most (but not all) of the visible liquid should be gone from the pan. Remove from heat and allow to cool while you create the cake batter.

Step 2—Mix batter with one-bowl mixing method: Whisk eggs until slightly frothy. Add brown and white sugars, oil, salt, and baking powder, and whisk until well blended. Sift the flour into the bowl. Stir only enough until a smooth batter forms; do not overmix or you will develop the gluten in the flour and your cake will be tough instead of tender. Batter will be loose.

Step 3—Pour batter into pan and top with apples and honey: Pour the loose batter into the prepared pan and gently tilt the pan back and forth until the batter coats the bottom of the pan in an even layer. Using a fork, gently begin to pick up small amounts of the shredded, cooked (and cooled!) apple topping (from Step 1), leaving behind any visible liquid. Drop the apples in small mounds across the batter in the pan. Using the fork's prongs, gently separate these mounds, spreading the shredded apples into an *even layer* all the way across the top of the cake batter. Drizzle the final 1 to 2 tablespoons of honey over the cake top. (If using raw honey warm it a bit for drizzling consistency.)

Step 4—Bake: Bake in a well-preheated oven at 350°F for 30 to 40 minutes. The time will depend on your oven. Cake is done when the batter has turned golden brown, and a toothpick inserted into the cake comes out free of batter. *(Tip: The cake center will take a bit longer to cook than the outside edges but take care that your cake's edges do not overcook.)*

Step 5—Serve: Cool the cake in the pan. Gently run a knife between the cake and the pan sides that are not covered with parchment paper (to loosen the cake and prevent sticking); and then use the parchment paper "handles" to gently lift the cake onto a cutting board or serving platter and slice into squares. Ice cream and whipped cream make tasty toppings for this cake. If eating dairy-free, try **WHIPPED COCONUT CREAM.** Learn how to make it in the recipe guide to this book. Download it at Cleo Coyle's online home: coffeehousemystery.com.

**From Clare, Matt, Madame,
Quinn, Franco, Esther, Nancy,
Dante, Tucker, Punch, and
everyone at the Village Blend . . .
May you eat and drink with joy!**

Don't Miss the Next
Coffeehouse Mystery
by Cleo Coyle

For more information about the Coffeehouse Mysteries and
what's next for Clare Cosi and her merry band of baristas,
visit Cleo Coyle at her website: coffeehousemystery.com.

ABOUT THE AUTHOR

CLEO COYLE is a pseudonym for Alice Alfonsi, writing in collaboration with her husband, Marc Cerasini. Both are *New York Times* bestselling authors of the long-running Coffeehouse Mysteries—now celebrating eighteen years in print. They are also authors of the national bestselling Haunted Bookshop Mysteries, previously written under the pseudonym ALICE KIMBERLY. Alice has worked as a journalist in Washington, DC, and New York, and has written popular fiction for adults and children. A former magazine editor, Marc has authored espionage thrillers and nonfiction for adults and children. Alice and Marc are also both bestselling media tie-in writers who have penned properties for Lucasfilm, NBC, Fox, Disney, Imagine, Toho, and MGM. They live and work in New York City, where they write independently and together.

CONNECT ONLINE

CoffeehouseMystery.com
CleoCoyleAuthor
CleoCoyle